GUARDIAN

T.S. PEDRAMON

This book is dedicated to my family, who patiently bore my excessive unavailability while I worked to produce this volume at break-neck speed.

This book is also dedicated to all those who wish to adventure, who desire to do great and brave things. May you find ways to expand your horizons and stretch yourselves to make the world a better place, even if—especially if—your lot in life seems mundane at times.

Acknowledgements

Thanks to my wife, my children, and my sister, who played integral roles in the development of this book. They acted as sounding boards, helped brainstorm, and offered general support. My wife patiently allowed me to occupy the dining room table with a 5'x3' world map, which greatly facilitated planning this novel and the future volumes in the series. Of course, I also have to thank everybody who bought book one in this series and have looked forward to this installation in Allabva's story.

Further thanks to those who beta read for me and gave me invaluable feedback to ensure this book is as fun as it can be. And special thanks to all the subscribers to my newsletter and to the *Grendhill Chronicles Podcast,* both of which give me a frequent connection to the outside world.

Contents

NIGHTSHADE
2
UNICORN
GUARDIAN

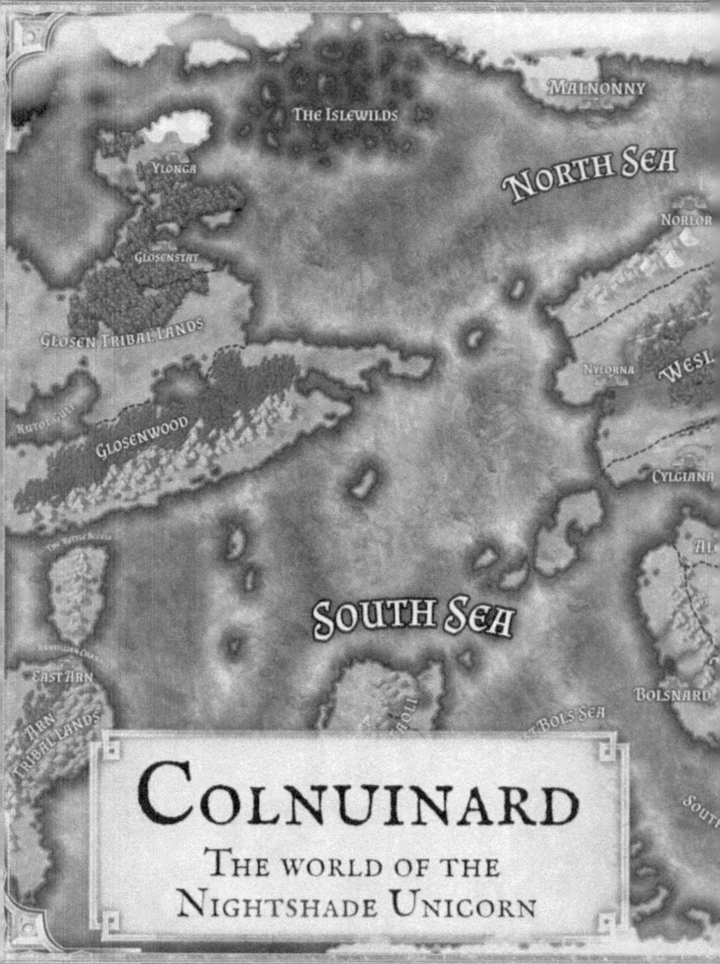
The Islewilds
Malnonny
North Sea
Ylonga
Glosenstat
Glosen Tribal Lands
Nylorna
Kutot Gulf
Glosenwood
Cylgiana
South Sea
East Arn
Arn Tribal Lands
Bolsnard
Bols Sea
Colnuinard
The world of the
Nightshade Unicorn

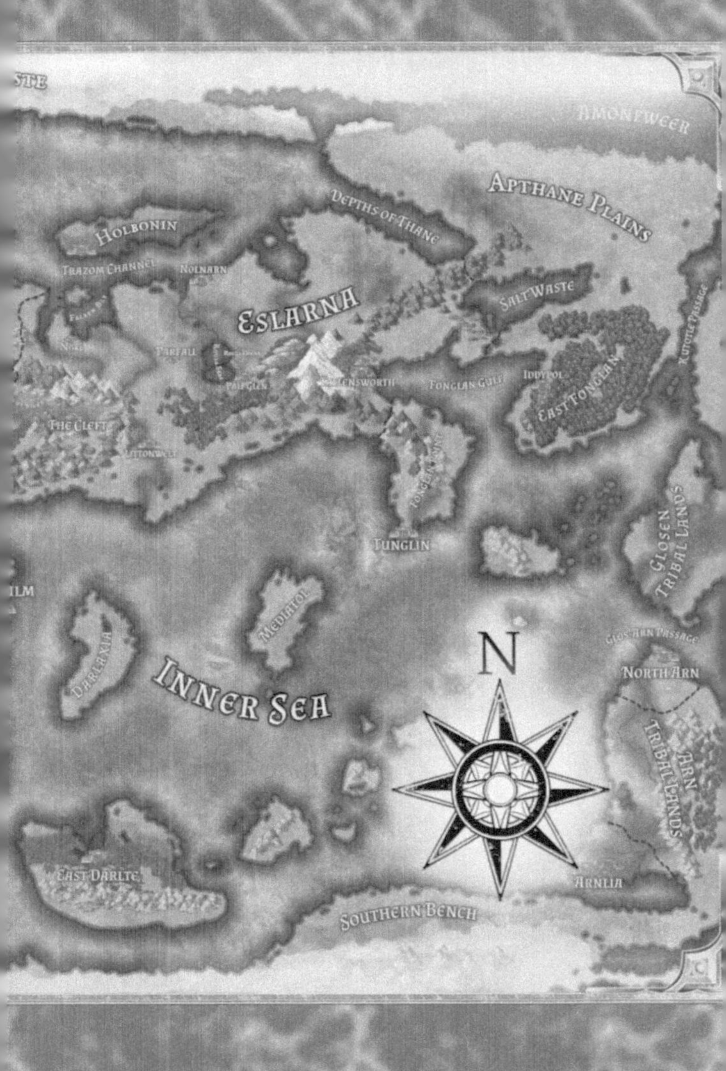
STE
AMONFWEER
APTHANE PLAINS
HOLBONIN
DEPTHS OF THANE
TRAZOM CHANNEL
NOLNARN
SALT WASTE
ESLARNA
KUTOBE PASSAGE
TARFALL
IDDYPOL
FONGLAN GULF
EAST FONGLAN
PALEGUN
LENSWORTH
THE CLEFT
LITTONWALT
GLOSEN TRIBAL LANDS
TUNGLIN
ILM
GLOS'ARN PASSAGE
MEDIATOL
N
NORTH ARN
DARLAXIA
INNER SEA
ARN TRIBAL LANDS
EAST DARLTE
ARNLIA
SOUTHERN BENCH

TRAZOM CHANNEL
FALREN BAY
NORL
PARFA
NIGHT RIVER
THE CLEFT
LITTONWELT

COLNUINARD:
ESLARNA
THE DISAFFECTED
TALLENS ROAD
ROULA DOCKS
PALF GLEN
TALLENSWORTH
N
SOUTH SEA

Prologue: The Storm Breathes

Several Months Ago

A young woman walked westward across the ice, her straight dark brown hair hanging about her round face as the wind whipped it back and forth. Her eyes, steel-gray with a touch of brown next to the pupils, stared ahead as she trudged silently in the cold.

The woman didn't know her own name. She didn't remember where she came from or where she was going. She felt like the clothes she wore might mean something, but she had no recollection of what that might be.

In fact, she had no coherent memories at all. But while she didn't have any words for where she was going or what she was doing, she knew what she felt.

First and most noticeably, she felt cold. She comprehended the bitter cold that nipped at her fingers and reached in through her clothing to stab at her sides.

Second to the cold was her hunger. She had no idea when she had last eaten, or if she had ever eaten, for that matter. She perceived that it must have been some time ago.

Her eyes felt dry. She had to keep wiping her nose of its drippings caused by the cold. She could feel fatigue in her legs and soreness in her feet as she walked ceaselessly westward.

But despite her shivers, hunger, and overwhelming tiredness, she felt a directive, an impulse, something coming from somewhere outside of herself, commanding her to walk. To walk this direction.

She put the yellow orb of the sun on her left and endlessly placed one foot in front of the other. The sun moved in the sky, dipping below the horizon and rising again as day and night continued their perpetual chase. At times the sun was ahead of her, at times behind, but she kept its incessant dance to her left.

At intermittent intervals the young woman could make out impressions where the ice clung to tiny cushions of drifted snow, semicircular impressions that went ahead of her. She felt an impulse to follow these impressions just as much as she did to maintain the sun on her left. More so, if she was honest with herself. She *had* to follow these impressions, these prints.

As she walked, she wondered what her clothing said about where she came from. The colors were bright, not faded. She found that she wore a necklace made of a hard, cold material, some parts of it silvery and some of it a yellow color. It had many intricate shapes, and in moments when the woman felt less exhausted, she took the necklace off of her neck and admired the intricate design on the pendant.

Her clothing did not add to the discomfort brought to her by the frigid temperature, or by the force of gravity to her feet and legs. Rather, the clothing fit her very well, gently hugging her form where it ought to be snug and giving her plenty of room to move where she needed more space. Her boots were thick and rugged, but caressed her feet as she stepped onward, as if she were walking on pillows. She wore trousers and a tunic which, while simple in function, were quite elaborate in design. She had a small coat that was all but covered with embroidery. The entirety of her outfit appeared to have been designed to be worn together, with flowing colors lining up from one garment to the next to create the impression almost of being one full piece.

The final thing that kept pulling this woman's attention, that kept calling her to wonder what it was and where it came from, was an object she held in her hand. It had been there during the moment she came to herself, realizing that she existed and that she needed to walk westward, following the prints in the snow.

It was a curious rod that had the appearance of bone. This rod was about the length of her forearm and the palm of her hand combined, and was a slender cone, broad at one end, the width of three fingers at the base and tapering along its length to come to a fine point at the other end. The other feature she noted was that the rod was a spiral. It sported ridges as if it had been fluted and then twisted so that the ridges gracefully turned as she traced the length of the rod from point to base.

The young woman with the steel-gray eyes didn't know what this meant and didn't know what it was. But she believed the rod was granting her survival.

As the wind pulled at her clothing and forced its way through the weave and against her skin, she felt the extreme cold of the freezing weather. It seemed that it should overtake her, overwhelm her, and drive all other sensation away, all other thought away, until it consumed her and she fell to the ground, dead.

But that didn't happen. She seemed to have enough heat in her, or somehow her clothes kept her warm enough. But even though she did not know where her clothes came from, or what this object was in her hand, she felt that it gave her an energy that kept her warm, kept her alive.

The young woman kept her intense gaze forward as she marched on, ever westward, staring into the sun's light as it set ahead of her in repetitive monotony. After walking for many days and nights, the young woman saw a dark speck on the horizon.

As she neared, it slowly grew and formed into multiple specks, which, still growing, formed in turn into the shapes of people. The young woman stowed the bone-like rod out of sight inside her coat.

There were two people closer to the woman than the rest of the group, gathered around a hole in the ice, with several miscellaneous pieces of gear scattered around them. Although the rest of the group was too distant to be sure, the woman supposed that the others must have similar gear with them. One item seemed to be a tool made of metal—she recognized that thought wordlessly, realizing that the tool fell in a class of materials that also included her necklace—with a sharpened part that twisted like the rod she had hidden, but was not formed into a cone.

The woman guessed the two closer people had used the tool to make the hole in the ice. Or had started it at least, as now it was too big to have been created only with that.

A thick rod—wooden, she recognized, though still without words forming in her mind—lay nearby that measured most of the height of a man. At one end of the wooden rod was a flat leaf of metal. A shovel, she knew. The shovel's blade looked to be about as broad as the hole was wide.

She turned her attention to the two people in front of her, who were looking at the woman expectantly. The pair of strangers had rods of cane with lines leading down through the ice and into dark water underneath. As she approached, they looked at her curiously and moved their mouths, making sounds that she did not understand.

"Hello there, lost one," the older one said in a voice that was lower than the woman's own. She didn't comprehend his words.

These people also had a look to them. Their features differed from what she observed on her own hands. They were larger, coarser... Men. These were men. She decided she liked men, and wondered how best to use them.

One looked young, like her. The other was older, with creases showing where he had formed his face into a smile many times over many years. She stared at them, her drive to walk west now interrupted by the curiosity of encountering other living creatures.

The older man spoke again, the woman still not understanding his words. "Hello, lost one," he repeated. "I said, how are you? My name is Aptluk. Aptluk", he pronounced again more slowly, patting his torso. "And this is my son, Punuk. Do you come from around here?"

The younger man spoke. "I don't think she does, Father."

"Of course she doesn't," Aptluk replied to his son. "Look at her clothes and her face. She's much paler than we are. But you've got to be polite."

"I suppose," Punuk shrugged.

The young woman continued to stare. The two men in their furs didn't appear to be in a hurry to go anywhere or accomplish anything except to stand around this hole with their lines going down into it.

"How did you get here?" Aptluk asked. "Were you sailing and ran aground during the blizzard two weeks ago?"

Silence.

"I hope not. That was an unnatural storm. Quite bizarre lightning, I thought the world was ending!"

The woman stared back.

"You want some fish?" Aptluk asked. "We have some already. Maybe you like it cooked? How do you want it? We don't have any cooked here."

The young woman stared back.

"Alright, you're a quiet one. Look, I'll, I'll serve you some," Aptluk offered.

He turned to a bag he had nearby and pulled a fish out of it. Kneeling on the snow, he lay the fish down and pulled a knife from a pocket on his trousers to cut it. He fileted it, speaking the whole time.

"In our country, in Ylonga, we like to fish."

"Father, that's obvious," Punuk said.

Aptluk ignored him. "I like the char fish. Punuk here prefers sculpin. But we can agree on salmon. All of them are good, truly. Some you just have to prepare right. And depending on what kind of fish it is, you may need to cook it or not. This one right here, it's good just like this."

Aptluk hadn't finished skinning and filleting the fish, but he was able to cut a piece out, and he handed it up to the young woman. "Here you go, lost one. It's good. Try it. Salmon."

The woman reached her empty hand forward and grabbed the piece of fish. She turned it around and smelled it.

"You eat it. Look." Aptluk cut another piece and held it up to show that it was the same as the piece he had handed to the newcomer. Then he brought it to his mouth and took a bite. "It's good. Eat."

Hesitating slightly, the young woman raised the chunk of fish to her lips. It did smell as if it would keep her alive, perhaps even strengthen her. She bit the flesh and noticed that it was soft, and she could chew through it easily. Giving a soft moan of relief to celebrate the end of her hunger, she swallowed and took another bite.

The nameless young woman decided to stay with Aptluk, Punuk, and their people. Her urge to follow the semicircular prints in the snow abated, while she realized she needed assistance, at least for a bit. Looking at the matter from a practical standpoint, they could provide food when she had none.

As she stumbled through using her mouth to form their language over the next few weeks, it became clear to anyone near enough that she was picking up their tongue with extreme rapidity. While she assimilated their words, she took advantage of the opportunity to learn about them, to learn how their society worked. These were the Ylongans, and it was soon evident to the woman that Ylongan society was rather loosely defined. There was no single leader, nor any group of nobility vying for control. Instead, the one thing that was deeply ingrained in their collective consciousness was that a person could only begin to have any significant sway in the community at around the age of forty years, as faces wrinkled and bellies grew larger.

The nameless woman with gray eyes did not know her own age, but when she looked in a mirror she could tell she didn't look like she was approaching forty—that was for certain. As the days turned into weeks among the Ylongans, the young woman's now-vanished desire to follow some ephemeral tracks in the snow was replaced by a marked inclination to have others bend to her will. Being too young to bear sway among them, she realized that she had to leave the Ylongans behind.

The steel-eyed girl used her hosts for what they were worth while she was with them. Aptluk was kind and generous, and the nameless girl was all too happy to take advantage of his kindness. Punuk eyed her hungrily, so she used that as much as she could, teasing him with alluring glances when no one was looking, and when she thought it would entice him to do her bidding.

But their usefulness to her could only go so far. In the end, she had to leave. She wouldn't gain a foothold among the Ylongans for at least a dozen years or more if her youthful appearance had any say in the matter, except by proxy. Just as she tried to get Punuk to do her bidding, she could always hope to manipulate and bend the will of others in her favor. But nowhere in the short term would she be given a serious voice to drive the community, and even if she could buy the cooperation of an elder member of society—or even several of them—it wouldn't satisfy her desire to call the shots.

The young woman made her plans quickly and selected a day for her departure. When the time came and her hosts were asleep, she quietly filled Aptluk's favorite shoulder bag with food, a knife, various provisions, and the clothes they had found her wearing. She had begun wearing Ylongan clothing to keep her unique threads from wearing out and to blend in a little better, even if her face still set her apart. The young woman knew that some people would disapprove of her actions—taking what was generously offered and then, greedily, whatever she desired on top of that. But she didn't trouble herself with these trifles of morality. She had survived who-knew-what, and she intended to keep surviving. She would survive on her terms, in her own way.

The Ylongans had mentioned the tribes to the south, in the Glosen lands. She thought she might try her hand there, see what their society was like, and work her way into that. She didn't know what gave her this directive, where she had gotten the idea to follow the prints in the snow, or the desire to command. She felt driven by a formless force outside of herself, and sometimes she felt like she caught a ghost of a memory that might tell her where she came from and what her clothes meant. But she knew that what this apparently-outside force was guiding her to do filled her with excitement. It filled her with a yearning from within to topple whatever structure may be in place and stand on top of it, victorious. Then she would form the world according to her *own* desires.

With this thought, she happily robbed Aptluk and the lonely Punuk, and stole away in the night toward the south.

The young woman wandered. She roved through woods, across meadows, over bridges traversing rivers, always going either west or south. She had left the kind people who had found her without ever formally choosing a name. She never did remember her name, so Aptluk had kept calling her "lost one." Thus she drifted south toward the Glosen tribes.

The Ylongans that she set at her back talked about the Glosen tribes as inordinately political. There were twenty-six tribes, they told her, all of them vying for position over the others, and within each tribe, the members vying for renown. That sounded to the steely-eyed girl like a place where she could work.

She avoided unwanted encounters, traveling on roads when she found that it suited her purpose, but scurrying out of sight at the first hint that anybody was coming. She traveled for two weeks on the provisions she had stolen, using some as bait to catch fish as she went along, until she hit a point where she had passed enough people and seen enough buildings and carts to decide that she had some choice in whom she met. She wanted to choose people she could work with, people who might understand a little bit of what she wanted to achieve. She swung west, keeping distant from Glosenstat, which was an Ylongan city despite the name.

She was aware of and felt a strengthening connection to...something. An influence, another mind, that seemed to guide her, to tell her that what she wanted to do, she wanted to do quickly. She couldn't afford to fall among simpletons who couldn't help her, nor among anybody whom she couldn't manipulate in just the right way. She needed somebody a little bit like herself, greedy and conniving. Things needed to be done with finesse. So she kept watch and observed people to choose carefully.

The young woman silently approached a couple, a man and a woman, from behind. They picked their way through the woods, looking for specific plants. The woman wore a colorful outfit bound about the waist by a roll of cloth, a hood holding back her straight black hair, while her husband's hair was held under a solid blue cap which matched his outer garment.

To reveal herself intentionally, the lost girl stepped more heavily now, not trying to mask her passage. The couple ahead of her paused. The woman turned her head and saw the steel-eyed girl.

"What are you doing here?" she asked directly.

"Whoa, easy," the man said. "No need to get up in arms, Ani'irad." He turned to the nameless girl. "What is your name?"

She stared back wordlessly. She hadn't understood what they said at first. These were Glosens, and the Glosen language was not the same as the language of the Ylongans. But there were some commonalities.

That final word, she had understood: "name." She didn't have one, so she opened her mouth and said what Aptluk had called her when he found her, and had continued to call her while she was with them.

"Lost one," she said in Ylongan. "I am Lost One," she repeated.

"Like... Jashdin," Ani'irad replied in Glosen. "Is that what you said? Jashdin?"

The steel-eyed woman saw that Ani'irad understood that she was calling herself "Lost One," but her pronunciation of the Ylongan term was poor, laden with the Glosen accent, and came out sounding different. She doubted that the other woman knew what her new name meant.

"That works," Jashdin said in Ylongan. "Yes. I am Jashdin."

"Well, Jashdin," Hal'rad said, "Ani'irad did ask you a question. What are you doing here?"

Jashdin cocked an eyebrow. "You seem like my kind of people," she said in Ylongan, knowing that the Glosens probably still wouldn't understand her.

"I guess you don't speak Glosen," Ani'irad said.

Jashdin shrugged, trying to look non-threatening. It was easier to look natural now that she had the extra layers of clothing she had brought from the Ylongans.

"Look, I don't know what she's up to," Ani'irad said to Hal'rad. "Let's shake her and head back."

"I don't know if we'll be able to lose her," Hal'rad said. "She approached us intently. Jashdin, do you understand me?"

Jashdin shrugged again, holding her hands out.

"Alright, well, you go that way and we're going to go this way," Hal'rad pointed, first one way and then the other. "Come on, Ani'irad, let's go."

Hal'rad and Ani'irad started walking away from Jashdin.

Jashdin didn't want to lose them. She had been watching them and decided that these were the people she needed. So she followed.

The couple turned.

"Jashdin, go that way," Ani'irad said.

Then they turned again and walked in the same direction they had begun, and Jashdin immediately followed again.

"Alright," Hal'rad said, stopping. "Are you lost? Fine. Let's take you back until you can find your own way again."

Jashdin followed them, never turning away until they reached their home. She would work her way into their lives for the immediate future.

She didn't speak Glosen, but she had known what they were doing that day. They were looking for poison.

Hal'rad was a leatherworker, but his pieces weren't the most desired in the area. She saw how he looked at the old leatherworker in their village because she'd been watching from a distance. Hal'rad wanted him gone. He probably wasn't trying to kill the old man; he just wanted him too sick to work. He wanted him to decide that he needed to leave and set up shop somewhere else. Or, something like that.

So Jashdin had followed them and attached herself to them. They were begrudgingly kind enough to share their dinner, and they allowed her some floor space to lie down on that first night. In the morning, as Hal'rad set about his work, she came into his workshop and sat next to him, picking up tools.

"Hal'rad," Jashdin said, awkwardly imitating the sounds in the Glosen tongue and calling his attention as he tried to ignore her.

Hal'rad turned his gaze to Jashdin. "I'm going to ask you what my wife said yesterday. What are you doing here?"

Jashdin stared back at him through and shrugged innocently. "What this for?" she asked in Glosen, grabbing a tool.

"Be careful with that," Hal'rad said, taking the implement from her. He lifted an eyebrow appraisingly. "You speak Glosen?"

"Starting. What that is for?"

Hal'rad studied the curious expression on Jashdin's face before answering tentatively. "It's a stamp. Look, you get the leather wet like this." He grabbed a piece and dipped it in a bowl of water he had brought, working the moisture in with his fingers. "Then you set it in place, and you apply some pressure." He grabbed a mallet and hit the back of the tool a few times, forcing the tip into the leather as he tapped it repeatedly. "When you're done," he pulled it away, "you get the design of the stamp imprinted on the leather."

Jashdin nodded, looking at the wavy impression left on the scrap. This seemed easy enough.

She continued quizzing Hal'rad in broken Glosen, grabbing this tool and that, asking him what each was used for. As she watched him answer each question, she listened carefully and expanded her nascent command of his native tongue.

The Glosen language appeared not to be a sister tongue to the Ylongan language, but they had been in proximity for some time, so some words carried over, like "name" had the day before. Jashdin assimilated Glosen even faster than she had the Ylongan language because of these carryover words.

As she passed the time in her self-appointed apprenticeship to Hal'rad, she rapidly improved her broken Glosen over the next week and a half. Then she started spending more time with Ani'irad. Ani'irad was something of a busybody in her village, which was one of many settlements among the Bas'naya Glosen tribe. Jashdin observed her, time and again, sticking her nose into this neighbor's or that neighbor's business.

This is exactly what Jashdin had come along for, though. She immediately and deliberately inserted herself into their lives, and Hal'rad and Ani'irad tolerated it because Jashdin helped with the work around the house. It turned out she was not just extremely gifted with the languages she was picking up, but adept with her hands as well.

Within three weeks, her skill with the leathercraft nearly caught up with Hal'rad's work. He noticed this, of course, as his habit was to work sloppily, not really caring about the quality of his work, only caring to turn a profit. So while Jashdin began to rival Hal'rad, he worked harder on each piece that he produced, increasing his quality.

It didn't truly matter, of course. Jashdin didn't care so much about the leatherwork; she just needed a rationale to be here, a reason to be allowed to stick around and see the ways of the Glosen people. Her reluctant hosts didn't make a point of showing her, but Jashdin made a point of studying them.

She paid attention to the styles in the leatherwork. She saw how people dressed, and she saw what they cared about, what symbols they liked to wear in their jewelry, what dishes they liked to cook. Particularly, she observed *why* they chose what they did. Analyzed their motives.

Jashdin studied, making mental notes with the rapidity and precision and thoroughness as only she could. She knew she was unique now. She had found herself merely weeks ago, and since coming across other people, she had seen that she could pick up their languages at a rate that alarmed them.

While Hal'rad and Ani'irad allowed Jashdin to be around because they were glad to make a profit from selling the leatherwork that she produced while mimicking Hal'rad's work, in truth they were serving her without knowing it.

Over the next few weeks, Jashdin talked more and more with Ani'irad. And to conspire with her.

"I have...plans," Jashdin confided in her hostess one day while she helped her prepare the evening meal.

"You're going to make a building?" Ani'irad asked.

"No," Jashdin blinked. She had used the wrong Glosen word; a rare error coming from her. "Not blueprints. Plans." Both words translated as one into Ylongan.

"What kind of plans?"

"We will rise, you and I," Jashdin said.

"Rise in what way?" her hostess asked, searching Jashdin's eyes before turning back to her task.

Jashdin scoffed at Ani'irad's naivety. "Look, you and poor little Hal'rad, you're dreaming too small."

"What do you mean? He's just a leather worker. How grand are we supposed to live on his earnings?"

"Ani, let's be frank. I know you were looking for nightshade the day that you found me."

Ani'irad blinked and looked sideways at Jashdin, then turned her eyes back to the dough she was kneading. "That's ridiculous. What makes you think we were looking for nightshade?"

"Because I watched you for a few days before I showed myself in the woods," Jashdin said.

Ani'irad's face paled. "No, you couldn't—" she trailed off.

Jashdin laughed at Ani'irad's discomfort. "Have no fear—it's not like I'm going to tell anyone you want to get rid of the old leatherworker. That's fine. I don't care about that. Like I said, you and Hal'rad are dreaming too small."

"Dreaming too...? Alright," Ani'irad said, the fear erased from her semblance and replaced with curiosity. "What are you proposing? What are you trying to do?"

"Ani, come now. Wouldn't you like to be in charge around here?"

"Of course, who wouldn't? But it's not like we can do that. My husband is a leather worker, as I already said, and I keep the house. In charge of what? It's not like I'm going to rule over anybody."

"Don't be daft," Jashdin said. "Look, you garden. That's the good little housewife thing to do, right? But your garden grows. You produce well, you cook, and your dishes turn out well. You're smart." Jashdin wasn't at all conflicted about the contradiction in complementing her hostess's intelligence in the same breath that she called her daft. As long as it worked. "Hal'rad is, well, you're right. He's a leather worker. I didn't say anything about *him* being in control, though. I'm talking about you and me."

"What, in control of the Bas'naya Glosen?" Ani'irad asked, scandalized at the scale of the thought, but with a hungry look in her eye just the same.

Jashdin grinned. "That's more like it. But I have my sights set higher than that."

"How high?" Ani'irad asked, not paying much attention to her work now as she rolled the dough.

"Let me worry about that for now. Getting control of the Bas'naya Glosen is going to take some resources that you haven't had at your disposal. Until now."

"Yes, you mean like a smarter husband?"

Jashdin sighed. Maybe this wouldn't be as easy as she thought. "I'm not saying that wouldn't help. I'm saying..." she sought her words carefully. "Come. Join me in the woods tonight. Put your little husband to bed and we'll go out, and I'll show you something."

"How do I know you'll be able to pull this off?"

"Do you know anybody else who can pick up a language and a trade as quickly as I? Have I not shown myself to be capable?"

Ani'irad frowned, but nodded. "Alright. Why me?"

"I already said you're smart," Jashdin said. "You're capable. Now, understand, I will be the one truly in charge, but you can be next to me. You will be my assistant, my second in command. And I know you don't love gardening or cooking. Unless I'm wrong about that last point, of course?" She let the question hang in the air.

"No, I'll gladly leave them behind," Ani'irad said hastily.

"Good," Jashdin continued, "so you follow me, and I'll make it so you never have to cook and garden again. You'll be able to do whatever you want. Just help me mold people and their opinions. You promise to do that, and I'll give you power."

Ani'irad nodded. "Alright. Let's go through the evening like normal, and when Hal'rad is asleep we'll go out, and you'll show me...something?" She sighed and kept kneading the dough.

Jashdin smiled to herself. Not so difficult, after all.

It was a dark night, overcast and with no moon. Jashdin had planned for this night specifically because of the moon phase. It had to be dark for this to work potently. She didn't recall how she knew that, but know it she did. She had a sense that once she was more practiced at the task she was about to attempt, she would not need the dark of the darkest night. But for now, she needed every advantage that she could get.

"Where are we going?" Ani'irad asked suspiciously.

"You'll see," Jashdin replied as she led the way into the woods.

"When?"

Jashdin ignored Ani'irad's question. "What do you know of the fae-birds?"

"Silly creatures," Ani'irad answered derisively, stepping over tree roots and ducking under low-hanging boughs. "They flit from here to there."

"Yes. And how do you catch a fae-bird?"

Jashdin had to lead Ani'irad on. She wanted to give the other woman a job, charge her with a specific task in order to build their influence. No, Jashdin's own influence, she mentally corrected herself. But her follower would need to see an example of what they were doing.

Ani'irad blinked. "You can't catch a fae-bird; nobody can. They just pop out of existence and then pop back in somewhere else."

"Too true," Jashdin said. "Unless you have a net made from the coat of a woolly rhino and the mane of a unicorn."

Ani'irad laughed, showing disbelief. "Are you serious? You have a net somewhere lying around, and you're going to try to catch a fae-bird? Are we going to break our ankles or our necks here in the woods, in the dark? This is your grand *blueprint*, is it?" She stressed the word "blueprint," mocking Jashdin's momentary lexical confusion from earlier in the evening.

Jashdin blinked, trying to practice patience. Unsuccessfully. "Of course not. In fact, I already caught a fae-bird."

"You expect me to believe that?"

"You should, but I don't expect it. Not until I show you."

This silenced Ani'irad and she and followed Jashdin wordlessly as they went deeper into the woods. After a few moments, she spoke again. "Are we going to see this fae-bird right now?"

Ah, so she can catch on, Jashdin thought. "Yes. We're walking to the fae-bird right now. I will show it to you. I will show you the net. And then I will make my proposition."

"Proposition? How did you think to make a net out of rhino fur and unicorn hair?"

Jashdin had learned that unicorns had another name, that the Ylongans preferred that other name, nearly throwing fits if anybody called them unicorns. The Glosen tongue had similar-sounding terms: *unicorn* was a basic physical descriptor, whereas *Nomord* was said to be the proper name for the horned equine race. But the Glosens weren't so offended by the common descriptor. Jashdin thought the whole affair a rather tedious one.

"Simple enough," Jashdin said. "The hard part was getting a hold of some unicorn hair."

"I was about to ask about that—where did you get it?"

"Don't worry about that. I have my ways. But no, I didn't gather it myself."

"Why woolly rhino? Why a Nomord?"

Jashdin scowled at Ani'irad's use of that last word. She knew Jashdin didn't like to dignify the creatures with that name.

"As I said already," Jashdin drew out impatiently, "it's simple. The rhino brings strength, and the unicorns are inherently magical, just like the fae-bird. If you want to capture something that gets away using magic, you must use magic as well."

Jashdin heard some pitiful peeps coming from the bush ahead that she was leading her companion to. They closed the final few paces to get there, and Jashdin crouched down to probe under the bush. She reached in and grabbed hold of a wooden rod, then pulled it toward her. As it came, she stooped and then sat down, gesturing for the other woman to do the same. She might as well let her in on some of her secrets.

Ani'irad hesitated, but then sat down next to the bush, facing Jashdin.

"We'll be here several minutes at least, I think," Jashdin told Ani'irad. "Get comfortable." She took a deep breath before proceeding. "I feel like I'm not quite alone," Jashdin said.

"Well, you're not, obviously," Ani'irad replied, opening her arms in a gesture to indicate herself.

Jashdin rolled her eyes. Ani'irad was really the best she could find, and she still wasn't that smart. She took another breath, then continued.

"Obviously, I am not alone right now because you are with me. What I mean is this: you know what I told you. I found myself walking across the ice. I came across some people, and I left them behind. But while I was walking across the ice and after leaving those people behind, coming here, I did not feel alone. I feel like I have something guiding me. A voice, a feeling. An impulse. What's the word? I'm still not great at your language. When you want food..." She paused for the word to come to her.

"Hunger?" Ani'irad guessed.

"Yes!" Jashdin said, eyes lighting up. "There is a *hunger* that follows me. It comes with a certain intuition. It tells me what to do. I do not know what this force is," she raised an eyebrow, leaning in. "But I like it. I don't care if it's good or bad, I like it. It feels powerful."

"And...?" Ani'irad asked.

"And I knew that I needed to catch a fae-bird. I knew that I needed to do something with it. I knew how to approach," Jashdin paused. "This hunger didn't tell me to use a rhino's coat or a unicorn's mane. I thought of that myself, but I had this feeling that I needed something of this—flavor?—this type. Anyway, it pays off."

Ani'irad stared back at Jashdin, waiting for her to get to the point. Jashdin said nothing more, but instead turned back to the wooden rod, pulling it completely out from under the bush. There was a loop at the end, with a woven net attached to that loop. A bird was trapped in the net. It had been still while undisturbed under the bush but now it flopped helplessly, trying to escape. It blinked in and out of visibility, but every time it reappeared, it remained in place, always trapped inside the net of rhino and unicorn hair.

"There, you see?" Jashdin said, proving it to Ani'irad, whose eyes had enlarged to the size of dinner plates.

Jashdin couldn't see the colors of the bird's plumage at the moment, and she knew that in this dim light, Ani'irad couldn't see them either. But she could make out shades, light and dark, and the shape of the bill. It had ridges on the upper and lower portions of the beak, leading to gentle spikes before coming to the point. It was unmistakably a fae-bird.

Ani'irad looked down at the bird in the net, then back to Jashdin.

I've got her eating out of my palm, Jashdin thought. "Now watch this," she said aloud.

She reached under the ring of the net while keeping it down on the ground, and put both hands inside, taking hold of the bird in one swift motion. Having placed one hand on the bird's body and one on its head, she suddenly twisted, breaking the fae-bird's neck in an instant. It looked as if it wanted to make a final cry but couldn't, and as the two women watched, life quickly faded from its eyes.

Ani'irad looked on in disgust. Jashdin didn't care. She was doing what she needed to do. She now pulled the fae-bird out of the net and held it up in front of her, pronouncing words to herself, to the bird—now dead—and somehow, although secretly and softly, to the whole world. Jashdin didn't know ahead of time what she needed to say; she was following the bidding of this amorphous hunger.

"This is *my* power. It once belonged to another, but I have conquered, and I have taken, and now it is mine. I will do as I please with my power. It is my right. This is my power. Let all who would challenge me wither."

Then, opening one hand, she took the bird's carcass by the head with her other hand and used the point of the bill to pierce the skin of her open palm. She made three dots in a row forming a line, and then two more dots to either side, forming a cross. Piercing her hand four more times, she finished with a ring of eight bloody points centered around a single dot in the middle.

"This is my power," Jashdin repeated. "Let it permeate my blood." In a moment she suddenly felt fast, felt inexplicably light. She laughed. "This..."

Yes, it was done.

"This, yes—Oh. Watch me," Jashdin said to Ani'irad, then vanished and reappeared standing a couple of paces behind where she had previously sat. Ani'irad looked up at her, stunned, mouth agape, the words momentarily shocked out of her.

"Was that—" she began to say once she had found some words. "Was that how?"

"That was proof, dearie," Jashdin interrupted. "That was proof. I am now a Lemnerox—one with power I have taken upon myself." A sick grin bled across her face. "*Now*, let's talk about our ambitions. You want to go farther, right? You want to be in charge of the Bas'naya Glosen tribe. And you will, in time. But for now I will send you west, and you will start working for us there. I will work here; you build a following in the west."

"How am I supposed to build a following?" the other woman asked, confused. "What kind of following? How—why will they follow me?"

"Because, Ani'irad," Jashdin explained, taking out the twisted, tapered, fluted rod, "you will be something known as a Binterox."

Ani'irad's eyes locked on Jashdin's hands. "How did you get a unicorn horn?" The implication hit her like a ton of bricks. "How did you *kill* one of the Nomord?"

Jashdin shrugged, then Shifted out of visibility and reappeared again, sitting cross-legged right in front of Ani'irad. "I don't know if I did. I have no—"

"You can't just go around doing that!" Ani'irad interrupted, leaning back. "Do you know how unsettling that is?" She breathed heavily in surprise despite the fact she had been sitting still for a while.

Jashdin pursed her lips. She should still tread lightly with the woman, apparently. "I have no recollection of killing one, and it would be quite the feat, wouldn't it? Anyway, there's something odd about this horn, don't you think?" She leaned her head to the side, gazing carefully at the object that she held, then handed it over to Ani'irad.

"What...what am I supposed to be seeing? What am I looking for?" Ani'irad said, glancing back and forth between Jashdin and the horn in her hands, holding it gingerly as if it might bite her hands off if she weren't careful.

Jashdin divulged something else without fully understanding how she knew it. The fluting was twisted counterclockwise from the tip down, the reverse of what the Nomord were known to have. That meant...

"That horn is from a Nomord stallion."

Ani'irad gasped as though burned, throwing the horn to the ground in front of her, then scrambled to stand. "You must be mad! They're all mares, there's no such thing as—" Ani'irad stopped herself, then resumed her sitting position, though she leaned away from Jashdin again.

Jashdin could see the wheels turning in her would-be protégé's head. She spoke softly, giving the other woman a path through the mental morass.

"You claim to want power. Influence. You're already thinking a little outside the box, only too small. I've just shown you how to take the power of a fae-bird. That's real power. Combine that with the right words in the right situation and it becomes real influence, too. But no human can truly wield a magical ability, right? And yet—"

Jashdin vanished again to drive her point home, reappearing standing a couple of paces away.

"Here I am," she said, holding her hands out to the side. She stayed solid, stepping back toward Ani'irad and sitting cross-legged in front of her. "So if that was possible after all, is a male unicorn really so far-fetched? Is it inconceivable to take its power as well?"

Ani'irad didn't back away this time, instead sitting up, closer to Jashdin again. "How do you—?"

"Look at the spiral. It goes the wrong way."

"Oh." Ani'irad raised both eyebrows. "Tell me what a Binterox is, and tell me... I think I'm beginning to sense the scale of your dreams. Tell me what to call you."

Jashdin grinned with pleasure, the feeling of power heady in her mind. "Call me the Oracle—" She stopped, sensing what to say next. ”—of the Alvewimon. Of the Dragonspeaker.”

Chapter 1

Disoriented

Last Week

"That's all of it!" Delgan Dlorovin whooped as he pushed earth on top of the end of the furrow. "Planting is over. Tomorrow I'm reporting to Master Ntoffel's forge."

"Good work, son," his father commended, pulling his hat off to wipe his brow. "Let's go home and get some dinner in you. You'll want to make sure you have your strength."

"True," Delgan admitted, biting his lip. As ready as he was to get started, he wondered if he would struggle with a blacksmith's heavy work. "Well, at least today and yesterday were all maize. Planting the wheat the day before starting my apprenticeship? No thanks. Dragging the harrow is plenty of work by itself. I don't want to show up with sore muscles on my first day."

"But you'll certainly show up with sore muscles on your second day," Master Dlorovin teased. More seriously he said, "I suppose you're glad we did all the ploughing before seeding, then? You've had a few days of relatively easy work."

"Yes," Delgan nodded. "I am glad."

He and his father grabbed their empty seed bags, heading out of the field and down the lane toward the house.

"You're welcome."

"What?"

"You know that I usually like to plant as I go. This year was different. That was for you."

"Oh. Thank you. Umm... Father, do you think I could pass by the Roalkes' house?"

"That's kind of out of the way, don't you think?" His father looked at him mirthfully with the question of *why* written on his face.

Delgan bit his lip again. "Yes, but I just kind of want to check in and make sure—"

"What, that she's still interested?"

"Well—"

"Don't worry, Delgan. If Allabva said she'll come to dinner, then she'll come. Two days left, she'll come."

Delgan's face flushed. He did want to check in, but there was time right now and he also simply wanted to see Allabva. Now maybe his father wouldn't let him go?

"But I was thinking, maybe she doesn't like what we make for dinner, and—"

Master Dlorovin interrupted his son with a laugh that rose from his belly. Reaching for Delgan's seed bag, he spoke what the young man wanted to hear.

"Go! Don't worry about it."

"Alright," Delgan emitted, face lighting up. "I'll just touch base with her and—"

"Go on, I'll cover for you. But don't come home too late. You need your energy for tomorrow."

"Thank you!" Delgan called back as he trotted off ahead of his father.

He took a side path in the direction that would take him through the town, with a pronounced bounce in his step all the way to the Roalke house. Their orchard was on the opposite side of town from the Dlorovin farmstead, but to Delgan it felt like a very brief walk to get there. On the way, he thought about how things had been going.

He'd been riding high spirits ever since Allabva had danced with him at Greenstone Observance, most of a week before. He had noticed when she and Brelin Blyckwan had lined up behind Aulbwin and Yalrou Tonalstga. Delgan had been disappointed that his place in line meant he would dance with Yalrou instead of Allabva. He had accepted his fate.

There was nothing wrong with Yalrou. She was a fine young lady, Delgan supposed. That is, if one didn't mind the stuffy, suffocating air with which she did anything. Her carefully practiced indifference to anything that other people found to be interesting and exciting told Delgan that he ought to look elsewhere for good companionship. Other than that...well, he could suffer one dance.

Then, right before Mistress Tunnigan kicked off the evening's proceedings, Allabva and Brelin had switched places with the Tonalstga twins.

Delgan had done all he could to restrain the stupid grin that hit his face in that moment.

True, he had been standing next to Alvern, so when Allabva and Brelin switched with the Tonalstga twins, that also meant that Brelin would dance with Alvern. It was probably her idea, not Allabva's. But the switch had happened. And if it just so happened to provide a convenient outcome for Delgan, he wouldn't complain.

So he had danced with Allabva, and it had gone quite well. They talked candidly and she really appeared to enjoy herself. It only got better from there.

They had eaten their dinner together at the Observance. Allabva had asked *him* to dance some more. Then she accepted his invitation to dinner, and even turned around and invited him over to dinner at an earlier occasion.

The following night, Delgan had gone over to the Roalke house. Things had continued in a very positive tone. She seemed pleased with his loaner-gift of his grandmother's flute. Her eyes said that she liked the gesture and being entrusted with it, even though she tried to refuse it out of politeness.

Since then, Delgan had spent the past week's daylight hours working on the farm, and the evenings stressing about whether Allabva would like the Dlorovins' presentation of a meal. He was eager to plan something that would bring her back again and again, and keep her in his life.

So now he headed over to see her, not only because he had a bit of free time. The dinner planning was a perfect excuse for the visit. And, while he took advantage of the opportunity for a brief period of companionship, he could verify if the dishes he had planned would be acceptable.

With great anticipation to see Allabva—the genuineness of the personality in her eyes, the full curls of her hair, among many other pleasant aspects—Delgan rapped on the door and waited.

It was longer than he expected before the door opened. Didn't Allabva's brother, Mellier, always like to answer the door? Perhaps he was out back in the orchard.

When the door did open, Mistress Faethlen Roalke stood in the doorway, a concerned expression on her face as she looked at Delgan.

"Is Allabva here?" Delgan asked.

Mistress Roalke pursed her lips. "Why don't you come inside?" She stepped away from the doorway, leaving him room to enter.

He did so, following her into the house and finding a seat on the couch as his hostess placed herself on a chair in front of him.

"No," she told Delgan, answering his question. "Allabva couldn't be here right now, as you might have expected." Her voice sounded vacant. Distant.

"Can I ask where she is?"

"I'm not sure where she is right now," the matron replied. Her expression shifted halfway to consternation. "Did you not receive my message?"

Something was wrong. Allabva wasn't just gone for the moment. Delgan felt something inside him sink from his gut down into his feet.

"What message?"

Mistress Roalke paused, bringing one hand up and dragging it down across her face before talking. She spoke haltingly. "I sent you word. Allabva had to go. She had to take care of some business. Umm, yes, she had to leave." Her eyes were turning red.

"What happened? What kind of business?" Delgan puzzled aloud, now full of questions he hadn't imagined before knocking on the door. *She can't be going to sell any fruit,* he thought. *They don't have any yet; it's too early in the season.*

Allabva's mother didn't respond.

"Is she going to market downriver?" Delgan probed. "When will she return? Is there something that I can help with?"

"No," Mistress Roalke shook her head. "She had to go on business elsewhere. I don't properly know where she was headed."

"When will she be back, then?" Delgan pushed, trying to get something, anything, from Allabva's mother.

"I don't know," her voice cracked. "I don't know where she's gone, I don't know when she'll be back."

"Did she leave alone?"

"No. No. She left with—" Mistress Roalke hesitated, "—a protector. She'll be fine."

Delgan raised an eyebrow. His hostess didn't sound convinced at her own words.

"She'll be fine," she repeated. "She'll be back."

"*When* will she be back?" Delgan asked again.

"I don't know." Now the woman sounded defeated, tears welling up in her eyes. "I don't know when she'll be back."

She left to take care of some business. With "a protector," Delgan thought. *What kind of business is it?*

"And when she's done with her business, she'll come home," Mistress Roalke recited, seeming to talk more to herself than to Delgan. "When she's done with her business, she'll come home, and everything will all be alright."

Delgan was still trying to put this together. *A protector?* "So she's—is she going to make it back for...?" He left the question hanging in the air.

"No," Mistress Roalke shook her head vacantly, "I don't think she'll make it to dinner two days from now. That's why I sent you word. All we can do is to trust her to take care of that business, and then come back home."

What kind of trouble—no, danger—is Allabva in? Delgan thought. *Her mother is concerned for her safety, not just trying to save face.* Out loud, he asked, "Can you tell me what sort of business she's taking care of?"

"You wouldn't believe me if I told you."

Delgan raised an eyebrow. "A year ago, I wouldn't have believed a story about red lightning tearing the sky open."

Mistress Roalke smiled wanly. "Nor I. Still, this is a little different from that." Her eyelids lifted suddenly, a realization striking her. Then, whatever it was, she suppressed it just as quickly. "This is different." Again she sounded like she was convincing herself.

Delgan sensed that his hostess did not want to say more. He desperately wanted to find out all she knew. What was it about mentioning the red lightning that caught her attention? But Delgan decided to err on the side of maintaining polite relations with the woman across from him. She insisted there was nothing to be done right now. He could visit again another day; perhaps then she would be open to telling him more. So, swallowing his confusion, Delgan stood to go, but something else nagged at his mind.

"Does Allabva have...?" He gestured to his neck.

Mistress Roalke understood. "Yes, I'm sorry we didn't get the flute back to you. She had to leave in somewhat of a hurry, and neither one of us thought of it while she was preparing to leave. I remember seeing the chain around her neck as she left, though."

Delgan nodded. "Good. I hope it can do her some good and comfort her on the road." He took a breath to strengthen his next words, taking a page out of Mistress Roalke's book and trying to convince himself. "I know she'll be back in no time."

He walked himself home, emotionally detached, trying to make sense of what Mistress Roalke had told him, and trying to reconcile the mystery of Allabva's absence with her promise to come to dinner and return his grandmother's flute to him. He had lent it to her both as a token of his affection, and to provide her an extra reason to come see him. Now she was gone who-knows-where, and the flute with her.

It seemed to Delgan that perhaps he should have been worried about losing the flute after all. All those years growing up, he had broken and lost necklaces holding the flute, but never lost the flute itself. It turned out that all it took was a crush on a young woman: he lent the flute to her, and it was gone. But he wasn't upset about the flute itself; he was upset about Allabva being gone.

He didn't walk home by the most direct route. He couldn't face his family yet; he would have to tell them Allabva wasn't coming to dinner. Obviously, none of them would be as upset about it as he was, but he didn't know if he could truly face that reality yet.

After meandering through and around outside of town, he finally set his face toward home. Upon arrival he was immediately ushered in to dinner before it got cold. His siblings had already eaten and gone to bed.

In still-stunned silence Delgan sat down by himself and began eating mechanically, not even noticing what was on the plate. He still needed his energy for tomorrow, for his first day of his apprenticeship.

Delgan's father walked in. "You're awfully quiet, son."

Delgan made a noncommittal sound acknowledging that his father had spoken.

"Everything alright?" his father asked.

"Sure," Delgan delivered a single word response.

"She can't come, can she?"

Delgan looked up, startled. "How did you—? No, she can't come," he admitted slowly, mentally guarding himself against probing questions as to why.

"Well, maybe another time," his father said, sounding unconcerned.

Delgan was glad that it wasn't phrased as a question. "Yes, maybe another time," he echoed.

"Have another plate," his mother inserted, leaning in from the kitchen to deposit another serving of food in front of Delgan. "I need your mouth to be on full duty if the Roalke girl isn't coming to dinner.

Delgan nodded his thanks, then glared at the spot where his mother disappeared around the corner. It was nice to be cared for when he couldn't be troubled to even taste the food while he was eating it, but that didn't mean she had to say things out of hand like that. After silently inhaling his second helping, he left the table and went to bed.

Delgan awoke suddenly in the morning, eyes snapping open. He was wide awake and today was the first day of his apprenticeship. Yet he lay there for a good while, dreading having to face the world with the knowledge that Allabva wasn't coming to dinner tomorrow. And the stark uncertainty of whether she could ever come.

Her mother hadn't told Delgan what kind of business Allabva had gone to take care of. She had only expressed trust in her daughter. What an odd thing—trust. He turned that over in his mind.

He *thought* he trusted Allabva. Growing up in the same village, they had played together sometimes, and she had always seemed to want to do the right thing. He believed that Allabva wouldn't lie, wouldn't act nefariously.

But what did trust really mean now? She wasn't around to say a single word, whether truthful or not. Mistress Roalke had said that she trusted her daughter to take care of her business. She obviously wasn't talking about money, sales, or contracts. She was talking about accomplishing some vague task, then.

No matter how Delgan poked at the problem in his mind, he couldn't hope to guess what that task was. It was a mysterious unknown. Allabva had apparently left town to do something specific. *Something* important.

Even if Allabva's mother couldn't—or wouldn't—tell Delgan where she had gone or what she had to do, as he thought about it, Delgan found himself agreeing with the older woman. All he could do was to trust Allabva to take care of whatever it was she was doing, and then return someday.

All that was in the context of how to regard Allabva. But what happened to them: Delgan and Allabva? Would they still court? Would she still be interested? What if she were gone for years? Would Delgan even want to wait that long?

He heard noises from elsewhere in the house, his family getting up and getting ready for the day. He tried to put these things out of his mind. Where was he now? He was back home. He was in the Cleft. He was...left behind.

He thought of the song the Nomord-enchanted flute played on command. He had learned the song's words, or at least a version of them. It was an old song, so it was sung differently in different places. He hummed and ran through the words in his head, swapping the pronouns to reflect his situation with Allabva:

In the cool shade of the mount,
My love came to call in the morning, (to
me)
And I knew not when she'd return,
So I held her forever that day.

Take me there, through the ash and pine,
Take me there, to the desert or sea,
Wherever you go, do not leave me here,
I will not be parted from thee.

O'er the deepest, bluest sea,
My love went to sail in the morning, set
free,
And I stayed all alone in the shade,
Wishing I could share her embrace.

Take me there, through the ash and pine,
Take me there, to the desert or sea,
Wherever you go, do not leave me here,
I will not be parted from thee.

In the darkest, fiercest war,
My love was affrighted to leave me, (weep-
ing)
And I feared she might cease to be,
And could never come back home to me.

Take me there, through the ash and pine,
Take me there, to the desert or sea,
Wherever you go, do not leave me here,
I will not be parted from thee.

In the cool shade of the mount,
My love came to call in the morning, (to
me)
I had known not if she'd return,
So I held her forever that day.

In the cool shade of the mount,
My love came to call in the morning, (to
me)
And I knew not when she'd return,
So I held her forever that day.

Delgan scrunched his face while he thought of the words. War? He certainly hoped Allabva wasn't getting tied up in anything where people intentionally harmed each other. Delgan was glad there were no wars nearby that he knew of. Both Eslarna, wherein the Cleft lay toward the west, and Weslan Fields, which occupied the western half of the continent, had been peaceful for as long as Delgan knew.

He shook his head, pulling himself from his meditation. He really wanted to see Allabva, but he couldn't right now. When he could do something, *anything*, to change that, he would. For now? What he could do was to continue living. He could learn his trade.

Rising from his bed, Delgan hoped that he would make a good impression on his first day as a blacksmith apprentice. Getting dressed in smart-looking clothes and hoping to impress his new master, Delgan idly daydreamed of living on the micro-continent of Darlte. It was said that apprenticeships started at twelve years old there, or sometimes younger.

He envied his hypothetical other self who would probably be a journeyman by now for having several years under his belt. But at the same time, Delgan was glad to have the chance to grow up before beginning his trade. What would he have done with the build and musculature of a twelve-year-old, trying to learn the trade of a blacksmith? He was already concerned about being strong enough now, and he was fully grown.

Maybe his hypothetical other self would have taken advantage of the years to develop his muscles, so now the real Delgan was at a disadvantage. Realizing that he was thinking circularly, he set out on his day. He stuffed a few mouthfuls of breakfast down his throat and headed to Mastered Ntoffel's shop.

Delgan knocked his knuckles against the door tentatively.

His father had mentioned to Allabva at Greenstone Observance that Delgan's apprenticeship would start as soon as their wheat and maize were planted. Planting finished yesterday, so here he was, standing on Master Ntoffel's doorstep, scrubbed and dressed to make an impression.

The door swung open and Anastine Ntoffel smiled at him.

"Come in, Ruldern's expecting you. He's already in his shop out back."

She motioned Delgan into the house and he entered, feeling self-conscious, an outsider to the Ntoffel household, though he had spent his childhood within a stone's throw of this place. He had been to the forge a number of times, accompanied each time, so he'd never had a reason to approach the house.

He breathed deeply as he followed Mistress Ntoffel through to the back, smelling eggs and potatoes in the air. He put the scent out of his mind and tried not to look too pointedly at any of the decor on the walls, concerned that too much interest could be viewed as snooping.

"Come on, come on." She stood at the back door, gesturing for Delgan to follow her out.

He did, seeing the long outbuilding with multiple doors on the same exterior wall. The short side of the building faced toward the house, with the row of widely spaced doors facing the open yard behind the house. Delgan could hear a repetitive metallic ping coming from the near end of the building.

Mistress Ntoffel opened the first door. The pinging turned into a pounding immediately, echoing in Delgan's head. His hostess walked in and he followed her into the darkness inside. He immediately tripped on something that his hostess had apparently stepped over.

Releasing a muted shout, Delgan caught himself before he fell to the ground.

The pounding stopped.

"Sorry!" two voices proclaimed in unison.

"Sorry," Master Ntoffel's voice repeated, "I forget how dark it is in here if you're not used to it."

"And I'm used to it," his wife said. "I should have warned you to step over that slug."

A slug? Delgan thought. It had felt large and solid, nothing like a slug.

Mistress Ntoffel apparently could see well enough to read his confused expression as she helped him to his feet. "That's the terminology," she explained, pointing at the object he had tripped over. "You'll learn. It's that hunk of iron. We use it to prop the door open."

"Are you alright? Are you ready to work?" Blacksmith Ntoffel looked at Delgan appraisingly. He eyed Delgan's smart outfit with a question apparently on his mind, but he said nothing.

"Yes, Master Ntoffel." Delgan tried to sound confident. "I'm here and ready."

"No doubt," the blacksmith said simply. "Call me Ruldern. Master Ruldern in public, but here in the shop we don't need to be so formal. I'm sure your farming upbringing has laid the foundation for the physical strength and work ethic required in this trade. Now it's my job to help you truly develop them and hone them to what this craft requires."

That sounded a little foreboding to Delgan.

"Thank you, Anastine. I'll take it from here."

"Alright. I'll have breakfast ready soon," Mistress Ntoffel nodded cheerfully. She left Delgan standing in the doorway.

"Close that door. I need to be able to s—" Master Ntoffel began. He stopped himself and placed an object Delgan couldn't identify on the front of the furnace next to himself, the tip of it in the fire. "Never mind. I need to show you what you're doing today."

Dressing smartly had been a mistake. In retrospect, it was obvious, though Delgan had been so focused on making a good impression for his new master that he didn't really think about it. Smithing, with the various tasks that Delgan would soon learn, was heavy work and tended to get one dirty. He had already known this, when he took a moment to remember passing by the smithy countless times before throughout his boyhood, but he hadn't realized it would be to this degree. In his thinking about impressions, he had hoped in vain that he'd be able to keep his clothing somewhat clean.

Master Ruldern had him shoveling charcoal all throughout the day. The master blacksmith had stated that the charcoal needed to be moved from one shed to another, bringing it closer to the forge and making room for the next delivery. By the end of the day, Delgan was sure not even his mother would recognize him coming home, so he stopped by a stream on the way home to wash his face. His trousers and sleeves were covered in charcoal dust, and he hadn't even approached the forge itself. He imagined that when he did, he would quickly be covered in soot and ash.

The next day Delgan showed up wearing an old set of clothes, expecting more of the same type of work. He wasn't disappointed. Although Ruldern didn't assign him to relocate an entire shed full of charcoal again, his master apparently had no shortage of menial and repetitive tasks to give him.

This time Master Ruldern welcomed Delgan into the shop and handed him a set of chisels. "You're going to sharpen these," he said simply. "Over there—" He pointed at what looked like a grindstone, then stopped himself. "No, sorry. Not there. The mechanism that turns the grindstone broke last month, so you get to file them by hand. There is a set of files over there."

The older man grabbed a file and showed Delgan how to use it.

"You swipe it across like this. Nope, nope."

Delgan had grabbed a file and started imitating the master's movements. Apparently, he imitated wrong.

"No, in this motion." Master Ntoffel stroked along from the handle of the chisel toward the tip repeatedly several times. "And when you're done, it'll look like this."

He grabbed another one from a pouch on his belt and held it up for Delgan to see, pointing at the tip.

"See that? Now check how sharp it is with your finger. You feel that? It needs to be sharp enough to do the job, but it's no razor. Got it?"

Delgan felt the tip of the chisel and nodded. The blacksmith continued.

"I need to run over to the butcher shop this morning. Keep the family fed, you know. I'll be back around midday. Anastine is in the house if you need anything. Have fun."

With that simple introduction to the day's work, Ruldern departed, leaving Delgan alone in the smithy.

Great, Delgan thought, *now I get to be alone with my questions, and nowhere to properly exert myself to work out my frustration about the mystery with Allabva.*

He sighed, then bent over the workbench and started to file.

Present Day

Jashdin left her hut among the Nafet'elu Glosen, leaving Silomat asleep. She had work to do and didn't want him slowing her down.

Stepping out into the spring air of the central Glosen tribal lands, she yawned and stretched in the morning light. It filtered down to her through the trees, casting shadows that were rapidly shortening as the sun climbed. Her hair hung over a striped coat that fell to her knees, worn over a woolen dress dyed a deep blue, and brown leather boots.

Spotting the remains of the boar still on the spit from the night before, she remembered her hunger. Ducking back inside the hut, she rifled through papers on the table that served as both dining set and desk.

Where's that stupid fork? she thought, moving correspondence aside.

She moved a letter she was drafting to send to East Arn, and another she had received from a recent contact in the Glosenwood. Stupid tribal king of the Tahonu Glosen didn't want to ally with her. So what if the southern lands had an arrangement and fancied themselves a federated land? The Glosenwood had only existed for thirty years as a political entity, composed of eleven of the tribes. Jashdin aimed to merge all the Glosen tribes together, both in the tribal lands and in the Glosenwood. Under her leadership, of course, but she couldn't tell King Yon'ir'fan that.

King, Jashdin scoffed. More like head chief, among the eleven chiefs that led their tribes in the Glosenwood.

The beauty of the morning couldn't touch her rotten mood. Something had happened last night. Something wrong. Everything was wrong.

Well, no, not everything.

Some things were progressing well, despite her nagging feeling she was missing something important from her memory loss.

She had made some good progress since joining the Nafet'elu, or Wetwood Glosen, a month ago. She'd left the Bas'naya, or Ringwood Glosen, once she felt she had a good network of followers established. Combine that with Ani'irad's progress in Eslarna, and things were coming along nicely. Ever expanding, she was now in the Wetwood and was looking to gain a foothold in the plains next.

She'd found Silomat Veliti'Mon, the man among the Nafet'elu with the most stone-cut face and dark hair, and started romancing him. It didn't bother Jashdin that he already had a family when she found him. All she had to do was orchestrate an excessively *warm* experience for them, and act convincingly so Silomat believed she was doing everything she could to rescue the family while their hut burned down around them. Then he was all hers, no complications.

Jashdin still couldn't remember her original name or old life before stumbling into Aptluk and Punuk. That didn't matter. Silomat was taken with her—nobody could say Jashdin wasn't physically beautiful—and with his late family out of the way, Jashdin assumed his family name because it was the most convenient thing to do.

Stupid Rockwood Glosen, Jashdin thought, throwing aside another letter and finding a fork and knife. She walked back outside and stood next to the spitted boar, cutting meat off and eating it straight. The steel-eyed woman reflected on styles of living. This village was a cluster of several rings of huts gathered around fire pits for cooking. The Nafet'elu weren't as refined as the Bas'naya Glosen, but they sure knew how to cook a pig. She'd teach them what they lacked, given a bit of time.

Once Jashdin was joined to Silomat and officially in the Nafet'elu tribe, she'd gotten to work building her status and Silomat's. A few carefully-placed knives, some flattery and some insults here and there, and Silomat was now right hand to the chief. But he took orders from Jashdin, naturally.

Alright, she thought, *so it hasn't been all bad.*

And she had the fae-bird's power. She could jump up to a few dozen paces away in a blink, and she could manipulate her appearance ever so slightly. She needed more power if she wanted to do anything more difficult than hiding a mole or changing her eye color, though.

The mammoth she'd killed, lunging in close to stab it before using her new ability to Shift suddenly out of reach again, had made her stronger, though only half again more than her natural strength.

Jashdin wondered if she'd wasted that Nomord horn on Ani'irad, rather than consuming its power herself. She felt sure it would have boosted her abilities significantly. Not to mention transferring the unicorn's own power to her.

Silomat had seemed a little wary of Jashdin's practices at first, but once she'd helped him augment his strength by half as well, he'd wisely decided to keep his mouth shut.

Along with sending Ani'irad to Eslarna, Jashdin had sent other followers to Adlis-Taoli, Darlte, and the Arn tribal lands. Shy on resources, she hadn't yet sent anyone to Weslan Fields. She hoped Ani'irad would send a delegation to gather her people there.

Jashdin felt like she had every right to do this, of course. She was the Oracle, was she not? *She* was receiving this direction, not anybody else.

So, yes, many things had gone well.

But she still felt angry.

The night before last, Jashdin had woken up with an inexplicable sense of fury. The other mind, the Alvewimon, was mad. Without being able to articulate why, Jashdin felt that something was wrong with Ani'irad.

Then, even though last night began well—that red lighting, oh, that *glorious* lighting! It felt so good, the Alvewimon felt so powerful, right before and during those sky-splitting moments. It was euphoric, intoxicating. Almost enough to overcome her foul mood—then the second wrong thing happened, canceling out the positive feeling she had obtained from the red lightning.

Jashdin had trouble describing it to herself, aside from that the connection to the external mind was weakened. It was nearly missing, now. What was she supposed to do without that guide?

A child came out of another hut and ran past her, evidently excited to be somewhere.

"Hey, dense paw-dust," Jashdin barked at him. "Fetch me your mother."

Jashdin needed to send the child's mother to get—She searched for an idea—to get some herbs. That would do it. Jashdin would call for a specific herb, hard to get, and demand a certain quantity that would take the woman hours to collect. She'd think of some way to twist the poor mother's arm into doing the chore, and she would take her child with her.

Then Jashdin could have some time alone to lead on the other woman's husband and take her mind off of whatever was wrong with her Oracle connection. She'd already gotten a silver bracelet from him before, and she always had a hunger for beautiful trinkets. He wasn't too hard on the eyes, either.

After this much-needed diversion, once she'd gotten rid of this unsettling feeling, *then* she could get some work done today, and worry about whatever it was that had the Alvewimon so upset and distant.

A thunderclap woke Delgan, though he heard no rain.

"What in the—" he heard his father's voice down the hall.

Delgan looked to the window, transfixed by the red glow that split the sky overhead. Over several seconds the red lightning twisted, roiled, fought to remain, and then faded.

It was still dark outside, though morning light had begun to illuminate the night.

Again? This strange lightning had first happened months ago, then the second time came a bit over a week ago. To happen so soon, with no explanation...

That red lightning, which Faethlen Roalke appeared to think—or know—had something to do with Allabva's disappearance. Mistress Roalke hadn't been very specific, but Delgan believed Allabva had departed the day following the last red crack in the sky.

His thoughts wandered aimlessly for several moments about his upcoming work at the smithy today. He thought into the future, wondering what it would be like to design a puzzle made of iron.

Then the sky lit again, the same brilliant red fissure tearing across the sky he could see in the window. Delgan's room shook threateningly while he jumped out of bed and approached the window. Snakes of red vibrating sparks stretched from horizon to horizon as he looked on.

As the light dimmed back to normal, Delgan resolved to dig for answers. He started getting dressed. He'd visit the Roalke orchard before going to the forge today, even if it made him late.

Delgan made his way to the kitchen, grabbing a few morsels as quickly as he could. He heard his parents moving about and wanted to leave before they came to talk to him. He didn't.

Master Dlorovin entered the kitchen just as Delgan left.

"Good morning, Father. I'm going to head out early today."

"Don't you want a good breakfast?" his father called after him.

Delgan was already outside. He turned to hold up a bit of fried bread he was chewing on, not breaking stride. "I'll be fine!"

He would get it all out of Allabva's mother this time. Every detail she knew, he would know before the sun left the horizon.

Where was Allabva Roalke, and why did she leave the Valley of the Five Moons?

Chapter 2

The Summit Above the Aspens

"What must I do?" Allabva repeated to the Nightshade Unicorn.

The large horned equine loomed over her, intimidation and foreboding emanating from his very being. Despite his fearsome appearance, Allabva knew that she was supposed to trust him. Trust him, and work with him.

It had come as a shock that not only did the Nightshade Unicorn exist, but that he and the Shrongelin were one and the same. The Shrongelin was another creature of legend, usually recounted as if he were human, or at least humanoid. He was supposed to carry a sword, or an axe—clearly weapons that required hands to wield them. In legend, the Shrongelin was a great benefactor of humanity. Allabva was raised on stories that the Shrongelin had carved the valley she grew up in, that he had given humans the capacity to feel joy. Some stories even held or hinted that the Shrongelin was the Creator.

The Nightshade Unicorn, on the other hand, was understood far and wide to be terrible, a denizen or harbinger of calamity. The beast appeared and ruin followed. He ate children or brought devastation to crops. And when a person left childhood, she learned that there was no Nightshade Unicorn.

And yet, here he was, standing in front of Allabva. Hronomon the Forerunner, another great Nomord, had led Allabva to the top of this mountain to meet him.

Allabva had grown up in the Cleft, properly called the Valley of the Five Moons, occasionally seeing Nomord from afar. She considered herself privileged that she had briefly chatted with one of them.

Then, on the same day when Allabva had reached the age of majority in the Cleft, she was approached by Nomord. A male Nomord, shattering her preconceptions. No, breaking the preconceptions of anybody she had ever met. This Nomord who approached her was Hronomon, the Forerunner. He spoke to her briefly while she gathered rosemary and then left, promising to return. The white Nomord were known for being flighty, not for being capable of planning ahead.

But just as he said, he came to her again, this time in the middle of the night. He roused her from slumber to call her on an immediate quest to save the world.

She had crossed the countryside with Hronomon at an exhausting pace, was abducted by a band of men who distrusted the Nomord, escaped her captors, and scrambled up the side of a mountain. She was pursued by those who would cause her harm.

As she and Hronomon reached the top of the mountain, the Summit Above the Aspens, a pack of wolves had assaulted them. Fierce and strong, Hronomon had fought them off to protect Allabva with his dying breath.

Now, in this moment, Hronomon lay lifeless on the ground at her feet. Allabva stood over him, wiping tears from her eyes. Because of him, she had reached the top of the mountain, and had bonded with none other than the mythical Shrongelin in a brief ceremony.

Now Allabva knew that the Shrongelin was not the Creator, nor had he been around since the beginning of the world. Just as Hronomon meant *Forerunner*, Shrongelin meant *Guardian*. He stood in between the world and an evil force known as Sacalai.

Sacalai had ravaged the world before the Nomord forged the Construct and imprisoned her. The Construct was an enchantment cast by cooperation between Ta-Nomord and Gha-Nomord, female and male. They knew the prison could not last forever, and thus the Construct designated and charged a Forerunner and a Guardian with standing at the forefront of the world's defense against Sacalai's attacks.

Sacalai's incessant and manic barrage of rebellion against her physical and spiritual constraints took a toll on this Guardian, the Shrongelin, both mentally and physically. His mood soured, his coat soiled to coal black, his perception of character twisted, and he became the Nightshade Unicorn.

Every few millennia Sacalai broke loose and had to be re-contained, the Shrongelin expending the last of his magic, rendering himself mortal, to forge the world's shield again by guiding the magic held within the Construct. Cycle after cycle, a Shrongelin was rendered powerless and mortal. A Guardian being spent, his Forerunner would step into his role and become the new Guardian—the new Shrongelin—and another Gha-Nomord would become the new Forerunner, or Hronomon, and the cycle continued.

The current Hronomon, whom Allabva learned moments ago carried the name Eretuquein, had found Allabva and brought her here, to this place on top of the world. And now, as Hronomon lay dead at her feet after succumbing to his wolf-inflicted injuries, she was to continue her quest with the Nightshade Unicorn, crushing her grief under the heel of duty.

"What must I do now?" Allabva repeated in a loud and clear voice, staring into the Shrongelin's deep midnight eyes. "Your Forerunner, my friend, is gone. I will *not* let him die in vain. Show me where this Sacalai is, and I...I will tear her to shreds." She breathed, calming herself.

The Shrongelin's bond gave Allabva strength. She knew she was powerful now. But if she really thought about it, there was no way that she could hope to stand up in a one-on-one battle against Sacalai. Sacalai had sent the wolves against Hronomon, she guided the Disaffected, whether they knew it or not—

"We—" the Shrongelin interrupted Allabva's thoughts but stopped suddenly, looking down at her feet. No, he was looking behind Allabva.

Allabva whipped her head around and looked down. The Nomord at her feet twitched. His eyes opened and he coughed.

"Hrono—Eretuquein!" Allabva exclaimed in amazed disbelief, dropping back to her knees to cradle his head. "You're alive. How?"

Hronomon wheezed, righting himself and bringing his hooves underneath him as he twisted, then shakily stood as Allabva backed up to give him room.

"I don't—yes, I do know," he said, realization dawning on his face. "It is the Construct. The Construct..."

"What?" Allabva said. Despite knowing something about the Construct, she didn't understand how it could have healed Hronomon right now.

"It is a cooperative enchantment. Any male Nomord could bond a human, up to three usually, but the Construct modified that bond in the case of the Shrongelin's Companion. He can only bond one human at a time, but this bond is stronger. Both Ta-Nomord and Gha-Nomord had forged the Construct together. The Ta-Nomord brought to the Construct the ability to heal; Gha-Nomord brought influence over the weather and influence over minds. The Shrongelin—"

Hronomon started to cough again.

The Shrongelin spoke in his place. "The same Construct which brought the Ta-Nomord magic to you moments ago and healed you of your wounds, you brought to Hronomon. *You* have healed him."

"But how can this be? She cannot carry the magic." Hronomon puzzled, looking at the Shrongelin.

They shared a quizzical expression and then looked at Allabva.

"What Companion have you brought me," the Shrongelin asked Hronomon, "that she can heal you? Allabva, are you not simply human?"

"Of course I am," she shrugged. "Hronomon knows where I came from. That's where I've always lived. Both my parents grew up in the Cleft. That's where my ancestry is: in the Valley of the Five Moons."

"In the Valley of the Five Moons," the Shrongelin repeated flatly.

"You know it?" Allabva asked.

The Shrongelin snorted. "Of course I know it. I just didn't know the current name you use for it. I'm thousands of years old, girl. I know most places around the world."

"Oh," Allabva said. "Right." Hadn't the Shrongelin seemed almost cheerful a few minutes ago? *Why did your mood change?* she wondered.

The Nightshade Unicorn—the Shrongelin—turned to Hronomon. "How was your journey, Forerunner? Arrived a little late, didn't you?" he said in an accusatory voice.

Hronomon didn't appear to take any offense. "I found her late—"

The Shrongelin cut him off. "Did the Guides lie to you? Was their information bad about the cultures of this modern world?"

Hronomon shook his head. "No, the Guides' information has been accurate. The one did indeed send me to his home country. The people speak his language, and just as he said, they are known for their honest character."

"Then the problem was?" the Shrongelin pressed impatiently.

"A suitable Companion was not to be found in the first region I searched," Hronomon said. "As a result, it took me longer than expected to find one. When I found her, I approached her, vetted her, and then called on her at the first opportunity to depart."

"The problem, then?" the Shrongelin said more pointedly, more slowly.

"We had ground to cover."

"If that's it," the Shrongelin said, "then why do I find her damaged, weak, barely able to stand? And you, yourself, were already injured before the pack of wolves attacked you, Hronomon."

Hronomon nodded, acknowledging their injuries. "Sacalai has already built a following. We encountered a small band. They weren't well organized, but a larger camp was close to the base of this mountain. They followed us up and posed a real threat," Hronomon said matter-of-factly.

"Then the calamity that comes may be more trying than those that came before," the Shrongelin said. "This is just perfect. I'm so glad that the world rests on our backs, that it will be our fault when the Construct finally fails."

Is that sarcasm from a Nomord? Allabva thought, surprised.

"Your pessimism is not helpful," Hronomon chided the Shrongelin. "I have brought you a good Companion, have I not? I can tell you that she fits the bill exactly. Her strength in this role will be an asset against the forces of Sacalai."

"How can you be so sure?" the Shrongelin retorted. "She is untrained, physically weak without the bond, too young to know anything useful—"

This time, Hronomon interrupted the Shrongelin with an edge of impatience in his voice. "And yet, here I stand before you, healed by the magic of the bonding that comes with the Construct."

The Shrongelin countered, "This is only the bonding—the moment when the power of the Construct flows through—that is what healed you."

"That may be true," Hronomon admitted, "but I stand here nonetheless." Legs now sturdier than before, he stepped closer to Allabva.

"Remember the burden the Guardian carries. His is not an easy load," Hronomon replied.

"Sorry," Allabva said to the Shrongelin, realizing she was going to have to exercise some patience with her new legendary escort. "But aren't you glad that Eretuquein is alive?"

Hronomon cocked his head at the mention of his true name. "Yes, that was my name, though I'd forgotten it. How—how did you know it?" he asked Allabva.

She gestured at the dark unicorn standing next to them, and Hronomon nodded, acknowledging the obvious.

"Of course, I'm glad he's alive," the Shrongelin answered sharply. "That doesn't mean we have an easy mission ahead of us. Since you asked, let me tell you."

He took a breath, appearing to take great effort to exercise patience with this ignorant human Companion, then continued.

"We have to go down this mountain, easily enough done. You and I descend on the east side, toward Tallensworth, as the Guides told us the city is called."

"What are the Guides?" Allabva asked.

"A few men we consulted who told us things," the Shrongelin said. "We must find favor with the overduke in Tallensworth. Then we'll find a ship and get on it. We will voyage on the sea to find the leaders of men and women. We will journey to make allies against the coming of Sacalai before she bursts forth from her prison."

"What?" Allabva asked, alarmed. "I thought we were supposed to stop her."

"Just listen," the Shrongelin replied. "Yes, we will stop her, but we cannot prevent her from breaking out. What we have to do is put her back once she's out, and so we shall. She will burst out of her prison in power. We can't stop her right there. She has a stronghold in the north. Perhaps you have heard of Amonfweer."

Allabva's eyes widened. "Nobody goes there."

"As well they shouldn't," the Shrongelin said. "Those woods, as expansive as they are, are impossible for humans to pass unaided. As I said, she has a stronghold. It is based hundreds of leagues through those woods. She has already begun to turn the hearts of men, to twist them, to drive them to envy and strife. Many will follow her. Many will side with her in this battle."

"Battle?" Allabva asked.

The Shrongelin stared her in the eye, daring her to interrupt him more. How was she supposed to work with this character? He was too dark, too angry.

He continued, "The Forerunner will head west on land while we travel south and then west by sea. We have mere months remaining before Sacalai breaks the walls of her prison. When she does that, just as we weakened her this morning... She will recover. When she breaks free, I will be weakened, and by our bond, you will be weakened. We must build our forces so that when she breaks out and makes her way to the Amonfweer, we can stand long enough to make our offensive. We must gather our forces and bring them to the Apthane plains before the Hateful Wood, and unite the world against her."

"Build our forces? Where are we going first?" Allabva asked. "And how am I supposed to fight? I don't know how to fight."

"I will teach you," the Shrongelin said. "I will make sure you know how to fight."

"How do you know how to train a human to fight?" Allabva wondered aloud.

"I have studied," the Shrongelin said. "I was previously Hronomon. I knew I would be the Shrongelin. I knew I would have this mission. After the last Shrongelin sealed up Sacalai four thousand years ago and was rendered mortal by virtue of having used every ounce of his magical power to do it, his Companion, who had been a great fighter before he was bonded, taught me. He came with us back to the Islewilds, and I studied under his tutelage for over twenty years."

"How was he such a great fighter? I thought you needed a young companion," Allabva asked.

Hronomon nodded. "Yes. Relatively young. As I told your mother, somebody who can withstand the journey. Your predecessor was twenty-eight years old, and despite his relative youth, he had risen in military rank in his homeland before the last breaking occurred. He was a regimental commander and had gotten there because he was known for his great ability and his great capacity to love."

"That is beside the point," the Shrongelin interrupted. "The point is that I will teach you to fight. You will be ready. First, we must get down this mountain, recruit Tallensworth, then put ourselves on a boat."

"Find her some food," Hronomon interjected.

"What?" the Shrongelin said.

"Find her some food. She must be famished. She hasn't eaten in a couple of days."

"No, I'm—" Allabva started. "Actually, you're right." She felt an intense pain in her belly.

"You didn't make sure she was fed?" the Shrongelin asked Hronomon in a disappointed voice.

"I did what I could, given the situation," the Forerunner replied. "We were beset by enemies. Sacalai seems stronger this time." His voice fell as he said it, sounding discouraged.

"I'm sorry," the Shrongelin said, changing in attitude and stepping forward tentatively. "I have felt it too. Although my battle has been mental and spiritual, I see you have fought the same intensity of struggle physically. Very well, my old friend. Is there any modification to our plan that you would propose?"

"No," Hronomon said. "We'll stick to the plan. We rendezvous in Cylgiana."

"I have seen firsthand that the Guides gave us good information. You visit your stops, I'll visit mine, and we will raise an army to keep Sacalai on her toes."

"If you say so," the Shrongelin said.

"Shrongelin," Hronomon chided, "you must maintain optimism. You have to believe that we can win, at least this round. Do your part, then pass the duty on to me, and the world lives another few thousand years."

"Of course, I'm doing my part," the Nightshade barked. "I'm up here, am I not? I bonded this Companion you brought me."

"I know," Hronomon nodded. "I know. But try to be gentle with her. As you said, she is young and she needs to learn to survive."

The Shrongelin nodded.

Hronomon turned to Allabva. "Be patient with him. He bears a burden I do not envy, though one day it will be mine. Heed him and push yourself harder than he will push you. The world may depend on it. But remember what I told you before: be yourself. Trust your own instincts. Keep your own moral compass."

"Yes, Hronomon—Eretuquein," Allabva nodded. How was she supposed to say goodbye to him? "I will see you again?" she asked hopefully.

"Yes," Hronomon said. "Do your part. Prepare and be ready to lead. Remember that to lead is to serve."

"To lead is to serve," The Shrongelin echoed Hronomon's words somberly.

Allabva looked back and forth between them, perceiving this to be some manner of farewell among the Nomord. "To lead is to serve," she repeated.

"Farewell, Forerunner," she said, leaning forward to put a final hug around her friend's neck. Then she bent to pick up her things from the snow.

"Wait a second," Allabva said, a realization hitting her. She turned to Hronomon. "You're going west? Across the continent?"

"Yes," he replied. "More or less back the way we came, except this time, I go in public, not in secret. This time, I attract as much attention as possible."

"Wow." Allabva couldn't think of anything better to say. "The secrecy really was just to get me here safely."

"Of course," Hronomon replied.

Allabva blinked. "Yes, I didn't doubt you. It's just that now it's really driven home. We made it here. I made it here and formed the bond, and now..." Allabva looked down at her hands, flexing them into fists. "Now I feel the strength of the bond. I guess it's fitting that we move on to the next phase, isn't it?"

"Yes," Hronomon replied.

"Hronomon," Allabva asked, not sure of what he would think, "may I call you by your name now? I mean, your real name, not your title."

"Yes. But if you talk about me, make sure people know the Forerunner is traveling; the Forerunner is finding strength to follow the Shrongelin."

Allabva laughed at Hronomon's serious demeanor. "Of course, Eretuquein." She paused, thoughtful. "You know, that still feels too formal. How about 'Tuki?'"

"Tuki?" Hronomon snorted.

"Yes, I think it's cute," Allabva said. "It fits you."

"It is cute, and it fits me?" Hronomon tried to reconcile his image of himself with Allabva's new nickname for him.

The Shrongelin laughed darkly. "Yes, *Tuki*, it fits you. Ha, ha, ha!" His laugh didn't sound real. It was something other-worldly, foreboding, even though Allabva knew his character to be benevolent at its core.

"Alright, Companion," the Shrongelin said, "it is time to—"

"Wait," Allabva interrupted. "Tuki." She chuckled to herself, grinning. "That's right, it's gonna stick. Tuki, can you tell my mother I'm alright?"

The white coated Nomord pursed his lips. "I won't be there as fast as we got here," he said at last. "My route, though essentially going back the way we came, will venture far and wide. Remember, I'm trying to contact as many people as possible."

"That's alright," Allabva conceded.

"Very well, then," Hronomon said. "I will find your mother and let her know that you made it here safely, that you have progressed to the next stage of your journey. Now, by your leave, I will depart back down the mountain the way we came up. Shrongelin, until Cylgiana."

"Yes, brother," the Shrongelin replied, "until Cylgiana. Come, Allabva, it is time to begin. We may not be in as much of a rush as you were on your way here. Now we have weeks or months to play with, not mere days. However, we have a lot to do. He looked at Allabva through narrow eyes, blinking, judging her. "I suppose your puny human body is hungry," he said.

Allabva raised an eyebrow at his manner, then nodded truthfully.

"Just one question, then."

"What's that?" Allabva asked nervously, not sure how to behave around this grisly Nomord. How did you act when you came face to face with legends themselves? He was both Nightshade Unicorn, the foreboding beast, portent of doom, and the Shrongelin, benefactor of mankind.

"Do you like strawberries?" he asked in a deep, rumbling voice.

Allabva blinked. "What?"

"Do you like berries?"

"Yes, of course," Allabva replied, intrigued at his pitch.

"Good. I know a good patch. It should only take us, oh, probably most of today to get there. No, wait. I almost forgot. You're bonded now. We'll be there in a few hours, as long as you're not too hungry already."

"No. Well..." Allabva said, "yes, I'm famished. But yeah, I could run." She bounced on her toes, testing her bond-enhanced strength. "Oh, wow. Yes, I could run quite a while, I think."

Chapter 3

Downhill

They set their march at a run, jogging down the trails, Allabva hopping up and down from one foot to the next, never having felt lighter in her life than she did at this moment. And yet, hunger tore through her. This sensation was powerful; she knew she needed to eat.

She smelled the berries fifty paces away, before the Shrongelin stopped and pointed them out.

"You'd better get some before I eat them all," he said, immediately leaning down to take a bite.

Allabva was surprised once more at his behavior; it was such a contrast from how Hronomon had acted. But as Hronomon had directed her to, she would exercise patience with the Nightshade.

She put his manner out of mind and dashed forward to nab her share. She found blackberries, still rather green and unripe, and she set about immediately picking them and shoving them in her mouth.

She found she was at a disadvantage against the Nomord, for he didn't pick out just the berries, preferring instead to bite off the entire section of bush wherever there were berries. Allabva started gathering berries more recklessly just to keep up. She pricked her finger several times in her haste to grab the berries before the competition got to them. Soon enough the bushes in front of them were picked clean.

The Shrongelin nodded at some red spots on the ground behind Allabva. "You can have those, though they're wild strawberries. I don't care for them myself. They taste like water, but they may provide you some nourishment." He turned away dismissively and stood a short way off while Allabva picked at the wild strawberries.

The Nightshade was right; they did taste like water, with not much flavor of their own. Still, Allabva was hungry, so she ate several. She stopped when the Nightshade nickered at her. She looked up, expecting some explanation.

"We have more time than you did before meeting me at the summit, but don't take all day."

Allabva sighed, then stood. "Of course." She jumped ahead of him and dashed down the trail, making a show of being ready to do her part and not shy from the challenge.

He quickly caught up. They looped down the trail, side by side where permitted, and where it didn't, one would jump ahead of the other, each of them daring the other to push the pace faster.

"Fool human," the Nightshade said impatiently. "You can't keep up with my pace. I know what you're doing. You're just trying to impress me."

Allabva rolled her eyes. "I'm just trying to do my part," she said, beginning to wonder if she should worry about impressing him after all. "I'm trying to show you that I'm ready. I can do what we need to."

"You can show me that when the time comes," he said. "For now, I'll slow it down for you." His words seemed to claim that he was doing something kind, but his tone made it an accusation. *I'll slow down because you need me to,* he seemed to say.

I can definitely tire of this attitude, Allabva thought.

"Those berries weren't enough, were they?" the Nightshade said.

Allabva pounded along beside him without answering his rhetorical question. Of course, they weren't enough. She was starving.

"There is a walnut tree ahead."

"But it's not the season for walnuts," Allabva protested. "There won't be anything there."

"Maybe you can find something on the ground," the Shrongelin replied. "They have thick shells. There's bound to be something edible."

Allabva sighed and advanced to the tree, performing a cursor search of the ground. She found several intact shells, but as she broke them open, she wondered why they were so soft and easy to break. Were the shells rotted away, or was it the strength of the bond? It didn't matter. In disgust, she tossed them away as she found the insides to be decayed or eaten by ants. She stood.

"I could go for nuts if there were any. Chicken would be perfect right now. I need something meaty."

"What about fish?" the Shrongelin suggested.

Allabva winced. Fish didn't tend to be her favorite.

"There's a stream up ahead," he said. "You might catch something there."

"How will I catch any fish?" she asked. "I don't have any fishing line or traps."

"That's up to you to figure out," he said. "Fish aren't part of my palate."

Allabva pursed her lips and continued jogging forward. As she came around a bend in the trail, she heard the stream the Nightshade had said was there. She continued running until she came to it. There was no bridge, although the footpath they followed continued on the other side of the stream. Whether she wanted fish or not, she was going to have to wade through the stream.

Without bothering to sit down, Allabva bent over to remove her boots and socks. She walked forward, placing her things on the stream bank, including boots, travel bag, walking stick, and the bow and quiver of arrows she had lifted from an assailant on the way up the mountain. She looked at the bow for a moment. Could she shoot a fish? No, she decided. She didn't have the necessary skill with the weapon.

She tested the water with her foot. Very cold. But she had to eat. Holding the skirt of her dress above her knees, she gingerly stepped into the water and found her way toward a pool where it was deeper than in the rest of the stream. She could see fish moving around in there.

Standing stock still, Allabva watched carefully and looked for the largest of the shapes she could see moving under the surface. She chose her target and slowly crouched down closer to the water and held her hand at the ready.

This is crazy, she thought. *How am I supposed to catch a fish like this? I should make a trap.* But instinctively, she followed her current plan. Feeling the right moment, she struck suddenly, reaching down with her free hand and snatched at the shape. The fish bolted, but Allabva still managed to grab it. In one try, she caught it with her bare hand.

She pulled the fish from the water as it wriggled and tried to shake free of her grasp. It threatened to break free and jump back into the water. Reflexively, she held it by the tail and smacked it against a rock. It stopped moving and hung limp in her grasp.

"You moved quickly," the Nightshade observed, walking up beside the stream. He didn't voice it as a compliment, but Allabva would take what she could get. Though, it seemed right to pass it back.

"I am going to blame your bond," she said happily. "I don't think I was ever so fast before."

"That, I can believe," the Shrongelin said gruffly, then turned his head to look down the trail. "Don't take all day with that fish."

Allabva was determined not to let the Nomord's sour mood get to her, but she was puzzled as to how she would eat it. "How am I supposed to cook it?" she said out loud. "I don't have any flint or kindling to make a fire."

"As I said before," the Shrongelin repeated, "*how* is up to you. You didn't need a line to catch it. Maybe you don't need a fire to cook it."

Allabva swallowed, raising her eyebrows. "Eat it raw?"

She already didn't prefer it, even if it was cooked. Taking a deep breath, she stepped out of the stream and grabbed her knife. Sitting down to brace her forearms on her knees, she cut the fish open down the middle of its belly. Then, setting the knife aside, Allabva pulled the skin apart to reveal the flesh underneath. Scowling, she took a bite and grimaced as she did her best not to chew it before swallowing.

It wasn't...absolutely awful, she supposed. It was somewhat edible. Allabva hated thinking that the poor thing had been alive just moments before, and she didn't let herself spend any thoughts on what parts of this fish she might be eating. Gingerly, she took a second bite and swallowed it again without chewing. She choked down two more bites, minding the flavor less with each one, but still disliking it. Having taken large bites and seeing that they were a significant part of the fish, which wasn't very big to begin with, she decided she was done and tossed it back in the creek.

"Alright, Shrongy," she said. "I've had some meat. Let's keep going."

The Nightshade paused before replying, eyeing her darkly for the impromptu nickname. "Are you sure that is enough?"

"For now," Allabva affirmed, nodding. "I've got another half day in me." She picked up her things and then waded across the stream to the other side, where she wiped the dirt off her feet before putting her socks and boots back on. "You said we're going to Tallensworth? Let's go."

"Don't get too used to this new strength," the Shrongelin told her as they trotted along.

"What do you mean?" Allabva said.

He took a moment longer to answer, apparently trying to respond thoughtfully. When he did, it was a backtrack.

"No, *do* get used to this strength. You'll need it, and you need to learn to use it well."

"Won't I do just that?" Allabva asked. "I'm experiencing it now as we bound down this mountainside. I caught that fish with my bare hand, right? Aren't I getting used to it already?"

"To be frank," the Shrongelin replied, "yes, in a way. But you will need to learn to fight, and you will need to learn when to hold back and when not to. Obviously, if you fight against humans and you don't want to inflict mortal damage, you will need to hold back. To do that skillfully, you will need to know the bounds of your strength. Also, when we go up into battle against Sacalai, you will need to know exactly when and how to apply your full strength."

"Won't I do that just by, you know, hitting as hard as I can?" Allabva asked.

"No," the Shrongelin replied, "except in appropriate moments. But you need to have balance to do that. You need coordination. You need to develop your speed."

"Alright, how do I do all that?"

"With practice," the Shrongelin said, "you will learn. I will train you."

"But how can I ever practice using this full, augmented strength? Won't I break things when I don't mean to?"

"Not if I take your strength away," the Shrongelin said.

"How do you take it away?" Allabva asked, surprised that this was possible while the bond was in place.

The Shrongelin stopped talking, leaving her question unanswered as he watched the valley ahead of them. From their vantage point, they were able to see two Ta-Nomord. It was uncommon to see two Nomord at the same time.

All the while that Allabva grew up, she had believed all Nomord to be female and all to be of fickle temperament. Everybody knew the Nomord possessed the power of speech but either did not care to hold a conversation with humans or didn't have the temperament or focus to do so.

Allabva had recently learned, when her traveling with Hronomon began, that there were male Nomord, called Gha-Nomord, and that both the Ta- and Gha-Nomord had engaged themselves in an epic impasse, periodically battling against the evil Sacalai when she escaped from her prison every few thousand years. They did this within the umbrella of the Construct, a magical structure that both female and male Nomord had enacted as a framework to set up a prison for

Sacalai. This Construct set the foundations for the prison and shield protecting the world from Sacalai's power. It also had the side effect of masking many of Hronomon's memories, which he would need to regain before he became the next Shrongelin.

It also kept the male and female Nomord separated from each other, both physically and spiritually. The Ta-Nomord wandered the world in a mental haze, partly existing in another realm. They pulled the world spiritually away from the evil influence of Sacalai. Meanwhile, the Gha-Nomord maintained the prison to confine Sacalai. Thus, while she remained imprisoned, the male Nomord resided together to hold the prison on the isle of Mascaldinig and, spiritually and mentally, out of view of the female Nomord. The Ta-Nomord were utterly unable to perceive the presence of any male Nomord, even if they encountered them in the flesh.

Right now, Sacalai's prison was aging and weakening, creating the haste to get Allabva bonded to the Shrongelin and trained for battle, and to rally the armies of the world at the fields of Apthane.

Allabva watched the Shrongelin looking out at the valley and viewing the two Nomord. "You must miss them," Allabva said empathetically.

He scowled at her, then turned back to the valley slope below them.

Of course, he misses them, Allabva told herself, *but with his permanently sour mood, he won't admit it.* It was deeper than that, though, she realized. Although this fearsome and yet benevolent beast was still alive, he had already given his life to stave off Sacalai's inevitable victory for one more cycle.

He was just yet another volunteer in a whole line of Gha-Nomord who had stepped into the role, first as

Hronomon and then as Shrongelin. The current Hronomon, Eretuquein, had significant holes in his memory, but he had told Allabva that once the current Shrongelin had fulfilled his mission and had re-imprisoned the evil Sacalai, he would exhaust his magical power and be rendered mortal. He would live out his days, if he were lucky, and die of old age.

The two beautiful creatures the Nightshade watched on the slope below them would remain in the world indefinitely, along with all the other immortal Nomord who survived the coming battle and desolation. After the battle and Sacalai's reimprisonment, the female Nomord would be returned to their state of innocence until the prison would burst once again. Likewise, the male Nomord would all return to Mascaldinig, guarding the prison both physically and magically for another period of approximately four thousand years. Then, tragically, the cycle would repeat. Sacalai would escape again, and another Companion and Shrongelin would re-imprison her.

But the best-case scenario was still unacceptable. Allabva shook her head. Even if they won the day and no Nomord were slain in the battle, this one standing next to her was already a casualty of the war. He was doomed to spend his power and live out a mortal life. Every repetition of the cycle of the Construct slew a Shrongelin. And while human civilization and the rest of the world would live on to forget this battle and this calamity, Sacalai would be one step closer to winning her age-old war of attrition. One day, she would break out of her prison for the last time. One day, the world would finally fall to her forever.

Allabva's heart shattered. It was hopeless. Why even fight? She grew weary on her feet, and her frame shook, wanting to repose. She trembled and wobbled on her feet in a daze.

The Shrongelin turned his head and looked at Allabva in alarm. Then, with smugness, he laughed—*laughed* at her.

"You feel the tiniest sliver of my burden, girl!" he said. His voice rose. "You feel the weight of a single ounce of my suffering. Be glad you do not feel the pounding, the constant blows, as Sacalai screams and batters at the walls of her prison to be shaken." His voice lowered again. "Yes, you feel a tiny sliver. Maybe you can begin to understand. All you have to do is multiply that a hundredfold and carry it for *four thousand years*. Then, you will know."

The black-coated Nomord harrumphed and resumed his march down the mountain without another word. Allabva didn't think he would be answering any more questions for now.

Chapter 4

Open Air

Two days after leaving the summit, after they had been on the road for several hours, Allabva realized that this experience was in stark contrast to her travels with Hronomon after leaving the Cleft. The bond seemed to help her sleep warmer, but the difference she noted was in how the Nightshade didn't seem to take any side roads with consideration to avoid human traffic. They were coming down into the foothills and spending less time on switchbacks, and the Shrongelin's distinct coat would never be mistaken for one of the numberless white Nomord that the people of the world were used to seeing from time to time.

"Nightshade, do we not need to be concerned about people seeing us travel together? Or seeing you at all?"

"Let them see," the Nightshade said gruffly. "Hronomon would have exercised caution with you, yes? If you were attacked before the bonding, you could not fight back. Now you are stronger. And Sacalai's attention will be turned somewhat, not to mention that we are enjoying at least a few days of her being weakened."

"Her attention is turned?" Allabva asked.

"She tried to prevent our bonding. Now that it has already occurred, she will shift her focus to trying to win our ancient war."

"How does she try to do that?"

"Gathering her forces," the Nightshade said, sounding as if he were having to exercise great patience while explaining a basic concept. Then his patience shifted into fatigue. "She gathers her forces, we gather ours. We meet in the northeast, where we have always met."

"Why is it always the same place?"

The Nightshade growled. Allabva hadn't ever known a horse to growl, but at least one Nomord could. "She has a stronghold in the north where she makes her stand."

"Is that where her prison is?"

"Her prison is in the north, yes," Nightshade said in exasperation, "but that is at Mascaldinig, an isle apart from anything else. Her stronghold is beyond Amonfweer."

Allabva thought for a moment. "If you know where she's going to go, why can't you head her off?"

The Shrongelin chewed for several moments on nothing before answering, this time without showing impatience.

"Several factors. My brothers and I are holding the prison as long as we can. That requires the bulk of us to remain at Mascaldinig. Our sisters are not capable of mounting a fight until the prison bursts and their minds return fully to this realm. Together, we are constrained to wait."

"Oh," Allabva said.

"Even more compelling than that, Sacalai is far more powerful than any of us, and has always proved herself to be a nearly unbeatable foe. Even when we do combine, she has placed defenses to make it impossible for us to approach her stronghold unless we are at our full strength. Until we are all gathered in a single force, only then can we—"

"What's that?" Allabva exclaimed, pointing off the road to the right, some distance away, where she could see a massive animal slowly reaching up to grab foliage from the trees. "I didn't know they lived here. I mean, I knew they lived on the southern coast. I'd heard stories. I didn't know they lived this far east. And, wow, I can't believe how large it is!"

The Shrongelin examined Allabva with an annoyed gaze, bored with the sight of the ground sloth that had Allabva fascinated. After a moment, he simply looked at the road ahead of himself and replied nothing while they continued at a trot.

Allabva continued watching the sloth for several minutes as they progressed closer to it. She wanted as good a look as possible at this new sight, though they wouldn't come terribly close to its position off the road. Having easily grabbed a mouthful of branches and leaves from its chosen tree, it bent back down and rested with all four paws on the ground while it chewed pensively. Allabva burned the image into her mind, determined that this, and everything else she encountered, she was bound to protect from Sacalai's ravaging.

When she turned her eyes back to the Shrongelin and saw him waiting for her to finish gawking, it was her turn to be annoyed. She was confident that she was less annoyed than he looked, though.

"What? I can't enjoy new sights?"

"Of course you can," the Shrongelin drawled. "Just like any other young foal probing out into the world for the first time."

Allabva had had enough of this. She had to work with this Nightmare Unicorn, but she didn't have to enjoy every aspect of his personality.

"You're right," she said, "I'm very young, not yet a month as an adult. I've never seen one of these animals before, so I find it interesting. There's nothing wrong with that, is there? Besides, aren't we trying to protect that as well?"

"As everything else, yes," the Nightshade relented.

"Well, I like it," she concluded, sad that she wasn't seeing eye to eye with the Nomord, "even if you don't care."

The Shrongelin inhaled deeply, then exhaled heavily. "I do care, Companion. I will fight to protect humans, to protect Nomord, and to protect the wordless beasts of this world. But did not my Forerunner talk to you about duty? I have a duty. And now, as you agreed to the terms of the bonding atop the Summit Above the Aspens, *you* have a duty. This duty burns above all and will require every sacrifice."

Allabva saw that the Shrongelin was going to be as single-minded as his Forerunner was. She felt a need to break that attitude, or at least soften it. "Shrongelin, do you—" she said aloud, pausing to turn to him and make sure the question drove home, "Don't you have a name?"

"You may call the Shrongelin," he said gruffly, eyes wide at what Allabva perceived must have been some kind of breach of protocol.

"I know I can. And I know that if I were to translate it into Eslarna, I can call you Guardian, right?"

The Shrongelin nodded once.

"But what is your *name*?" she pressed. "You told me Hronomon's name."

"We believed him deceased. It was appropriate to render honor to him."

"He still has a name, even if he's not dead, and so do you. So, what is? You remember it, don't you?" she jabbed.

The Nightshade didn't answer.

"You know your name, don't you?" Allabva pressed again.

"I do," he confirmed. "But I will not share it with you at this time. We must focus, and my individuality is entirely secondary to the world's plight. We must prepare, and we must fight."

"I know that, but apart from your duty—" Allabva began.

"My duty is all that I have," the Nightshade growled.

Allabva sighed. This was similar to a conversation she'd had with Hronomon, except that this time, it was more aggressive. "I know that. Your duty is very important to you and to the world."

"It is *all* that matters, until Sacalai is back in her prison," the Nightshade interjected.

"In some regards, yes," Allabva conceded. "But I want to know—who are you? Hronomon—Eretuquein—you and he both. You're so tied up in your duty. And...and that's not bad," Allabva said. "I agree that it is important. Vital, truthfully. But *you* matter too. So, who are you? What is your true name? What do you like to do? Can't you remember life before this war?"

The Nightshade wasn't hearing it.

"Help me imprison Sacalai. Help me save the world one more time, as has been done many times before. Then, when I am mortal, when I no longer carry the title of the Guardian or the responsibility that comes with it, when all I have left is my name and my weakened mortal body, then you will learn my name. For now, you may call me Shrongelin, or Guardian." He finished with a finality that told Allabva she wouldn't get anywhere.

She kept her mouth shut.

"I would appreciate it if you stopped prattling on with this nonsense," the Nightshade warned, giving her a glare even more intense than before. "We will focus on our mission."

Allabva mourned the Nomord's emotional stoppage, caused by ages of hopeless struggle. She took several deep breaths to calm herself. She knew she could trust Hronomon. Hronomon had come to her with the special gift of the Forerunner, able to perceive the nature of one's soul with the touch of his horn. He had gauged her and found her to be what he considered a good match to be the Companion for the Shrongelin.

Allabva was still trying to figure out what that meant. But when Hronomon had seen inside her mind, she had also seen inside his. She knew she could trust the Forerunner. Eretuquein—Tuki, she thought of him fondly. They'd become friends, right? She knew she could trust him, at any rate. And Hronomon had said to trust the Shrongelin and to be patient with him.

Allabva mentally put on some thicker emotional coats. The Shrongelin had been rather rude, but she knew implicitly that they were fighting on the same side. Or at least, she knew implicitly that Hronomon believed they were fighting on the same side. Allabva believed it as well, but the thought made her cast a sideways glance at her black-coated traveling companion. What if his gruffness exceeded his judgment and bearing? Could the Nightshade Unicorn inadvertently be pushed to behave, to act, in a manner that was not beneficial to the world?

Allabva shook her head, trying to put the thought out of mind. If that were the case, then the world really would be lost. The Construct—all the memory, all the plans that she assumed they had laid carefully—depended on the Shrongelin acting in tandem with his Companion to stop Sacalai.

Frustrated, she ran in silence for some time. She would find a way to reach him sooner or later.

Now the sight of the ground sloth was long behind her, but she wished she could see it once again. She looked down the road ahead of them, missing the mountain vistas they had enjoyed over the past couple of days. At least she felt closer to everything down here, closer to life.

A few hours after leaving the forest behind, Allabva began to see fences marking farmland on either side of the road, as well as the occasional farmhouse nestled between rows of planted crops or pastures with cows or sheep. She wondered how the people here dealt with the monstrous ground sloths and. Surely, they must break fences sometimes. Thinking of that, she noticed the fences were generally taller and looked like they had been built with thicker beams than she was used to seeing back home.

A question occurred to Allabva.

"Shrongelin, why are we going to Tallensworth specifically?"

The Shrongelin slowed to a walk and gave Allabva a long sideways stare. "Yes," his deep voice finally relented. "If I'm going to work with you, you need to understand many things. The Guides came to us."

He shook his head. "No, I need to start before that. They are a few sailors that came to our island. Without them, every cycle in the Construct, we male Nomord are bound at Mascaldinig. It has been my home for many thousands of years now. We reside close to Sacalai's physical prison to hold it as long as we can.

"When it is coming near to breaking, the Guardian and the Forerunner venture into the world. The Guardian always goes directly to the Summit Above the Aspens. That location is protected from Sacalai's memory, so it is always the same place. The Hronomon, the Forerunner, searches abroad, looking for the right personality to bring to the Shrongelin. I admit, it is something of a blind search, as the face of human civilization changes greatly in the amount of time that we are gone. The Ta-Nomord are among humanity, but without their wits about them, they are useless to guide the search. When we have a Companion, or thereabouts, we begin raising forces.

"That also begins as a blind search. We attempt to determine which lands to go to that are most likely to yield faithful and valiant troops. Sometimes we have more success than others, and other times the battle that we face is particularly difficult, as we find ourselves racing, marching troops across the land at breakneck speed to assault through Amonfweer to the fortress of Sacalai before she gains too much strength and becomes insuperable."

The Shrongelin lowered his head. "Last cycle was one such occurrence. I was the Forerunner, and..." he searched for words.

Was the Nightshade Unicorn being introspective? Maybe Allabva had broken his shell. Then the look vanished. His gaze turned again as hard as steel.

"I feel shame for not bringing the Companion to the previous Shrongelin faster than I did. I feel shame for failing to rally enough forces fast enough to make it a stronger battle than I did. We barely won. But we did win, and I have felt

Sacalai's poundings against my mind as a reward. I suffer, but duty is all there is."

Allabva raised her eyebrows and blinked. Back on the duty kick, was he?

"Alright," she said aloud. "How about we discuss these plans? The Guides—"

"Yes, the Guides," the Shrongelin recovered quickly. "Three sailors who lived with us for a time. They were able to tell us about the outside world. They told us what nations have strong armies and navies. They told us of the culture of each nation, and we did our best to hazard a guess at which of these cultures would be most likely to stand strong against the mental influence of Sacalai. As a result, we were able to set a proper itinerary, a route that we will travel, beginning with Tallensworth. It is hopefully both the quickest route we could plan and yield the best results militarily, in order to bring a significant force to bear at the battlegrounds at Amonfweer."

Allabva took a deep breath. It sounded like a big responsibility. "I'm game," she said cheerfully, putting on a mask.

Part II: Society Again

Chapter 5

Dusty Pot

"How much farther do you think it is to get to Tallensworth?" Allabva asked the Shrongelin that evening.

"Probably a day and a half," he said.

"So that means two more nights, I suppose," Allabva voiced. "Now that we're down off the mountain, I know I won't sleep as cold as I did the last two nights. But it wouldn't hurt if I could find a bed for a few hours and sleep properly."

"Sleep in a bed while you can, young one," the Shrongelin said.

Was he trying to brush her needs aside as insignificant? Still, poorly behaved or not, Allabva reminded herself he was fighting for the same team.

"What do you mean?"

"I mean exactly what I said, young one. Sleep in a bed while you can."

She'd been right. It was his name for her. *Now smile through it,* she told herself. *Just smile through it.*

"Right. Until when?"

"Until we're on campaign toward Amonfweer. You'll sleep when and where you can once we're in the field of battle or on the way to it. There will be times when you'll be glad to have half an hour just to call the grass your bed."

Allabva wasn't sure how to respond to that, so she didn't.

Then she caught an inviting smell. Allabva wasn't sure what food it was, but it certainly smelled like a hot prepared dinner. She could see a building in the distance with a sign out front. It was too far to make out what the sign had on it, but she felt sure that this was an inn.

"I think I just spotted my bed up ahead," she said, hopefully. Then she fished for her coin purse...

Oh, no!, she thought, *those men robbed me.* Tuki had forced them to return her bag and staff to her, but her coin purse hadn't been in the bag when Hronomon had forced them to return it to her.

"I don't have any coin," she said aloud. "But even if I had enough, people out here probably only take hafender, so the thaler I had before wouldn't do me any good anyway."

Her companion shook his head. "If I know humans, they'll take your shiny little discs, no matter what. They might value them less if they don't look the same as the coins they're used to, but they'll take them."

"I'm afraid that doesn't help me right now," Allabva lamented.

"Well," the Nightshade turned, his menacing face now looking mischievous, "how about you start recruiting?"

"Recruiting? I'm not any kind of leader yet."

"It's going to happen sometime. Might as well happen now."

"But, recruiting? How?"

"I'll hang back. You go in alone."

"What? Just because I'm strong enough to defend myself doesn't mean that I can go in there and just convince them to give me a meal and a bed," she protested.

"No. Don't go begging. Go bargaining."

His face now bore a sick grin, if Allabva could imagine that expression on a horse's face. He was enjoying this, whatever it was he was thinking of.

"Bargaining? With what?"

"Go tell them you'll arm wrestle them for your supper. Make a bet. Have some fun with it."

Allabva felt the color drain from her face at the imagined embarrassment. "Arm wrestle for my dinner? How could I?"

"You don't know how to arm wrestle?"

"Yes, but that's just so brazen. That's not me. That's not who I am."

"Don't tell them all about your feelings inside. You don't have to give them your name. Just tell them you're the Companion. Start building a reputation for the Companion. It will serve our cause."

Allabva's eyebrows almost rose off her face, trying to hold on to each other for dear life as they scrunched together.

"Arm wrestle for my dinner?"

"That's what I said," the Nightshade reiterated with poorly masked glee. "Don't worry. I'll be within earshot. If there's any real trouble, you'll be able to fight them off for enough time until I get there."

Allabva thought about it. She supposed that was true. Unless...

"What if somebody pulls out a knife?"

"Then push it away. They won't be fast enough to catch you unaware as long as you're on your guard."

Allabva felt deflated. She didn't like the beast's idea, but she didn't have a better one. And she smelled that food—beef, mutton, potatoes, carrots. There was even some fish in there, and she was hungry enough that it smelled good to her. She *needed* that food.

"Fine. I guess I'll meet you—"

"On the next rise," he finished for her, "beyond the inn. In the morning, as early as you wake up. I will not come and wake you, but remember that the faster we get to Tallensworth, the more time we will have to work with, and the more effective we will be with our efforts."

Allabva tossed her hands high in the air, shaking her head in surrender. Then she left the Nightshade Unicorn behind and jogged the half-league ahead of her until the inn.

Allabva approached the small inn and gave the front of it a look-over. It was a log structure with a different type of roof than she had seen back in the Cleft or in Palf Glen. In Palf Glen, most of the roofs were thatched or shingled. This roof appeared to be shingles from a distance, but as she neared, she saw the shingles were chunks of wood. A lone horse was tied to a post in front of the inn.

She looked at the sign, which she was now close enough to read. It said *Dusty Pot,* but the image drawn on the sign was obviously that of a barrel. She figured this was due to regional differences. "Pot" must be what they called a barrel here.

Feeling the strangeness of what she was intending to do, she reached up and idly thumbed the necklace from which Delgan's flute hung. She was supposed to give it back, he'd said. It was his way of making sure she followed through on her word to come to dinner. Allabva wholeheartedly wanted to, but then Hronomon had shown up on her doorstep in the middle of the night and she hadn't even had a chance to say goodbye to Delgan before she left. She twisted the cord around her finger, then pulled her finger out and let the weight of the flute pull the cord straight again. She repeated the action, heaved a sigh of determination, and stepped inside.

Inside, Allabva found a medium-sized dining room with tables set about for guests to sit at while they ate. There were only a couple of people seated at the tables—one with a plate and the other with a bowl, spooning some kind of soup into his mouth. Allabva stood there awkwardly, trying to determine the best way to go about this. She would obviously have to talk to the proprietor and shouldn't bother these guests, but she didn't see any proprietor at the moment.

The door opened at the side of the room, and a young man walked in. His blue shirt was buttoned up the front, but had no collar. His trousers appeared to be held in place by a kind of drawstring rather than a proper belt.

"Welcome, miss," he said. "Jaldren's the name. Were you needing anything, Miss..." he prompted.

"Allabva," she replied, not thinking of the Nightshade's suggestion of calling herself the Companion. It sounded silly to her. "And I don't have any Tallen hafender, so I don't know if you'll take my money. I'm afraid I don't have much."

She couldn't force herself to challenge him to an arm wrestle out of the blue, could she? There needed to be some kind of paradigm of a game or some friendship already between them for that.

"Well, what do you have?" he asked.

Allabva stammered. "Actually, I don't have anything."

Jaldren looked her over. "You look tired, and you look like you've been traveling a lot. I could probably bring you a piece of fruit."

Allabva gave him a half smile. *Every bit of food would help,* she told herself. "That'll work. And..." She stalled. Embarrassed, she almost didn't go on. "If you'd like, I could play a tune on this," she pulled the flute out of her blouse, "in appreciation for the piece of fruit, of course," she said.

He eyed her appreciatively. "Don't want a handout, huh? I can respect that. I don't think we need any entertainment, but you'd be welcome to provide some. And to be honest, I am curious to hear what you have to play."

Allabva secretly wished she hadn't felt the need to offer anything. She barely knew a single tune with the instrument, and she played that haltingly.

"Right," Jaldren said. "I'll be right back."

He disappeared back into the kitchen, and she could hear his voice come through the door. "Mother, there's a traveler with no coin. I'm going to give her an apple."

Another voice responded. "Alright, Jaldren. Just don't give her more than that."

"No worries," he said.

Jaldren reappeared with an apple in one hand and an orange in the other. Allabva had to restrain herself to keep her eyes from popping at the sight of the fruit. Maybe she didn't realize how hungry she was, or perhaps the bond with the Shrongelin added to her senses, but she could smell the orange as soon as it appeared. And she would much prefer that to the apple, which was dark red and looked like it might be bruised, but she restrained herself. When Jaldren proffered her the apple, she accepted it graciously.

"Have a seat," Jaldren said, gesturing to a nearby table and then seating himself. "If you don't mind sharing, I'm curious about your travels."

Allabva sat and stared back at him. "I... I'm not sure. I don't know if—"

"Come on," he said. "People come through here all the time. It's not like you're gonna surprise me with something I haven't heard before."

Allabva knew for a fact that her story was something Jaldren hadn't heard before. "Well," she said, wanting to turn the exchange elsewhere, "how about... how about if I arm wrestle you? And if I win, then I don't have to tell you anything."

Jaldren did a double take. "You—you really don't want to tell me anything, do you? Well, alright," he eyed her up and down. "And if I win, then you tell me where you spent last night, or what direction you came from. That's it."

"Alright," Allabva nodded slowly. "Very well." She put her right elbow on the table and opened her hand, placing her left hand holding the apple under her right arm so she could use her left arm as balance.

Jaldren copied the movement and took her right hand in his while he set himself up. "Alright, on three," he said. "One, two, three."

Allabva could feel the pressure on her palm from his attempt to down her hand to the table. She felt the pressure, but she how light it was surprised her. She looked at their hands clasped together, then up at Jaldren, who appeared to be surprised at how much he was having to exert himself and still achieve no movement.

Allabva felt bad and decided she couldn't just beat him like this out of the blue. It didn't feel right.

So, slowly, she allowed her hand to sink backward until her knuckles touched the table surface. Jaldren gasped at the effort he had applied, but then smiled. "Aha. Now tell me. Where did you spend last night, or what direction did you come from?"

Allabva sighed but returned the smile. She did want to be polite, but the smile was truly genuine. She was entertained, and it was nice to have some friendly human companionship for the first time since Doctor Noteh had put the salve on her feet several days before. Had it been a full week since then? Blinking, she opened her mouth. "I came down from Tallen Mountain. I spent the night up there."

Jaldren didn't reply but remained gazing at her expectantly with one eyebrow cocked, as if waiting for more.

"I just slept in a patch of grass and tried to use my cloak as a blanket," Allabva admitted.

"Ham hocks!" Jaldren said. "No wonder you look the way you do." His eyes went wide. "No, I didn't mean that. I mean, yes, you must—you look tired. I already said that. No wonder you look tired."

Allabva laughed. "I'm not offended. You're right, I must look horrendous right now," she breathed.

Jaldren looked relieved at not offending a guest, paying or no. Then he grinned. "I'll play you again."

"What?"

"Let's go again with another arm wrestle."

"What for?" Allabva said, pausing as she was about to take a bite of the unappetizing-looking apple.

"Come on," he said. "I see how you look at the apple. I look at it the same way. That thing came in from Iddypol or from—"

"That thing came in from Iddypol. It was picked weeks ago, and it traveled by ship to reach here. You don't want that apple; you want this orange."

Allabva shook her head. "The apple is fine, thank you. Besides, I heard your mother tell you not to give me anything more."

Jaldren laughed again. "Nope, I won't give you anything more. You'll win it from me in an arm wrestle."

"I see," she said, a grin crossing her face to match Jaldren's. "An arm wrestle for the orange. If I win, I get the orange. And if I lose, then what? I give you the apple back?"

"No, silly," he said. "If you lose, you tell me where you spent the night before last."

"Fine. Let's go."

Allabva set her hand again in the middle of the table, and Jaldren took it, setting himself in position for another contest.

She decided this time she would win. Jaldren seemed to want to give her the orange anyway. So, when he said, "One, two, three, go," and she felt the gentle pressure from his palm again, she slowly pushed her hand the other direction, bringing her palm down to force the back of Jaldren's hand onto the table.

When his hand hit the table, he broke contact while his face turned back from red to its regular shade. He pointed at her and said, "How did you do that? You were really hard to beat the first time, and the second time you looked like you didn't exert any effort to win."

He plopped the orange between them in the center of the table.

Allabva wasn't going to let this opportunity pass. She grabbed the orange, leaving the apple in its place in case Jaldren wanted to take it back, and immediately opened the skin and began to peel it.

"Sorry," Allabva teased. "I guess I just won. Besides, owing you an explanation wasn't part of the bargain, so I think I'm going to decline."

Now Jaldren looked at her with admiration. "Alright, then," he said. "Keep your secrets. And the orange," he nodded, gesturing. "But, hmm... best two of three. But this time, I get to use both hands. And if you *still* win, I'll bring you dinner and tell my mom you paid for a room, if you're looking for a place to sleep."

"What? No," Allabva said. "Don't lie to your mother. And remember, she told you not to give me anything else." She wanted the room, though.

Jaldren laughed. "Yes, but as I said with the orange, I won't give it to you. You'll win it off me. I'll smooth it over with Mother."

"I wouldn't want to stick around if there might be any problem," Allabva said.

"Fine," Jaldren said. "I'll go smooth it over first." He stood quickly and dashed into the kitchen. Allabva imagined she was probably drawing attention from the other guests, and she wished she could turn invisible for the moment.

This time, she couldn't hear what Jaldren said on the other side of the wall, but she could hear his tone of voice—excited—as he talked to his mother. When he came back, she followed, a middle-aged woman with straight dark brown hair, tan skin, and hazel eyes. She wore a dress that appeared to be made of two halves, such that it was one color in the front and another in the back, a tan-and-brown combination.

"Now this I have to see," the proprietress said. "Alright, young lady, you beat him here in an arm wrestle. He uses two hands and you win, you get dinner and free accommodations for the evening."

"Alright," Allabva said sheepishly. She chewed and then swallowed the bit of orange she had in her mouth. The fruit was already half gone in the moments it took for Jaldren to bring his mother out.

"Alright," Jaldren's mother said. "Let's have at it then, and see what you've got."

For the third time, Allabva set her right elbow on the table, with her left fist underneath her arm, her right hand held open in the air. Jaldren sat down across from her and prepared to take her hand for the arm wrestle. Allabva sat there coolly, waiting for the contest to begin.

The innkeeper made a funny expression. "You know what? This is interesting enough for me that even if you lose, I'll give you an entrée."

"Thank you—" Allabva said, but then Jaldren added his left hand to his grip in that moment and started pulling Allabva's hand backward. She resisted and held the spot. Jaldren grunted lightly and repositioned his weight so that he could pull with greater force. Allabva held the position and didn't budge. Jaldren's cheeks puffed out and he blew air through his lips, bracing himself against the table as he exerted himself further. Allabva felt the pressure against her palm, but it didn't feel like all that much to her.

Well, she didn't come here to sit as still as a statue all night, so she gently moved her palm toward her left side.

"No!" Jaldren said, trying to pull with all his strength now. Allabva continued, slowly lowering Jaldren's hands to the table. When his knuckles pressed against the wood, she stopped and let go. Jaldren was sweating and breathing heavily.

"Oh, my silver!" the innkeeper said. "Young lady, how did you do that?" Allabva shrugged sheepishly, trying as hard as she could not to be a spectacle, even though she had just done something that even she still found extremely surprising.

"Are you even sure you need the meal? You've certainly got your strength up. My silver!" the innkeeper repeated.

"Actually," Allabva said, "I could really use a meal. I haven't eaten much in the past few days. And, if you could, I would greatly appreciate some accommodations for the night, and then I'll be on my way."

"What did you say your name was?" the middle-aged woman asked. Allabva was feeling very self-conscious under the attention. She shifted her eyes from Jaldren to his mother.

"You can call me..." She almost got it out. She almost asked the woman to call her, "the Companion," but she paused. Her hesitation was due to how unnatural it felt to her, how she supposed she would be putting on airs, trying to give herself any sort of title. She was just a farm girl away from her orchard, and she had already given Jaldren her real name. "Just call me Allabva," she said at last.

Jaldren said, "Sorry, Mother. It took me a moment to remember. She told me earlier."

"Wow. And where are you from, Allabva? Do you have a family name as well?" Allabva froze. She didn't want to give her surname as well. She had already given her true given name, against the Shrongelin's recommendation.

"Companion," she said at last. Maybe these people would take it as some kind of surname.

"Allabva Companion," the proprietress tried out in her mouth. "Alright, well, beef or mutton?"

"Mutton, please, and thank you," Allabva said. She hoped the rationale for the free meal would soon be forgotten, despite her easy win at the arm wrestle.

"Potatoes and carrots?"

Allabva nodded.

"Alright, just give me a minute." The hostess wandered into the kitchen. "My silver!" Allabva overheard the hostess say one more time as she disappeared.

One of the other guests stood up, leaving a few coins next to his plate, but he didn't make his way to the exit. Instead, he came over to Allabva and addressed her.

"Allabva Companion? Can I say, 'the Companion?'" he asked.

She shrugged permissively. "Yes."

"Can I try to beat you in an arm wrestle as well?"

Allabva froze. She had already settled her dinner and a bed for the night. She didn't need anything else.

"Look here. Have a copper hafender for the attempt, and I'll give you two silvers if you win."

Allabva flinched at this. This could pay for dinner and a bed tomorrow night. "Alright," she said.

"Excuse me, Jaldren," the man said.

Jaldren moved out of the way.

The gentleman sat, dressed in a leather coat and hat. Allabva guessed he was some kind of farmer or rancher from the look of him. His beard reached halfway down his chest, with white streaks that marked his advancing middle age. Allabva would have placed him as probably a boy when her father was born. He settled himself and pulled one hand up. Allabva slowly placed her hand into the man's rather large palm.

"And I'm sure you won't mind," the man said, "since I'm the one putting up the coin for this little challenge, if I give myself, but not you, the privilege of using two hands."

Allabva gulped. She wasn't sure how her strength would compare to this grown man. She had heard that middle age for men brought decreased energy levels but greater brute strength.

"I'll be gentle about it if you promise to do the same," he smiled with a friendly air.

"Of course," Allabva said.

She felt him pull with just his right hand, slowly at first. She resisted the movement, and he pulled harder. He changed the angle of his wrist, trying to hook her hand in a way that would alter the angle of her elbow and make things much harder for her. She felt the change and perceived that she did have less leverage because of it, but she was still able to hold. The man's face turned red. He reached up with his other hand.

Allabva started to pull, the muscles in her arm flexing as she righted the angle of her wrist against his force. The man's brow furrowed in concentration. He leaned to his left, trying to pull with his weight. Allabva's arm still held position. She increased her force, applying more strength to her grasp. Allabva's legs started coming up off the bench she sat on, making her realize that her weight disadvantage was coming into play. She shifted her left hand underneath the table so she would have something to rotate her right hand toward.

The man heaved and hauled, but Allabva slowly brought the back of his right hand down against the table against his will. When his knuckles touched, he released his hold and collapsed into a slouch in his chair. He looked at Allabva in amazement. "Who are you, young lady, and what do they feed you where you come from?"

Allabva laughed. "Well, if you must know..." he trailed off, feeling strange talking about it. Her mission had been a secret between her and Hronomon ever since she left home. Her mother knew *why* she left, but not even her mother had known—not even Allabva herself had known—*where* she was headed when she left home. "Well, how do I say this?" Allabva said.

The man's eyes narrowed to slits. "You got some kind of secret, young lady?"

"It was until now." Then she forced it out. "A Nomord...stallion."

The man's eyebrows shot up. "Male Nomord?"

Allabva pursed her lips and nodded. "One of them gave me the strength."

The man's mouth hung open. "First you tell me there is a male Nomord, and then you tell me that he gave you this strength? Like some kind of... I don't know. Sure, the Nomord can heal, but giving you strength is something different."

"It is," Allabva admitted.

"So why did he do it, if you're so convinced it's a 'he?'"

"Oh, I'm convinced," she confirmed, eyes wide. "I've actually met two of them now."

"Really, now? You met them. As in, you talked to them?"

"Yes," Allabva confirmed.

"And they talked back? You conversed?"

"Yes."

"Why? How am I supposed to believe this?"

"I'm traveling with one. I traveled with one and now I'm traveling with the other," she said.

"Where is he now?" the man laughed, looking around and spreading his arms. Allabva was having trouble reading his manner.

"He's staying outside."

"Alright, Alright. You have this strength. I'll give you that, and maybe this Nomord stallion is somewhere outside," the man conceded. "But why?"

Allabva got very serious. She hoped the man would believe her. She started shivering, feeling exposed as though to the cold, as she opened up. "The world is in danger."

"Everything's in danger," the man countered. "It's always in danger. Why, the overduke of Tallensworth had to send soldiers up to Grinswolder last month to put down some highwaymen, and the Dukes' Council is always putting their fingers in this business or that, trying to control things."

"I'm sure it's like that in other countries, too," Allabva replied.

The man got quiet. "I've heard of these people called Disaffected, gathering up on the other side of these here mountains. That's a new thing in the world. They say they need to change the social order. I figure if you want to change the social order around you, you just go to another country and it's different there. Pick your favorite locale, and you're set."

"I see..." Allabva thought about her less than pleasant interactions with the five Disaffected who had abducted her on the road toward Palf Glen.

"Although," the man continued, "I've also heard tell that they specifically dislike the Nomord. They even refuse to call them that. They always call them unicorns, or horned horses, or beasts." He was mumbling to himself and looking down at the table. His eyes perked up, and he looked back at Allabva.

"Now you're saying there are male Nomord. So, what's going on? What's the full story?"

Allabva took a deep breath. She hadn't expected to be essentially recruiting to her cause right here in the Dusty Pot common room, at the first inn she came to.

"It's like I said," she answered softly, becoming aware that Jaldren was standing next to the table, intently listening as well. "The world is in trouble. I don't think I can tell you everything, but something is coming, and I'm trying to help the Nomord prepare the world for it."

"You're traveling far to do this? You look like you come from Weslan Fields."

"Close," Allabva said.

"Alright, fine. Some western part of Eslarna. I assume you're going to Tallensworth. You're trying to talk to the overduke?"

Allabva opened her hands in a gesture of innocence. "Guilty as charged."

"What's your plan when you get in front of him, if you get in front of him?"

"I'm not sure…"

Allabva didn't know what to say. If she said, "Nightshade Unicorn," or if she said, "the Shrongelin," either one was likely to gain some kind of visceral reaction. One was said in legend to be a kind of demon, and the other was believed in many places to be a deity. She settled on translating his actual title.

"The Nomord—the Guardian knows the plan. I don't know all of it. I only know the gist of it."

"Well, I'll be," he said. "And your Nomord buddy is hiding somewhere outside?"

"Well, I don't know if he's hiding," Allabva answered truthfully, "but I did say he's waiting outside."

"And now, after you've told me this..." The man leaned in across the table and lowered his voice. "You don't know me. How can you be sure you're going to be allowed to sleep well tonight, and not get yanked out of bed? Or stabbed? News like this is bound to make somebody mad."

"True," Allabva said. "But... Well, you felt me arm wrestle you. I can hold my own long enough for the Guardian to get here. He's staying within earshot," Allabva added.

"The Companion," the man repeated, letting his mouth hang open. "Well, I guess... I've got to go about my business. I've got leagues to cover before I sleep. Calving season, you know. Jaldren, you have a good one." The man rose. "My name's Scaltern Wold." He extended a hand to Allabva.

She took his hand.

Scaltern shook once, then released.

"Jaldren, give your mother my best."

"Of course," Jaldren answered, who had been sitting nearby and heard the whole conversation.

Scaltern departed without another word.

"The Guardian..." Jaldren began, sitting down in front of Allabva again. "What does he look like?"

She paused. "Well, like a horse with a horn coming out of his forehead," she said, grinning.

Jaldren rolled his eyes.

At that moment, Jaldren's mother came out of the kitchen again, carrying a steaming tray. She placed it in front of Allabva and said, "Alright, young lady, eat up. I don't know where you're going to put it, so much food, but I figure you need a lot to keep up that kind of strength."

Allabva locked eyes with Jaldren, who had witnessed the arm wrestle with Scaltern. He grinned knowingly, but his mother chose that moment to shoo him back into the kitchen. "Come on, come on. Let's leave our guest alone. She's earned it."

Jaldren disappeared behind the kitchen door.

The proprietress pulled a key out of her apron pocket and set it on the tray in front of Allabva. "Here you go. The room is up those stairs." She pointed at the far side of the common room. "It has the number two on it. If you can't find me when you're ready to check out, drop the key through that slit." She pointed out a hole in the wall next to the kitchen door. "Let me know if you need anything else. You can open the kitchen door and talk to us if you need to. You have a good evening."

The woman turned to address the other guest. "Miss Pelanuc, is everything alright?" she asked as she swiped Master Wold's payment off his abandoned table and scooped up his tray.

The other diner nodded and mumbled something Allabva couldn't hear.

Allabva pocketed the two silver and single copper hafender that Scaltern had left for her after the arm wrestle. Then she turned her attention to the delicious-smelling dinner in front of her with gusto.

Chapter 6

First Review

Allabva awoke the next morning and opened the curtain on the window to reveal the soft glow of dawn appearing on the horizon. She gathered her things and went downstairs.

There wasn't anybody in the dining room, but next to the kitchen door, a table held a tray decked with pastries and rolls. There was a small paper label next to them, identifying the price as a copper hafender for two.

Allabva took out the copper she won last night and placed it in a small bowl behind the sign. She heard noises in the kitchen, but it sounded as if the hostess and her son were busy. Allabva dropped her key through the slot next to the kitchen door. As she turned to go, the kitchen door opened behind her, and Jaldren's mother appeared.

"Miss Companion," she said, dipping in a slight curtsy. "Thank you for staying here. I hope you enjoyed it. I know Jaldren was entertained by his own defeat. Now, be sure to let people know how much you enjoyed the food and the beds, right? Assuming you did," the woman laughed congenially.

"Of course," Allabva reassured. "Thank you, Madam."

Jaldren leaned into the doorway from the kitchen side and looked at Allabva. "Goodbye," he said. "Maybe next time I'll win."

"Maybe," Allabva deflected and stepped outside.

The weather was brisk; she could see her breath in the cold morning air, but it was certainly warmer than it had been back home when she had left the Cleft. She wondered how much of that was due to the advance of the season and how much was due to the difference in location. The humidity in the air suggested it was more the location than the season.

She set her face east once more, nibbling on the roll she had taken from the tray. She set out at a fast walk, feeling the desire to move, but feeling self-conscious if she were to break into a jog. Before she reached the next rise to the east of the Dusty Pot, she heard a gruff voice.

"It's about time, young one."

Allabva rolled her eyes. Typical Nightshade Unicorn mood.

"And a lovely morning to you as well," Allabva said, perhaps adding a little too much cheer to her tone for it to sound completely devoid of sarcasm.

"You humans sleep *so much*," he complained. "And you sleep even longer without the Nomord bond. It's certainly long enough with it."

Allabva wanted to roll her eyes again. "Well, I've been running on empty for... a while. I had a proper meal last night and a proper bed. I feel so much better than I did before."

"Surely, you don't expect me to believe you slept so long. What were you doing? Oh, I know. You got a taste of winning at arm wrestling, and you went at it again and again."

Allabva sighed. "No."

"But you did arm wrestle?" he prodded.

"Yes, despite myself," Allabva admitted.

"Did you tell everyone you're the Companion?"

"Kind of," she said.

"Well, you're not 'kind of' the Companion," Nightshade said. "You *are* the Companion, and you need to grow into it. I hope you had some experience doing that."

"I suppose I did," Allabva said somberly. "There was a gentleman who wanted to arm wrestle me after he saw me beat somebody else. He asked questions, and I answered them. I didn't tell him I was traveling with the Nightshade Unicorn—I called you the Guardian—but I told him that there was trouble coming, and that we're traveling to prepare the world."

The Nightshade pursed his lips and then whinnied softly. "That is good. You need to get used to your role. You will fill it. Hronomon believes in you, and I believe in his faith in you. I haven't seen your mind as he has, but I trust him and his judgment." He paused. "I think. I just have to get used to the idea of trusting you."

"Do you have a particular distrust for humans?" Allabva asked.

"No," the Shrongelin said after a long pause. "I have a general distrust for those I don't know, who have not yet earned trust in my eyes."

"Is there any reason for that?" she asked.

"Yes," Nightshade said flatly. "You began to feel the tiniest sliver of that reason yesterday."

He stepped eastward, and Allabva paced along beside him. The Nightshade continued speaking.

"I use to not distrust so much. There is much I don't know about our adversary. The Construct has some unintended side effects, and some intended."

"They're not side effects if they're intended, are they?"

The Nightshade eyed Allabva with slight annoyance. "Every cycle, Sacalai rediscovers that the Guardian's meeting place with the Companion is at the Summit Above the Aspens. When she is resealed in her prison, that memory is taken from her again, by design. As a side effect of the memory-manipulating aspects of the Construct, none of us remembers what she was like before she came to power, nor how she was while we fought her once more. As far back as I remember, her influence and power were just there one day, and we had to stop her urgently. We held a council, and the Construct was founded. The first Mhosorem was the architect, but we all had a part in creating it."

Allabva idly looked over her shoulder at that moment while they crested the rise. The Dusty Pot was about to vanish from view. She saw Jaldren outside.

Apparently, he had just caught sight of the two of them. He had something in his hand that Allabva couldn't make out due to the distance, but as he gazed at them, it fell to the ground. His arm rose in front of himself, pointing at Allabva and the Nightshade Unicorn. She could just hear his voice, carried by the wind, "Mother!" it seemed to say faintly. Then she and the Shrongelin were beyond the rise, and the inn disappeared behind it.

"Right," Allabva said, wishing she could take the time to tell Jaldren everything that was going on. She reminded herself of the urgency of her journey. "How about we run from here?"

The Nightshade eyed her appreciatively. "I didn't think you would suggest it so soon. Lead on."

Was this how she would earn his trust—by persistently pressing on and proving her diligence toward their common goal?

The pair was now obviously within the realm of civilization once again, even more so than at any point since leaving the Cleft, except for when Allabva passed through Palf Glen. The road widened as it wound eastward, and they passed through a few small towns that day. Allabva was nervous about being seen publicly and openly traveling with the Nightshade.

While Allabva had mounted the Summit Above the Aspens with Hronomon and then descended with the Shrongelin over the course of several days, they had traveled mostly on narrow paths, without encountering many people. But now, after leaving the Dusty Pot, Allabva could tell they were approaching more populated areas.

It was early to mid-morning when they passed a farmhouse by the side of the road where a toddler was standing outside in her bare feet. The tone of her skin and color of her hair were similar to that of Jaldren, his mother, and Scaltern Wold. She stood there in white pajamas, gawking at the spectacle of a black-coated Nomord walking by.

Allabva took a moment to flash a smile and wave at the little girl.

The girl stared back. After a moment, Allabva realized that the girl wasn't staring at her at all, but only at the Shrongelin. Allabva looked to the Nightshade and then back to the little girl, who had hooked her finger on her lip and held it there, motionless.

"Lussie!" a woman's voice called from inside the house. "Lussie, where are you?"

The little girl blinked but still didn't move, keeping her eyes locked on the Nightshade Unicorn.

"Lussie!"

The door of the house opened, and the girl's mother stepped out to pick up her daughter. As she picked her up, she saw the Nightshade and yelped, nearly dropping the girl as she stumbled in shock. Wordlessly, she seized the toddler and yanked her inside, slamming the door in fright.

Allabva supposed they might get several such reactions as they encountered more people.

She heard the next people before she saw them.

Voices rang out, singing a steady, rhythmic song. As Allabva and the Nightshade rounded a bend, she saw a family working in their field.

As the family came into view, Allabva saw a mother, father, and three sons of various ages, along with a daughter. The father, mother, and two eldest sons wielded garden hoes in rhythm with the song they sang, while the younger son and daughter gathered weeds that the family dug up, tossing them to the side. The four older family members stood with their backs to Allabva, but the youngest two, who had mostly been bent down picking up weeds, stood up straight, facing her and the Nightshade.

"In the forest, somewhere in the red—" the boy sang, but then stopped, pointing at the Nightshade and laughing, seemingly amused by the sight.

The little girl looked up and also stopped singing, but stood more pensively. The father, noticing the distraction of his youngest children, turned his head to see what his son was pointing at. He continued to chop idly with his hoe and sing, but his eyes grew dark with puzzlement and then concern. Whatever this meant, he had decided it couldn't be good. The rest of the family then looked up, and the song died on their lips.

"You, girl," the father said directly to Allabva. "What is this? How did you put a horn on a mistreated black horse?"

"I am no horse," the Nightshade bellowed back.

The man's eyes popped wide open.

Allabva cast him an annoyed glance, then turned back to the man. "It's true. He's not a horse," she agreed, trying to smile away the Nightshade's ill demeanor.

"What is he, then?" the father asked.

"All unicorns are white," one son interjected.

"Nomord," the boy's mother corrected immediately, awkwardly. Then realization dawned on her face, and she whispered something to her husband.

The man grimaced, glancing at the Nightshade, and observed aloud, "All the Nomord are also female. Could this be...?"

Allabva jumped in, trying to repair the exchange before it spiraled into shouting. She held her hands up frantically. "If you've heard stories about the Nightshade Unicorn, this is not like that."

"Not like that!? Look at him!" The father demanded.

"Not like the stories," Allabva repeated.

"Then what is it?" the father demanded, dropping his hoe and forgetting his farm work. "The beast talks. He's obviously no horse. He must be some kind of demon. A horn doesn't make him noble like the Nomord. Be gone! Be gone!"

Allabva shook her head to herself. It was too late; the man was shouting now.

"We live a simple life. You won't curse our lands. Be gone," he said again.

"Sir, I promise, it is not I who will curse your lands," Nightshade defended. "It is not I who brings trouble, but trouble is coming. Be ready. In the coming weeks, you will hear a rallying cry throughout the land. Answer it and help. Every hand will be needed."

"Be gone, demon!" the man shouted again.

"It is not I," the Nightshade bellowed one last time. "I am not the torment that comes, but one does come. Come, Companion," the Nightshade said. "Let us not waste our time here." He broke into a canter.

Allabva ran after him and quickly caught up. Though he was not moving at his top speed, she was certainly traveling faster than any natural human could have.

"Ham hocks!" the woman cried out as Allabva left the family behind.

This region has some odd expressions, Allabva thought.

Thus, the morning passed.

Throughout the day, they encountered several people. Some stopped, talked, and listened to Allabva and the Nightshade, readily agreeing that if something threatened their home, they would stand and defend it. Others made rude gestures, holding one finger up to represent a Nomord horn and using the other to cross it—a symbol of rejection against the Shrongelin's and Eretuquein's kind. One person saw them coming and immediately turned and ran in the other direction.

Allabva jogged through the afternoon, holding her belongings under her arms, including her cloak. It wasn't because she was overheated from the exercise, but simply because the sun made it unnecessary. She was reminded of crossing from the Cleft toward the Roula Seas, before she met Fiewren and Banduchy. She had taken off her cloak then because she was hot from exertion on her journey. Now she traveled much faster, but found it much easier.

Allabva wondered how they were doing. They were good people, and she felt sure that they would be ready to accept Nightshade as the Shrongelin. Fiewren had taught Allabva the words to the song in the cool shade of the mount, the music of which she had learned from Delgan's flute that she carried on a chain around her neck. She might pull it out and hear its music now, but the bouncing of her running pace and the soft wind in her ears would have dampened her appreciation of the luxury.

At least the Nightshade was behaving himself. Mostly.

CHAPTER 7

GREENSTOCK

By the time evening came, Allabva and Nightshade determined that she would stop at the next inn for the night.

Allabva had seen every type of reaction imaginable during the day. Some people were simply fascinated that there was a Nomord with a black coat, treating it as if they had found a four-leaf clover. A few had screamed at the unknown. Most, though, kept their distance and looked at the pair with distrust.

There was a woman, however, who claimed she could tell that Allabva was good just by looking at her. When Allabva told her why this Nomord stallion was important and that it was crucial for her to travel with him to help the world, the woman nodded and handed Allabva five silver hafender to help her on her way. Allabva's eyes widened and she tried to decline the money, but the woman insisted.

The Nightshade grew increasingly irritable as the day progressed, complaining about delays as they stopped to talk to people. Allabva reminded him that he himself had said they weren't in as big a hurry as she had been with Hronomon, and he relented, but stayed irritable.

As evening approached, Nightshade indicated he would find some pasture space nearby for his dinner and again stay within earshot of the inn. As Allabva approached, she saw the name of the establishment: *The Greenstock Tavern and Public House.*

Stepping inside, Allabva noticed immediately that it was more lively than the Dusty Pot had been.

There was an elderly man with a lute on a stool across the room from the entrance. Next to him was a young redheaded man playing a flute. *He's certainly not from here,* Allabva thought. Everyone here had a certain complexion and a nose with a rounded point, while the young redheaded man had a more angular nose and a lighter complexion than Allabva herself. The older man played the lute and sang, while the people in the tavern sang along with him.

Allabva stood awkwardly, unsure whether to choose one of the two empty tables and seat herself, or wait to be seated. Just as she was about to take a seat, a middle-aged man wearing a black tunic and a red apron stepped up to her.

"Can I help you, miss?" he asked. His eyes flicked to her clothing and her curly hair before returning to her eyes. Allabva wondered if he found her clothing interesting, or if he was just noticing that it was different from that of most of his patrons.

"Yes, please. I'd like dinner and a room for the night."

"Alright, Miss...?"

Allabva hesitated. "Companion," she finally said, feeling odd using this assumed surname. But it wasn't inaccurate, so she figured there wasn't any real problem with it. At least this way, she didn't have to disclose her full real name.

"Miss Companion?" the man repeated. "You can call me Master Blackwood. I'm here to serve you. It's fried flat steak over pasta with tomato sauce tonight, if that sounds alright with you."

Allabva's stomach growled. She hadn't eaten anything all day except the pastry from the Dusty Pot.

"I've never tried it, but yes, that sounds fine," she said.

"Alright, that's half a silver hafender for the dinner, charged now, and we can arrange your room later. Unless you need dual accommodations?"

"No, thank you. Single is fine."

"Ah, good. We have single rooms to spare."

Allabva fished out a silver hafender and handed it to Master Blackwood. He reached into an apron pocket and returned a smaller silver coin. She looked at it in her hand as he walked away. It was stamped with the word "Weslan Crown." She was momentarily surprised that something called a "crown" was worth less than a hafender, but then she remembered her lessons growing up.

The Cleft, with mountains separating it from the rest of the nation of Eslarna, had taken to using Weslan both Eslarna thaler and Weslan Fielder money since they could travel up and down the river into Weslan Fields. Meanwhile, Tallensworth had taken to minting its own coin. She wondered if this far east, they would accept any Weslan Fielder money. She supposed they probably would have accepted her Eslarna thaler after all, if she'd still had them.

Realizing that Master Blackwood hadn't directed her where to sit, Allabva chose a seat nearest her and did her best to make herself comfortable.

"Not from here, are you?" a young woman Allabva's age spoke to her from the next table. She had straight, dark brown hair bound up in waves cascading down the back of her head, and her blouse and skirt were modestly decorated with yellows and browns. The young man she was with looked over at Allabva and smiled politely, seemingly indifferent about Allabva's presence.

"Yes," Allabva replied, smiling back and hoping it looked genuine. "I'm not exactly from here."

"That I can tell," the other girl replied. "My name is Lesala, and this is my husband," she chuckled, "Jonatlu. We're not from here, either. We come from Greengate. I suppose you don't know where that is. It's a small town outside Tallensworth, over on the east side. It's right on the water. We love it, but since we just got married, we thought we'd take a little trip up to see the mountainside."

"Ah," Allabva acknowledged, smiling at Lesala's barrage of personal information. "Yes, I'm heading to Tallensworth, myself. I've never been, so I guess I'll see what it's like."

"Oh," Lesala said. "Wait a second, wait a second. Let me try to guess. Do you come from Nolnarn?" She laughed nervously. "I'm guessing you're from the other side of the mountains, but I don't actually know many places there."

Jonatlu laughed. "That's an understatement," he said. "Lesala knows her geography like I know how to read the language of Adlis-Taoli."

Allabva genuinely smiled this time. Few people outside of Adlis-Taoli could speak that language. The Taolians tended to keep to themselves. They allowed visitors from other lands, but only as visitors, never permanent residents. Their culture was said to be very structured, but their society was closed to outsiders.

"No," Allabva replied to Lesala with a laugh. "I'm not from Nolnarn. You have to go a lot farther west than that, not north, to get to my home."

Jonatlu looked from his bride to Allabva. "Are you from Weslan Fields? I can see your skin isn't as light as people from Nolnarn, so you must be from farther west."

"Not exactly," Allabva said. "I'm actually just as Eslarnan as you are, just from the west side of the country."

Jonatlu squinted. "But...so you are from Norl? You don't look it; you're not very blonde."

"No," Allabva smiled. "I'll give it away."

"The Cleft," Jonatlu guessed.

"Aha," Allabva confirmed.

"That makes sense," Lesala said. "Wait, if you haven't been here, then you must not be very familiar with all the pasta they have in the Tallen High Dominion." She looked at Allabva excitedly. "We have so many kinds of pasta."

"And so many kinds of seafood," Jonatlu added. "Whether you take that as good news or bad, it is what it is."

"Alright," Allabva said. "I guess I'll make of it what I can."

"What brings you to Tallensworth?" Lesala asked as she took a bite of her food, something soft and white oozing out of an edible envelope. Lesala kept talking with her mouth half full. "Wait, let me guess. It has to be the food. You came for the pasta, right? Like this? We paid extra for this."

Allabva looked at the dish. "That doesn't look like what Master Blackwood described to me."

"It's not," Lesala said. "We ordered this special and had to pay extra because it's not the regular offering tonight."

"What is it?" Allabva inquired.

"Pasta shells stuffed with cheese. It's the best. You should try it sometime."

Jonatlu must have been curious to find out the answer to the question his wife had asked. "So, we know it's not the pasta. What does bring you to Tallensworth?"

Allabva took a deep breath. She hoped this question would become easier to answer, but right now, it certainly wasn't. "I am trying to gain support for a cause," she said slowly.

"What cause is that? If you're trying to get something changed and your home region can't handle it, why don't you petition to Nolnarn?"

"Well, it's not that kind of change," Allabva said. She thought for a moment. "I guess... maybe it is that kind, at least partially."

She leaned in close to the couple, scooting her chair over to their table. "Have you—" The music stopped right then, and the room went silent. Allabva bit her lip, glancing around before lowering her voice further. "Have you heard of the Disaffected?"

Lesala's face went blank, and Jonatlu's brow furrowed with concern.

"Yes," he replied in a low voice. "There's a camp up north, right within a couple of days of Palf Glen."

"That's right," Allabva said. "Well... Do you know what they're all about?"

"Yes," Jonatlu said, frowning. "My older brother went to join them. I don't..." His eyes shifted. "I don't agree with their thinking. They're looking for big changes all across the land. I mean, sure, I don't always love the overduke's decisions, right? But no government's perfect, I think."

"What do you have to do with the Disaffected?" Lesala asked.

"Do you know what they think about the Nomord?" Allabva said.

"Yes," Lesala answered. "They don't like them. They think anybody who trusts the Nomord is an idiot."

"I think that's ridiculous, though," said Jonatlu. "They never hurt anybody. If they do anything to people, it's always a good thing, right? Like healing."

Allabva nodded. "Let's say that I'm helping the Nomord."

"How are you doing that?" Lesala asked, intrigued.

Allabva heaved a breath, stressed at coming out in the open with this information in a crowded room full of people, even if most of them couldn't hear her. "I'm traveling with one," she said.

"Really? Where is she? Is she outside?" Lesala interrupted.

Allabva blinked. "Umm... yes, he is outside," she repeated, "staying out of sight until the morning." *I hope,* she added mentally.

"Ah," Jonatlu said with a good-natured smirk. "So naturally, it's something that we can't confirm. *He* is just staying out of sight."

"That's right," Allabva said tiredly, "I said 'he.' I can't show him to you, but I can prove something is weird about me." She prepared herself to begrudgingly follow the Nightshade's suggestions.

"Oh, really? How?"

Glancing around, Allabva leaned in to put her arm on the table. But just then, Master Blackwood returned with her dinner, interrupting the conversation.

"There you are, miss. And if you have another silver hafender and a half, I'll go make up your room."

More expensive than the Dusty Pot, Allabva noted. She figured it was because they were closer to the big city. She pulled out another silver hafender and the silver crown Master Blackwood had given her earlier.

The music picked up again, this time playing a slower tune that Allabva recognized—well, kind of. It sounded like "Five in the Morning, Five at Night," but only the chorus, and it switched to a minor key. Allabva grabbed the fork and knife she had been provided and looked at her food. Deciding it was too hot to eat yet, she set down her utensils and scooted the plate to the side, offering her arm to Jonatlu in an arm wrestling position.

"Arm wrestle me," Allabva invited. "I'll beat you easily."

"Alright," Jonatlu said, looking to his wife and then awkwardly placing his hand in Allabva's. He started with a sudden jerk, but he didn't get very far. Allabva halted his motion quickly, and brought the back of his hand down to the table smoothly, if not too rapidly.

"Ah," he said. "How did you do that? Here, let's go again." They wrestled again, this time with him using both hands. "There's no way... How? You're cheating somehow."

Allabva held her hands up innocently. She stood, took off her coat, and hung it with her cloak on a hook against the wall. Returning to the table, she rolled up the sleeves of her blouse so Jonatlu could see her bare arms. "I have nothing to hide here," she said frankly. "You want to go again, now that you can see it's just me?"

"Yes, in fact I do," he said.

Lesala got up as well, smiling. "I'm going to help."

Allabva shrugged. "Alright." She stopped and looked around, conscientious. "Can we block the view? I don't want to show the whole room."

Lesala positioned herself so that if anyone wanted to see what was happening, they would have to come around and place themselves rather close.

Allabva arm wrestled Jonatlu a third time, this time with Lesala's help, and handily beat both of them.

"Unreal," Lesala said. "Then what does this prove?" she asked, looking to Jonatlu for help.

"It proves...that something is weird," he said.

Allabva nodded. "I know that's all it proves, but I'll tell you what it means, even if I can't prove the rest. I'm traveling with one of the Nomord—a stallion. They can do an enchantment that makes a human stronger. I got my strength from somewhere, right? That's where."

Jonatlu shook his head. "Wow. Now, what are you doing against the Disaffected?" he asked, putting two and two together.

Allabva sighed heavily and then leaned in close again. "It's not so much against the Disaffected; it's against who they—"

Footsteps plodded nearby, and Allabva stopped talking, looking up.

"I saw that," said a rough voice that belonged to a large man with beads braided into his beard. "I want to try."

"Try what?" Allabva tried to play dumb. "My food? I haven't even tasted it yet."

"No, I want to arm wrestle you."

"I think I'd rather not," Allabva said frankly.

"Look, I've heard of you. Scaltern was here early this morning. Said he traveled through the night because he had to get home for calving. You must be Allabva Companion, right?"

Allabva felt a chill run up and down her spine, the hair rising on the back of her neck. She was a stranger in a strange land, and she already had a reputation here. Fearing what bad could come of it, but hoping for the best, she swallowed her doubts.

"That's right," she said, her voice shaking. "I... I still would rather not arm—"

The man plopped a gold hafender on the table. "I said I want to try. Does this get me in?"

Allabva blinked. "I'm not here to raise—"

"Look, I figure whatever you're trying to do, that gold will help you do it when you get there. So, can I give it a go already?" he asked expectantly, grabbing a chair from a nearby empty table and placing it so that he could sit across from Allabva.

"I..." Allabva stammered. The gold surely *would* be useful at some point. "Alright, I suppose."

Allabva stared pointedly at Jonatlu and Lesala, hoping they understood what she had told them in confidence and wouldn't spill it all out to this newcomer.

"Alright," she said. "Just once."

"That's all I need," the man replied, putting his arm on the table.

Allabva took his hand, and the man jerked her hand suddenly, without warning, bringing it within inches of the tabletop before she reacted. But then she stopped the motion completely and started pushing in the other direction. The man grunted and immediately reached up with his other hand, pulling harder. Allabva simply continued to rotate her forearm until she brought the man's knuckles in contact with the tabletop, then let go.

The bearded man gasped as the match ended. "Allabva the Companion," he said. "Companion to whom?"

"Just call me Companion, please," Allabva said firmly, trying to keep her given name off of the stranger's lips.

"Hey!" the man piped up, calling to the entire common room, "we've got a contest over here. Allabva Companion doesn't want to arm wrestle, but if you give her enough shiny, she'll give you a try. I bet she'll win too, against any of you!" His voice carried loudly over the music.

Allabva's eyebrows shot up in shock as she shook her head, protesting the declaration. "No, no," she said softly, fearing the attention. Then she heard the Nightshade's rude laughter in her mind. He seemed to like it when she was ready to work against her own fatigue and face the challenges their mission might bring. She remembered him seeming disappointed in her and in her entire species when she shied away from anything.

No, she told herself. *I will not back down. I will show this Nightshade I can face discomfort, whether that's a cold night under the stars or the eyes of everyone in this room.*

She realized the bearded man was laughing, apparently thinking he had told some great joke.

Taking a deep breath, Allabva stood. "That's right," she said. "Every word he said is true. I don't want to arm wrestle you, but I'm willing to."

She looked down at the gold hafender on the table. She didn't want to make it too expensive for everyone.

"One silver hafender, and you get to try. Beat me, and I'll give you two. I'll match you one for one. Now, if you'll excuse me, since I wasn't inviting the attention, I'm going to eat my dinner."

Allabva sat down and picked up her fork and knife. As she started to cut her thin fried steak and the long thin noodles underneath it, she heard the room recover from the man's outburst. Some corners of the room laughed, and others seemed to carry on with their conversations. Allabva tried to ignore them as her ears burned.

She took the first bite of her dinner and froze, raising her eyebrows. She turned to Lesala. "This is good. I've had noodles before, but not pasta like this."

"Oh, that's nothing," Lesala said. "I'm telling you, try the stuffed shells or baked tubes with the soft cheese."

Allabva chewed and swallowed, then took her second bite. "Tallensworth has a lot of pastas, you say?" she asked the young couple.

"That's right," Jonatlu said. "As a region, we're crazy about pasta, and some of us are crazy about the seafood," He nodded to his wife.

Allabva's stomach sank a little when she heard a coin drop on the table in front of her. She looked up and saw a burly woman with a sneer on her face.

"There's no way," the woman said. "Come on, let's get this over with. I don't know what that man thinks he's saying. He must be weaker than he looks, but I've got you. I'll get you squared away"

She didn't. Allabva squared her away and quickly returned to her pasta, pocketing the woman's silver coin. The pair of musicians on the far side of the room had picked up a more unfamiliar song—a striding ballad telling of the conquering of Eslarna a thousand years ago. Allabva recognized the tale from history, but she hadn't heard this tune before.

As the song reached its climax, she heard two more coins plunk down on the table. She supposed the challengers felt inspired by the ballad. No matter. She handled them each in quick succession and continued with her dinner.

During the next song, four more people came to challenge her, and she pocketed another four silver hafender. Finally, as this latest song concluded several minutes later, the lute player stood up while the flute player looked up at him.

"For newcomers, my name is Trinva Yalben and I have an idea," the entertainer said. "We've all seen this remarkable young lady best several of you in an arm wrestle. I say, let's challenge her in bulk! Surely we can handle her in cooperation."

Allabva almost choked.

"Here's the game," the entertainer said. "I propose that she allow us up to five at once, to try to defeat her. Five of us each contribute one silver coin, and if we beat her, then..." He paused for effect. "We ask that she matches us on the table. Miss Companion, are you game?"

Allabva counted on her fingers rapidly, decided she could easily make it through tomorrow, even if she lost five silvers. She nodded.

"Alright. I nominate you, and you, and you," the bard said, pointing to the bearded man who had already arm wrestled Allabva, and two other challengers in the room who looked the most muscular. One of them held his hand up to decline, apparently not wanting to pay into the pot, but another readily took his place.

"That makes four of us. Now, Lamtor, why don't you join me?" The entertainer turned to the flute player sitting on the stool next to him. The redhead boy looked surprised at being roped into the task. He appeared nervous though, not unwilling.

"Lamtor, you take point. You over there, you take anchor. The three of us in between... Well, let's figure this out."

Yalben guided the flute player Lamtor into the seat across from Allabva. She proffered her hand, and the other four challengers lined up, ready to help pull Allabva's hand toward defeat.

"We'll start this slowly to make it interesting," Bard Yalben said. "First, everyone, you have to pay into the pot."

He pulled out two silver hafender and placed them on the table, turning to the other three challengers to do the same. Once that was done, he turned back to his apprentice.

"Lamtor, go ahead and take her hand, and we'll start slowly, right, Miss Companion? No sudden slamming of hands. We're going to ramp it up and see just how strong you are."

His manner was very congenial and lively. Somehow, he made her smile in spite of her nervousness at being in the spotlight.

Lamtor took her hand awkwardly; his hand was cold, which surprised her. Hadn't he just been playing his flute, and that would have warmed it up? Lamtor looked up to the master entertainer for guidance, but the bard simply looked back at him expectantly.

Lamtor began to pull.

Allabva resisted, not allowing him to gain any ground. Instead, she half shrugged and pulled the other direction.

As soon as she did, the bard jumped in with both hands and started slowly pulling back toward the back of Allabva's hand.

Allabva resisted and again started winning the contest.

"Next, join in," Yalben grunted as the third challenger jumped in, the whole common room watching.

Allabva felt the tug increase, opposing her. The same with the fourth. It genuinely became difficult at this point, but still she slowly gained ground toward the tabletop surface.

Finally, the fifth challenger joined the contest. There wasn't room to put his hands directly in, so he leaned in and grabbed the fourth challenger's forearms, pulling.

Finally, they had her. The mass of hands started traveling, pulling Allabva's hand backward and slowly, gradually, brought it to rest with the back of her knuckles on the tabletop.

The entire room gasped a sigh of relief, letting go of the tension as Allabva's face released its red hue.

"Well," the entertainer said, wiping the sweat from his brow, "there we have it. She's not so strong, right? It only took five of us to best her!" he grinned, looking around the room to the sound of hearty laughter.

"Lamtor, how about you take a break? Blackwood, if we can get a drink over here?"

"Coming up," Blackwood nodded from behind the bar, already moving to pour the drinks.

"Now, Miss Companion," the bard continued, grinning, "pay up, pay up."

Allabva nodded and reached into her pouch, feeling a mix of relief and amusement. She had worried the crowd might think she was trying to take advantage of them. Happily, she pulled out five silver hafender and placed them on the table.

The entertainer picked up the coins and distributed them. As he did, it became clear what sort of man he was. He pocketed only two of the hafender, replacing what he had contributed, and handed the extra two to his apprentice.

"I believe you've learned something today," he said, patting Lamtor on the back. Lamtor, still catching his breath, managed a nod and a grateful smile.

"Thanks," Lamtor replied quietly as he pocketed the two silver hafender, his face a mix of exhaustion and admiration.

The bard turned back to Allabva, his jovial demeanor still intact. "Miss Companion, I hope you'll stick around a bit longer. It seems that you easily entertain a crowd as just as well as we can!"

Allabva found herself breathing deeply, her heart still racing from the exertion and the sudden attention. While Yalben continued to entertain the diners, urging them to give her some space, Lamtor leaned toward her, a look of amazement on his face.

"How did you do that?" he asked, his eyes wide with curiosity.

"Do what?" Allabva replied, feigning ignorance once more. "I lost, didn't I?"

Lamtor scoffed. "Against five of us! How did you even hold out that long?"

Allabva gave a small, tired smile. "I think I'm going to excuse myself now," she said, glancing around the room. She spotted Mr. Blackwood entering the dining area and approached him. "Is it alright if I finish my dinner in my room?"

"Of course," he replied, gesturing welcomingly. "Just make sure you don't wander off with the dishes in the morning," he smiled.

"Naturally," Allabva said with a nod. "Thank you, sir, and excuse me, Lamtor." She looked over to the next table. "Goodnight, Lesala, Jonatlu."

Allabva turned away, gathering her walking stick, coat, and cloak, along with her travel bag and bow, and grabbed the plate still mostly full of food.

Master Blackwood handed her a key with a number scrawled on a scrap of parchment.

Seeing no stairs nearby, Allabva walked toward the back of the room, where an open hallway revealed a row of numbered doors. She located her room, grateful for a bit of privacy and a chance to eat in peace.

Chapter 8

The Touch

As she settled her things and she heard the music start up again in the common room, Allabva set her coat and cloak on hangers on a dowel in the corner, so they wouldn't get crumpled through the night. There was a writing desk and chair in another corner.

Although her feet had been better off ever since the moment she had bonded with the Shrongelin, she did still feel some chafing in spots.

But what about her dinner? Allabva decided quickly. She removed her boots and socks immediately and set them to air out. She had washed both pairs last night at the Dusty Pot, so tonight she would just put on fresh ones when she left in the morning. She was warm enough that she wasn't uncomfortable unshod, despite the slight chill that hung in the evening air.

Barefoot, she sat down at the table to finish her dinner. She could take the time to savor it.

It was perfect. Both the meat and the pasta filled a different type of hunger Allabva experienced while healing and running across the countryside all day. Her muscles needed to be refreshed. There was a knock at the door just as she finished.

Allabva wasn't expecting anybody, so this caught her somewhat by surprise. She rose and stepped toward the closed door, asking, "Who is it?"

"Lamtor," came the reply. "I really hoped to talk to you about how you did what you did."

"I understood that," Allabva said patiently, "but I believe I excused myself for the evening."

"No, it's alright," he said. "It's alright," he repeated. "I..." Hesitation. "I can see the Touch in you."

Allabva's eyebrows rose. If he could see it in her, why hadn't she noticed it in him?

She threw the door open and looked intently into Lamtor's eyes.

He stood there, saying nothing.

Allabva must have been too busy with the attention around her in the common room. But it was true; she could see it now. Lamtor's eyes held a gentle sparkle, something that told of experiencing a connection with something outside of the natural order for humans. She studied his face for a long moment. There was a certain agreeableness there that reminded her of Delgan.

"So," she said finally, "you know it's true. I can see it in you as well, but what were you hoping to talk to me about?"

"Your strength," he said, perhaps growing tired of her standoffishness.

"Right," Allabva said flatly.

Then she changed her mind about opening up to him. After all, if a Nomord had willingly come into physical contact with the boy in front of her, that told her that at least, at some point in his life, he had demonstrated a kind enough disposition to have earned that trust from one of the magical creatures. She stepped back a pace, allowing him to step into the doorway from the hall.

"I got my strength from a Nomord—" Allabva began, but Lamtor interrupted.

"I...um..." he stammered. "I wanted to show you something." He reached into his pocket and pulled out a brooch.

It had several small, pointed, diamond-shaped turquoise stones set in a ring, pointing out from a transparent red stone in the center, giving the effect of a flower.

"I think," he said hesitantly, "this may make more sense to you than to anyone else I've met." He paused, holding it in the air between the two of them. "This was my mother's. She passed away from consumption when I was seven."

As Allabva stared into Lamtor's eyes, she couldn't help but feel that he still felt the pain of it at some level, although he now related it as if it were mundane information. He looked at the brooch, turning it over in his hands, studying it, as Allabva imagined he must have done thousands of times over the years.

"I'm sure it's important to you," Allabva said, "and I'm sorry for your loss. But... Why show it to me?"

"Why indeed," Lamtor answered. "Well... My mother was to be buried wearing this brooch. My father had her dressed for the interment with this resting below her neck."

He stopped again. Allabva waited for him to continue.

"I never told anybody this before," he said at great length, pausing again.

Allabva waited patiently. "Go on," she prodded gently.

"My father..." Lamtor choked. "Said he couldn't bear the sight of it. He'd given it to her as a wedding gift, see. He tucked it behind her burial clothes." Lamtor swallowed as if choking on a particularly large morsel of food.

"I was a kid, you see," he continued. "I was little, and I wasn't done seeing it. We were getting everything ready to bid her farewell, and there was a moment where everybody was busy, and wasn't next to the coffin with me. So I pulled the brooch back out, and I held it in my hand. I'd played with it often when I was a toddler; my mother always allowed me to with a smile. And I remembered that—I associated the brooch with her, with spending time with her."

Allabva nodded understandingly. "I think I understand somewhat," she said. "My father's been lost at sea for several years, and I hold on to any memory I have of him. I have some toddler shoes that he bought for me, just because he thought I would look really cute in them. There's no real reason to hold on to them."

Lamtor looked at her appreciatively, gratefully, then breathed deeply. "Before anybody else came back, a Nomord walked into the clearing where we were going to bid her farewell at the burial grounds. She walked up to me and lowered her head, looked into my eyes, looked into *me*. She didn't say anything. But then she brought her horn down, brought her face close enough for me to touch. And I did, because I was amazed to be so close to one. And then she touched the tip of her horn to the brooch. It felt warm after she did it, and then I knew... I couldn't put it back."

Now Allabva breathed deeply. "Yes, I suppose that would put a different light on it."

"I'm pretty sure my father knows I have it," Lamtor said, recovering from the tender moment. "But he's never talked to me about it, and he doesn't know it was touched by a Nomord. But I think he understands. For him, it would carry more meaning about what he lost, but for me..."

"It's more about feeling cozy and safe," Allabva finished for him, nodding again. She waited for him to see if there was some other reason he had come.

"That's not why I'm showing it to you," Lamtor continued. "I mean, yes, that's all special for me, right? Except... Except the Nomord...blessed it, I suppose. After she touched it, if I'm holding it, I can tell when somebody's lying," he said at last.

Allabva's eyebrows went up. "Really?"

"Yes, but it's not so powerful as to make it obvious all the time. I kind of have to pay attention. But if I am paying attention and somebody speaks the truth, it just kind of feels right to me. Whereas if they're lying, that feeling isn't there. I just feel empty about what it is they're saying."

Allabva stared calmly at Lamtor. "Well—" she said.

"Right," Lamtor interjected. "You must think I'm mad. A brooch that tells me if somebody's lying? I must be making it up, right?"

"No, I don't think you're mad," Allabva started, but was interrupted as a pair of voices came around the hall corner from the common room. Lamtor stuffed the brooch into his pocket immediately as Jonatlu and Lesala came down the hallway.

"Oh, hello," Lesala said, seeing that Allabva had her door open, talking to Lamtor. "I am so glad you're still here. I wanted to talk to you more."

Allabva felt standoffish. The newly married couple wasn't part of her conversation with Lamtor, and she doubted the boy was ready to share everything with them as well.

"Well, Allabva, I think we were just going to part ways now, and—"

"I want to know more," Lesala interrupted. "I *must* know more, please."

Allabva breathed deeply, locking eyes with Lamtor. "I don't think I can... I mean, I need to get to sleep..." she exhaled, defeated. "Tell you what." She made eye contact with Lamtor again. "I have something to share with all three of you. Come on in. We'll close the door."

Allabva stepped back to let her three guests enter the room and sat on the edge of the bed. "I don't really have anywhere to sit for everybody, but there is the one chair," she began said apologetically.

"No problem, we'll stand," Jonatlu said, shaking his head.

"Alright," Allabva said. "I don't think I'm going to tell you anything more about my strength with the Nomord, but I think you'll appreciate this."

She pulled the small silvery flute out of its hiding place on her necklace under her blouse. She felt awkward, wondering if Lamtor had been hoping to develop any romantic bond with her. She had no intention for that.

"I learned this song recently—This isn't my flute. It belongs to somebody back home, and he lent it to me. I need to get it back to him—But I learned this song." She omitted the fact that she heard the notes first from the flute magically playing itself. "Maybe you'll recognize it; maybe you won't."

Allabva put the flute to her lips and played. She chose a slower tempo, hoping not to mess any notes up due to lack of solid memory with the instrument. She played through one verse, the chorus, and another verse of "In the Cool Shade of the Mount" before stopping.

Lamtor seemed to stand there somewhat awkwardly, wondering why Allabva had chosen to show them the flute and the song that she played.

"Yes, yes," Lesala said. "That's... oh, I don't remember the title, but that's a song about lovers, right, where one of them has to go away?"

Allabva nodded. "Right, and the singer doesn't want to get left behind, but she wants to travel with her lover wherever he goes. I—"

"So romantic," Lesala said, hugging Jonatlu closely. "Do you have somebody like that? Let's always be like that, Jonatlu."

"Of course," Jonatlu said, smiling at his wife.

Allabva ignored the question Lesala had shot at her before the last thing she'd said to Jonatlu. Better to redirect. "Now to explain," she said, "this flute was touched by a Nomord. It belonged to the boy's grandmother. And ever since then..." She trailed off, then held the flute firmly in her hand and said, with conviction, "Beware the wolves."

Shock appeared on the faces of Jonatlu and Lesala, while understanding blossomed on Lamtor's face as the flute played "In the Cool Shade of the Mount" by itself. The young couple stared, awestruck, while Lamtor leaned back, his mind apparently working overtime about something.

Allabva stopped the music after a verse, uttering, "Beware the wolves," again.

"Wow," Lesala breathed.

"This flute has been a great comfort to me over the past few weeks since I left my home," Allabva said. "I was supposed to give it back to its rightful owner, but I had to leave home in such a hurry that I didn't get the chance. I have to return it to him someday, so that means I have to make it back home. In the meantime, it makes me think of him."

Her heart ached for Delgan. As the days passed and time passed, she grew more appreciative of him, having begun to imagine him filling a place in her life. They had just begun to explore that possibility in the form of a formal courtship when Hronomon called her away. Allabva hoped Delgan would forgive her for leaving.

"But the flute has another function," she said. "You heard what I said to activate it. That is a reminder. I... I had a run-in with real-life physical wolves several days ago."

"How did you get away?" Lesala asked.

Allabva breathed in and out, tucking the flute away. "Maybe you won't believe this, but a male Nomord protected me from them."

"What?" Lesala said, leaning forward in interest.

Allabva thought of the Shrongelin waiting for her outside to continue the journey in the morning. She couldn't stay up having a long conversation.

"I'd like to tell you more if there were time," she said, trying to compress the background into one breath. "All I can say right now is that Nomord stallions exist, they've kept themselves away from the world for a long time, and now they're coming to help us face some trouble that's on its way."

Jonatlu now gave his attention to the new turn in conversation. "What kind of trouble?"

Allabva raised her eyebrows in anxiety. "I don't know many details yet. Dangerous trouble."

"In Tallensworth?"

Allabva returned Jonatlu's intense gaze, concerned her news might worry him greatly.

"Apthane Plains, mostly, but I think it will be everywhere."

"You can't just tell us something like that out of the blue," Lesala said.

"I'm sorry," Allabva apologized. "Just try to be prepared."

"How?" Jonatlu asked.

"I don't know yet."

"But…" he pressed.

Allabva thought of the Nightshade again. "Anyway, I still have more traveling to worry about. I should be getting to bed, if you'll excuse me."

She stood, and the young couple, understanding her intent, slowly turned to leave the room.

Lamtor stalled. "Can I talk to you about one more thing?" he asked.

"Of course," Allabva allowed.

"I'll just be a second." Lamtor moved to close the door behind the couple.

Jonatlu paused to look back, making eye contact with Allabva.

"It's alright," she assured him.

"Whoa," Jonatlu laughed, realizing the ridiculousness of being concerned for Allabva's safety with only one other person in the room. He turned and left.

Lamtor closed the door behind Jonatlu.

"Um," Lamtor reached into his pocket again, once more pulling out the brooch, "I think you should have this," he said.

Allabva's eyes opened wide. "No, that's an heirloom. That was your mother's. You need to keep it."

"No," Lamtor said, shaking his head decidedly, "you need it more than I do. I don't know exactly what you're doing, but you're obviously favored by the Nomord. You're away from home. You're headed somewhere to do something that you imply you must have to do. Don't tell me this wouldn't be useful." He held the brooch up between thumb and forefinger.

It was Allabva's turn to shake her head. "No, it certainly would be helpful," she stammered, "but you—"

"You need to have it," Lamtor repeated. "Come find me someday. Maybe at some future time, I'll be a full bard and you'll be able to ask for me by name. When Allabva Companion calls, I will come, even if you can't give the brooch back. It doesn't matter why you call. Whatever the Nomord needs you to do, I will assist however I can."

He held the brooch in the air for her to take.

Allabva stalled.

"I never told anybody I had this, so no one else will miss it," Lamtor added. "Anybody who knows it exists thinks it's in the ground already, so this is fully my decision. You take it and use it. Stay safe."

Allabva slowly held her palm out and allowed Lamtor to place the jewel in it. "You as well," she said slowly. "I can't give you the flute in return for the brooch, because it's not mine to give. But you'll remember that I said, 'beware the wolves,' right?"

"I will," Lamtor said.

"Do that. Beware the wolves," Allabva finished, "and watch out for the Disaffected."

A curious expression struck the young man's face. "The Disaffected? Are they..."

"They're wrapped up in this somehow," she said. "I don't have it all figured out yet, but there are..." She took a deep breath. It still felt weird to go share, after she started her mission in secrecy. "There are hard times coming," she warned. "Not just for this area, or for all Eslarna, but for the world. Wherever you see the Disaffected, go the other direction."

"Alright," Lamtor replied.

Allabva looked down at the jewel in her palm, hefting its weight. "Have you met any Disaffected yourself yet?"

"No."

Allabva furrowed her brow, squinting at nothing. "I..." A smile cracked the edge of her mouth. "I don't believe you," she said.

Lamtor's face broke into a wide grin. "Good. Then I'll tell you this: I have met a few. A couple of them seemed disagreeable, but some of them seemed like normal, average folk. And one... one seemed downright charitable."

Allabva paused, as if she were tasting the air surrounding this information. "That is true," she said. "I can feel it... The brooch, I mean. It's somewhat subtle, though, but it's there."

"Good," Lamtor said. "Take your own advice, then." He turned to the door. "And beware the wolves. Thank you for letting me know; thank you for warning me that there will be trouble, even though you already had the brooch when you told me, so I can't confirm that by its power. I see the Touch of the Nomord in your eyes, and I trust you. I'll steer clear of the Disaffected, and you watch your back."

Lamtor stepped toward the door but turned back, narrowing his eyes at Allabva. "You have a plan?" he asked.

She nodded, breathing, sighing. "Or rather, I have a Nomord escort, and he has the plan."

"Good," Lamtor said. "I'm glad you're not alone. Will I hear of you again?"

Allabva nodded, very solemnly this time. "Most certainly. I said there will be trouble, and there will be. I don't know if you'll be able to stay out of it, or if anybody will be able to stay out of it completely."

"Where will it be?" he asked.

"I don't think I can tell you that," she avoided. "Not yet. Just go about your life for now, and beware those wolves."

Lamtor turned slowly to the door again. "Very well, Allabva. Have a good night." He opened the door and let himself out without another word, leaving Allabva alone.

She felt exhausted now. Her body wasn't particularly tired, but this conversation had taken a heavy emotional toll. As raw emotions rose to the surface, Allabva dropped to a seated position on the bed, then lay down, still in her clothes, and went to sleep feeling a great emptiness.

Chapter 9

Second Review

Allabva awoke in the morning, feeling a certain apprehension and excitement mixed together. She and the Nightshade were supposed to reach Tallensworth today.

Allabva had ventured outside the Cleft before, but always downriver to the west, into Weslan Fields, so that even though she was now still nominally within her homeland, she anticipated new and exciting sights. As she gathered her things to depart, she touched the flute through her blouse to feel its cold presence against her sternum. And now, very conscientiously, she felt the presence of the brooch in the pocket of her coat.

At first, she'd only had to worry about keeping Delgan's flute safe. Then, Hronomon showed up, and now she had to worry about saving the entire world. The last thing she needed was the added responsibility of somebody else's prized heirloom under her care.

Nothing to be done for it now, though, she told herself.

Allabva tapped a pocket sewn into her bag and heard a clink. At least she didn't have to worry about money for a few days on her way into Tallensworth. Although she hadn't sought the spotlight or the attention that winning all those arm wrestling matches brought her last night, the bearded man's gold piece would certainly help her on her way, and she wouldn't have to go into town wondering where she would get her next meal.

All set to depart, she left her room and found her way back to the common room down the hall, where she found Master Blackwood bringing water in through the front door from the well outside.

"Leaky buckets, but I'm glad you're up," the innkeeper said in a rush with wide, alarmed eyes. "I was going to have to wake you, otherwise."

"What?" Allabva said, confused. "Why?"

"Right. Thank you for coming, Miss Companion, but you must be on your way now. I can't do business with your, um, friend out there!" He turned curtly and disappeared into the kitchen.

Now more confused than before, Allabva continued out the door. She came face to face with the Shrongelin.

"We need to get moving," was all he said by way of explanation.

Master Blackwood stepped out the front door tentatively, carrying his now-empty water pail. He looked up at the Nightshade and back to Allabva. He wore an accusatory glance. "This creature knows your name. What is it doing here?"

Allabva took a deep breath. "Master Blackwood, I'd like you to meet...the Shrongelin."

Blackwood choked.

"Also known as the Nightshade Unicorn," Allabva finished.

The innkeeper sputtered. "How? How? There is no Nightshade Unicorn," he finally insisted.

Allabva shrugged, shouldering her bag. She gestured at Nightshade. "Nightshade here would beg to differ."

The innkeeper's face contorted with confusion, facing the reality right in front of him. "How dare you imply—or outright claim, even worse!—that this beast and the Shrongelin could be one and the same?" he exclaimed.

Allabva nodded coolly. "It took me by surprise as well. But it turns out that 'Shrongelin' is evidently a Nomord word. It means 'Guardian.'"

"Guardian?" the man asked.

"Come, Companion," the Nightshade spoke.

Master Blackwood winced at the sound of speech coming from this intimidating equine. "You're *his* Companion?" he asked dumbly.

Allabva nodded.

Nightshade started to walk off.

Allabva leaned to go, but felt the need to finish the conversation with Master Blackwood in some fashion. She handed back her key.

"The Guardian has been protecting the world for thousands of years," she told him. "Soon, the force he has been protecting us from will break free, and he has to lock it up again. There are hard times coming, Master Blackwood, I'm sorry to say. Be as ready as you can."

"Hard times..." the innkeeper echoed.

Allabva tried to give him an encouraging look. "If you'll excuse me, I need to help the Shrongelin prepare the world. Farewell, Master Blackwood," Allabva called as she waved, then began to trot, then to run after the Nightshade.

They ran harder today, dashing past houses and any passersby that didn't get in their way without stopping to talk.

"How did it go last night?" Nightshade asked as they ran.

Allabva rolled her eyes. "I accidentally made a spectacle of myself."

The Nightshade made an awkward sound halfway between a grunt and a whinny.

Allabva was starting to understand Nomord expressions a little better, but this one surprised her. "Are you laughing at me?" she asked.

The grunting chortle became more pronounced.

Allabva looked over at her escort and saw mischief in his eyes. "Are you glad that I was uncomfortable?" she confronted him.

His laughing stopped for a moment. "Not exactly," he said, then his laughter continued. "Maybe a little."

"Nightshade," she said, "I did not go in there to call attention to myself. I thought I was just going in to get a good night's rest so we could continue on our way."

"I know," he said. "Isn't it great?"

"Isn't what great? I was truly uncomfortable in there. Every eye in the room was on me."

"Yes, well, that's what you get for being stronger than five grown men," Nightshade laughed.

Allabva flushed. "If you must know, I wasn't. They beat me when they teamed up—five of them."

"Give it time," Nightshade said. "The bond is still settling in, and you haven't trained at all yet. By the time you face Sacalai, you'll likely be stronger than ten or fifteen men."

Allabva whipped her head to the side to look at the Nightshade for a moment, then turned back to watch where she was running. "When I face Sacalai? I thought I was your Companion; I thought you were facing her."

"We will both face her."

Allabva supposed that made sense. "Alright, but what's this about enjoying my suffering?"

The Shrongelin gave her a sideways glance. "Look, princess, suffering happens. What you experienced last night was mild discomfort. You'll experience real suffering before we're done."

"Well, sure," she replied indignantly, "but it feels like you set this up to make me suffer."

"I didn't, but what if I did?" he said defiantly. "Like I said, you'll suffer worse. This was nothing. You were never in any danger, were you? And look at it this way—what did you do with it? Did you overcome it?"

Allabva stalled for a moment. "I fled from it," she said. "I left the room when I got a chance."

"Aha," he said. "'*When you got a chance.* You did not leave too early. You did what you had to do, and then, when able, you did what you needed to. I'd call that overcoming."

Now Allabva looked at the Nightshade in a different light. What she thought was derision—and she still felt it was—had somehow morphed into encouragement. How did that make any sense?

Whatever, she huffed silently, and ran on. The Nightshade was quite different from Tuki.

The two ran in silence for a long time. Allabva grew curious as it appeared the Nightshade sometimes slowed, then sped up again as if he were distracted. After overthinking it a while, she finally decided there was nothing against her asking questions.

"What's on your mind?" she asked him.

Nightshade looked at her for a moment and continued running. "We have to talk about what we're doing in Tallensworth," he said. "You will enter the city alone. What happened last night and the night before were practice rounds. Not for the arm wrestle itself, of course, but for gathering attention. You traveled in secret with my Forerunner. But although we have traveled in the open and we are allowing ourselves to be seen, we haven't announced ourselves. In Tallensworth, we push it to the next level."

Allabva wasn't sure she liked the sound of this. "What do you mean by the next level? I'm not going to go around, hollering that the sky is falling, am I?"

"No," Nightshade said matter-of-factly, "but you will intentionally draw attention to yourself. Go and challenge people to arm wrestling matches. Win them. Gamble for money, or not. It doesn't matter. Just attract attention by doing what everyone else thinks to be impossible."

"Alright," Allabva said. "I guess I can arm wrestle. But I can't simply be a show-off. That just isn't me, and gambling isn't my way."

"Whatever suits you, as long as it works," Nightshade said. "At this rate, we'll reach the city by mid-afternoon."

"Mid-afternoon?" Allabva asked in surprise. They were going fast enough that she started to feel a slight ache in her legs, which hadn't happened over the previous few days. "Then why don't we slow down?"

"Because," the Nightshade answered, "you need to visit as many taverns or public places as you can. Go to one, gather everyone's attention, drop your name as Allabva the Companion, and then leave. Go to the next, and repeat."

"What if there's trouble?" she asked. "If you're outside the city, wouldn't it be possible for a crowd to overwhelm me before you can get there?"

"It is possible," Nightshade admitted. "We should have some signal. Do you have any sort of small trinket on you?"

"I have this," Allabva said, pulling Delgan's flute out of her blouse.

"Yes," Nightshade said. "I recall that you played that on the mountain before I fought off the wolves attacking Hronomon. Hold it out in front of you."

Not knowing what to expect, Allabva complied.

The Shrongelin flicked his head down and lightly touched the flute with the tip of his blade-like horn.

"Now, when you give it a blast, that will carry its tone to me from a distance. Let's try it out," he said.

He took off galloping suddenly, surprising Allabva with his speed. She had seen horse races, but their top speed was nothing to match the Shrongelin's.

"Blow three hard, short blasts on your flute when I stop running," he shouted back.

Soon the Shrongelin was just a speck on the horizon, just large enough for Allabva to know the moment when he stopped and stood still.

She put the flute to her lips, thinking this would sound awful, as normally happened when one blew on the flute too hard. But the Nightshade seemed to want her to play as loud and hard as she could, so that's what she did.

Allabva didn't hear any musical tone coming from the small instrument, shrill or not. Instead, she only heard the wind moving through it. After she played her three short blasts, she saw the Nightshade start trotting back toward her while she continued forward. This took several minutes due to the distance he had gained ahead of her. When they met up again, he nodded.

"That will do," he said. "I'll be able to hear that from outside the city, no matter where you are in it. But we'll set the distress call at three repetitions of three short blasts each."

Allabva nodded her head. "That'll work."
They ran on.

INTERLUDE I

Chapter 10

West and North

Nolder Lawgrin opened his tent flap to look out at the Disaffected encampment early in the morning. He had arrived here a week or more prior with four other men.

Previous to coming here, Nolder had decided to travel with Nillan Protfund, as the man had expressed many ideas that Nolder agreed with readily, particularly around distrust of the Nomord. The mere thought of the Nomord was enough to make Nolder shake his head in frustration and get Nillan riled up in anger. They had both been beyond upset when one of the white beasts stopped their wagon on the way to this camp, after which Nillan had chased the beast and the girl it traveled with up a mountain, while Nolder stayed behind.

At a younger age, Nolder might have acted similarly to Nillan. He certainly felt that he had plenty to be upset about. But these days, his bones ached and his muscles complained when he did something too strenuous.

He still considered himself fairly active. He had walked several hundred leagues in the last month or two and ridden in a wagon several hundred more. He was able-bodied. But his age was nipping at his heels, encouraging him to wisely temper his passions, reining them in so they wouldn't do him any harm, except on occasion when he consciously made a calculated decision to allow that to happen.

The morning air helped him. Nolder thought it smelled fresh and lifted his spirits. *When you get through a good portion of the day's work in the morning, you feel like your time was well spent,* he thought.

Stretching and yawning, he grabbed the jar and the metal pitcher sitting on a table next to his cot and made his way along between the rows of tents to a well that had been dug before he'd shown up at the camp. Fetching some water, he washed his face and hands, allowing the runoff to splash into a shallow trench in the ground that led downhill, away from the well and out of the camp.

When Nolder finished at the well, he returned to his tent, bringing another jug full of water with him.

In his tent, he sat down on the rickety chair they had provided him when he arrived, and ate a simple breakfast of dried sausage and apples. Then it was time to set about the day's work.

Nolder normally thought of himself as a straightforward and simple man. He had never vied to be the mayor of his hometown, nor sought great academic honors. He just wanted to take care of himself and his family. Well, what family he had left. But the way life had played out, he'd had experience balancing account sheets for a merchant lord's shipping enterprise.

Now, when he arrived at the Disaffected encampment several days before, they had asked him what skills he could provide, and he had answered truthfully. So, now they had him scouring and balancing accounts.

Nolder opened the books on his portable table to where he had left off yesterday. Maybe today he would finish this set and move on to something that would help him feel like he was making more of a difference. There were so many things that needed to be corrected in this world, the least of which, he thought, were the numbers in his books. But he knew they made a difference in this camp, and he wanted to help out. He sighed. Before he jumped into this, he needed a little something...

The aged man stood and stepped outside of his tent again, stretching some more as he did so. He looked around and saw a white speck on the small rises going up into the foothills of the nearby mountains. He squinted. That speck—could it be? No, he decided it was nothing but some rocks.

He did a few more stretches, preparing himself to face the day's work. Then he took another look.

No.

The speck was moving, and impossibly fast, too. That was no rock formation, after all. As he watched it and tried to gauge the distance, he shook his head. This was moving too fast to be a wild horse. It was one of those cursed Nomord.

Nolder furrowed his brow in suspicious anger. This was odd behavior, even for Nomord. It must be the same one that had stopped their wagon on the way here and forced them to release the girl.

This Nomord was up to something; Nolder just knew it. He now knew, having learned personally just less than a day before arriving at the camp, that the Nomord were not all mares; there were Nomord stallions as well. He had no way to confirm it, but he felt sure of his suspicion that this was the same Nomord stallion that had faced his group that day, had stared them down, and dared them to counter it.

Nolder took a moment to wonder if he should report this immediately. He shook his head. There was already plenty of excitement around here. He'd pass the word on, right after assessing what his books and figures would demand of him today. That way, when people got excited, he'd have a reason to excuse himself and not fall behind.

Lifting the flap, he ducked back into his tent and sat down to his work.

Tylonus raced over the ice, Vlon and Pontil huffing along on either side of him.

"Can we stop and rest already?" asked Pontil.

Pontil was the youngest of them, but Tylonus was in the best physical condition due to Pontil's fondness for drink and aversion to hard work. The young sailor was still useful despite that. The three men charged along behind the Nomord called Rhaslemonor, with whom they had bonded some months before. Due to their bond, they trotted along faster than any human would have been able to naturally. The bond not only increased their maximum physical strength but also gave them stamina, so they were able to charge on for half a day at a time before they had to stop and rest.

"Quit yer yappin'," Vlon replied. "We got places to be, young buck. You ain't hear me complainin'. But you do hear me wheezin', don't you?"

Vlon wasn't in as good shape as Pontil was, despite his age. In his years, he had learned the value of hard work, and it showed. But Tylonus could see sweat beading and running down Vlon's face as they ran.

"Come on," Pontil begged. "Let's stop, and Rhas can give me some water, and we'll have a little bite to eat, yes?"

"We stop when Rhaslemonor and I say so," Tylonus said. He looked over at Vlon again. Although Tylonus insisted on himself deciding when they would stop, he truly didn't want to wear them out.

Vlon pursed his lips and nodded at Tylonus. "It's probably about that time," he grunted.

Tylonus sighed. He didn't want to stop. He needed to get the news to the Shrongelin in Cylgiana.

Something was wrong with Sacalai's prison. He and his three companions—humans and Nomord—had gone into the great chamber underground where the great evil force known as Sacalai had been contained for the last few millennia. They should have seen shifting images inside the prison sphere, never holding to one shape. Instead, they had seen a menacing beast with thick, woolly fur and two sick horns on its nose. The woolly rhino had spoken to them, had taunted them.

Tylonus whistled the signal for Rhas to stop running. The four of them slowed to a trot and then a walk.

"This is a brief halt," Tylonus directed at Pontil. "You know we have to push on."

While Vlon and Pontil breathed heavily and wiped sweat from their brows, Tylonus was doing some of his own heaving for air. Their Nomord escort breathed easily. Tylonus knew their pace hadn't been difficult for him, and he could go on significantly longer with his longer legs. He was a mythical Nomord stallion, after all.

Tylonus thought while the men reached into the bags strapped to Rhaslemonor's back and extracted food and water. Tylonus reached into a bag and grabbed a handful of grass and offered it to the Nomord.

"No, thank you," he said, turning his head away and flaring his nostrils, sniffing the air. "Something is wrong." He turned his head back and forth, eyeing the horizon and sniffing deeply.

"What is it?" Tylonus asked, stowing the grass back in the pack.

Rhaslemonor shook his head. "The air is wrong. It smells…"

Tylonus sniffed as deeply as he could. Tylonus inhaled as deeply as he could.

"I don't smell anything. It just smells like…" He trailed off, trying to catch a hint of a scent.

"Seawater," Rhaslemonor pronounced at the same time as Tylonus and Vlon. Rhaslemonor raised his head up and down in agitation.

"Seawater," he said again. "It's too close. If we can smell it this close, then…the ice will be getting thinner. And perhaps—"

"Can't you just call another storm?" Pontil interrupted.

Rhaslemonor raised his brow, if that's what it could be called on an equine face, turning his gleaming, twisted horn to point at Pontil as the sunshine glistened off his white hair.

"Have you no memory?" he said. "Yes, I can bring a storm, to an extent. Not of this magnitude. You were there when I and all of my brothers at Mascaldinig called up this storm. You were there, months before when we did the same, but with the Shrongelin's and the Hronomon's aid. It took *all* of us to call up a storm large enough and freeze enough of this ice so the Forerunner and the Guardian could walk to shore. No, I alone cannot freeze the sea, apart from a light frosting and perhaps a few individual ice floes."

"How bad do you think it is?" Tylonus asked. "Do you think we still have passage?"

Rhaslemonor shook his head slowly.

"I cannot say for certain."

"Then let's continue," Tylonus said firmly. "We have to get the word to the Guardian and the Forerunner. Whatever Companion they have selected will also have to know of this development. And if we have to swim a few hundred paces, so be it."

"A few hundred paces?" Pontil shouted. "In this icy weather? Are you mad?"

Tylonus rolled his eyes. "Young man, remember your current enhanced strength."

"Of course, but I would never swim in water this cold at all without this strength. With it, maybe I could do half a dozen paces."

"You'll do as you're told," Vlon grunted. "I thought you'd learned a few things since the Armadillo wrecked."

"Yeah, I learned the Nightshade Unicorn is real," Pontil back talked.

It was Vlon's turn to roll his eyes. "Yes, that's true. But you'll do as you're told. Besides, you also learned the Nightshade Unicorn is one of the good guys."

"If you can call him that. Right grumpy, that one is," Pontil mused.

"Are you done eating or what?" Tylonus pressed.

"Hey, give me a few minutes," the young sailor protested. "Give me a few. I need some more water, too."

"I think you're done," Vlon said, grabbing the waterskin from Pontil's hands and shoving it back in the bag on Rhaslemonor's back. "You heard the man. We got places to be." Vlon turned to Tylonus. "But perhaps a few more minutes—minutes—rest to let us get this down."

Tylonus nodded patiently, handing the waterskin back to Pontil. "A few minutes."

A few minutes later, the three men and their bonded Nomord continued westward, heading for the continent. The Nomord led the way, having traveled on hoof to and from Mascaldinig many times before, as the cycle of the Construct played out against Sacalai.

As they loped along, Tylonus, who was not a sailor, but a hopeful merchant of fortune in recent years before the *Armadillo* wrecked, felt a suspicion that their route was not a straight line but that it meandered somewhat, deviating back and forth across a westerly direction. He saw Rhaslemonor glance back at them in a manner which he had not used before their last stop. Tylonus squinted, but he couldn't see anything different on the landscape of ice and sky.

Finally, he saw it ahead of them, where the white on the ground gave way to light aqua and then to a deeper shade of blue. The ancient horned equine slowly came to a halt and turned to face the men.

"I'm afraid it is useless," he said. "I perhaps could go on alone. I do not know how wide the water is, but we cannot cross it on the ice."

"What?" Pontil complained. "We can't get across?"

"I thought you were rather averse to swimming anyway," Tylonus accused.

"I am, that I am," Pontil said. "But I don't want to be out here on the ice forever, now do I? I want to get across already."

Tylonus sighed. "Rhas, you have no idea how far it is to get across?"

Rhaslemonor shook his head slowly. "It has to be at least half a league."

"We'll never make that," Vlon laughed.

Tylonus slouched his shoulders, then fell to his knees, bringing one hand to his forehead, rubbing his brow through his glove while slamming his other hand on the ice in a fist. "We have to make it," he said, frustrated. "How can we not make it?"

"Hey, sometimes, 'tis what it is," Vlon said.

Tylonus looked at him sharply. "That may be true, but I can't accept that. I have family out there somewhere. I *will* give the Shrongelin and his Companion every opportunity to beat this Sacalai and keep my family out of danger."

Tylonus noticed Pontil idly scuffing his boots in the snow, wandering off a little by himself.

He turned his attention back to Vlon and Rhaslemonor. "We have to make it," he said. "There has to be some way."

Pontil coughed. Tylonus turned his attention back to the young sailor again. He was suddenly acting a little odd.

Vlon also turned his attention. "You have something to add to the conversation?" the veteran seagoer asked.

Pontil took a deep breath, then let it out. "Well, I suppose we could. I mean, maybe we can go back to Mascaldinig and..."

"And what?" Tylonus prodded.

"And get my...boat," Pontil said.

"Your boat?" Tylonus and Vlon said together.

Pontil shrugged. "Well, I suppose... Well, you know, I didn't know when we were going to get off that island, so I started... I don't know... I started making one."

"You started building a boat? When?" Vlon asked, surprised at this isolated incident of motivation coming from Pontil.

"Oh, you know, basically whenever I had a free moment. You guys give me a lot of free time, you know. You don't involve me so much in the planning with the Nomord. So I figured I would just get off the island eventually."

"Oh." Tylonus and Vlon echoed each other.

"I mean, I've had plenty of time, haven't I?"

"I suppose you have, at that," Vlon said. "And it's big enough for the t'ree of us, uh, the four of us?" he corrected himself, gesturing with one arm to Rhaslemonor.

Pontil nodded firmly. "Oh, yes. You see, there are some strange animals on the island. I wanted to trap them, and maybe stuff a few and bring them back with me wherever I wound up. I could probably sell them and live pretty well for a while."

Tylonus's face was flush. "And you were going to tell us this, when?"

"Oh, I don't know. Before I left, I guess."

"You guess." Vlon said flatly.

Pontil looked at his feet, then back at the other two men. "Well, do you want it or not?"

Tylonus shook himself with relief at the prospect of success. "Of course. Of course, my man. You've saved us. You've saved the world, maybe." He lunged forward to embrace Pontil, then stepped back, holding him by his shoulders. "Maybe it was late, but it's still alright. There's still time, right?" He looked to Rhaslemonor. "Alright, well, let's head back."

"And I suppose we're not in such a hurry anymore, are we?" Pontil said.

"Now, there you're wrong," Tylonus said. "Since we couldn't make it across on foot, we're in more of a hurry than ever before. Let's go! Last one back on the island is a lame turtle."

Tylonus began to trot, and then to run eastward. Vlon and Rhaslemonor joined him immediately. Tylonus looked over his shoulder expectantly and saw Pontil begrudgingly begin moving his feet and start jogging behind his companions.

Part III: Settling In

Chapter 11

Entry and Orientation

Allabva stopped running along with the Shrongelin when they came within sight of the city Tallensworth.

"Enter on your own," Nightshade directed. "Meet me outside the northwest gate at third strike daily, otherwise blast your flute if you need to contact me urgently. Remember the distress signal if you are in danger. We should part ways now so you don't raise suspicion entering the city. Let them get to know you carefully. This will probably take several days. Your goal is an audience with Overduke Afaln Pymseet."

"Do you know what he's like?"

Nightshade pursed his lips. "The Guides told us this city is very structured. I expect its ruler to be the same way. His family has ruled the High Dominion of Tallen for the last hundred and fifty years. I cannot tell you more."

"What do I say I need to talk to him about?"

"Anything that will get his attention. The Disaffected gathering just beyond his backyard, perhaps. When you get an audience, let me know. I will come, and together we will seek to curry favor and organize the economy and output of this region for our cause."

Allabva turned to go, but her escort spoke to her again.

"Remember, you need to be bold. Your comfort is irrelevant. All that matters now is duty."

Then the Nightshade was off, galloping north, swinging wide of the city. Allabva was left to her own thoughts as she closed the remaining leagues to the west gate. There were two sentries monitoring traffic at the gate, but they appeared to be letting people pass through without much hassle. They noticed Allabva, though, and one of them spoke to her.

"Hey, miss. Come from out west?" His words were carefully pronounced, more separated than the speech of people in the Cleft. His uniform sported a blue-dyed leather jerkin covering a white shirt with pressed creases, loose-fitting trousers, and sturdy boots.

This fit the well-kept look of the stone walls behind him and the impression Allabva had gotten of the city overall.

"Why do you come to our city?"

Allabva was slightly taken aback at the directness of the question, but the other sentry spoke before she could answer.

"And your name, please?" He turned around, taking a seat behind a desk under an awning, and pulling out a book and pencil.

"Um, Allabva Companion," Allabva answered, "and I seek an audience with Overduke Pymseet."

The sentry with the book smirked to himself, bringing his hands together and resting his elbows on the open logbook. "An outsider looking for an audience with the overduke himself? You don't appear particularly noteworthy. Why do you think you deserve an audience?"

"Because I have something important to discuss." Allabva couldn't start rambling about male Nomord here, and she didn't want to mention the Disaffected if she didn't have to.

She felt like that was probably not the right route to take, anyway.

"Miss, look," the sentry said. "You want an audience with the overduke, you have to go through different layers to get there, especially with Southmarch coming up in two weeks."

Allabva wondered what Southmarch was, but didn't interrupt to ask.

The sentry continued. "I don't know what kind of chaos you come from out west, but here there are rules, and we follow them because they bring us stability. This is a city of order. If you want to get this started, you have to go through me to submit the proper channels, of course. It starts right here. But you're not convincing me. Your garb is foreign, but otherwise makes me feel quite blasé. You look like you try to take care of your appearance, but you're obviously a common enough traveler. You have a bow, so perhaps you hunt: nothing out of the ordinary. Would you bring a weapon with you into the presence of the overduke?"

Allabva hadn't thought about that. "No, if I don't have to—if there's a rule against that—then no, I'll leave them behind, of course," she stammered, trying to show a spirit of cooperation.

The guard leaned back in his chair. "Look, Miss..." He glanced down at the book to see what name he had written for her. "Companion—and I don't know what kind of surname that is—Miss Companion, you can enter the city, but I'm not submitting that request."

Allabva was flustered. She had to get that going. "I am..." What could she do? Well... "You've heard of the Disaffected, right?"

"Yes," the sentry replied, "but I don't think wherever this goes is going to help you get that audience. What about the Disaffected?"

Allabva hesitated. "Well..." she stammered.

"Do you have any information, or what?" the sentry pressed.

"Not per se," Allabva said, "but they're not up to any good."

"Lady, tell us something new," the other sentry interrupted sarcastically.

Allabva threw her hands up. "Fine. What if I told you I talked to unicorns?"

"I'd say use their proper name to show respect, and anybody can claim that," the guard smirked again. "Move along, Miss Companion," he said with derision.

The other guard tried to push Allabva, but she stood firm, and with her enhanced strength, the guard didn't have any real hope of moving her if she didn't want to be moved.

"Alright," Allabva said. She hated to pull this card. "I'll arm wrestle you for it."

The guard who was trying to push her along into the city stopped while he buckled over to laugh along with his fellow sentry.

"Arm wrestle me for it?" the seated sentry mocked. "You're what? *Maybe* an adult," he said, eyeing her up and down. "You're a twig. I've been eight years on this guard force, and I don't skimp when it comes to strength building." He flexed a thick arm to show her.

"Alright," Allabva said. "I see that. It's... It's ridiculous, isn't it? And yet, here I am. So, I ask that if I can beat you in an arm wrestle, you submit that request for me to get an audience with the overduke."

The sentry blanched. "You know what, Miss Companion? I will do that," he said at last. "You beat me in an arm wrestle, and I will submit that request. I will include my recommendation that it be ignored, but, fair enough, my superior will have to see it. And you know what? I'll tell him I'm only submitting it because of a dumb contest."

"That's fine," Allabva said. "Shall we get it over with?"

"Wait, you're serious?" he guffawed. "Hold on, just let me calm down."

After the two sentries were done laughing, and several people who had been passing through gathered around stopped to watch the spectacle, Allabva borrowed a second chair from the guard post and promptly but gently defeated the much larger man in a contest of muscle.

With expressions markedly less jolly and more appraising, the men took down the details of her request.

"Where are you staying in the city?"

Allabva blinked. She hadn't thought she would need to provide that information, and didn't know it yet herself.

"Miss Companion," the seated sentry droned, "if this request is to be honored, the magistrate needs to know where to find you. If you haven't made billeting arrangements yet, you can add those details later. You have three days from eleventh bell strike this afternoon to provide that information to the west district office, or your request will be scrapped. If you really want to see the overduke, I'd recommend updating your lodging tomorrow morning. If you do it today, they won't know anything about your request yet, as we deliver it to that office at the change of our shift. If you do it after tomorrow, it won't be fresh on the clerk's desk, and it might get lost in the bureaucracy." The guard looked at her admonishingly. "Go tomorrow morning, and take this. You'll need it for them to match you to the request."

He dragged a blade across the paper, separating a section from the bottom where he had scrawled a request number which was duplicated at the top of the page he still held on the desk.

Awkwardly trying to act as if nothing much had happened, Allabva thanked the sentries, accepting the slip of paper, and entered the city while they finished preparing the audience request. Allabva knew some people were staring after her as she walked down the street, so she made the first turn she could, then another, to lose the eyes on her back. Glad to regain some amount of anonymity, although she wore the clothing of an outsider, she asked a few passersby if they could recommend an inn.

After the first recommendation, she realized that although she could follow the directions to get there, she had no concept of where it was situated in the city. She mentally scrapped that information and asked for directions to a cartographer instead.

A small bell chimed as Allabva stepped through the door into the mapmaker's shop underneath a sign displaying *Whistlecomb's Marvelous Maps.*

"Just a moment," she heard from a dark region inside as she tried to allow her eyes to adjust to the dimmer interior. Getting her sight, she assessed her situation. Books and rolls of parchment paper surrounded her, standing tall in boxes.

"Just a minute," the voice repeated, sounding like it belonged to a decidedly elderly gentleman. "I'll be right there," he said.

Allabva coughed, resisting the urge to cough more in the dusty shop.

"Yes, how can I help you?" The old man came around the corner from behind some shelves, adjusting his spectacles to look up at Allabva.

She gave him a smile, making it as genuine as she could. "Master Whistlecomb?" she asked.

"That's me," he said. "What can I do for you, Miss... Miss?"

"Roalke," she said, assessing him to be harmless, and feeling happy to give somebody her real name, rather than the impersonal title that the Shrongelin gave her. When she did feel the need to give the title of Companion, she tried to pass it off as a surname, but she hadn't felt that way about it. Not yet, at least.

"Alright, Miss Roalke, how can I help you today?" Master Whistlecomb said.

"I need a map of the city," she said.

"Ah, new here?"

"Yes," she confirmed.

"Well, I can get you your basic city map. Here's one, and this one's just a single copper." He pulled a small roll of parchment from a box that was full of rolls the same size. Evidently, this was some kind of base offering.

"Ah..." He unrolled it and laid it on the counter between them.

Looking down, Allabva saw that the drawing was rather basic. It divided the city into quarters, but it didn't give much information other than that and the major streets. Allabva pursed her lips. Her winnings from the previous night's arm wrestles would surely let her do better than this.

"Thank you, Master Whistlecomb. Do you have anything a little more detailed?"

He raised his eyebrows appraisingly. "How much more detailed?" he asked.

"Well…" She paused and thought for a moment. The way the Nightshade had described her mission here so concisely, it sounded rather basic. But she knew there were many details she would have to figure out that just hadn't been discussed openly yet. "I think I'll need one with significant detail," she said, "as much as you can fit on a sheet about this size." She motioned her hands a little broader than her shoulder width, square.

"Ah, alright," Master Whistlecomb said. He turned around and looked among the cubbies in the wall behind him. Finding the correct cubby, in which there were only five rolls, he grabbed one and, turning back around, spread it out on the countertop. Allabva raised her eyes.

"Now, this—this is a lot better," she said.

"Alright, and it'll cost you five and a half silver hafender."

Allabva thought the price seemed rather high, but she supposed it was proportionate to the amount of work that went into creating it. She pulled her coins out and saw that she didn't have enough silver.

"Can you break a gold piece?"

"Of course."

The shopkeeper disappeared behind a wall and Allabva heard him shuffling around. He reappeared soon with some silver pieces, placing them on the counter. Allabva spoke while he counted four hafender and a Weslan Fielder crown as change.

"Master Whistlecomb, sir, I think I need a little bit more than the map by itself. Can you talk me through it? And keep the other half silver for your trouble," she added.

Master Whistlecomb frowned at the thought of being paid extra without providing more maps, but kept the crown, pushing only the hafender toward her.

"I'll talk you through it, no problem. What kind of artisan mapmaker would I be if I couldn't talk to the quality of my maps? Alright, miss..."

He leaned over the counter, bringing his face close to the map, and explained the legend. While he talked, he pointed out every major part of the city and characterized which corners she may not want to go to for her own safety, and where to find the best services for a tailor, a baker, and the like.

Allabva looked around the shop. There were maps of more than just the city here. She could see there were maps of the entire Fonglan Gulf, as well as greater Eslarna. Looking around some more, she spied maps of the entire Glosen lands, maps of the South Sea and Inner Sea, of Mediatol, of Darlte, and every other place in the world she could think of. She would have to come back here when she had more coin, she decided.

Master Whistlecomb finished his explanation, after which Allabva asked for a recommendation for a good inn.

"Well, you could try the Medicine's Roost," he said. "They don't typically have a lot of vacancy this time of year, what with the festival coming up, but they might still have room for you. They might be a little expensive for you, but I don't know what their exact rates are. You go ask them, and if you can afford it, it'll be a perfect place to lay your head."

"The Medicine's Roost?" Allabva asked, verifying the odd name.

"That's the one. It's over on Indoque Alley, which comes off of Indoque Street," he said, pointing at the map. "Of course, most of the Alleys are up a little further north in the city, the way they're named, but go to Medicine's Roost. Its location is just right to keep you safe and not pay too much."

"And what's this festival coming up?"

"Southmarch," the elderly man smiled. "You'll have a great time, I'm sure."

He seemed to think Allabva had some idea what Southmarch meant. She didn't want to press it right now.

"Thank you, Master Whistlecomb," Allabva expressed her gratitude, gathering her map and leaving the shop with another ding.

What a kind gentleman, Allabva thought, wondering if he had family living with him, or nearby, for that matter. She hoped he wasn't all alone in his advanced age.

Allabva directed her steps as the old cartographer had recommended, and found the Medicine's Roost on Indoque Alley, as he had indicated. It was a tall inn, having been built upward due to the congestion of the city. It stood three stories tall, and was no less wide from side to side, or deep from front to back. Some of the buildings in town were made of stone, but this one appeared to be of a material that imitated it—perhaps some kind of plaster over wooden beams. The material had been molded into shapes, imitating the faces of stones and the grooves in between them. She had seen other buildings like this in the city, but among those, this one was done particularly well, giving off an impression of sturdiness, as if it truly were stone.

Allabva paused, stopping where she stood. She had just come around the corner, bringing the recommended inn into view. As she saw people coming and going, passing by in front of the inn, all she could think about was how differently they were dressed from herself. Looking up to her right, she saw a sign with clothing carved on it, and a label that said *Vilna's Fashions*. She quickly ducked inside.

While the Nightshade wanted her to draw attention to herself, Allabva felt less eager to do so. But if she had to do it, she would prefer to be noticed when she was ready and had a plan to follow.

Allabva looked around inside the shop. There were racks with men's coats and trousers, as well as women's dresses, and an interesting bag-like garment. Allabva had seen those worn by many of the children running around the city. There were a few of these bag outfits that appeared to be in adult sizes as well, but based on the stylized creases and frills sewn into them, Allabva supposed they weren't exactly intended for blending in.

She made her way to one of the racks of dresses and started flipping through. Here was a shade of deep burgundy she had seen on a few of the women, and there, a cream accented with black.

Allabva checked the coins in her bag. She would need to conserve them. She still had to check into the inn and pay for her room there, even if it was just for one night. Then, after an afternoon of hypothetical arm wrestling, she could come back and pay for a longer stay. But she needed to keep at least one night's fare in her pockets.

She turned away from the dresses, wondering if there was a less expensive option. *Maybe a shawl,* she thought, *especially if it will cover my hair.* Curly hair was not common in this area, and it wouldn't hurt to make her shade of hair less immediately visible, too. Maybe she could even hide her bow and quiver under the shawl until she got to her room. She could be noticed for what she did once she was ready to be noticed, not sooner.

As Allabva's eyes fell on a shelf with several shawls folded, she shook her head, knowing that she couldn't cover her hair. The women didn't do that here, at least not that she had seen in this time of year. She would stick out like a sore thumb if she used a shawl in that manner. But, thinking of what she had seen on the townswomen as she walked through the city, perhaps she could still hide the distinctiveness of her clothing.

Allabva selected a light shawl from a stack of identical ones, light brown with a border of tassels extending an inch or two around the fringe. Having made her selection, she felt the freedom of mind to realize that she was probably being watched.

"Can I help you, miss?" Allabva turned her head to see a woman standing behind a counter, pen in hand, and an open notebook before her. Perhaps Allabva wasn't the only one who had just come to herself.

"Just the shawl, please," she said, pulling it from the shelf and walking over to the counter. She spied something else behind the counter. "And one of those coin purses," she said, pointing.

"Of course, miss," the shopkeeper said. Allabva wondered if this was Vilna herself, or if the woman was someone employed by Vilna. The woman—Vilna, or Vilna's clerk, or whoever she may be—named a price that was at least half again more than what Allabva expected.

Allabva tried not to let her eyebrows rise as she reached into the pocket inside her bag and pulled out the requested amount, trying not to wonder if this was a special price charged extra to out-of-towners. But she knew she needed these items.

After paying, she stuffed the coin purse in her bag and draped the shawl over her shoulders, carefully positioning it so it covered the most area of her back, hoping to pass unnoticed and be thought of as fairly commonplace. She bemoaned the fact that she wasn't able to cover her bow and quiver. She stepped back out into the street. As she did so, a bell chimed in the distance nine times.

Ninth strike, Allabva thought. She knew it was later than Nightshade had planned for her to get about her business. Still, she had to rent her room at the inn before she hit any taverns.

"Well," she thought, "here goes nothing." Hopefully, people wouldn't remember her clothing and recall that the Allabva from the Cleft entered this particular inn.

Allabva stepped inside the Medicine's Roost. She crossed the common room to approach a counter at the far side, in the back of the room. A woman was there, whom Allabva assumed to be the matron of the establishment, hanging keys up on little hooks fastened to a board with numbers marked over them. The woman turned to Allabva and raised her brow appraisingly.

"Yes, madam. How can I help you?"

Madam, Allabva noticed mentally. She supposed the woman was just being overly courteous, as she might for any customer. Allabva was aware of how young she was, and she certainly didn't feel like a "madam."

"I'd like accommodations, please," she said.

"Of course, madam..." The woman paused expectantly.

"Companion," Allabva filled in. "Allabva Companion."

"Yes, of course, madam. Is there a Master Companion traveling with you today?"

"No, just me."

"A single, then, I presume?"

"Yes, please."

"Alright. I'm sure you'll find our rates agreeable." The woman nodded toward a sign next to her with room prices listed. Allabva glanced at the bottom of the list to see the lowest fare.

"That will work fine," she said. "Do I need to pay now, or...?"

"Oh, no," the woman said. "A young mistress such as yourself needn't worry about the rent in advance. We'll just settle accounts when you check out, if that works for you."

Allabva nodded. She could pay the price of the room right now for one night, but she would need to obtain more money in town before she could pay for any more nights. Still, she knew that wouldn't be hard with her newfound strength.

"If you'll follow me. I am Mistress Tofan, by the way," she said, grabbing a key from one of the higher hooks on the board behind her. She then led the way down the hallway to the left and up two flights of stairs.

Allabva thought there would probably be a decent view from the third story, and she wondered why they would put one of their budget rooms up top. Perhaps in this town, one had to pay extra for the more convenient ground floor.

"And, here we are," Mistress Tofan said. "Your key, madam. Now, we do serve dinner—it's not included, but it's available after the eleventh bell strike. Of course, you're welcome to join us. Visitors staying with us get a slight discount on the meal, and we offer a complimentary pastry and two eggs any way you like them in the morning."

"Thank you," Allabva said.

"Just let me know if you need anything," the matron said hurriedly, and then vanished down the stairs.

Allabva held the key in her hand, feeling the small weight of it in her fingers. Then she inserted it in the lock of the door in front of her marked with the same number, and turned the key.

Opening the door, she found a sight that rather surprised her. This room was far nicer than the rooms at the Dusty Pot or Greenstock. It wasn't any larger—she could blame constraints of the urban setting for that—but the pastel-painted walls and exposed rafters gave quite a pleasant appearance.

Stepping across to the window at the far side of the room, past the four-poster bed, Allabva looked out the window and down at the view of the street. She saw over the rooftops across the way and off into the hills to her right. She could just make out the coastline on her left, so her room faced west or southwest.

Shaking her head and wondering how the inn could provide such a nice room at the affordable rate she had seen on the sign in the lobby, Allabva settled her few things, leaving her bow and quiver leaning against the wall, as well as her staff, which was truly just a walking stick. She sighed to herself at the prospect of leaving the comfortable room and beginning the surely uncomfortable task ahead. She had no idea where to even start.

Chapter 12

Blank Slate

Allabva's room offered a desk and chair with a modest amount of gilding on the surface of the desktop. There was also a small mirror sitting on the desk, which she grabbed and studied herself in. Her hair was mildly disheveled despite the hours of running, but her face was something quite different from how it had been when she left home.

Allabva had left home scrambling cross-country for the sake of the world and for her own life. She had also missed several meals in the process and exerted herself to the utmost in order to accomplish the mission Hronomon brought to her. But now, as she took a pause at the first place that she could consider to be a destination since leaving home, she really looked at herself. Her face was thin—not quite gaunt—but her features had hardened in a short period due to the conditions of running across the land, hunger, and stress she had experienced. It was a somewhat subtle change, but it was undeniable, nonetheless. At least her hair wasn't the complete tangled mess it had been a few days before, prior to her first stay in one of the inns.

"Alright," Allabva blinked, pulling herself out of her reverie. It was time to be about her business. She tucked some stray strands of hair behind her ears, settled her shawl over her shoulders, adjusted her money purse under her belt, and headed out the door. For the first time in her life, she was to be actively looking for trouble, like it or not.

She considered going for a simple walk to see where it took her. She was hungry, but she knew she had to make it a working meal: wherever she ate, she needed to be making contacts among the inhabitants of this city, and hopefully adding to her coin purse so she could afford her room at the Medicine's Roost.

Allabva approached the first tavern she came across in the docks district with some trepidation. She had come this way on purpose, assuming that anywhere there would be sailors relaxing and unwinding, there would be gambling. She read the sign over the door: *The Blank Slate*. Thinking of the almost-required task of arm wrestling, she idly brought one hand to the opposite upper arm and flexed the muscle against her palm.

Allabva stepped inside. She could hear singing, the sound carrying through the closed door. She opened the door, and the song came sailing out at her as she stepped inside. Glancing around, Allabva couldn't see the host or hostess in the room.

"Seat yourself, miss," a voice called to her. She looked and saw a man with a tidily trimmed beard sitting at a table. He nodded to her and gestured at the empty tables, then turned back to his menu. Appreciating the friendly gesture, Allabva picked one of the tables and sat, picking up a card waiting for her there with the names of dishes written on it.

Allabva took another look at the man. Although he was seated, she could tell he was tall and lanky. He didn't look very intimidating. Then again, Allabva didn't need to feel intimidation from any men these days, thanks to the bond with the Nightshade. The man smiled back at her kindly.

Allabva turned to her menu after acknowledging his glance. She wasn't here to draw attention to herself by looking at people. If she listened to the Nightshade, she was here to find her way into their games and catch their attention with her abnormal strength.

Reading the menu, the first thing she laid eyes on sounded exquisite to her, until she noticed the second thing listed. As she read down the page, almost everything sounded good. She realized her hunger was doing this to her. Even the things she had never heard of sounded good, since she was willing to try just about anything right now. At least she wasn't as hungry as she had been a couple of days ago. That had been difficult to endure, but this was a simple, everyday appetite.

Allabva hastily settled on the second item on the menu and then pretended to keep perusing as she turned her attention to the conversations around her. Feeling self-conscious about being a stranger in town with a different complexion and garb, she reminded herself of the shawl on her shoulders, trying to believe that it added a sufficient touch of locality to her appearance.

A man appeared, wearing a shirt with buttons running up the front and an apron over his trousers. "Madam Delegate," he addressed her.

Allabva cocked her head. What had he called her?

"Madam, would you like to order?"

It was late afternoon. "Are you still offering midday meal?"

"I can check if we still have any of those items left over, but I don't believe so."

Allabva worried that she was wasting the man's time, sitting there unsure of herself, unsure of what to eat, unsure of how to approach attracting attention like the Nightshade wanted her to do, but still in a manner that would be palatable to the locals' sensibilities and not get her thrown out. Or worse yet, have her and the Nightshade's mission cast in a bad light and ruin efforts moving forward. She stalled, turning the card over and looking at the dinner side.

She was hungry, but she was supposed to visit multiple places, and she didn't want to make herself sleepy before she was done for the night. That meant it had to be something light. "Umm..."

The waiter cocked an eyebrow. "How about the vegetable soup and some toasted bread, yes?" he suggested to her.

Allabva nodded. "Yes, please."

Anything to move the afternoon forward and start making things happen in a sensible manner. The waiter nodded and ducked into the kitchen.

Another customer rose from his seat and walked out the door. That left Allabva, the bearded man nearby, and a couple on the far side of the dining room in an otherwise empty tavern. As she started to doubt whether she should be in this establishment at this time of day if there weren't many people to meet, the bearded man spoke to her again.

"You really aren't from around here, are you?" he asked.

Allabva shook her head. "No, sir."

"It seemed like you were confused when the waiter called you 'delegate.'"

"Yes," Allabva admitted. "I thought he must have said 'delicate,' but I don't think I look particularly—"

"No," he said, interrupting, and confirming the word, "it was 'delegate.'"

"Well, why would he think—?"

"As I said, you're not from this region, are you?"

"I already said I'm not," Allabva replied, "but I'm trying to blend inasmuch as I can. See, I'm wearing what I've seen other ladies wear—"

"Miss, if you don't mind," the bearded man said, "let me explain the confusion. You've seen other women wearing that brown shawl, and so you thought it's a point of fashion. It's not fashion; it's appointment."

"Appointment?" she asked. That was not the word she was expecting to come out of his mouth. She slipped her hand into her pocket to grasp Lamtor's brooch.

"Why, yes. The shawl marks the Ladies' Council all over the High Dominion."

In the High Dominion...? Suddenly Allabva understood. "This shawl means something here, in all the lands governed by the overduke, doesn't it?" Her face flushed red.

"It does," the bearded man confirmed. "And you come here wearing it, along with clothing obviously not from Tallensworth. So what are we to conclude, other than that you were appointed as a delegate from one of the outlying areas?"

It was all true. Allabva felt her red face now turning white as she hastily removed the shawl. The couple on the far side of the room chuckled to themselves, and Allabva started feeling her ears burn.

"No, no," the bearded man soothed. "Don't take it off now. It's only the three of us still in here, and the waiter. He'll treat you extra nice for it. But you could run into some trouble out in town if somebody thinks you're trying to impersonate a delegate. But I saw you come in. You're obviously from outside of the overduke's lands. Just take it off when you leave here, but for now, leave it on so you don't have to explain to the waiter."

Allabva nodded, settling the shawl back into place. She needed new clothes immediately. *No,* she shook her head. Not immediately. It probably wouldn't be so bad if she stuck out a little. She just needed to stop looking like she was impersonating one of these delegates. Allabva didn't even know how large the Ladies' Council was. She had seen several ladies wearing the shawl, so it must not be too small of an organization. And she supposed they didn't keep track of each other across long distances on a personal basis. That meant that, so far, none but the three other patrons in this tavern knew she was wearing it erroneously. Maybe she could sell it back to Vilna's Fashions tomorrow.

Taking a deep breath and blowing it out through puffed cheeks, Allabva watched as the waiter returned and placed her meal in front of her, then left her alone. She glanced again at the bearded man, then paid attention to what was before her. It wasn't quite what she expected. She had supposed in her mind, subconsciously, that there would be potatoes, celery, and perhaps beets and spinach. What she found instead was mostly squash, both green and yellow, along with onion, which she had expected, and small bits of carrot. The seasoning smelled different from back home, but it still smelled good. The bread sitting on the plate next to her bowl of soup was sliced and then toasted on either side, although it looked like it had been prepared before she arrived and wasn't very fresh now.

Allabva ate her soup, dipping the toasted bread in it to soften it and spread the flavor of the soup onto the spongy texture. She ate quickly, trying to forget what was still true at the moment: she wore the brown shawl in front of strangers.

Somebody entered the tavern. Allabva had placed the door at her back, so she had to glance to see the person walking in.

She didn't notice anything peculiar about the newcomer, and looked back to her food while the newcomer called out, "Hey, Jalcon! Give me some of that shrimp stew."

The waiter heard the man from inside the kitchen. "Coming right up, Bilner!" he called back.

Allabva glanced at the bearded man, who gave her an understanding look, shaking his head. She understood his meaning: *No need to worry about Bilner. No need to remove or adjust the shawl.*

Allabva finished her soup and toast, stood, and left payment on the table next to the bowl. "Do people do this here?" she asked the bearded man nervously, pointing at her payment.

The bearded man simply gave her an encouraging nod and a slight wave with his fingers. Allabva turned, feeling very relieved, and stepped outside the Blank Slate. She grabbed the shawl off her shoulders and rolled it up so it wouldn't be recognized, tucking it under her arm.

You need to be bold, Allabva could hear the Shrongelin's voice in her mind, dispensing derision for her timidity. Allabva hung her head and massaged the back of her neck with one hand. Then she looked back up at the tavern sign. As before, it still said, *The Blank Slate.*

Be bold, she heard again. *All that matters right now is duty.* Shaking her head and appreciating the message from the tavern sign, she tried to internalize the advice often given by her father, years before. When something bothered her, he always told her to let it roll off like water off a duck's back.

"Like water off a duck's back," Allabva said aloud, wishing her father were here in person to say something more calming and encouraging.

The Shrongelin could give his direction and orders as much as he wanted, and he might be right about every scrap of it that he said, but that didn't magically make Allabva feel good about it all.

Allabva's mother had done a magnificent job of filling the roles of both mother and father after her husband vanished. But the truth was—and Allabva knew that Mother was aware of it—that no matter how expertly she compensated, Father's absence could not be filled completely.

"Like water off a duck's back," Allabva repeated again. Even if her father was lost and drowned in the depths of the sea, she could still carry him with her right now. She lifted her head. It was still only late afternoon. She had plenty of time left in the day.

Standing where the building next to the tavern jutted out in front of the Blank Slate, creating a blind spot on the other building's side, Allabva pulled out her city map to find the nearest market. She needed to get rid of this shawl, but she didn't have to take it back to the original shop. If she sold it this afternoon, she could use the money to patronize the next tavern she went to, and perhaps use her coin to loosen the purse strings of those who fancied themselves strong. Few people liked to place a bet if they were the only party going in on it.

Allabva shook her head again, this time at the irony of the situation. Hadn't she always regarded gambling as a low habit among people? And now that the greatest threat in the world was facing civilization—even though civilization was unaware—Allabva was using gambling, of all things, as a means to gather attention and ultimately protect the world.

Allabva had talked to Tuki about morality and discussed whether the end justified the means. Ruefully, she realized that now she was engaging in what could be considered morally relativistic. Allabva thought as she walked, setting her route toward an open-air market she had seen on the map.

But I'm not gambling with hope or a desire to win and take advantage, she thought. *I'm engaging with others how they wish to engage, in order to garner attention and thus to meet with the overduke and achieve success for everyone's benefit. I would not do this if I could see another way.*

With that thought, she determined to try to look for another way, but to proceed as planned otherwise. The Nightshade's plan would keep her off the street because it could pay for bed and roof, and keep food in her mouth until they could reach the next phase. Allabva didn't have to like it, and there was no reason to suppose it impossible to find another solution.

Some time later, Allabva arrived at the market, the sun sinking behind her. It was late afternoon, moving into early evening.

Chapter 13

Market

Allabva entered the market, smelling bread and meats, as well as the sweet and tangy odors of fruits, some of which she did not recognize. As she looked around, she noticed the market had been built into a square with proper stone buildings around the perimeter, and straight lines of stalls going up and down the middle in rows.

Allabva took a turn to make a loop around the edge of the square first, then she would start going down the rows. She needed to find a booth trading in textiles. She felt some urgency, as she saw shopkeepers closing up their stalls for the evening. However, some stayed put, so she continued her route.

Presently, she found a booth offering textiles and jewelry. She stopped to address the man sitting slumped on a stool and leaning against the back of his stall.

"Hello, sir," she started.

The man stirred, then opened one eye. She had the sun at her back, causing him to squint and blink in the sunlight.

"What do you want?" the man said tiredly, eyeing her out-of-town clothing. "I don't have anything to match your outfit. Everything I have comes imported, up from Fonglan Point."

"Oh, that's alright," Allabva said. "I need to sell this shawl."

"Sell it? What do you want?"

Allabva named how much she had paid for it. The man laughed.

"That's not going to work, miss. Maybe shops in the high streets charged you that much for it, but I hope they proved the quality. Let me see it."

He sat up and leaned forward, and Allabva handed him the ball of cloth. Inspecting the shawl, he countered her price.

"That's far too low," Allabva protested.

"That's half regular retail," he said. "If I'm going to be here and help you, I have to earn somehow or other. You're not going to get a better deal from anybody else here."

"But I paid—" Allabva tried again.

"Tell you what," the man said. "I'm tired and I want to go home. I'll give you half what you paid, not a copper more."

Allabva pressed her lips. "Alright," she said. "I'll take it."

The man reached into his coin purse and pulled out several coins, handing them to Allabva. She counted them and then looked back at the man.

"You're three coppers short."

"Of course I'm three coppers short," he said. "I'm going to have to pay taxes when I sell this, aren't I? Tax collectors come through here all the time. There's no getting around it."

Allabva felt sure the man was taking advantage of her, probably due to her out-of-town clothes. She huffed, taking the money, and walked away.

As she walked away from the man's stall, she spotted another stall selling clothing at the end of the row. Maybe the other stall would have something that combined the local styles with Allabva's aesthetic sense. She wouldn't have the money for a full outfit right now, but she could come back tomorrow.

It appeared that people in the other stall were packing up. A young woman pulled a rack of clothing toward a cart and heaved to load the rack onto the cart. She moved it out of the way of a display behind it, showing a red dress hung up, cut in the local style.

Allabva's eyebrows rose at the prospect, but as she walked forward to look at the dress more closely, a middle-aged woman folded the display in half, bringing the top forward and then down, hiding the dress from view. Then, like the younger woman, she heaved the display onto the cart.

Allabva quelled the dismay inside her. *No matter. I'll come tomorrow and see about that dress, or perhaps a similar one.* She continued forward, deciding she might as well get a closer look at the other offerings they had while they were still in view.

She quickened her step. She wanted to be able to talk to this pair, who appeared to be mother and daughter, before they were gone. It was too bad she didn't sell the shawl to them instead. Surely, they would have given her a better deal, despite what the man had said.

"Good afternoon," the older woman said as Allabva approached. "If you liked what you saw, we'll be here tomorrow morning."

Allabva nodded. "Thank you," she said. "I'll try to come by."

"Right. Well, if you'll excuse us, we still have things to pack up."

Allabva inclined her head, about to bid them farewell and continue to walk through the market. But then the Nightshade entered her mind again with his, *Be bold.* This probably wasn't what he was thinking about when he said that, but

Allabva didn't think it would matter too much. She worried that she would be troubling them, but she only wanted to ask a simple question.

"What's a good place to eat? Your favorite tavern?"

"Oh, I don't—" the mother started, then she shook her head and turned back to her work of packing up her wares.

"Ooh," the younger woman said, "are you from out of town? You should definitely go to the Coughing Badger."

"The Coughing Badger?" Allabva smirked at the funny name for the establishment, but it seemed odd names were the rule rather than the exception.

"Absolutely! I'm Jilona, by the way," said the young woman.

"Nice to meet you. I'm Allabva. Where is the Coughing Badger?"

Jilona stopped loading to give Allabva directions from the marketplace. The Coughing Badger wasn't particularly nearby. Allabva pulled out her map.

"There it is," Jilona said, pointing.

"Alright, Jilona, come on, let's get back to work," the older woman prodded.

"Yes, Mother. Nice to meet you, Allabva. Oh, and I hope to see you tomorrow," Jilona said, turning back to packing and loading.

Allabva pored over her map. This would take her over to the east side of the city, but that wasn't necessarily a bad thing. It just meant she would have to walk longer to get there. It might even be a good thing, as it would force her to get to know more of the city as she went. She could even take a different route coming back, thus forcing herself to see more shops and taverns, and encounter more of the people.

She looked to thank Jilona and her mother one more time, but they had already finished loading and were pushing and pulling their cart away by hand. While she watched, Jilona looked back and Allabva waved. Jilona waved back, then turned to heave the cart over a bump.

Allabva browsed the market a while longer, eyeing some of the weapons warily and wondering if she could ever get to be as comfortable carrying one as the guards she had seen at the gates of the city. Real weapons always seemed so heavy and bulky. Even the bow and the quiver that she had carried down from the mountain after their archer had been forced to surrender them had felt awkward in her hands. She had gone so far as to use the bow, trying to hit one of the men pursuing her, so it wasn't for lack of intent. Shrugging to herself, she supposed it was probably all for want of instruction and practice.

Allabva also stopped to watch at the booth of a luthier, which had been built into a permanent structure at one of the permanent side walls, with a kiosk facing into the market. The luthier sat repairing an instrument at the table in front of him. Allabva could see into his shop behind him, with instruments arrayed in various stages of manufacture and assembly. These were all stringed instruments; none were winds like Delgan's small flute that she carried around her neck, but the sight still made her wistful and homesick.

Delgan wasn't truly a woodwind player though, his specialty being keyed percussion. Allabva laughed to herself as she continued walking. She knew that Delgan played most of his music on the little xylophone he had brought over to her house a few weeks before, but she doubted that he would consider himself to specialize in any instrument. It wasn't his chosen profession. Delgan must have started his apprenticeship to the blacksmith by now, Allabva thought.

She held her hand just below the neck of her dress for a moment, pressing the cold metal of Delgan's flute against her skin to remember him.

Then she felt hungry again.

"I guess it's that time," she said aloud to no one, feeling slightly happy-go-lucky. "Time to get some real food in me and stop feeling this hungry. Have to fill these cheeks out."

Pulling her map out for another glance, Allabva visually verified the route and then set off.

Chapter 14

Coughing Badger

It took Allabva three quarters of an hour to get to the Coughing Badger. She could have gotten there a lot quicker, but she preferred walking to avoid making a spectacle of herself in front of the whole city by running.

When she arrived, she could see it was a much livelier place than the Blank Slate had been. It was larger and in a more affluent part of the city. Standing outside, she could hear music from within, whereas the Blank Slate had also been an acoustic blank slate.

Walking inside and looking around, Allabva didn't see a counter for a hostess or host to take down names or party sizes as people arrived. This tavern provided tables of different sizes, so that two or three people could sit together at a smaller table, and larger groups were also accommodated.

Allabva sat herself at an unoccupied, small, round table and waited. A young boy came to the table; Allabva thought he couldn't have been more than twelve years old.

"Good evening, miss," he said in a boyish soprano. "What's your name? I'm Andamaln. What can I get you?"

Allabva didn't have to think about this one. "You can call me Miss Companion." She felt odd giving an adult salutation.

She had come of age, but it was still a recent thing. "What's your best pasta on a budget?" she asked.

"I'd have to go with the baked tubes."

"Sounds good to me."

"We'll get started on that right away, Miss," the boy said, then dashed off to another table. Allabva heard him say, "Everything good, folks?" before he disappeared into the kitchen.

"And is there something *I* can get for you, miss?" Allabva heard a man's voice say. Its owner sat down across from her without invitation. He wasn't exactly as young as she was, but he was still youthful—perhaps in his low- to mid-thirties.

Allabva hid a grimace. Even if she weren't hoping to get back home to court Delgan properly, there was an age gap with this guy, and he still wouldn't have interested her, regardless.

"I think I'm alright, thank you," she tried to put him off.

"I like your cloak," he said. "Some of the guys here probably think it's weird, just because you're from out of town, but I can tell you've got some class."

Allabva choked back a groan. *No.* "I'm just here to—" Allabva stopped herself. As far as this man was concerned, she was only here to eat her dinner and be on her way. But even though that was as far as he needed to know, it wasn't exactly true. She rephrased, "Let me receive my meal and eat in peace."

"I'm sure I could make the experience all the more pleasant," the man said with a smirk.

"No, thank you," Allabva said firmly.

"Here, here, like this. Oh, my name's Jimlarnt, by the way. As I was saying, I can make things more pleasant just like this.

Hey, waiter! Andi!" he called the young boy back. "Bring us two of those pul-pul banana drinks," he ordered.

"Right away, sir," the waiter said, scurrying off again.

"You're going to love it," Jimlarnt said to Allabva.

"But you don't even know if I—" Allabva tried to say.

"—If you drink?" Jimlarnt said. "Don't need to know. It's fresh. They call them pul-pul, and they chill them with ice that they bring down from the mountains. Isn't that great?"

"Sure," Allabva said uncomfortably. "Look, Jimlarnt, I'm just not interested. You're not going to get anywhere sitting here, so why don't you just go on your way and leave me alone?"

"Because I know the look of a thirsty girl when I see her," Jimlarnt said, still smiling that infuriating smile. "That's why I already ordered you a pul-pul."

"Well, Jimlarnt, I'm seeing someone, alright?

"Is it an official, proper courtship?"

"Well, not technically."

"Well, then I'm sure the beau wouldn't mind." Jimlarnt leaned in. "Look, Miss..." he prompted for her name.

"You can just keep calling me miss, if you must talk to me at all," Allabva said, growing annoyed. She reminded herself again that she had nothing to fear from him.

Andamaln showed up with the two pul-pul drinks. "Here you go, sir, miss," he said, disappearing again just as quickly.

"See? There you go, I did that for you," Jimlarnt said, grabbing his own drink and taking a swig. "Mmm, I love that. It's fruity, creamy, and just delicious all around. Why don't you try it?"

Allabva rolled her eyes. "I've already asked you to leave twice, I believe."

"Come on, you haven't given me a good reason."

"Fine," Allabva said, truly irritated now. She glanced around at the crowded tables. Would nobody else intervene? Might as well give him a hint he ought to stay clear. "I'll show you exactly why you should leave."

"Oh, you'll show me?" Jimlarnt mocked. "I'm sure this will be real good."

"I'll show you," Allabva repeated. She set her arm on the table, ready to arm wrestle, her elbow planted and her hand in the air.

"Ho-ho, holding hands in public already, are we? You're really coming on to me now," Jimlarnt laughed, putting his elbow on the table and reaching for Allabva's hand.

She yanked it back, scowling openly at him now.

"Hey, you want to hold hands? Let's hold hands," the man put on a feigned hurt expression.

Allabva didn't know how he could keep his voice that smooth while his words were so sticky and slimy.

"We arm wrestle," Allabva said. "I win, you leave."

"And when I win?" Jimlarnt laughed.

Allabva blinked. Of course, Jimlarnt was going to lose, but he didn't know that yet. He needed an incentive to engage in the contest.

"If you win, then I leave," Allabva answered. She set her arm back on the table, and Jimlarnt reached for her hand again. She pulled it out of reach one more time and repeated, "I win, you leave the table and leave me alone."

"Fair enough," Jimlarnt laughed, "but if I win, you're welcome to stick around. I'm not going to force you to leave."

Allabva rolled her eyes, then took Jimlarnt's hand.

He yanked immediately, trying to pull her hand down toward the table before she had a chance to react. Unfortunately for him, she was several times as strong as he, so halting his progress was as easy as blinking. She did so, and Jimlarnt's body shook as he encountered the unexpected, arresting resistance.

Then Allabva started pushing the other way, slowly, enjoying the intense shock on Jimlarnt's face as he tried harder and harder to pull her hand backward. He finally stood to grab their hands with his free hand and pull, using the strength of his legs. One corner of Allabva's mouth pulled to one side in a half-smile as she showed her immunity to his best efforts. Then she calmly and steadily lowered his hand against the table.

Suddenly, Jimlarnt grew angry, grabbing his drink and throwing it at the floor. Glass shattered and creamy liquid splattered wide.

"You cheated!" he accused, pointing at Allabva. "You cheated!"

Allabva shrugged. "Maybe. Is it cheating to be stronger than you?"

"You can't be stronger than me! You cheated!"

"Whatever," Allabva sighed. Then she turned halfway as she prepared to stand. "I think I'm done with this place."

"Huh. So you admit it, then? You cheated?" Jimlarnt accused.

Allabva turned back. "No. How would I have cheated? I'm just stronger than you are. You lost. The terms were that you would leave the table, and leave me alone."

"Yeah, the terms weren't about anything about you cheating," Jimlarnt growled.

A couple of men from the next table over stood and turned to Jimlarnt.

"We overheard the whole thing," one of them said in an accent that was new to Allabva's ears. "You agreed to her terms. Young lady, why don't you repeat those terms one more time, and the young man *will* abide by them." He gave the rude intruder a dark look.

Standing by the table, it was clear that the two newcomers would be more than what Jimlarnt could handle. They towered overhead, whereas Jimlarnt was sitting. Allabva doubted whether she would come up to the sternum of either of these men if she stood in front of them.

"Yes," Allabva said, hoping not to have to repeat it again. "We agreed that if I won, you would leave the table and leave me alone."

"Fine," Jimlarnt said begrudgingly, looking at the newcomers. "I'll go find another table."

"Ah, no, you don't," said the other newcomer. "I'm afraid the young lass misspoke. I'm quite sure the terms were that if she won, you would leave, and not come back to the Coughing Badger again."

"What? No way, that's not what—" Jimlarnt protested, but the man interrupted him.

"Isn't that what she said, Walrus?" he addressed his friend.

"Yes, Tank, that's surely what she said," Walrus replied. "And this blister here agreed to not come back to the Coughing Badger again. Ever." He stepped in closer and Jimlarnt leaned back.

Tank smiled down at Jimlarnt. "Oh, don't worry, son. We'll take care of the bill; we're nice like that. You go on now. Have a good evening."

Jimlarnt lunged to grab Allabva's banana drink as well, apparently wanting to cause more destruction, but Tank and Walrus grabbed him by the arms and escorted him out as gently as a pack of wolves takes down a young buck, shoving him onto the street before he could try to renegotiate.

Allabva sat in her chair, still shocked at the spectacle and the unexpected drama.

"Ah," Tank said, walking back to her table, "young lass, don't worry about him. He won't bother you again. And don't worry, we'll be here."

"I think we like you," Walrus said.

"I thought we would," Tank joined in.

Allabva breathed in and out slowly, trying to digest what had just happened.

"Hey, Andi," Walrus called out, "if you don't mind, put these two banana pul-pul on our tab, and the glass as well."

The young waiter, clear at the other end of the dining hall, turned his head to the party and nodded acknowledgment.

"Lass," Tank said, "it looks like you're here all alone. Would you like to come and sit with us? Just to have some company—no obligation, of course." He held a hand up, palm out, signaling that it was her decision.

"Well... I mean..."

"Ah," Tank said. "Walrus, don't let's be lazy now. Come on, grab your tray."

Walrus grabbed his own tray from their table and brought it over to Allabva's table. "Look, young lass, we'll sit here for this meal so nobody else bothers you. Then you'll be done with us, if you wish. We won't follow you. We won't ask you for anything. We're just here to make sure you don't get messed with again."

"Thank you," Allabva said meekly.

Tank laughed. "Huh, as if it would matter, Walrus. You saw her sort him out. She beat him in a fair arm wrestle, and he cheated. *He* cheated, not her."

"Ha, ha, ha," the two large men laughed together.

"Oh, that was great. Hmm," Walrus said, "alright, maybe we lied. I will ask you one thing."

Allabva cocked her eyebrow sportingly, her mouth turning from a grimace into a smile at the men's antics. "What's that?"

"No, wait. Two things," Tank said. "Two things we ask. We must."

"Oh yes," Walrus echoed. "Two things. Number one: you attempt to genuinely enjoy your beverage."

"They are, indeed, delicious!" Walrus said, filling in Tank's words.

"But banana is just the beginning," Tank said excitedly. "They have coconut pul-pul, date pul-pul, apricot pul-pul—"

"And number two—" Walrus interrupted.

Tank took the hint to get back on track. "Number two, you let us try and arm wrestle you."

"We'll pay you," Walrus said. "We'll pay you just for the chance."

"I can't offer much, though," Tank said. "Our wives wouldn't be happy if we threw money away unnecessarily. But I'll give you twelve coppers."

"I'll give you fifteen," Walrus showed his friend up.

Now Allabva rolled her eyes, laughing a genuine laugh. "Well then, gentlemen," she replied, eyeing the waiter coming out of the kitchen and carrying a tray of what looked like what she had ordered, "I will ask two things of you."

"And what's that, young lass?"

"Let me eat my dinner first, and tell me why you're each called what you are."

"Oh," they both laughed together, "Of course, of course."

"Build up your strength; you'll need it against us," Walrus added with a smile.

"Will she, though?" Tank mused aloud, pausing to ponder. "That certainly was impressive. I look forward to the contest, Miss...Companion." He must have overheard when Allabva gave that name to Andamaln.

"Allabva," Allabva supplied gladly, smiling confidently as she removed her hand from her pocket, knowing these two men were sincere. "You can call me Allabva."

"So, what brings you to town?" Tank asked. "If you don't mind."

After providing her given name, Allabva now mentally pulled on the reins. She knew these men were genuine and forthright with her at this moment and posed no threat here in the tavern. But that didn't mean they would immediately help her with all her efforts. Everything here was a whirlwind as she got used to the new sights in this unfamiliar city.

"Actually," Allabva replied, "I think I'll keep that to myself for tonight. The details, at least. I'm basically here to talk to people."

"Ah, well, mission accomplished," Walrus said boisterously, slapping the table and making it shake.

Allabva was glad she was holding her drink, worried it might topple from the motion if it had been on the table. She had to laugh despite herself.

"Yes, I suppose so. I'd like to tell you more."

"You can tell us tomorrow," Tank butted in. "We'll be here again. This is where we unwind."

"I see," Allabva said. "And what is it the two of you do?"

"I'm a carpenter," Tank said. "I do it all. I make furniture, frame houses, whatever people need. I may work with my muscles, but I'm powered by my stomach! My wife likes to say I'm as large as a cistern because of that, so you can see why I am called Tank."

"And I am a stonemason," Walrus answered. "I help out whenever they need repairs on the palace walls, the city walls... But most of my work goes into setting up..." He trailed off. "Anyway, my brothers started calling me Walrus when I was young. Love you swim, you see, and I'm not such a small man, either." He grinned with mirth.

Allabva looked at the two men's bulging muscles with new appreciation. "Any clue what that Jimlarnt guy does?" she wondered aloud.

"Don't know, don't care," Tank said. "I'm terribly intrigued to know how *you* got to be so strong, though."

Allabva smiled wanly. "Maybe I'll tell you tomorrow. But you gentlemen helped me get rid of the nuisance, so, of course, I'll entertain your arm wrestle. But the money is not necessary."

"Now, of course it is," Tank said, looking offended and glancing at Walrus to confirm. He started counting on his fingers. "We can tell you're new in town. Your clothes aren't from around here. Your face says you've been traveling. You're vague about why you're here, and you're traveling without an escort. So, you're not here on any highfalutin' government business. You're no noble. I figure you could use some spending money."

The carpenter pulled out his coin purse and counted out twelve copper hafender. He glanced up at Walrus, who was also counting, then counted out three more to make it fifteen. "Here you go," he said. "Thirty coppers to beat us in an arm wrestle. But," Tank laughed nervously, "try to be a little gentle on me, eh?"

"Always," Allabva nodded.

Each man took his turn trying to beat Allabva in a simple arm wrestle. Neither used his left hand to pull harder. She could tell they were clearly stronger than most, but she still handily defeated them.

"What an enigma you are," Walrus said slowly, wiping the sweat from his brow after losing. "You're barely there at all, and yet you possess this strength." His mouth hung open, and she could see his tongue playing with his teeth as he tried to puzzle it out. "I know there's something about you," he said. "Whatever it is, I'm going to find out—through the proper means, of course, meaning you volunteer the information," he added, holding his hands up to show innocence.

"As if you could—" Tank interjected with a laugh, unable to finish his own sentence.

Walrus acknowledged the comment with raised eyebrows. "No, no persuasion, no coercion. And I won't be stalking you. No worries. No need to fear that. But if you'll come here again tomorrow, I'd love to talk more and find out whatever you feel like you want to tell us."

Allabva looked from one man to the other, then inclined her head gently. "I think that sounds nice," she said. "As I said, I'm here to talk to people. You are people, aren't you? But—" She glanced out the door, which had been propped open. It was now fully dark outside. "—I think I'll be on my way for now. I'll come back here tomorrow and enjoy your company again, if you don't mind. But I need to get to know the city and meet more people while I'm here."

"Well, there are more people right here in this tavern," Tank said with a grin, protesting her departure.

"That's true, but I need to get to know the city better overall."

"Well, but," Tank sputtered, "if you leave and we stay here, who will watch after you?"

Allabva shrugged and held her hands out. "I just beat both of you in an arm wrestle, didn't I? I'll watch after myself," she said simply.

"That, you will," Walrus repeated, sounding unconvinced.

"Doesn't mean somebody couldn't poison you, or stab you in the back," Tank added.

"That's true," Allabva said. "I'll just have to be careful. Gentlemen," Allabva stood, "thank you for helping me ward off the creep. Thank you for giving me somebody to talk to for a bit. And," she frowned, considering, "if for some reason we aren't able to find each other here again at the same time, I'm staying at the Medicine's Roost. You already know my name."

Allabva stood awkwardly, trying to remember if there was a local gesture they used instead of a handshake, which she wasn't familiar with.

Tank laughed. "We're not so formal. Don't give us any ceremony." He reached out his hand and grabbed hers in a firm handshake.

Allabva suspected that a week prior, this grip would have seemed much more constricting than it did now. She smiled, then turned to Walrus and shook his hand as well.

"Gentlemen, until tomorrow." She turned and walked out into the night.

Chapter 15

Slight Detour

Allabva stepped outside the Coughing Badger into the night, wrapping her cloak around her shoulders. It wasn't as chilly as it was back home, but there was still a certain coolness to the air.

She began to wander, deciding to go south and east—or as well as she could judge without the sun. The Coughing Badger sat on a rise in the city's streets, so she could see the harbor, toward which she oriented herself. She could pull out a map if needed, but right now, she thought she would explore and see where it led her.

A light drizzle added to the cool of the night, tickling her nose and dusting her eyebrows. Not wanting her hair to get tangled and wet before she went back to the inn and slept in that same tangle, she pulled her hood up over her head. She was aware this diminished her field of view and how much of the night's sounds she could hear.

It seemed to Allabva that the soundscape was filled with the light pitter-patter of raindrops and her own footsteps, neither of which concerned her. She had only made a few turns after leaving the Coughing Badger when she heard sudden running footsteps, followed by the two feet stomping the earth in unison, then a moment of relative silence.

Alarmed, Allabva's eyes widened, and she ducked forward to escape the shroud of her hood. Time seemed to slow as she felt sure the follower would successfully tackle her to the ground. But as she ducked forward and pushed off her left foot to twist on her right, she made nearly a full turn before seeing her assailant fly past, directly through the space she had occupied a moment before.

Allabva blinked, realizing the Shrongelin's gift had saved her from being hit from behind, if not fully tackled. The other form crashed to the ground with a thud, then sprang up, muttering angrily.

"No way you can do that," the shape said in Jimlarnt's voice. Allabva sighed in exasperation as the form launched itself at her again.

"Why won't you leave me alone?" she said, sidestepping easily as the man once again unsuccessfully attempted to tackle her.

"You're mine," he said, grunting as he picked himself up again. "I don't have to go back into that tavern to get to you. I knew you would come out sooner or later." He paused for a moment, straightening up and looking at Allabva. "We got off on the wrong foot. Why don't we go and find another place? Come with me to the Duke's Diner. It's a good place, and it doesn't have meddling busybodies like those oafs back at The Badger."

Allabva rolled her eyes and shook her head. "No."

She turned to walk away, but Jimlarnt reached out and grabbed her wrist. Allabva froze and looked down, considering her options. She sighed deeply. "You're not going to leave me alone unless I go to that diner, are you?"

"No way, beautiful. You're mine," Jimlarnt repeated.

"Well," Allabva breathed deeply again. *Am I really about to do this?* she thought. "I suppose I'll go there with you."

Jimlarnt grinned—a sickening sight. "I knew you'd come around. Here, let's do it the proper way." He stood jauntily on his feet and held his elbow out for her to take.

"No," Allabva contradicted. "Let's do this the improper way. I'm not going there with you as your consort. I'm going there with you as my baggage."

She shot her hand forward, grabbed his wrist, and pulled. He was yanked forward immediately, and he complained with a grunt.

"Wait, no," he said.

"Oh yes," Allabva replied, holding his left wrist with her left hand. With his torso now facing the ground, she grabbed his right shoulder with her right hand from behind, twisted him upright again, and slid her hand down to his elbow. She then let go of his left wrist and grabbed his left elbow with her left hand while Jimlarnt faced away from her involuntarily.

"What are you doing?" he said. "Help!"

Allabva growled. "I can't believe this." She reached forward, snaking her right arm around the front of his torso, then up with her left hand to cover his mouth. "Look, we're going there because the embarrassment in front of that crowd wasn't enough to convince you to leave me alone. I want to talk to *your* people."

Allabva felt moisture on her left palm. Were there no depths below which this scoundrel would not dig? She released him with both hands and looked around for somewhere to wipe his saliva off her hand. She grabbed his sleeve and wiped it there, then shoved him away from herself.

"Lead the way. Walking, unless you want to get tired. You run, I run. Don't worry, you can't lose me. But we're going to the Duke's Diner, right now."

"Yeah, whatever," Jimlarnt said, finally turning to leave her presence voluntarily.

But Allabva had decided the situation had gone beyond that point.

Jimlarnt broke into a sprint down the street.

Allabva looked around her for something hard, but not too hard, to throw at him. She bent hastily, took off her boot, and hurled it. It sailed through the air and struck heel-first on the back of Jimlarnt's head, and he crumpled. Knowing she hadn't thrown it hard enough to knock him out, she jogged forward to the man still lying in a heap on the ground. She reached down and turned him over onto his back, revealing a new bump on his forehead, showing that he had hit his head on the cobblestones when he fell.

"Alright, you dog," Allabva said, grabbing Jimlarnt by the arms and pulling him up. "Let's go."

When she had him in a standing position, she held his torso up with one hand while bending down and reaching behind one knee with her other arm. Then she straightened, picking him up easily. She could probably carry his weight with one hand, but his size made that awkward. So, she set out walking in the direction Jimlarnt had chosen to run in, with him lying across her shoulders.

Jimlarnt continued to struggle, though feebly now. She held him in place while walking toward a patch of lamplight cast into the street from another tavern down the way.

"Put me down, you witch," Jimlarnt said, evidently finding new strength within himself as his Shrongelin became more pronounced. Allabva complied, setting the man on his feet.

"Now just leave me alone," Jimlarnt said, turning to flee once more.

I've come this far. We're going to see this through, Allabva thought. "Not now," she said aloud. "I said I want to talk to your people. I am going to do that." She held onto his shoulder and then delivered a light blow with her other fist to his belly.

He looked at her smugly. "I knew you weren't that strong," he said.

She hit him again, harder than before. She didn't want to hurt him, but she needed him to submit.

The second blow made Jimlarnt wince, but he still tried to pull away, so Allabva hit him a third time, harder again than the second. His wince turned into a groan.

Hoping that would be enough, Allabva bent down, reached an arm behind his knee, and picked him up on her shoulders again.

"Just cooperate, please," she said, wondering momentarily if it was wrong to be polite to someone who so clearly didn't deserve it. *No,* she assured herself. *My dignity lies in how I treat others. I will use only the minimum amount of force necessary.*

Walking to the lit building ahead saw that it wasn't a tavern, but a large house. She had only come here to ask directions to the Duke's Diner, but didn't want to intrude on anyone's private space. Deciding not to disturb someone's evening at home, she walked on past.

Just beyond, she encountered a man and a woman walking the other direction toward her. They were well dressed, as though perhaps they had come from some social event.

"Excuse me," Allabva said to them. "Can you point me to the Duke's Diner?"

The couple looked at each other, the question obvious in their eyes, then back at Allabva. "The Duke's Diner? Why are you going there? That's not really the sort of place…"

"That's where he wanted to go," Allabva said, pointing her thumb at Jimlarnt on her shoulders.

"That's quite the load you have on your shoulders," the man said.

"Sure is," she confirmed. "Anyway, I don't actually know this guy, but he mentioned that place, so that's where I'm going to take him."

"Young lady…" The man with graying hair looked at his wife again, then back at Allabva. "I'm just not sure that's the kind of place you want to go to."

"Fair enough," Allabva said, "but I think I can hold my own."

"I'm just not…" the man stammered. "Why don't—well, look, we live just right over here." He pointed at the house with the lights on that Allabva had mistaken for a tavern. "Why don't you bring him over here, and we'll send for somebody to take him wherever he wants to go?"

Allabva looked down at her feet, wondering how much to tell them and how much they would believe. "Look, I know this is weird," she said, "but this man was harassing me. He wouldn't leave me alone. You can see that I sorted him out, right?"

"Well, if you—" the gentleman started.

"So, I'll tell you what. You give me directions to the Duke's Diner, and I'll be back here in two hours, so you know I made it out of there safely."

The man balked. Allabva felt Jimlarnt turn his head stupidly into the conversation.

"Look, why don't you just put me down?" Jimlarnt said.

Allabva complied roughly, letting him fall to the ground. Then she pulled out her map and handed it to the couple. "Look, just point to where the diner is. I'll take him there, talk to his acquaintances, and let them all know why it's in his best interest to leave me alone."

The gray-haired man looked at Allabva, appraising her only now—seeing how she had dropped Jimlarnt, and realizing she had not appeared weighed down by his mass while she held him.

"Well... alright," he finally said, indicating with his finger. "It's down Salmon Street, just past where it crosses with the south market and Greenwood Avenue."

"Thank you," Allabva said, taking the map and lifting Jimlarnt back onto her shoulders, before taking the map back in one hand. Walking away from the couple with her load hanging helplessly on her back, Allabva looked at the map, deciphered her current location, and made her way to the Duke's Diner.

CHAPTER 16

DUKE'S DINER

Allabva walked up to the Duke's Diner sometime later, just as she began to feel the slightest fatigue from carrying Jimlarnt on her shoulders the whole way. She had grown up in a small town and had seen large cities on rare occasion, but she could instantly tell that this tavern was not the kind of place she wanted to visit. In a neighborhood where most buildings were constructed with stone walls and wooden roofs, this one had mostly wooden walls with peeling paint and large bare spots where she could see the wood rotting even in the dim lamplight.

The windows had small panes crisscrossed with wood. Three panes were cracked, one shattered in a spiderweb pattern but still held in place, and one pane was nearly missing entirely, with a few pointy shards clinging to the edges. The sign was quite faded, and she had to come close to read it, knowing which building to look at only because she knew exactly where to expect to find the place.

No music drifted out of the broken window and onto the street, but there were rowdy voices. Looking through the windows and into the establishment, Allabva could see a crowd of men seated at various tables, engaged in animated conversations. She saw one man gesture crudely as he told another man something. The smell of alcohol hit Allabva in a wave while she was still several paces from the door.

Jimlarnt suddenly struggled again, this time more desperately than he had at the beginning, trying to break free—clearly not wanting the crowd inside the tavern to see him like this. Allabva held firm and didn't let him go, even as he started hitting her face. She reached up, grabbed his hands, and held them fast while she walked through the door sideways, pushing Jimlarnt's head in first so he couldn't block her entrance by kicking the door frame with his feet.

A few of the men inside—there were no women—looked up and laughed.

"Ho," one said, "Jimlarnt's found himself a girl. Tell us, Jimlarnt, what's she like?"

Allabva rotated her shoulders, letting go of Jimlarnt and letting his momentum carry him to the floor. She turned with a scowl to the man who had spoken. "I don't know what kind of company this man keeps, but I do know he doesn't keep company with me."

Another man laughed. "Oh, she's got some spirit. She has some spice to her, you know?"

Allabva glared at this man, too. Then she looked down and gave Jimlarnt a kick that she wouldn't have been strong enough to give him a week prior. He coughed and rolled over, trying to get away from her. She let him go.

"Say that again if you want to get what he got," Allabva said to the last man who had spoken. "I wish to mind my own business this evening, and this man harassed me. He named this place as his favorite hangout. I defy—"

A man close to Allabva reached his hand out as if to caress her cheek. She grabbed his hand without diverting her gaze, then pulled it toward herself, turned to face the man while he stumbled in close, and then shoved him with both bond-enhanced hands. The offender sailed across two tables while other patrons dodged out of the way.

"Please do not try anything else," Allabva dared the crowd.

Nobody said a word, though a couple of men still sneered.

"I was told this city was a place of order," Allabva said. "I didn't expect to be harassed and harangued by the likes of him. Or any of you."

"Do you believe this girl?" one man in the crowd said to another. "Comes in here like she's the boss."

"I'm nobody's boss," Allabva retorted, "but I will protect myself if I have to. I have no compunction against doing so, and I exhort the rest of you, as his peers, I assume, to teach him how to behave. Maybe yourselves as well."

She spent a silent moment weighing the situation and chewing her lip while she continued to stare them all down. Allabva could walk out now and find a different place to learn more about the city, and hopefully earn a few coins. But chance had brought her here when Jimlarnt had decided to harangue her back at the Coughing Badger.

Allabva looked at the men, now feeling a momentary liberating sense of latitude to do whatever she felt she needed to, now that she had experienced the Shrongelin's gift firsthand in her own defense. Perhaps she should get to know the city's underbelly just a bit. Scowling again, she sat, took a seat at the nearest empty table, and waited for the staff to approach her.

"Don't bother getting up, Jimlarnt," one of the men said, motioning to some of those around him. His lips cracked into a grin. "You and me is going to settle our score right now. Gentlemen, clear the spot."

The other men that he had gestured to moved a couple of tables out of the way, leaving the man standing next to

Jimlarnt, still crumpled on the floor, in the center of a square conveniently marked by colored stones that decorated the floor of the tavern.

"Here's mine," the man with the score said, tossing a silver hafender into the square on the floor. "Where is yours?"

Jimlarnt looked at his challenger with contempt. Jimlarnt himself was of somewhat average build, a little on the tall side and well-rounded out. His challenger came up to Allabva's nose, she would hazard a guess, and was less than stocky.

"Don't worry, Holwan. I'll sort you out," the larger of the two said, trying to shake off the weariness from Allabva having beaten him. He pulled himself from the floor, tossing a silver coin to match Holwan's into the middle of the square.

No sooner had Jimlarnt thrown his coin out than two other men each tossed a coin into the square.

"I'll split that," one of them said.

Jimlarnt looked at the two of them, picking their coins up and tossing them back. "No. His silver is all mine. I don't need nobody else getting in this."

As soon as Holwan finished saying this, he plowed into Jimlarnt, who held his ground and pushed Holwan back. The two men grappled for half a minute as the room watched, some men wearing grins and some wearing sneers. Finally, Holwan pushed Jimlarnt hard, which resulted in Jimlarnt stepping outside the square.

"How the mighty have fallen," Holwan spat in Jimlarnt's direction, picking up both silver coins. "I knew I should have challenged you more than one silver piece."

Huffing, Holwan gestured to the waiter. "Bring me a Fonglan," he said, naming the beverage of his choice.

The waiter, who Allabva realized was standing right next to her table, replied, "Be right up," but then turned to Allabva before going to the kitchen to retrieve the drink.

"Miss, what will you have?"

"Do you have any stuffed shells?" Allabva asked.

"Tomato sauce or squash?"

At least it sounded like the food might be decent. "Squash."

"And your drink?" the waiter asked.

Allabva wasn't familiar with the local drinks she would enjoy. "Do you have chamomile or hibiscus?"

"We have hibiscus, hot or cold."

"Cold, please," Allabva said, and the waiter scurried off.

Holwan sat down across from Allabva, but unlike Jimlarnt's imposing posture at the Coughing Badger, Holwan slumped back in a slouch.

"Really, lady? Hibiscus?" Holwan asked. "We just both beat the same guy, and you're not going to have a proper drink with me?" He emphasized the word "proper," and Allabva understood he meant to get drunk.

Allabva eyed the man, trying to judge whether he was worth the time to talk to him. "As long as you don't behave like your friend Jimlarnt did," Allabva replied, "You're welcome to stay and have your drink. But if you want my opinion on what a proper beverage is, I think I'll stick with my hibiscus for tonight."

"How about a proper drink another time?" Holwan pressed.

Allabva almost laughed. She didn't fault him for a little persistence, not even in this seedy tavern. His manner was altogether different from Jimlarnt's.

"If I guess correctly at what exactly you're calling a proper drink? I personally don't do that," Allabva said.

"Not ever?" Holwan asked.

Allabva shook her head. "Not ever. It's not how I was raised. I've seen it ruin lives back home."

"I can respect that," Holwan mused. "And where exactly is back home? You come from Nolnarn?"

Allabva shook her head again. "I think I'll keep that to myself, thank you. Even if I might have told you otherwise, Jimlarnt over there made sure I wouldn't be in the mood to open up socially to anyone tonight."

"Shame," Holwan said. "I'd be real curious to know how a girl like you managed to whoop Jimlarnt. He ain't the smallest guy around."

Allabva said nothing while Holwan seemed to wait expectantly for an explanation.

"Thanks, by the way," Holwan continued. "I never could have bested him if you hadn't softened him up first. I owed him one, too."

"You owed him what?"

"A whoopin'," Holwan answered simply. "That man's a cur. We've crewed on the same ship these last six months. You ever been down to the Colnarn Protectorate? Fantastic fruits down there. Anyway, Jimlarnt has no respect for nobody. He thinks he's all that; just because he can wash up nicely he feels like he belongs in nicer taverns uptown. I think you did us all a service tonight."

Holwan looked around the room, then laughed as another two men, inspired by Holwan's bout with Jimlarnt, stepped into the square, tossing silvers on the ground.

"Oh, this will be good," Holwan said. "Them's Jutan and Natjan. They don't have no complaints with each other; they just want to go at it with someone. It's great fun for them. I'll split that!" Holwan shouted, tossing a silver into the square. "I'm for Jutan."

"I got Natjan's back," said another man, tossing a coin in himself.

"You should throw one in for Jutan," Holwan said.

Allabva demurred, holding up her hand. "No thanks. I think I'll just sit here and wait for my dinner."

"Fair enough," Holwan said.

Jutan and Natjan wasted no time in lunging at each other. Soon enough they arrived at blows, punching anywhere from the waist up, both of them wearing a grin while they fought each other.

"That's barbaric," Allabva observed.

"It's great exercise," Holwan said excitedly, still panting from his thirty seconds in the square with Jimlarnt. "Gets the heart beating and keeps us strong for when we go back on ship."

"Do you have to be strong to go back on ship?" Allabva asked, thinking of her father and hoping he may only be lost somewhere, and not drowned in the sea.

"Well, there's no test," Holwan said, "but if you got weak, you're gonna suffer for the first few weeks while you get your sea legs again and gain some muscle. The sea and the wind don't forgive easily. They'll yank a halyard right out of your hands, or shove a boom into your head and knock you unconscious at the same time it pushes you into the drink. It's a lot safer going out to sea if you're stronger."

Allabva looked over Holwan again, reevaluating what she had taken to be a scrawny form. What she saw now was well-defined and taut muscle, lean and pure.

"How long have you been a sailor?" Allabva asked as the waiter left drinks on their table.

Holwan took a swig of his Fonglan. "Past five years," he spat. "Wanted to see the world."

"And have you?"

He shrugged. "I've seen a fair amount. Been near everywhere in the Inner Sea. My favorite is the Northern States in the Colnarn Protectorate. They have the best food. Well, the best fruits. If you want to talk about all food..."

Allabva sipped her hibiscus. It was cool and refreshing, but way too sweet. When they made hibiscus tea back in the Cleft, they didn't use half as much sugar as the drink now in her hand.

"And what about you? What do you do?" Holwan asked.

Allabva found herself getting into the conversation and quieting her internal alarm that had brought her to the Duke's Diner with Jimlarnt on her shoulders. She would remain cautious, however.

"My family owns an orchard. That's the business I know. If you want to grow the best apples and cherries and peaches around, I'm your girl for that," Allabva said. "My father always—" She stopped herself. She was about to say *knew*. "My father always knows exactly when to prep for winter, exactly where to trim and prune, so I learn whatever I can from him. It's a good life."

"Do you ever get restless?" Holwan asked. "Want to go see the world?"

"Oh, I don't know," Allabva sighed. "It *sounds like it would be fun. Of course, I'd be curious to see different places, but I always felt happy enough back home."

"Then why are you here in Tallensworth?"

"My reasons are my own," Allabva avoided.

"Fair enough, fair enough," Holwan repeated. "I gotta say though, I still wanna know how you managed to best Jimlarnt and carry him in like that."

Something troubled Allabva. "You don't seem... well, you seem curious, but you don't seem as surprised as other people have been. In fact," she said, looking around the room, "I've seen shock at my strength elsewhere, but nobody here seems to be so disbelieving of that on my account. Why is that?" she mused.

"Well, I'll tell you why," Holwan said.

Allabva brought her eyes sharply back to Holwan. "Yes?"

"Well, we've seen upped strength before."

"You have? Where? How?"

"It happens. People get it from eating rasselbock."

"Rasselbock?" Allabva puzzled.

"Oh, you know," Holwan explained, "we have the same thing here. Something similar at least—the jackalopes. Rasselbock are pretty much the same thing. The horns are a little different, though."

"People eat jackalope?" Allabva asked.

"Again, it's a little different. It's rasselbock," Holwan repeated. "But yeah, it tastes great. Like rabbit."

"Yes, I've known people to eat rabbit," Allabva said, "but I've never known anybody to even catch a jackalope, let alone kill one. It doesn't seem right."

"What doesn't seem right about it?"

"Oh, you know," Allabva pieced together. "It'd be like the Nomord or any other magical creature."

Holwan's eyebrows rose. "I think the Nomord are a different case," he said. "They're more intelligent. Not like rasselbock. Rasselbock are clever, but they're not going to open their mouths and speak anytime soon."

"Does it have to speak to show that it's intelligent?" Allabva challenged.

"I don't know, but it's a real practical way of drawing the line, I suppose. Anyway, thing is, rasselbock are crazy about—"

"And how do they give people strength?" Allabva asked, interrupting Holwan.

He blanched momentarily. "Well, I guess it's just in the meat, although it's as tender as a well-prepared tuna steak."

Allabva blinked. She had heard of tuna but had never tasted it. Holwan's mention of the meat being tender made her curious to try it.

"Anyway, rasselbock and jackalopes are both super strong, don't you know? They're territorial—between themselves and with deer. That's why they have the antlers, to be able to fight off the deer. And they do," Holwan said, puffing out his cheeks and blowing air out his lips. "Have you ever seen a jackalope fight a deer?"

"Can't say that I have," Allabva shrugged.

"Anyway, yeah, so people eat rasselbock, and it ups their strength, but only for a few minutes. You came in here looking hungry, so I don't suppose you ate any. Wait a second," Holwan stopped, blinking. "You couldn't have eaten any, not this far north."

"What do you mean?" Allabva asked.

"Well, that's what I was saying. To catch a rasselbock, they're crazy about cas fruit. It's this fruit that grows in the southern Glosen lands and in the northern Colnarn Protectorate. You get some cas and use that as bait, you can trap yourself a rasselbock. Only thing is, we can't seem to get the cas to stay fresh, so you can't travel anywhere with it. And rasselbock meat doesn't store, either—it goes bad within a few hours."

"Hmm," Allabva said. "Well, you're right. I didn't eat any rasselbock meat."

"I know I'm right, that's what I'm saying," Holwan agreed. "But all I'm saying is, this crowd here might not know how you got so strong, but we have seen enhanced strength before."

"I see."

Just then, the waiter came with Allabva's pasta shells stuffed with cheese and baked in a squash-based sauce. It looked overcooked, but still good. Allabva inhaled deeply, enjoying the aroma before she dug in.

"You seem like a decent person," Allabva said, logging in her memory that there were rough types with good hearts.

"Thank you," Holwan said flatly. "Is that a compliment to me individually, or an insult for the whole room?"

"Oh, no," Allabva backtracked. "I was just thinking, in contrast with Jimlarnt over there."

"Noted," Holwan replied. "Well, if you set the bar that low, then I must agree. I can't look too bad next to that. I'd still say your type probably doesn't belong in a place like this," he assessed Allabva. "I try to treat other people right, but I admit I am rough around the edges, and so are most of these guys. Make sure you take care of yourself and watch your back in this part of town."

"I'll keep that in mind," Allabva said around a mouthful of food.

"Alright." Holwan jumped up from his seat as Jutan finally pushed Natjan out of the square of floor tiles. Jutan picked up the silver hafender on the floor, which had grown in quantity to eight pieces as four more people had chipped in.

He divided the eight pieces between himself and those who had bet in his favor.

Allabva looked at Natjan. Both he and Jutan were breathing heavily after their struggle, which had lasted several minutes. But both men wore smiles pasted on their faces, in addition to the bruises they had just given each other.

How is this crowd going to help me get an audience with the overduke? Allabva thought to herself. *Am I just wasting time?*

Be bold, she heard the Nightshade say again. Feeling annoyed and challenged, as if the Shrongelin were here, watching her and expecting her to fail, Allabva stood.

"Excuse me a minute," she said to Holwan. She stepped into the square where Holwan had bested Jimlarnt, then held her hands out in an open gesture.

"Who's game?" she called to the room. "I bet I can push any one of you out."

She waited nervously for a response while pulling out her coin purse, unsure of whether she could give a favorable impression. That was the question, as there was no doubt she could win. The room was quiet. Finally, one of the crowd stood up and walked toward her.

"My name is Liblan," he said. "What's yours?"

Liblan stepped into the square and dropped a copper at Allabva's feet. Allabva looked down, wondering at the color of the money.

"Why copper? Wasn't the going rate at least one silver?"

She reached into her own coin purse, pulled out a silver, and threw it down.

"Oh, a copper versus a silver," somebody else said. "I like that." He tossed in a copper as well. "I'm for Liblan."

Liblan was medium tall, with broad shoulders and a stocky gut, though not overweight. Allabva looked at the copper from the second man, then back up to Liblan.

"Alright," she said. "I guess we... Are there any other takers?" she said.

"If that's all you need," another man said and tossed in two coppers. "I'm for Liblan."

"I'm for the girl," Holwan said, tossing a copper in.

Several other men voiced their support for Liblan, tossing coppers into the square. There were enough now that Allabva wondered if she might slip on the money during her bout with Liblan, despite knowing this wouldn't be much of a challenge for her.

"Alright," said Liblan. "Let's go."

He tried to place his hands on Allabva's shoulders, but she grabbed his wrists and pushed.

He spread his arms out, trying to reach around her back to gain control, but Allabva pushed against him to force him back.

Liblan allowed his forearms to be pushed back while he bent his arms, rotating his shoulders to bring his torso closer to Allabva. Then he ducked his head down rapidly toward her face.

Allabva's eyes widened, but she dodged the blow easily enough, receiving it on her shoulder rather than in her face.

Then Liblan heaved with his weight advantage.

Allabva felt herself pushed off balance. She had resisted his shove and hadn't changed her stance, but his size was able to push her back. Using her foot as a fulcrum, Allabva bent her legs, allowing herself to fall to a squat rather than be pushed out of the square. Then, at the same time, she let go of her opponent's arms. Still squatting, she rotated to one side to place her shoulder in Liblan's gut. Then she shoved forward and up.

This time, Liblan was placed off balance, and with enough momentum, he tottered backward out of the square.

Allabva was victorious, but the cheers she hoped for from the crowd didn't come, nor were there any boos from those who had just lost their wagers.

"Well, there you go," Holwan said, picking up the coppers. He handed most of them to Allabva, keeping a smaller portion for himself. "I figure our winnings are proportional to the wagers we put in, so here's my part," he said, stuffing the coins he still held into a coin purse.

Allabva wondered at what had just happened, said "thank you" out loud to the crowd, and then sat down to continue eating her dinner wordlessly. A couple of men moved the tables back into the space that had been used for the matches, and she heard chairs scrape against the floor while men stood up to pay their tabs and leave as she finished her food.

"What just happened?" Allabva asked Holwan. "Why did everybody only put in a copper? They gave you silver, and for Jutan and the other guy—" She couldn't remember his name.

"You're a girl," he said.

"So? Are the rules different?"

"No, but they feel bad betting against you."

"Why did they do it? Why didn't they bet for me?"

"Not sure. Take that back, I am sure," Holwan reversed. "They still thought you were going to lose. Liblan's a big enough guy, bigger than Jimlarnt. Maybe you managed to beat Jimlarnt, but you're still a girl. And they didn't think it was likely for you to beat Liblan. But hey, you still got your payout, right?"

"I guess so," Allabva said.

"So, are you coming back here again?" Holwan asked nonchalantly.

"I don't know. Maybe. At the very least, I know it's here. It's not my favorite tavern so far," she sputtered out, hoping it wouldn't offend Holwan. He didn't appear to be affronted in any way. "But I think I can see what this place offers. I don't know if my business in the city will call for me to come back here, but I wouldn't say it's impossible."

"Well, if I'm not here, tell the waiter to say hi to me. What was your name, again?" Holwan asked Allabva.

"I think after everything that's happened tonight, I'll keep that to myself, just this once."

"Fair enough," Holwan said one more time. "Well, you have a good night." He stood, turning to the waiter to pay his bill.

Allabva finished her food quickly after that, washing it down with the too-sweet hibiscus tea. She paid for the meal and headed back to the hotel, stopping by the large not-a-tavern house to tell the helpful couple that she had made it out safely.

She walked through the streets, referencing her map by moonlight a couple of times to find her way back to her inn. She entered quietly, not wanting to disturb anyone, and silently made her way to bed.

Interlude II

Chapter 17

Disillusioned

Nolder sat patiently outside the large tent that served as an assembly area in the camp of the Disaffected. He thumped his hand occasionally on the side of the stump upon which he sat, but mostly, he sat idly and wondered about the conversation going on inside. Although he could hear rumblings of voices, the tent was large enough, and those within were far enough from any edge, that he couldn't make out what was being said inside—not that he particularly cared about the details.

When he had come into the camp, he was interviewed by members of the Disillusioned—the core sect within the Disaffected in the camp. He understood that any large organization needed to keep track of its members in some fashion, and to keep records of their capabilities and responsibilities. Right now, Nillan was undergoing his interview inside, the same as Nolder had when he arrived.

As it turned out, Nillan's interview was scheduled just before an open meeting of the whole camp. Nolder was curious to learn what would be said at this meeting, aside from the fact that they would potentially induct new membership into the Disillusioned. Nolder had gone to the trouble of joining the Disaffected movement, and decided he had a vested interest in observing how it was run, and in knowing what his leadership might ask of him.

So, he sat and waited while others milled about outside the tent. Eventually, the hum of voices inside ceased, and the tent flap opened a moment later. Nillan walked out with a self-satisfied grin on his face.

"You look like you feel that went well," Nolder said to him.

"Of course it did," Nillan retorted.

"How can you be so sure? Did they tell you what they planned? Did they assure you that you would be welcomed into the Disillusioned?"

"No need," Nillan said smugly.

"Oh, no?" Nolder questioned. "You know something I don't?"

"Only that they listened to me with rapt attention," Nillan boasted. "I had those saps eating out of the palm of my hand. Just get ready for me to be elevated when this meeting begins."

"If you say so," Nolder muttered.

The tent flap had closed behind Nillan when he exited, and voices could be heard from within. But after a few moments, the flap opened and a woman stepped out. She turned to walk alongside the wall of the tent, following it to one corner. When she reached that corner, she stood and waved at somebody who was outside Nolder's view along the adjacent side of the tent.

Nillan watched the woman pass, hungrily staring after her with a smirk. Nolder groaned internally at Nillan's lack of discipline and decorum.

"Did you see how she looked at me?" Nillan asked. "She'll be mine within the week, for sure."

"Whatever you say," Nolder repeated.

At the woman's wave, a bell clanged out on the other side of the tent, inviting the camp to the open assembly.

Nolder stood, his knees and back creaking as he did so. Despite being free to walk around the camp when he liked, he spent much of his time sitting to carry out his duties. It made him somewhat miss his cross-country trip with Nillan and their other companions. The journey had afforded him plenty of opportunities to walk along the way.

Nolder followed the more eager Nillan into the tent and ignored the man as he boasted to other members of the camp. Nolder looked around curiously, wondering if Halmon, Tunbloth, or Qurast might be around, but dropped the thought and sat by himself among the crowd.

Camp members were given several minutes to file into the assembly tent, which was significantly larger than any other tent in the camp. However, it still did not fit all the members inside. Nolder was glad to have been there early to make sure he could witness everything firsthand.

Eventually, the bell outside the back of the tent sounded again, and a man stood to call the meeting to order. A moment later, another man entered, whom Nolder recognized as the one who would have rung the bell, crowding past the entrance to make his way in. He walked toward the first man, who stood in front of the gathered assembly, joining him at a table where eight other people also sat.

The first man raised both arms in the air and spoke.

"Greetings, brethren and sisters. My name is Marlson Bontaln. This is a special meeting of the Assembly of the Disaffected. For anyone new here..." He looked around the tent slowly, as if to silently ask each individual if they were new. "We have become Disaffected with the social structure of our land. We recognize, as others have not, that our leadership behaves selfishly, offering opportunities, contracts, and wealth to their friends and family. This is the foundation of the change we seek."

A murmur of assent sounded throughout the tent.

"Before we go further, we will recite the oath. All rise."

Nolder stood, as did the rest of the crowd. He mimicked the speaker and those around him in lifting his right hand in front of himself, balling his hand into a fist. Marlson spoke, and the crowd repeated after him:

"I am Disaffected. I am free, my eyes are open. I claim independence of thought, of motive. I have become Disaffected with petty superstitions that cloud minds and set the Nomord on a pedestal. I swear that I will work to open the eyes and minds of others, to liberate all people from societal constructs that hamper individual freedom. We are meant to do as we like in all situations. I am free, for I am Disaffected."

Marlson lowered his fist, and the crowd lowered theirs, taking a seat. Marlson continued addressing the group.

"We recognize, with the upcoming festivities to take place in Tallensworth, that this preferential treatment of their friends and discriminatory attitude against those outside of their circle has long been traditionally connected to the creatures called the Nomord."

A man in front of Nolder leaned forward in his chair and spat on the ground at the mention of the beasts. Nolder turned his head to see who it was. It was Nillan, of course. But while Nillan's passion was obvious and on display at all times, Nolder did not believe his own hatred and distrust for the creatures was any less.

The man at the front of the room raised his arms again to calm the grumblings that had started.

"The uninitiated may think it odd for us to share our distrust of these…" He paused, his face contorting into a grimace. "Unicorns. But there is a reason we are called the Disaffected, is there not? We have seen sorrow, we have seen frustration, we have seen injustice. And somehow, it seems almost always that this is caused by, allowed by, or implicitly endorsed by those white, four-legged snakes."

The man's voice grew louder. "I believe that in the old stories, when we hear of dragons, it was none other than these so-called 'noble' creatures, as we all know there are no scaled, winged dragons." He drew the word out. "Dragon is the more correct term for these beasts, for it conveys force, nonchalance, even malignancy toward everyone else, as they satisfy their own sanguineous appetites."

He took a deep breath. "But that is not what we are here to discuss today. The duplicitous nature of appearing benevolent, when they are indeed downright sadistic, must be reserved as a topic for another time."

He took a breath, then continued. "If you are here in this camp, you have probably heard that we have recently lost the Wise. I, Marlson Bontalan, and the other members of the council, will announce a new Wise today. Before that, we will cover our more routine items that arise as part of our regular business. Seer Juilna Branne will lead us through events and membership."

Marlson nodded to a woman to his left, who stood in turn.

"Thank you for coming here today," Juilna said, addressing the assembly. "Since our last meeting, we have had fifty-three new arrivals who have been interviewed and are hereby admitted to official membership of the Disaffected. Please bear with me and hold all welcomes or other comments until the end. Our new members are…"

Juilna lifted a sheet of parchment from the tabletop and read off names.

"As your name is read, you are invited to stand and let the rest of the membership know you. We realize that not all new members will be present in the tent. If you see them out in the camp, be sure to greet and welcome them to our new order."

As she read the names, people around the room stood to be recognized, including Nolder, Nillan, Qurast, Halmon, and Tunbloth. Some bowed outright, while others nodded their heads or lifted a hand awkwardly to wave. One woman gave a deep curtsy with a flirtatious grin that would surely draw several of the younger men to speak with her after the assembly.

At length, Juilna finished reading the names and set the parchment down.

"We are also elevating three members to the Disillusioned," she said. "One of them is a newcomer within the last week."

At this, Nillan turned his head and looked at Nolder with a sneer that said, *See, I told you I got in. Tough luck for you, old man.*

Juilna continued. "These members will please stand and be recognized. To the crowd, I give you instruction that you will address these new Disillusioned members as 'Seer' when you speak to them. As Disillusioned, per our new traditions, they have seen past the social structures and other lies in our modern society, and we feel confident that they will skillfully aid in the work to replace these archaic institutions with a social order that guarantees fairness to all.

"Without further ado, Aumelle Calda, please rise. Everyone, a round of applause for Seer Aumelle."

The room complied, after which Juilna raised her arms to call for calm.

"Thank you. Secondly, Nogtad Zoldril, please stand. Congratulations, Seer Nogtad. Seer Aumelle, Seer Nogtad, please come and join the ranks of the Disillusioned at the front of the tent."

Juilna waited to speak until after the applause for Seer Nogtad had died down.

"Before I tell you the name of our third new member of the Disillusioned, I will tell you a bit of his background.

"He traveled a long way to get here, coming from northwestern Weslan Fields. Before he left his home, he was instrumental in removing a generational baron in his hometown who ruled his small realm with an iron fist. Although our Disillusioned newcomer and one of his traveling companions achieved this transition peacefully, the council is confident that he and his companions will do whatever is needed to effect change, ensuring that it will be lasting and benefit the most people. And be the most effective in removing the—" she sneered as she said the next word, "—*unicorns* from influence.

"After achieving this feat, he and his companion traveled, gaining three more companions along the way. They managed to do so while needing to avoid attention, as it was necessary for them to liberate a horse and cart from their prior handlers under the old order."

Juilna grinned conspiratorially, and snickers could be heard throughout the crowd.

"While avoiding attention for what we estimate to be some fifteen hundred leagues, they took under their custody a young woman who displayed suspicious behavior. The council commends them for their intent to bring the young woman here for questioning. Alas, that did not happen, for it was soon revealed to them that this girl was directly in league with...a Nomord stallion."

Juilna enunciated the last few words, vocally punctuating them as she accentuated the consonants.

Shouts arose from the crowd and chaos erupted. Nolder wasn't the least bit surprised by this. His own face grew beet red with anger once more at the memories that councilwoman Juilna had invoked. He heard shouts of "Impossible!" and "They do not exist!" from around the assembly.

Juilna raised her hands, trying to bring order back to the crowd. Marlson stood to assist, pounding his fist on the table. Then, realizing he had a gavel sitting on the table next to him, he grabbed it and rapped it on the hard surface several times.

"Order!" Marlson shouted. "Order! We are not savages as they are." He scowled at the room. "Councilwoman Seer Juilna, please continue."

Marlson sat down, and Juilna opened her mouth again.

"As I was saying, they were unable to bring this young woman with them here today because of the direct interference of a Nomord stallion."

She quickly held up her hand to hush the crowd as it began to rumble again. "For those of you who say that the unicorns are all mares, I share your skepticism," she said patiently. "That is all I have ever seen, and that is all I had ever heard of—until now. There are no fewer than five witnesses here in this camp assembly right now," Juilna said forcefully. "I already read their names as new camp members. I now repeat them and ask them to stand together to testify. Nolder, Nillan, Qurast, Halmon, and Tunbloth.

Nolder and his travel companions stood.

"Gentlemen, you say you saw a male unicorn. Is this true?"

"It is," they answered together.

"How close would you say you came to this male unicorn?"

This time, their answers differed from each other. "Five spans," said one. "Three spans," said another.

Then Nillan raised his voice, "It kicked me down!" he said angrily. "One of those beasts behaved violently, directly at me, using force, proving what we all knew—that they always wanted to, anyway."

"Thank you, Nillan," Councilwoman Juilna said, nodding. "Thank you," she repeated, nodding to all five men. Four of them sat down.

"It kicked me!" Nillan repeated, attempting to garner additional attention.

"Thank you, Nillan," Juilna repeated, gesturing for him to sit.

The man ignored her.

"It stood in our way and told that stupid little girl to unhitch our horse, and then spooked it so we would have to chase after the horse! Then the girl left with the unicorn."

"Thank you, Master Nillan," Juilna said a third time.

Nillan finally sat, looking pleased with himself and holding his chin high proudly.

"As I was saying," Juilna said pointedly, turning to the crowd again, "they were not able to bring the young woman with them due to interference from one of these beasts. But they bring us valuable information, such as direct accounts of a violent encounter with a Nomord. Whatever is brewing in high society, we must be on the right trail to upset their way of life if they would send one of these previously unknown males to cement themselves in place."

Juilna went on, "After these five travelers were separated from their charge, they continued on their path, undaunted to come here. Surely all of you heard the commotion on the afternoon when they arrived. They spoke about the male Nomord, and most people did not believe all of what they said, correct? Nor did I, at first. But some did, and there was merit in investigating, either way. We assembled a posse and sent them after the girl and that...white donkey. The posse followed the girl and beast up Tallen Mountain.

"They were unable to retrieve the girl," Juilna continued, "but because of that posse, we have more witnesses of her traveling with the white mule before their progress was cut off by a rock slide at Marjon's Scree. It was after this point that we had no news of them—until yesterday, when Liceln returned. Liceln, I see that you're here. Why don't you tell the Assembly what you saw?"

Liceln stood. "It's as you said, Seer. The girl was traveling with the beast. I was one of the few who managed to make it past Marjon's Scree. The unicorn shoved me really hard, pushed me down, and they threatened to kill me if I didn't stop following them. They stole my bow and quiver, too."

"Thank you, Liceln," Juilna said, nodding as Liceln sat back down. She addressed the crowd once more. "While some of you have heard their accounts, and while some of the group ascended the mountain with the posse and others stayed behind, the efforts of all are welcomed and recognized. They bring, as I said before, valuable information, but they also bring important skills to the camp of the Disaffected. After interviewing these newcomers and granting them membership in our ranks, the council has decided to go one step further."

Juilna glanced at Nillan, who wore a smug grin as she continued. "I already told you we were inducting three new Disillusioned today..."

Nolder looked at Nillan and saw him still grinning. The man leaned forward out of his chair, ready to stand...

"Nolder Lawgrin," Juilna announced.

Nillan froze, his face turning from smugness, to confusion, to anger.

"Please stand and be recognized, Nolder."

Surprised at hearing his own name, as he was not vying for a high position within the organization, Nolder stood. He nodded at Councilwoman Juilna, then turned to his right and left, nodding to the people around him as they applauded.

"Seer Nolder, you are welcome to join the ranks of the Disillusioned," Juilna proclaimed.

It was clear that many in the crowd were as surprised as Nillan had been. The applause was notably less enthusiastic this time, at first. Perhaps Nillan's bravado had led the Assembly to anticipate his elevation, just as he had himself. But then the sound of applause gradually grew for several moments, until Juilna raised an arm for quiet.

The tumult of the crowd died down and Juilna explained, "He is very new for a member of the Disillusioned, but during our interviews, it became clear to us that he has a keen mind and valuable experience. We want to put his skills to good use."

Marlson stood. "Thank you, Councilwoman Seer Juilna," he said, and Juilna sat. "We now return to the item of our organizational structure, after which we will discuss upcoming plans."

Nolder worked his way through the crowd as Marlson spoke, coming to the front of the room. There wasn't an empty seat set aside for him, but as he approached where the Disillusioned sat, a regular member of the Disaffected stood from his seat adjacent to the Disillusioned section stood to give him room.

Marlson continued. "The Disaffected movement was, until very recently, guided by someone we called the Wise. We now believe she was killed by none other than that same male Nomord up on the mountain last week." Anger contorted his face as he spoke, his thoughts daring the entire race of the Nomord to challenge him.

"We do not yet have a canonized procedure for replacing the Wise," Marlson continued. "Also, we, as the Council of the Disillusioned, have taken a first step today in elevating three of you to our ranks without the input of a Wise. But I digress.

"Among the Disillusioned, we looked at the Wise's pattern and influence. She showed a cleverness and ability to organize I have not seen in another. She also had a certain way about her—" he leered as he said this, slowly, drawing attention to the tone, "—which I know many of us had the opportunity to appreciate more than others." He coughed. "But of course, what I appreciated the most was her leadership.

"You see, Ani'irad, originally of the Bas'naya Glosen, impressed us all with her abilities and ambition concerning this continent. While some of us dreamed of reorganizing society in our hometowns, she aimed us higher and made us believe that we could solve the problems of egregious acts all over Eslarna and Weslan Fields. Additionally, she showed us *how.*" Marlson accentuated the word, glaring at all in sight. "The Wise showed us capabilities beyond human understanding and shared the means of achieving something similar."

Now the man took a deep breath, giving a look to another Councilman which Nolder would have pegged as envious. Then he turned his face forward again.

"She had quite an impressive impact on us, especially being an outlander herself. She assured us that a similar movement is taking place in the Glosen lands, as well. After considering the type of woman she was and the type of continued leadership we realize that we need, the council has come to the decision to elevate Seer Rauali Dinfolth to act as the new Wise of the Disaffected. Wise Rauali, thank you for allowing me to lead the meeting until this point," Marlson concluded, taking a seat.

A slender woman, much younger than Nolder but at least ten or fifteen years senior to the girl allied with the unicorns, stood and moved over to the center of the table while half the council shifted down to make her room.

Wise Rauali boasted lively green eyes and rosy cheeks among her wavy black hair. Despite her comely appearance, her gaze was intrepid as she looked around the room, and Nolder could sense that this woman also had ambition. The new Wise stood in front of her chair and leaned on the table to address the assembly.

"Thank you, Councilman Seer Marlson. Let's get right to it. We will fight injustice, and given the opportunity, we will kill the Nomord."

Some minor commotion arose in the assembly.

"That's correct," she said. "Given the opportunity, we kill Nomord. Let's make that clear, shall we? Do not hold back. If you have a chance, end one of the beasts... But that is not our primary goal. Principally, we must tear down the systems that oppress us. I have heard reports of the overduke of Tallensworth raising his farm tax, among other offenses." The

Wise paused to let the crowd internalize the news. "How does he expect his people to grow food?" she asked angrily.

"But there is more. Part of the harbor at Tallensworth is reserved for the nobles. Although some of you may have heard of this and lauded the act, the overduke has given special status to his blacksmiths. While I am glad for the blacksmiths individually, this is not good for his people. It is a detriment. By raising a few, he abases everybody else. How can he impose taxes and exclude his citizens, his subjects, from free trade by wiggling his quill over a piece of parchment?

"The haughty Emperor Holb the Second of old Eslarna gave Overduke Allvron Pymseet certain powers over his realm, which have been recognized in this land since that time, now held by Afaln Pymseet. Nobody should ever have these powers to begin with. Given the option, I would tear them all down today." She waved her hands in emphatic movements to show her passion for her words.

"We are yet a small movement. We number in the mere thousands, but we are growing every day. Before they know it, we will be tens of thousands, hundreds of thousands." She waved a fist in the air. "For now," she brought her fist down, assuming a calmer demeanor, "for now, we must take a softer approach."

A murmur of the crowd rose gently but was calmed when Wise Rauali raised a hand to quiet them. "I know we all want to see results immediately. But if our movement is to endure, we must carry ourselves circumspectly in front of the world. With this view in mind, we are sending three emissaries to leaders of this continent. While their teams are still being built, I will now name the leaders of each of these emissary groups.

"First, we must grow our numbers, so we will have Emissary Company One led by Seer Falb. You will head west, traveling rapidly into Weslan Fields. Seer Falb, you and your company will strive to influence those you meet along the way, but your primary goal is to establish a sister chapter of our organization in Weslan Fields."

"Seer Livim, you will lead Emissary Company Two, going north and west. You will travel to Nolnarn and approach the Emperor of Eslarna. He is not as strong as his ancestors were, and we will become the political force to replace the Empire."

"Finally, to address the problems right here in our own backyard, Emissary Company Three will travel to Tallensworth, led by Seer Nolder."

Nolder looked up sharply at the woman he now owed deference. He had been looking at the floor of the tent, kicking tufts of grass on the ground. Now, his head spun at the news.

"Seer Nolder," the Wise instructed, "you will travel with Seer Hugne as your principal assistant. Take your Emissary Company, and in whatever way seems effective to you, undermine the overduke. His behavior is egregious to the people. Face him directly, or run a grassroots campaign as you see fit."

Nolder saw a man who must have been Seer Hugne nod in acknowledgement. The man had a zealous look in his eyes and Nolder wondered if he would be an easy travel companion...or more like Nillan.

The Wise turned to nod at the two councilors who had addressed the assembly before she had.

"Thank you, Seers Marlson and Juilna. Emissary Company leaders, we will assist you in identifying the personnel for your camps, but you will be traveling out of here in very short order. Please come see us at the head table immediately after this meeting. Everybody, have a nice day."

Seer Rauali sat, and Marlson stood. "We close this meeting with the recitation of the vow of the Disaffected," Marlson said. "Everybody on your feet. Repeat after me:

"I am Disaffected…"

Seer Falb Relwater sat in the tent that counted as his office. He, like the other two emissary company leaders, had been surprised by this assignment, receiving no warning that it was coming before it was announced in front of everybody. He welcomed the opportunity to show what he could do for the organization. He sighed. He welcomed the opportunity, but did it have to come right now?

He shuffled through the papers on his desk. He had so many things to set in order before his absence from the main camp. There were so many things to prepare, and the Wise wanted him to leave tomorrow. He shook his head. Well, tomorrow he would leave, with as large an entourage as he could get. He would need significant numbers in order to place the mark of the Disaffected sufficiently upon the western half of the continent. Surely the Wise and the other counselors would send more help later, but Seer Falb didn't want to count on that. He'd read enough of history to know that remote campaigns often receive reinforcements too little, too late.

"Saneii," he called, summoning his assistant.

The tent flap opened, and her boot appeared. But then a deep voice said, "Excuse me," and a man strode into the tent without stopping.

"Brother," Seer Falb addressed the man. "May I help you?"

"Took the words right out of my mouth," the other man replied in a nasal voice. "My name is Nillan Protfund, and I am here to help you in any way that I can. You'll see soon enough that the only thing that outstrips my passion is my competence."

The man extended a hand for shaking. Seer Falb frowned to himself but then took the man's hand anyway.

"Pleased to make your acquaintance, Brother Nillan. So you want to know how you can help us, do you?"

"Absolutely, Seer Falb," Nillan replied. Something about this man seemed overzealous. Falb wondered if he should doubt how Nillan had ranked his own attributes and supposed that his passion probably came in ahead of his competence. Far ahead.

"Well, brother, we're glad to have all the help we can get," Falb said, setting his doubts aside and taking the offered help for what it was—at face value. "I'll tell you what you can do for me. You heard my mission. If you want to come and be in my emissary company, secure me fifty horses. I want to ride out of here with as many men and women as I can get. If you find those fifty, get me fifty more."

Nillan snapped to rigid attention. "Within the hour, sir. And if not, then by the end of the day."

He turned and was gone. Seer Falb was left blinking as Saneii walked in.

"What just happened?" he mumbled to himself.

"Sir?" Saneii asked.

"Yes, Sister Saneii. I'm going over to the council tent right now to see if they have their suggestions for my roster yet. Why don't you hold things down over here, and I'll see you in an hour."

"Of course, Sir," Saneii said.

"Oh, yes." Falb paused, turning back about in the doorway of his tent. "Never mind, Sister. I'll keep working on the provisions list. I think we'll be alright, but we may have to resupply before we cross the border. Not because of the border," Saneii jumped to over-explain, "just because that's a distance marker."

"Understood," Falb said, and walked in the direction of the assembly tent.

Chapter 18

Questing

Eretuquein, first known to Allabva as Hronomon, the Forerunner for the Guardian under the Construct, dashed across the countryside, bewildered at the recent sequence of events. He reviewed mentally.

The lightning came once Sacalai was nearly free. The fact that it came recently was no surprise. Thus had each cycle of the Construct occurred. But it was coming, if the first few bolts were any indication, more frequently than it had in times past. Was their old nemesis growing stronger? Did she have some advantage to help her win this time?

He threw that thought out of his head as soon as it occurred to him. But if she was growing stronger, then there was no end to his gratitude for the luck that had come in the form of the men Tylonus, Vlon, and Pontil. Their information may give the human-Nomord team the edge they would need to lock Sacalai up again, at least one more time.

The Forerunner had not traveled so fast while he was searching for the Companion as he did now. He had needed to pay attention to the pull that he felt to find the Companion, and also avoid appearing unlike the Ta-Nomord, which humans were accustomed to seeing around the world. Whereas he had previously imitated the inattentive behavior of his female counterparts, now he turned his intent into speed, running as only a Nomord could.

But as Eretuquein passed the landscape by in a blur, he thought more about the singularity of the Companion he had found for the Shrongelin. This young woman had a couple of interesting things about her. As Hronomon, Eretuquein had traveled to a land known for its good people and failed to find a proper Companion, but in the process, he felt Allabva's presence pulling him.

The time until the Shrongelin bonded his Companion was always a vulnerable and perilous time. Now that the bonding had taken place, Sacalai's influence was muted slightly, and the champion that he had found for the Shrongelin would be a mighty foe for anybody who tried to attack her. So he ran as a blur. He had paused, coming down the mountain, to observe the Disaffected encampment. It was larger than he had expected. Sacalai's influence on the hearts of men may indeed be stronger this time around.

This may have been cause for despair—except for the peculiarity of the Companion. Not only had she called him from hundreds of leagues away, but there, up on the mountaintop, she had healed him. As the Shrongelin had explained to his new Companion, she must have wielded some of the magic that was used to bond her to him. The bonding took place under the purview of the Construct, which had been forged by both Gha-Nomord and Ta-Nomord. If Eretuquein thought about it, this almost made sense. Almost.

But the truth was, it didn't. Where had that healing power truly come from? Undoubtedly, it came from the Construct—that was true, he thought, as he saw a city approaching on the horizon, growing larger. But he'd never heard of any of this magic leaking or overflowing in that manner. Had it come from her sheer determination? Or rather, had her sheer determination caused the magic to overflow onto him while it was fresh?

She very nearly gave her life going up the mountain to meet with the Guardian of the World. Eretuquein had no doubts that her heart and her mind were a perfect fit for her duties as the Shrongelin's Companion. So, if this somehow could cause that overflow of magic that had pulled Eretuquein himself back from the jaws of death itself, then he could harbor some hope in the face of these discouraging signs from the enemy. There was extra lightning. She might escape faster this time. Her followers were greater in number. Perhaps this would continue, and she would have larger armies when they met her in battle.

Well, try this one on for size, Sacalai, the Forerunner thought, using the human expression. *The Shrongelin has bonded a Companion under the Construct who is perhaps unlike any other before her. And so, just as I told her—she who now calls me Tuki,* he thought ruefully—*just as I told her, I will do my duty until my last breath. I will act without fear, even though I may feel it in my heart.*

He slowed from his kind's superlative speed, down to match a horse's gallop as he approached the city of Palf Glen.

Only a couple of hours after observing the Disaffected encampment, Eretuquein's hoof struck cobblestone, and he officially began the next phase of his mission as the Forerunner for the Guardian under the Construct.

Once he entered the town itself, he slowed to a canter, then to a trot. As he traveled the streets of Palf Glen, Eretuquein observed the buildings he passed, noting the Historium in particular.

The Guides had informed him this town wasn't big enough to have a university, and a library would not always necessarily possess the ancient knowledge he wished to bring the people's attention to. But many small- or medium-sized cities on the continent possessed a Historium, something of a cross between a library and a museum. There Eretuquein would go in a short while. There, he would announce that the calamity drew near, and gain some support to move against Sacalai. He would gather the people in front of the Historium, call for the people to choose a side, for a great battle was coming to them all.

But first, Eretuquein made his way through the streets, drawing casual glances from people who thought he was one of the Ta-Nomord simply engaging in an uncharacteristic urban pass. He drew more intense stares from those who realized he was no Ta-Nomord, and that he was not wandering at all. They would receive his explanation soon enough.

Eretuquein came to a stop in front of a house with a bench out front and a sign announcing the physician who lived there. He paused before pawing at the door with his hoof. Eretuquein wished he could make himself appear more...palatable to human settings. Less alarming. Other Nomord could; he could remember that. But like his own name had been forgotten, masked by the magic of the Construct, the knowledge of how to alter his appearance was lost to him until a future day.

Right now, the family behind this door merited thanks from the Forerunner for the assistance they provided to the Shrongelin's Companion.

Hoping he wouldn't deface it too much, Eretuquein pawed at the door.

Head Librarian Falndeg Tiweth walked past the gate sentries into the palace compound and made his way to the royal library, pulling a key out of his pocket and toting a tall mug filled with a steamy oat drink. He climbed the steps and approached the door, inserting the key in the lock and turning it. He entered, then pulled the doors closed behind him as he saw two guards take post outside.

Today would be a good day. The sun was just appearing in the sky over the east wall of the city, Falndeg had his oat brew with just the right amount of nutmeg, and just yesterday he'd finished cataloguing all the characters in the new scrolls found last year in some caves in the East Fonglan approach, south of the Salt Waste. With the characters' cataloguing complete, now he could dive into correlating words to try to decipher some meaning from them.

The script utilized several familiar letters, but also several that were quite foreign. Falndeg might have to write to his counterparts in Iddypol, Nolnarn, and perhaps even Bolsnard, to see what they could make of it. But that would require sending them facsimile copies of at least parts of the scrolls, which in turn would necessitate setting the library's scribes to perform the copy work.

Falndeg set his oat brew on his desk, considering. The university in Bolsnard had previously housed a professor of some renown, who always seemed to possess an uncanny familiarity with antiquities. Unfortunately, the man had set sail on a merchant ship a few years ago, and had never shown up in Malnonny where he was bound.

That irked Falndeg, apart from his obvious concern for the fellow scholar. Professor Rubiro had sallied forth to study weather patterns in the north to see if any connections could be made to predict cyclones around the world. Falndeg had looked forward to collaborating on the man's data to try to draw some conclusions. Poor man had probably been a victim of one such cyclone.

Research must continue, Falndeg reminded himself. It didn't necessarily have to stay put on one realm of thought—

A loud banging came on the doors at the opposite end of the library, breaking the librarian free of his pensive mood. He began walking across the vaulted hall with rows of shelves on either side to reach the far end.

Those doors were still locked. Falndeg arrived at the library early every morning and opened it up to the public. He enjoyed doing so, priding himself on sharing knowledge with anyone who sought it earnestly. He kept this up, day after day, despite rarely having a visitor arrive anywhere near as early as he opened up. Therefore, Falndeg reasoned, this should be quite the interesting visitor.

He opened one of the double doors, propping it with a chair, as always. The library, though located on the grounds of the royal palace of Overduke Afaln Pymseet, was intended for public access. As such, it was built with doors that faced the interior of the palace compound, through which Falndeg always entered in the morning, and this second set, which faced the street. These doors had no lock that could be left unlocked, and could only be opened from the inside. At the end of the day, he only had to pull them shut to do his part to secure the palace perimeter.

As he leaned out and settled the chair in front of the door, Falndeg looked up and saw a man standing expectantly. The visitor peered at the librarian out of green eyes set into a worn, middle-aged face framed by wavy, dark brown hair that was giving way to gray, as well as the week-old beard. He wore tired brown boots, torn woolen trousers, and a heavily stained and frayed cloak. Falndeg had to look again to notice faint ornamentation at the front edge of the cloak, running from in front of the man's knees, up to the hood and around to the other side, and back down to the knees. If it weren't for the man's overall scruffy appearance, Falndeg might have thought the cloak to be a mantle that carried some significance.

The librarian blinked for half a second, taking in the sight.

"Yes, come in," he said at last to the stranger. "I am Head Librarian Falndeg Tiweth. What is your name, and how can I help you today?"

"Call me Leaf," the stranger said, entering. "I'd like to read up on ancient folklore, if you have good reference volumes."

Leaf's speech was slow and deliberate, but delicate nonetheless, as if he possessed abundant experience speaking eloquently and yet feared making mistakes.

"Of course," Falndeg replied. "We do have some, both ancient primary sources and more recent copies, and rehashings of the old stories in even newer volumes."

"Perfect," Leaf said in his careful manner. "If you will be so kind as to show me your primary sources—"

"I'm sorry," Falndeg interrupted, "I can't let you handle those directly. I can show you copies and modern rehashings, but if you must see the primary sources, you will have to wait until one of the library's scribes is available."

"I understand. How soon will that be?"

Falndeg was caught off guard by the question. He meant to communicate that the primary sources were not accessible at this time.

"Well, as I said, that requires one of the scribes to be available for the task, not simply here at work. But they have their own tasks to take care of." *Like copying sections from the East Fonglan scrolls,* the librarian added mentally. "I can't say right now when they will have the time."

"I see. Well, then if you could show me your secondaries and rehashings, I'll try to make do."

"Right this way," Falndeg invited Leaf to follow him.

He showed the man up a flight of stairs and to a section of shelving, orienting him on how it was organized. Taking a few tomes off the shelf, Falndeg gave the visitor a quick run-down on the types of stories and lessons each one offered.

"Please," he finished, "don't reshelve anything. Our system can be a bit difficult for visitors to understand, so it's just for the best if you leave it out and we reshelve it ourselves."

With Leaf settled in poring over old books, Falndeg returned to his desk. The scribes were showing up. He gave them their tasks for the day and asked one to keep a discrete eye on the scruffy stranger upstairs.

Then he settled in and began to draft letters to the librarians or professors with whom he liked to share and collaborate. Rubiro's replacement in Bolsnard had turned out to be competent, but not nearly as sharp as her predecessor. Still, she would be included.

Falndeg was considering how best to present the scrolls and his questions for each of his contacts, hoping to translate the scrolls into any well-known modern tongue, when Leaf showed up in front of his desk, holding an open book.

"Yes?" the librarian asked, once again caught off guard.

"This one," Leaf said in his slow manner, pointing to a passage, "what does it mean?"

Falndeg took the book, turning it around. "The *Three Jackalopes*? That's a well-known story. One jackalope built a castle, another built a sturdy door, and the last one held the key. It's a classic children's fable about working together."

"Hm," Leaf said, rubbing his scruffy mouth nonchalantly, "I thought for sure it had more meaning to it. Why not three rabbits, or deer? Why jackalopes?"

"Because the storyteller liked jackalopes?" Falndeg guessed, wishing the stranger would let him get back to his work.

"I dunno," Leaf mused. "I think there was something special about the castle."

The man wandered off, leaving Falndeg alone.

The librarian continued his work, but only a few minutes later, Leaf returned.

"What's this story about the wicked king? It says his people caught the stars with kite string, and the stars put the king in a dungeon."

"Yes," Falndeg said impatiently, "and the people wanted to behead the wicked king, but his neck was made of iron. To be completely honest, I don't think there's any meaning hidden in that story. It's just a fun tale to entertain children before bed."

Leaf nodded. "Indeed, but I thought it was interesting that it says the wicked king dashed the stars against a wall before he was put in the dungeon. Can't you think of any parallels in real life?"

"I'm afraid not."

"Hmm. What if the three jackalopes were stars?"

With that odd question, Leaf turned and walked away again.

Falndeg shook his head. He would try to understand the man, but he doubted there was much of anything there to understand. He got back to his letters.

About half an hour later, Leaf once more stood in front of Falndeg's desk.

"What can I do for you this time?" he drew out.

"I was just thinking. What if there were really four jackalopes, and three of them were stars, and one of the three had to find the fourth jackalope?"

"What?" Falndeg let his face twist into an expression that would properly reflect the confusion he felt.

"I bet there's a primary source that says something like that," Leaf posited. "You should look it up. I would, but you don't want me handling those. Or, what if the fourth jackalope was really a fae-bird?"

Falndeg blinked, speechless, eyebrows pushing the ceiling up.

"Anyway, I have to get going," Leaf said to Falndeg's relief. "I'll see you tomorrow."

Falndeg hoped he didn't.

The man turned and walked to the opposite end of the library, departing out the street-facing double doors.

Falndeg shook his head. *Open to all true seekers of knowledge,* he reminded himself. Leaf may be way off the beaten path, but he appeared sincere.

Part IV:
Following Up

Chapter 19

Catching Up With the Nightshade

Allabva awoke intermittently in the night. At one point she awoke, partly thinking she should get up and start her day early as she often did back on the orchard, but although she could just see the sky outside the window beginning to lighten, she was overwhelmed with a feeling of exhaustion. She reminded herself that there was no pressing need to be up before the sun. Her late evening the night previous made her keenly interested in continuing to sleep. She turned over and continued dreaming.

Allabva's eyes popped open with the sound of a bell in the distance. She took a moment to orient herself. She was in Tallensworth. She had woken earlier—but why with such a complete feeling of fatigue?—and gone back to sleep. And that bell? It reminded her of the anvil she heard pinging sometimes when she passed Master Ntoffel's house, with his shop behind. Delgan. What was Delgan doing right now?

Coming to herself, Allabva looked at the light streaming in through the window. *The bell*. It surprised her that she had missed the first bell completely. Now she was at second strike, and she had to meet the Shrongelin by the fourth, outside the northwest gate, which her map informed her was called the Tallen Gate. She hadn't been there, so she wasn't sure how long it would take her to get there. Perhaps she had been up later than she thought last night.

Springing out of bed, Allabva grabbed her clothes and threw them on. Then turned to the desk, where the mirror was, and brushed her hair as quickly as she could. Eyeing her bow and quiver, she decided again to leave them here. She was in the city, after all, and if she were attacked, it would likely be from closer up, and she wouldn't need a long-distance weapon. Allabva made sure to tuck her knife into her belt, though, before she headed downstairs with her map in hand.

When she got to the common room, she saw that there was a large tray set out, although it had just one pastry left. She nabbed it and walked out the door into the morning sun. Putting the sun on her right in order to head north, she began heading through city streets, winding her way in the appropriate direction while she pulled the map out and folded it over in order to view her route from where she was to the Tallen Gate.

Munching on the pastry, she could see the city was wide awake well before she was, with people out and about conducting the business of the day. Soon enough, she arrived at the Tallen Gate and walked out, stepping past a pair of sentries manning a table, just like she had encountered outside the Westgate yesterday. They glanced up at her and gave her a "Good morning, miss," before apparently deciding she wasn't of any import to them. She was carrying no bags and must not have appeared to be doing anything suspicious in their eyes.

Wondering exactly where she would meet the Nightshade, Allabva continued on the road out of the city as far as she could go while keeping the gate in view. When she reached the farthest point, she stopped, looking around and thinking about her exploits from the night before. Just as her thoughts returned to her stomach, as that pastry had not been enough food to carry her through the morning, her Nomord escort appeared, stepping out of a thicket of bushes to one side of the road.

"Good morning," she greeted him. He ignored the niceties.

"What happened last night? What did you learn?"

Allabva shifted mental gears, adjusting once again to the magical creature's rudeness. *I might as well just make a list of it*, Allabva thought to herself. "I got a map of the city. I got a room at an inn to stay at. I visited one tavern called the Blank Slate. That didn't yield much of anything. I went to another, called the Coughing Badger, where I made a couple of friends. Also, I went to a market, but nothing important happened there. That happened before going to the Coughing Badger. And I went to another one called the Duke's Diner, where—" she paused, "I made an acquaintance and bested two men in front of everybody."

"An arm wrestle?" Nightshade prodded.

"No, actually. Although I arm wrestled somebody at the Coughing Badger. Oh, he was annoying. He wouldn't leave me alone, so I picked him up and carried him to the Duke's Diner. That's where everyone saw that I had bested him. The other one was more because they were all participating in a challenge, and I thought it might help to get noticed if I did the same."

"Did it?"

"I don't think so," Allabva said. "Nightshade, have you heard of the rasselbock?"

"Of course," he said.

"Have you heard of people eating them and getting en-hanced strength?"

Nightshade was silent for a moment. "Yes. But although I must admit I don't like the idea—I think I feel more kinship for other magical creatures than I do for horses—I don't see anything morally wrong with it, if you assume that hunting is part of the natural order of this world. Those people are out for a meal, thus the world goes. They get their meal, and as it happens, the rasselbock's magic is partially transferred to them. But it's very temporary. It is different from my bond with you, where I share my gift with you, and the gift is magnified between us. But it's not as though people eating rasselbock are stealing the magic from them. At least, not like—" he trailed off.

"Like what?" Allabva prompted.

"My Forerunner said you faced a Binterox."

Allabva nodded.

"That is a perversion, where one of us dies solely for the purpose of stealing our magic. That transfer is also permanent and lasts the lifetime of the thief who stole it. It is a senseless killing where no natural benefit comes from it." Nightshade softened. "Those eaters of the rasselbock are nurturing their bodies, and whether or not they do it for the purpose of the temporary transfer of magical strength, they engage in natural feeding. And I do not believe that the souls of the slain rasselbock are aggrieved as they would be if their magic were stolen by a Binterox."

Allabva chewed on this.

"Why do you bring them up now?" the Shrongelin asked. "Is that something they do here?"

"No," Allabva replied. "A sailor told me they do it in the southern Glosen lands and in the Northern Colnarn Protectorate States. He says there's no way to trap the rasselbock around here."

Nightshade thought long and hard before replying. "Very well. As much as I dislike the thought, it may be something to consider if there were some way to bring this effect to the battle lines at Amonfweer. But never mind that now, Companion. It doesn't sound like you accomplished a very large amount last night."

"Hold on," Allabva pushed back. "I would agree with that, but what exactly do you expect to happen? I thought it was a productive night. I learned some things about the city. I met some people who will help me network as I go back and meet their acquaintances, and I—"

"Fine," Nightshade interrupted. "Push harder today. Do more."

Allabva nodded. "Of course I will, but I was wondering... you only talked about going to taverns and arm wrestling to get attention."

"Yes, so?"

"What am I supposed to do during the day, when there won't be people in the taverns to talk to?"

Nightshade raised an eyebrow. Allabva didn't know that equine physiology could do that and now wondered whether it was a unique Nomord trait or if horses and donkeys could do it, too.

"Whatever you want," the Nightshade said. "You're the companion to the Guardian, bonded under the construct. You were carefully selected by the Forerunner. I know you won't do anything untoward, so go and do what makes sense to you. Keep our mission in mind, and if you can further it during the day, do so. But you'll be the judge of that."

Nightshade turned, facing the clump of bushes again. "Meet me here again tomorrow. We'll discuss as the situation progresses and plan your actions to get that audience."

"No," she had asked.

"I submitted the request," Allabva said. "When I entered the city yesterday, I had to convince the guard physically to submit it. Oh," she realized. "I need to go tell the district office what inn I'm at so they know where to find me when it is time, when they want to see me."

"And what inn is that?" Nightshade asked.

"It's the Medicine's Roost."

"Very well," the Nomord said, nodding his horned head and turning away.

"Wait," Allabva stopped him. Something he had said nagged at her mind. "Does a Binterox always slay a Nomord?"

The Shrongelin cocked his head, curious to Allabva's reason for asking. His answer came tentatively, "Yes."

"But there are other magical creatures besides the Nomord. Can a Binterox take their powers also?"

His mood shifted, putting on a pall of darkness and showing Allabva exactly why legends knew him as the Nightshade Unicorn. He tossed his mane menacingly at the topic as he reared up on his hind legs, seeming to pull the joy out of the sunshine around him. He brought his forehooves back to the ground and barked out the first part of his reply.

"Yes, it is possible." He took a step back, shaking his head downward as he tried to calm himself. It didn't appear to make much difference. "Sacalai's followers had all sorts of powers before the Construct was imposed upon them. But *we*, the Nomord, were the preferred race they chose to murder. *We*, who only desire benevolence upon all. *We* lost the most members before we managed to stop her!" His mouth stayed open after he finished talking, his breath coming heavily.

Allabva also took a step back, holding a protective hand up for her own perceived safety. She needed to know more.

"Why? Why did they want Nomord powers?"

The Shrongelin grunted. "I don't think they all did. There were those who preferred to fly, to cast fire, to dive below the ocean without the need to breathe. I think they spent little time perverting our set of abilities."

It didn't make sense. "But—"

"Because we are the unifiers of nature. We, as a race, can heal, can influence, can facilitate growth. We can bring things together. Our magic is a catalyst, an enabling force, for the betterment of all." His voice rose in fury. "That terrible being we call Sacalai *taught her followers* to steal what is ours and abuse it into serving their own pleasures. All they wanted was power, and they obtained it by murder!"

Allabva could taste the righteous indignation coming from the beast before her. She wanted to leave, but she still had questions.

"They took Nomord magic, and power from other creatures?"

The Nightshade reared slightly a couple of more times, bringing his hooves only several inches from the ground, calming himself before speaking again.

"Yes," he said at last, "those evil followers of Sacalai who were able, stole power from Nomord and from others. Those who could not kill a Nomord stole power only from other creatures. They were known as Lemneroces. A Lemnerox has much weaker power than a Binterox; our magic augments all the abilities of a Lemnerox; thus the distinction between that and a Binterox."

"What sort of creatures does a Lemnerox steal from?" Allabva asked.

The Shrongelin looked at her sadly.

"All kinds. Indeed, a Lemnerox can derive and extract his power from a natural, non-magical creature, if that creature is distinctive enough and carries a sufficiently notable characteristic. There was one man who could turn his skin hard, after performing a dark ritual while he killed hundreds of crabs and lobsters over a course of days. Obviously, magical creatures yield magical abilities to a Lemnerox with a single killing. But let us not dive into this anymore today. There will be more time when we sail."

Then he turned and disappeared into the foliage.

CHAPTER 20

LEAPING FROM OBSCURITY

A llabva walked back toward the city, and reentered without the sentries doing anything more than to look up at her. She wasn't sure if they recognized her from having exited half an hour before, but they acted as though they did, so she went with it.

Allabva made her way through the streets, pausing to ask a soldier if he could point out the location of the Western District office. Once she made it there, she was able to talk to the clerk, and he found her request paperwork quickly enough, scrawling in the name of her inn and bidding her a good day.

Allabva wandered the streets once more, this time loose in the city for the first time in the morning hours. Hungry, she checked her map and found the nearest market square, where she found a stall selling freshly cooked eggs and sausage wrapped in an envelope of bread. She bought one of those and a small bunch of grapes, and then strolled slowly around the market, looking at the wares, hoping to find clothing to replace her easily identified threads from the Cleft out West.

It wasn't that this marketplace didn't have anything good; there were a few decent offerings. But Allabva remembered the mother and daughter team from last night's market and decided to head there.

As Allabva made her way toward the market she had visited last night, she thought about her conversation with the Nightshade. Something troubled her about that, and how she had woken up in the pre-dawn light feeling so exhausted. With her gift from the bond, she should have handled the activities from yesterday without reaching that point.

Indeed, the previous two nights staying at the Dusty Pot and Greenstock, she hadn't felt that kind of fatigue, even though she had been running all day. Yesterday, she had only run about half the day before getting into town and walking all afternoon and evening. It didn't make sense that she should feel so drained, with no exertion to explain it.

And then, when she spoke to the Nightshade outside the city walls, he had appeared so dry and mechanical. He had still seemed ornery, though not as much as usual.

A wave of sadness and pain hit Allabva, and she thought of her home. Was mother worried for her? Was Delgan sad? And little brother Mellier, were his games so innocent and endearing in her absence? Allabva didn't know where this sudden reflection came from, but it troubled her greatly, causing her to stagger for a moment, gasping at the sudden shock of it. She gulped for breath and stumbled back to her feet. She hadn't even realized she had dropped to her knees.

"You alright, young miss?" A passing woman paused to ask her, offering a hand.

Allabva squinted at her through the memory of the mysterious event that had just happened. "I'm fine, thank you, ma'am." Allabva shook her head, glanced at her map, and, blinking, continued on her way. Was that her sharing the

Nightshade's burden again? Was this something Allabva would have to expect as she went forward?

"There's got to be some way to handle this," she thought, as she walked through the streets.

A few minutes after the incident, Allabva was feeling fine again and looking forward to speaking with Jilona and her mother at the market. She remembered the look of the dress she had spied across the way and hoped it would still be there so she could get a closer look today.

Allabva felt the ground shake underneath her as she heard a loud rumble from all around. She obviously wasn't the only one to feel it, as her shout was accompanied by several others around the square. Dust clouds sprouted from the stone walls of the permanent structures at the perimeter of the square. Looking up, she saw a small boy, half Mellier's age, who had been perched atop a wall at the edge of the square, stumble and pitch, throwing his arms in a pinwheel.

"Saeblin, get down!" A woman screamed at the boy just as he lost balance completely and fell.

Instinctively, Allabva dashed forward, knowing she was using strength and speed no normal human could, but not caring who saw her do it. A dozen paces off, she jumped into the air toward the child. As time slowed down around her, she felt herself rise, continuing forward, and she came to land on a balcony jutting out from the wall at the edge of the square, perched twice her height above the ground. Then she looked up at the falling boy and opened her arms. Reaching out over the edge of the balcony, she caught him by the leg.

The boy's mother stood on another balcony, a few spans to one side along the wall. "How did you do that? Oh, thank you! Please, just stay there. I'm coming," the woman said quickly, talking to Allabva and holding her hands out to emphasize her words. "Just stay right there. I'll be right over."

Allabva nodded curtly. As the woman disappeared into the wall, Allabva carefully lifted the boy's leg, bringing him up over the edge of the balcony, and turning him right-side up. Then she set him down on the floor of the balcony next to her. The child looked up at her and began to cry.

Allabva sighed. She knew she presented no reason for the boy to cry, but he didn't know that. "There, there," she said, calmingly, soothingly, backing up to give him space. "It's OK. Your mother's coming right now."

"Who's there? What was that?" A man appeared from within the house behind the wall, moving a curtain aside to step outside.

Allabva mumbled, "My name is Allabva," at a loss to explain how she and the child got to be there.

"Saeblin!" the man shouted at the boy, with surprise, not anger. "What are you doing here? How did you get here?"

Saeblin looked up at the man with tears in his eyes and wailed, "I fell."

"Fell? What, fell from your balcony?" The man cast his gaze back and forth between Saeblin and Allabva in utter confusion. "How did the two of you get here?"

"She jumped," the boy's mother shouted as she barged into the man's house from the other side, crossing through the interior to approach the balcony.

"Madam Lerran, what is going on? What was that shaking?"

"Earthquake," Madam Lerran answered. "Oh, Saeblin, come here. I've got you, my boy." The mother picked up her son, turning to Allabva. "That was incredible. How did you even—never mind. Thank you." She lunged forward, embracing Allabva in a hug.

"I have to know what is going on here," the man repeated.

"There was an earthquake, sir," Allabva replied meekly. "Saeblin here was walking on the edge of the wall outside. I don't know if it was the shaking itself, or if he got scared, but he tripped or lost his balance and fell."

"And she jumped and caught him," Madam Lerran finished.

"Jumped from where?" The man demanded again, sternly.

Allabva kept her mouth shut.

"From the ground," Madam Lerran answered finally, then pointed at Allabva. "She jumped up from the ground in the market square, clear onto your balcony, and caught Saeblin by the leg. Oh, Sae, I'm so glad you're alright. That could have killed you." Her voice turned to more firm tones. "I've told you before, you can't go climbing up there. Don't do that again, you understand me?" She held him out somewhat so she could speak to his face, then brought him back in for a hug.

The boy didn't answer but lay his head on his mother's shoulder, sniffling.

The man, whose name Allabva still didn't know, looked at Allabva distrustfully. "Jumped from the ground," he said. "What are you, some kind of demon?"

"She's no demon," the boy's mother insisted through her relief. "She saved my baby. She didn't even think about it, she just ran and rescued him."

"Well," the man sputtered, obviously not sure what to make of this situation. "I'm glad he's safe. Now, get out of my house, please.

"Oh, we're going, Master Casslen," Madam Lerran sighed, rolling her eyes.

"That's right, you are," Master Casslen agreed. "Leave me in peace. And how am I supposed to think you didn't need time to react to the earthquake? If you have the power to jump up onto my balcony from the ground, maybe you have the power to cause that."

Allabva's eyebrows rose. "No, sir."

"Are you sure? You—"

"I didn't ask a question," Master Casslen interrupted. "Please, just leave. I was just trying to enjoy my morning chamomile."

"Madam Lerran, I'm glad your son is safe. Now everybody, leave my house." He pointed into the house, ironically, as he said this, and Allabva understood that he expected her to use the regular exit.

Relieved not to repeat any superhuman feats in front of the man, Allabva gladly walked through his dwelling and out the other side, finding herself still a story above ground level on a catwalk.

Madam Lerran turned to Allabva. "I don't know how I can thank you. Do you want—"

Allabva held up a hand. "No, that's quite alright. Just—I have a younger brother not that much older than him." Allabva paused. Mellier was definitely larger and older, but in terms of Allabva's life, it was in reality only a few years' difference. She also noticed that the boy's mother was similar in age to Allabva herself—older for sure, but only by a few years.

"I don't need anything," Allabva finally said. "I'm just glad I could help. Saeblin, I'd listen to your mother and not climb up on top of the house again."

Allabva paused before leaving. "What's the fastest way back into the square from here?"

Madam Lerran told Allabva how to go around the row of houses, which were separated by interior walls, and enter the square from the nearest corner. Allabva thanked her and went on her way.

While she went, she wondered about people like Master Casslen, who appeared inherently distrustful, unwilling to believe that she was truly just trying to help. That made her wonder if Master Casslen had some sad experience which would explain his attitude, if Allabva just knew it. Taking this thought, she wondered what kind of experiences or inborn personality would lead somebody to join the Disaffected. Would Master Casslen join the Disaffected? Had he already? Or was he just overly cautious and protective of his home?

Entering the market square again, Allabva stopped herself. She was hungry, and as she had woken up late, it was the middle of the day. She could shop after finding some lunch. She preferred to go to a tavern and sit down rather than eat on the go. She had done plenty of that—plenty of being on the go, not plenty of eating—since leaving the Cleft, and now that it was in her power to do otherwise, she would.

Turning around to leave the square again, Allabva walked a couple of blocks before encountering a tavern with a sign out front that declared it to be *The Beet Table*, showing a pair of hands holding a knife and slicing a deep red vegetable.

"This is probably as good a place as any around here," Allabva mumbled to herself, and then walked in.

Chapter 21

Don't Hide

Allabva was greeted as soon as she walked in. "Right over here, miss," she was invited to a table, where a hostess pulled the chair out for her. "Have a seat and get comfortable. What can I get for you?"

Allabva thought of the tavern's sign out front. "What do you have with beets?" she offered.

"Oh, we've got a nice soup. I'll bring it to you with a side of toast from our daily beet loaf."

Allabva had never heard of a beet loaf, but she supposed bread could be flavored with any sort of thing. "That sounds good," she said to the waitress, "and some chamomile, if you have it."

"Coming right up, miss," the waitress said.

Allabva sat in silence by herself, watching people pass by through the windows and considering the other patrons as they ate their food. The waitress came back with Allabva's soup, toast, and a mug of chamomile.

"There you go, miss. Is there anything else I can do for you?"

"Well, as a matter of fact," Allabva said, "I'm sure you can see I'm not from here."

"Yes, I had noticed," the waitress laughed, "but as long as you like the food, then I don't have any issue with you."

Allabva paused. The waitress's tone sounded like she wasn't entirely insincere with her requirement that Allabva genuinely enjoy her lunch. "Yes, well," Allabva said, "I've come to town for a reason, and I'm trying to help my cause."

"Oh, what cause is that?"

"I'd rather not really get into it right this moment," Allabva avoided, "but my point is that I need to talk to the right people. Do you know of any resources, anywhere I can go, to try to get hold of somebody's ear who might be able to help in a big way?"

The woman's eyes narrowed slightly. "I don't know how helpful I can be without knowing what your cause is or what kind of help it needs. Besides, do you think I'd still be waiting tables if I knew how to get those connections myself? Enjoy your lunch," the woman said and left in a huff.

Allabva tried to shrug it off as she ate her soup and toast. It was good; she didn't have to feign her enjoyment of it. As she dunked the toast in her bowl of soup and sipped her chamomile, the waitress checked in on her partway through the meal, but didn't seem genuine in her concern to see if Allabva needed anything.

Saddened to be cut off from what should have been a positive exchange, Allabva told herself that perhaps this was Sacalai's growing influence in the world. She supposed some people might succumb in a big way, joining the Disaffected and even trying to kill Nomord and Allabva herself, while others might go under in little ways like this. She knew that everybody had moods, and it seemed to Allabva that in the large scheme of things, the trick was to bear one's burden gracefully when the difficult moments came, and latch on to the good moments when those arrived—trying to extend them and use them as the paint with which to cover the canvas of life.

Allabva hadn't heard of tipping being part of the culture here in Tallensworth. In each interaction she had had, those asking her for payment—whether for food, raiment, or services—had asked her for the specified amount directly. Nor had she observed anybody else leaving a tip. But when she left The Beet Table, she left extra coin on the table as a token of her goodwill, since the waitress hadn't addressed her directly for the bill.

Trying to hold on to positive thoughts only, despite the inexplicable wave of sadness that had hit her on the street, the earthquake, Master Casslen's attitude, and now this waitress's response, Allabva made her way back to the square. She thought of her mother, Delgan, and of Brelin and Mellier. Brelin would have said something snarky about the waitress. It would have been Allabva who said something calming and reassured her friend, but even though it would have been snarky, Allabva knew it would be funny, too. And that Brelin wouldn't intend it as truly malignant.

Thinking of Delgan again, Allabva pulled his grandmother's flute out from her blouse, where it hung on her neck, and tried to play a few bars of In the Cool Shade of the Mount while she walked. She missed being able to play the music openly. That was something nice about the open road—when nobody else was around, she could let the flute play itself and drink in the comfort without having to expend the effort to produce the music manually.

Allabva sighed as she walked into the market once more, then found her way to the booth where she had met the girl and her mother the previous evening.

Allabva wanted to stop sticking out like a sore thumb. Unfortunately, it did not appear this was going to be an option.

"Miss!" A voice hollered from a booth.

"Miss!" Another voice called nearby.

Cries went up throughout the lane she was walking down. These people had seen her jump, and obviously wanted any excuse to associate themselves with somebody who could do that.

"Would the miss like to buy a hat? Would the miss like to buy these leather gloves? More comfortable than any others you'll try! Discounted, half-price!"

Allabva turned around, intending to go back the way she came to the end of the square where she had entered and take another aisle down to the end. Apparently, that made no difference.

"Miss, try one of our new cloaks! Wouldn't the miss like a lovely scarf?"

Allabva ignored them, walking briskly to the other end and then finding the booth she had planned to go to.

"Jilona," Allabva addressed the daughter.

The girl turned.

"Allabva, is it true?"

Allabva's heart sank. Apparently, the word had been passed along with a description of Allabva.

"You jumped up onto one of the balconies and rescued the child?"

"Yes," Allabva said. "It's true."

"Wow. You must have drunk from Lee's Well yesterday or this morning, right?"

The question struck Allabva oddly.

"Lee's Well? I know nothing about it. Where is it?"

"Oh, Jilona," her mother rebuffed. She turned to Allabva. "It's a well near the center of town. It gives good, fresh water, but that's it."

"Oh no, there's more to it," Jilona countered. "I know because one time I drank from Lee's Well, and everyone else was getting sick, but I didn't. So every time people start catching cold, I make sure to keep some water from Lee's Well with me at all times."

"And yet, you still get sick," Jilona's mother said. "It was only that one time that you were spared, and everyone else fell ill."

"No, mother, don't you remember? Last fall, I didn't get sick then, either. You got sick two weeks later."

"Whatever that was, it was different. It was the next bout. I was just the first one to catch it."

"If you say so," her mother said, then smiled at Allabva conspiratorially.

"Well," Allabva said, "I don't even know where Lee's Well is, but no, it wasn't because of that. Even if I had some chamomile with water from there, I could have done it two days ago before I ever set foot in the city."

Jilona seemed disappointed, her theory apparently debunked.

Looking around, Allabva saw the occasional eye on her from people at other booths. At least these two seemed to regard her the same as they had yesterday.

"So, what exactly brings you back here?" the older woman said, getting to the point of commerce.

"Well, I was looking for some local clothes," Allabva said. "I want to match everyone else better."

The lady bit her lip. "Why?" she asked straightforwardly.

The question caught Allabva off guard. She hadn't thought there would be any question as to why she would want to dress like everyone else.

"Because I don't want people assuming things about me, or about why I'm here, before I get a chance to tell them myself. I don't want them drawing conclusions based on where I come from, or what they think they know about me."

The woman inhaled, then exhaled. "Miss, I think it's a bit late for that. Everyone in the square knows you jumped twelve feet in the air to save a child."

"No, fifteen," Jilona interjected.

Her mother ignored her. "A description of you and your clothing is going to be known citywide soon enough."

"So you understand why I might want to change that description of my appearance," Allabva said.

The shopkeeper shook her head. "Everybody knows you can jump, and everybody knows you did so to save a child. I don't see how that's a bad thing. True, they don't know your personality—except for that one thing. They know you want to help people, at least when there's danger. And they know you're powerful enough to do it. You want my advice? Own it. Keep your look. Maybe even make it more distinctive." She looked down at Allabva's boots. "Though those look pretty worn. You might want to replace them."

Allabva considered. "Thank you. I think I'll keep my same boots for now." She decided to hold off on buying a new outfit, even if she could afford it. She hadn't gathered much coin last night, after all.

"Do you have any socks, though?" she said finally. "I could use a new pair of socks."

"Right over here," the woman said, gesturing toward a rack with several piles of socks stacked on it.

Allabva quickly scanned the rack to locate the style she wanted: knee-length to protect her feet from the wear of her boots, entirely woolen so the socks wouldn't wear out quickly. She paused momentarily between a pair of brown and tan stockings and another of tan and green. This was an opportunity to at least make something of her wardrobe more local. Giving in to inevitability, Allabva grabbed the tan and green socks and turned to pay for them.

"What *does* bring you to town?" the shopkeeper asked Allabva, instead of telling her the price of the socks.

Allabva was taken aback but, once again, gave in to inevitability. She didn't have to tell the woman everything, but she didn't want to be standoffish.

"You wouldn't believe me if I told you," she replied.

"I wouldn't have believed you if you'd said you could jump to a second-story balcony from the ground, miss, but I saw you do that. I think I'm ready to believe whatever you tell me."

"Alright," Allabva said. "Are you friends of the Nomord?"

The woman scrunched her face into a quizzical look, glancing at her daughter, then back to Allabva. "We're friendly toward them," she said, "but it's not like we consort with them on a daily basis, or at all," laughed uncomfortably, "especially not here in the city. They stay out in the countryside. Anyway, why do you ask?"

Allabva took a deep sigh. "There's trouble coming."

"What kind of trouble?" the woman asked warily, glancing around the square. "Did the Nomord cause this morning's earthquake?"

Allabva blinked. She hadn't considered that question.

"I don't think so, but I can't say that for sure. I'm not talking about earthquakes, though," she said, shaking her head slowly.

"What are you talking about?" Jilona asked, stepping closer.

"One of the Nomord talked to me," Allabva said. "He told me there is somebody evil trapped in a magical prison the Nomord forged. Somebody powerful, and she's breaking out of that prison soon."

"Powerful like some kind of queen?" the mother prodded.

Allabva blinked again. Did Sacalai have political power?

"I don't know if she's some kind of queen," Allabva admitted, "but I do know she has magic at her disposal, and that she's strong enough that the Nomord are worried."

"That doesn't tell me what brings you here to this city," the woman said.

"True," Allabva breathed. "Nor have I told you where my strength came from that I could jump onto that balcony."

"I'm ready for you to change that," the woman offered, tongue in cheek.

Allabva laughed. "I'm traveling with one of the Nomord. He gave me the strength you saw this morning."

The woman's eye had cocked the first time at *Nomord*, but Allabva had said *he*. When she cocked her eyebrow again this time, Allabva nodded.

"Yes, *he*. Not all the Nomord are female. The males have stayed apart, on an island, maintaining the prison for Sacalai. That's the evil being who's supposed to escape soon. Anyway, we're traveling to... well, to talk to people and to rally forces against Sacalai when she does break out."

"They can't stop her from breaking out?" Jilona asked.

"They tell me they can't."

"*They*?" Jilona's mother prodded. It was clear the woman didn't miss much.

"I have traveled with two of the Nomord now," Allabva confirmed.

No need to confuse the mother and daughter with unnecessary information about Hronomon and the Shrongelin.

"So you're in town to talk to people," the woman summarized.

"Yes," Allabva supplied.

"People in power?" the woman guessed.

Allabva nodded.

"You're not going to get anywhere hanging around here," the woman said. "You mean to go knock on the overduke's front door?"

Allabva's mouth hung open, aghast at the thought. "There's no way I could."

"No, there isn't," the woman agreed. "Not literally. But you need to find your way there. Maybe not to the overduke himself, but at least to some magistrate or baron?"

Allabva frowned, concentrating. "I don't think a common magistrate would be enough," she said. "I traveled some way to get here, so I think the higher authority I can contact, the better."

"Sounds like you've got some sense to you, even if you jump up onto the balconies of strangers," the woman said.

Allabva remembered the socks in her hand. "How much do I owe you?"

"Not a thing. You saved a life today. The least reward you can get for it is a pair of measly socks, don't you think?"

Allabva's smile spread wide across her face. "You don't owe me a thing. Nobody does."

"No, but I want to, so the socks are yours."

Allabva's smile grew wider, even though she didn't know it could. "Thank you, that's very generous of you. Well, I suppose I should be going. I need to find the right people to talk to, who might be able to make some difference or, well, somewhere I can actually earn..." She paused, smiling. "A pair of socks."

"Are you looking for work?" the shopkeeper asked.

Allabva laughed nervously.

"I don't even know what I'm looking for," she said. "I journeyed to this town with the Night—" She caught herself mid-word. "... With a male Nomord, trying to talk to who knows who about who knows what. To make people do things to prepare who-knows-what, and who-knows-why."

Her smile flattened into a thin line across her face.

"But I will need some more coins soon."

The shopkeeper's eyebrows went up in concern as she fumbled with her money purse.

"How much do you need? Do you have enough to eat?"

"Oh, no!" exclaimed Allabva. "No, no, no. No, thank you. I don't need charity, believe me. You saw me jump, right? I know ways of earning some coin that I can resort to if I need to."

"Strong work," the woman replied. "That makes sense. Why don't you go down to the docks? They're always looking for strong backs to load and unload ships."

Allabva bit her lip. She hadn't considered that. She knew that getting boastful men to arm wrestle her had the potential to bring her coin quickly, but it hadn't even occurred to her to look for work that somebody actually wanted accomplished for hire.

"I might, at that," she said.

She remembered the socks in her hand once more.

"Madam, you just gifted me these socks?"

The woman nodded confirmation while monitoring a passerby looking at a row of hats at the front of the stall.

"Again, you didn't have to, but I note that I see different reactions. I saved that woman's son, and she said thank you, yet offered me nothing. I don't fault her for it—that's just an observation. But the man whose balcony I jumped up to did worse. His reaction was not only not generous; nor was it neutral. It was hostile and distrustful. Why do you suppose his reaction was so different?"

"Huh," the woman blurted. "If I could tell you that, I'd probably be more than a magistrate myself. All I can say is that people are different. They think in different ways. They act in different ways. And everybody thinks their way of behaving is natural and correct."

Just then, fifth bell struck.

"Miss, what did you say your name was?"

"Allabva," Allabva replied. "Companion's the name I've been giving people. Miss Allabva Companion."

"I wish there were more like you around. But if you'll excuse me, the district lord and lady will be coming through here in a few minutes. She often purchases a good amount, and unless you need to ask me something important, I'd like to have everything arrayed just so for when they pass."

"Very well," Allabva said. "I shall leave you."

She turned to go, and as she did, she realized this could afford her the opportunity to meet somebody who could potentially get her the audience she sought with the overduke. After pausing for just a moment, she continued strolling.

Chapter 22

Close Encounter

Allabva left the stall behind and wandered down the row and partway around the corner, almost out of sight. There, she discovered a sudden interest in rocks as she found herself in front of a trinket seller's stall offering buffed and sanded specimens of various colors and shades. Picking one up and then another, she examined them as slowly as she could while appearing to appreciate them in earnest. She kept one eye on the clothing stall of Jilona and her mother.

And she did appreciate the stones. There were beautiful hues of aqua, lavender, and auburn. Some had an internal structure that allowed some light to pass before being diffracted and reflected back out, whereas others were transparent all the way through or simply opaque, showing waves of different colors.

As Allabva watched, Jilona and her mother fastidiously arranged and rearranged their goods into perfect order, so as to draw the eye as much as possible.

After several long moments, there appeared to be some disturbance at the corner of the Market Square, nearest to where the booth of textiles she had visited was located.

Allabva continued to watch out of the corner of her eye as she examined stones and jewelry with stones set in them. Here was the necklace with the cat-eye brooch, and there was a bracelet lined with garnets. She noticed when there was a bustle over at Kilian's corner of the square.

A couple of soldiers appeared, flanking a short woman wearing an elaborate blue gown with gold trim on the sleeves. Allabva had half-expected to see the lady wearing a brown shawl identical to the one that she herself had worn by mistake the day prior, but she wasn't.

Behind the woman followed five adolescent girls, younger than Allabva.

"There she goes again, that old snoot," Allabva heard somebody say in the jewelry booth a few feet away. "Coming through here with her little protégés, as if she weren't ruining lives."

Allabva's ears perked up as she watched Jilona and her mother curtsy to the woman and her entourage in succession, gesturing to the items they suspected might tempt them into buying. The woman paused, and as she turned toward the display, the soldiers took note and assumed post, flanking the display and the booth, facing outward.

"Well, it's not only her," a voice replied to the first, this one deeper, but still a woman's. "She and her ilk aren't the ones who decree the law. You know that. It's the overduke. If she and hers want to enact some change, they have to get him to agree to it."

"Yeah, seems he agrees to all of their suggestions these days."

"You don't know that. We have no idea what other suggestions they might be making that he doesn't agree to," the second voice said with a laugh. "For all we know, things could be a whole lot worse."

"Don't you know it," the first voice replied. "Why, I was over at the Tank the other day, and they said there's a whole new set of rules coming down from on high."

"Yeah, and what would they know down at the old Tank?"

"I don't know. They have their ways of finding things out."

"They have their ways of making things up just as well."

Allabva turned, now sufficiently distracted from her observation of the lady. She had been wondering how to approach her, but now found herself getting more curious about the complaints of the women near her.

"Excuse me," she said. "What's this talk about a tank? What policies? What laws?"

"Oh, never you mind her," the deeper-voiced woman said, twitching her head toward the other woman in the stall.

"What?" the higher-voiced woman said. "You discredit all I'm saying, as if you don't know it's true."

"I don't know it's true."

"You know some of it's true," the deeper-voiced woman smiled.

"Yes, I know some of it's true. But I don't know about all of it." She turned back to Allabva. "The Tuna Tank. It's a tavern down the way. It's the biggest corner of gossip around this quarter of the city. If you want to find out the latest news—and the latest hogwash without knowing which is which—it's not a bad place to try. The food's good, too."

Allabva wondered about that. "Tuna?" she asked. "I'm not the biggest fan of seafood."

"Now wait," said the deep-voiced woman. "Honestly, you can't bash it until you've tried it," she admonished. "Every dish has its own flavor, and I know while some dishes have this distinctive fish flavor, tuna is light on that count. So I'd say keep an open mind and try a tuna steak."

"Steak?" Allabva questioned. "I've heard of fish filets, fish soup, but not fish steak."

The higher-voiced woman joined in. "Oh yes, tuna has a more neutral flavor, and it's a large fish, so you can get bigger cuts of meat from it. Obviously, the Tuna Tank specializes in it. You should try it out."

Allabva had to admit she was curious to try something new. "Alright, well, where is it?" she said, pulling out her map.

"Oh, of course, she has a map," laughed the deeper-voiced woman. "Like a proper out-of-towner, isn't she?"

Allabva smiled graciously at her own expense as she unfolded the map and held it up for the two women to point out where she could find the Tuna Tank.

"Right down yonder, leaving the square on Wharf Road. It's about half a league. You needn't make any turns; you just go straight there," the woman said, pointing.

Allabva thanked her and put the map away as one woman looked out of the booth and onto the alley between booths. Her companion spoke, "Of course, if you want to settle into the city and have people feel at ease with you, miss," the higher-voiced woman said, "I'd recommend this nice necklace with the cat-eye brooch I saw you looking at. It's a great choice and fits right in with the local fashion."

Allabva found the sudden change in conversation odd as she turned her gaze back toward Jilona's and her mother's booth. To her dismay, the noblewoman, her soldiers, and her apparent pupils were no longer there, and Jilona and her mother appeared to be assuming business as usual.

Where has the lady gone to? Allabva asked herself, looking up and down the alley.

A tap on her shoulder distracted her from the question as she turned her head, surprised to find two soldiers standing around her.

"Excuse me, miss," one said, "the lady has heard there is a heroine in our midst this morning, and she would like to have a word with you."

Allabva's mouth dropped open as she turned her gaze to see the lady standing there. She quickly lowered her eyes.

"I apologize," she said. "I'm not familiar with the local customs. Please forgive me if I do not respond correctly."

"Lift your head," the lady instructed.

Allabva did so.

"Do not fret about our customs," she added. "I understand people are different in different places. I have heard from others here something quite remarkable about you," she told Allabva. "Please, tell me in your own words what thing they are talking about that you did this morning."

Allabva hesitated. What exactly had the lady been told? Allabva certainly didn't want to open up and disclose anything supernatural about herself, but she also refused to lie or to cast aspersions upon someone else inappropriately.

"Madam," Allabva began, her mind racing as her heart galloped faster than she had with Nightshade by her side as they descended the mountain. "Madam," she repeated, "I do not wish to disappoint you, nor do I know what thing you have already been told. So, I do not know if my account will confirm that of another person or if I might confuse the lady with my own rendering."

The lady stared at her, waiting.

"I saw a child tumble," she said. "I saw him lose balance, so I ran near, and when he fell, I caught him. His mother approached me, and I set him down. Then she picked him up. That is as far as my involvement goes, Madam." Allabva finished awkwardly.

Allabva finished while the lady looked at her askance.

"And that's all there is to it?" the lady asked.

"All that matters," Allabva replied.

"All that matters," the woman echoed, looking at her younger companions.

"Yes, Madam," Allabva said. "The child is alive and well, and with his mother. That's all that matters, as far as I'm concerned."

"All that matters," the lady repeated again. "Very well. I commend you for your quick action to help another." She turned to her guard detail. "Come on. What we heard earlier was obviously..." she breathed deeply, "...an exaggeration. Let's go."

As the woman turned away, Allabva opened her mouth to try to ask for an audience, but she felt her throat catch. How was she supposed to do that? Simply bring it up: *Hello, Madam. I'm from out of town. Can I talk to you about the end of the world?*

Allabva clamped her mouth shut, shaking her head. That wouldn't do. Frustrated, she watched the woman's back recede ahead of her, wringing her hands. She wondered what Nightshade would say. How would he chide her? Precisely when would he call her a coward? Did the Nomord even use slang? Did they have their own slang words to use as insults?

Allabva looked down and kicked a stone. What was she even doing here in this city? Tuki had told her she would join the Shrongelin in a fight to save the world. She didn't want this fight. She wouldn't have nominated herself for it. But he had said she was the ideal match for the job at hand. He hadn't said anything about awkwardly failing to talk to people in a

city far from home. He hadn't told her at first how grumpy
Nightshade would be, nor that he would send her into this
unknown city all by herself.

Chapter 23

Going With the Grain

She wandered through the square, feeling that her task was futile and her efforts pointless. How was she supposed to get an audience with the overduke if she couldn't even talk to this seemingly minor noblewoman?

"No, no, no, no, no, no," she heard a man's voice saying.

Looking up, she saw him holding his hands out toward a couple of men while they unloaded sacks off a wagon and into his stall.

"No," the man protested. He wore a muted red tunic over brown trousers and sported a wide mustache straight across his upper lip. "I can't afford this. Take them back."

"We don't work for you," one man said. "Sorry. We're told to make a delivery, we make a delivery. If you have any concerns, take it up with our employer." He grunted, grabbing another sack and piling it on top of the others they had already placed. From the way he handled them, they were obviously heavy sacks.

The man stood, holding his hat in one hand and rubbing his other hand through his hair, then bringing both hands down to wring his hat once again. The two men unloading the sacks, apparently reaching the number they had planned, closed up the back of the cart. One of them made a note in a book he carried.

"And there you go, Master Jhalla," one of them said at last. "Ten sacks of rice and twenty of wheat. Master Krolln will send you the bill."

Jhalla stood silently and watched the two men mount their cart and flick the reins for the horse to pull them on their way. Allabva stood watching Master Jhalla as he watched the pair depart.

"Is something the matter?" Allabva asked, approaching the man.

"Oh, don't worry about it," Master Jhalla told her, stepping into his stall and sitting heavily on a stool. Looking up, Allabva read the sign over Master Jhalla's stall: *Farm Fresh Grains.* Allabva confessed to herself that she couldn't quite see the problem. The other men had come and dropped off this grain, which Master Jhalla was obviously in the business of selling. If he had stock to sell, why was he so upset? Wouldn't this keep him in business rather than harm him?

Looking around, she saw the fifteen sacks that had just been delivered sitting to one side of the stall, but she also saw other stacks of grain sitting nearby.

Master Jhalla looked up with an annoyed expression on his face. "If you'll excuse me," he said, "I'm trying to wallow."

"Maybe I can help," Allabva offered. "Is there anything I can do?"

The man quickly looked her up and down. "I don't think so. You see this day's delivery right here," he said, pointing at the stack. Then he pointed at more grain sacks inside his stall. "But then you see leftovers from yesterday and the day before. I have a supply contract with their employer that I will purchase a certain quantity of grain. If he drops it off, we negotiate the prices anew every year. So it's not like he's overcharging me, but it's here, and that means I have to pay for it."

"And people aren't buying enough of it?" Allabva guessed.

"It's not exactly like that," Master Jhalla said. "People don't really come to the market to buy a sack of raw grain very often. I sell a bag or two here and there, but most of my business is in distribution. I have the stall here in hopes of picking up more customers."

"So why can't you distribute what you have?" Allabva asked. "Won't your customers pay when you deliver, just like you have to pay when the grower delivers?"

"Well, yes," he said, "but I can't deliver it because I have to be here."

"Why do you have to be here?"

"It's a contract with the city," Master Jhalla complained. "If I don't man the booth that I rented, even if I'm still paying for it while it's closed, I could be penalized and pay a high tax. I'd lose more than I would gain by making these deliveries, and I can't modify the rent on the booth until the end of the month, forty-five days away."

Allabva mentally checked her calendar. It was true; Greenstone had flown by and they were now into Tanstone.

"Well, how did you make the deliveries before?" she asked.

"My son helps out," he answered, "but he fell under the cart a few days ago, so he can't walk right now."

Allabva's eyebrows rose in concern. "Oh, he'll be alright," the man said, "but his ankle is messed up right now. That leaves me to both man the booth and make the deliveries. I could try after hours when I can close the booth, but as you can see, over the past couple of days, I've only succeeded in making one or two."

Allabva noted that the previous two days' stacks were still nearly all the way up.

"Well, why doesn't your son man the booth while you make the deliveries?"

"We live outside of town," he said. "We don't own a cart, and it's too far for him to hop or for me to carry him on my back."

Allabva frowned. This sounded like a tighter and tighter situation the more she learned about it.

"Well, how about if I made the deliveries for you?" Allabva said.

"Miss, no offense, but I don't know you from the Lady Greenstone herself," Master Jhalla replied, shaking his head. "And besides," he added, "no offense again, but these sacks of grain are heavy. I'm not sure you could make it to the first delivery with one of them."

Allabva pursed her lips, thinking. She wanted to help this man. *Shrongelin be cursed.* Allabva widened her eyes in surprise at her own thought. Did she just think that about the Shrongelin? She had meant it about the Nightshade, but they were the same being, as it turned out. Was this sacrilege?

Allabva frowned again. How could she approach this problem? "Well, Master Jhalla," she spoke cautiously, "as it happens, I've realized that I need to buy some grain myself."

Master Jhalla flustered. "Want to buy some grain? Well, sure, I'll sell you grain, but what are you going to do with it—carry it on your shoulders?"

"Yes," she answered, smiling. "I'll carry it on my shoulders, and if I can't carry it, then you can have it back, but keep my payment."

Now the man frowned, unsure of what to make of this. "What are you getting at, young lady?"

"Never mind that," she said. "Just take my coin. I'd like to buy two sacks of wheat. How much do I owe you?"

The man sputtered some more, then named a reasonable price in coppers. Allabva fished out the requested amount and plopped them on the counter in front of the man. He shrugged.

"I still don't know what you're about," he said, turning to grab two sacks of wheat, one at a time, and place them on the counter. "Like I said, these are heavy. I'm guessing you're going to put them right back down if you can lift them at all, but I'll let you pay me just for the chance to try—but only because I'm in a bind."

"No worries," Allabva said. "But before I leave you, could you tell me—hypothetically—if I were to take these sacks of grain to one of your customers and come back to get more, where should I go first?"

The man laughed. "Ha! No, you're not taking my customers, and you're not inserting yourself into my business model. I don't have the coin to spare to hire a new hand, so if you don't mind, miss—no, no, no."

"Just once," she said. "I'll do this once. And if I never come back, then you made the right choice to doubt me. But if I come back and give you more coin for more grain, then let me make your deliveries today for free. No charge," Allabva said.

"And why would you do that?" Master Jhalla huffed.

"Because..." Allabva paused. "Because I've been in some tight spots myself recently, and right now I'm not... Well, in some ways, I am. But right now, I have the ability to help you, and you need the help. That's all there is to it."

"Yeah, whatever," the man said. "If you keep coming back, I'll keep selling you my grain if that's what you want to do. And then I'll send word to my customers by courier that I'm not able to deliver. I'm already two days late on some of them, but your coin will help me afford the courier."

"Alright," Allabva said. "It sounds like we have a deal. But, on one condition."

"One condition. I knew there was some condition. I knew you couldn't just be in this for me. What is it you want?" the man grumbled, pulling his arms across his chest. "As if you could help me catch up after two days. You're a young lass, barely wider than a piece of paper."

"Master Jhalla," Allabva repeated, "just tell me where your first customer is. That's my condition. That's all I need. I've paid you, this is my grain now, and it's sitting right here. But if you tell me where your first customer is, I'll come back and buy more."

Master Jhalla eyed her suspiciously, his gaze flickering for a moment back to his stacks of grain. The sight of his own backlog must have broken his resolve.

"Alright," he said at last. "First delivery goes to the East Wall Mill."

"Can you tell me where that is?" Allabva asked, pulling out her map. "I'm new in town."

"Well, it's on the east wall, of course," the man joked awkwardly. Then he leaned over her map. "It's right here. You'll find it just south of the Salt Gate—uh, the east gate, for newcomers to the city. If you get a little lost, find your way to the Salt Gate, then go south on Wall Avenue and ask where the mill is. They'll point you in the right direction."

"Sounds good," Allabva said, studying the route on the map.

"Wasting my time," the man muttered. "You're not even going to be able to pick them up."

"Good sir," she said, "I'll be back for more before you know it."

She grabbed one sack with both hands. It was no joke—the sack was heavy, and Allabva could tell that it was. But that registered in her mind intellectually, as a simple fact, not as a burden. She easily heaved it up onto one shoulder, while the man looked at her appreciatively.

"I'll give you one thing," he said. "You're stronger than you look, miss."

"Thank you," Allabva said as she calculated how to pick up the other sack with only one hand free. She palmed it around the middle and, pulling the edge up, rotated it as if it were a door on the ground she was opening. Master Jhalla leaned in to help, grabbing the two ends. He helped lift it into the air while she got her free arm under it. Then she looped her arms around it and stood up straight, separating herself from Master Jhalla, still leaning over the counter.

Nodding to the man, she turned and walked briskly away.

"Well, my silver," the man said. "I never—" Laughing, he added, "What if she does it, too?"

Here goes nothing, Allabva thought to herself. *I did that impossible jump this morning, and people saw that. Just like Jilona's mother encouraged, I shouldn't try to hide it. I'm just going to do what I can.*

With a hop in her step, she started jogging, carrying the heavy sacks of flour on her shoulders as people watched her pass in surprise. A quarter of an hour later, Allabva stood in front of the East Wall Mill, and the smell of flour filled her nostrils.

Allabva walked up to the mill with a feeling of relief. At least for the moment, she had removed the ambiguity of Nightshade's mission for her from her life. For this brief time, she knew what she was doing, and she knew that it was accomplishing good. As she approached the door, she realized she didn't have any hands free to open it. Carefully lifting one foot, she tapped on the door with her boot, hoping it would sound like a knock.

After a minute, the door opened, and a surprised matron looked up at Allabva and the bags she carried on her shoulders.

"Oh, miss," she said, "you must be about to drop those. Come on in quickly." The matron opened the door wide, and Allabva calmly strolled in.

"You can drop them on the counter here," the matron said.

Allabva rotated one shoulder down, placing the first bag gently on the counter, and then the second.

"Well, miss," the woman said again, "I must say I'm impressed. I don't know how you carry those bags like that. I know I couldn't. How can I help you?"

"Well," Allabva said, "I bring these bags from Jhalla's Farm Fresh Grains in the southwest market."

"Jhalla's?" the woman asked. "We wondered what happened to him; It's two days late. Where's the rest of it?"

"I'll bring it soon enough," Allabva said.

"Oh, are you with Avrekk?" the woman asked. Allabva figured that must be Master Jhalla's son.

"No," she said. "I'm just a new friend of Master Jhalla's, helping him out today."

"OK," the woman laughed knowingly. "I suppose Avrekk is around the corner, and he propped these bags on your shoulders for a fun joke on me."

"Well," she said, "do you want to bring it all at once, and then I'll pay you for the whole batch at the end?"

Allabva shook her head. "No. You see, I'm new, and Master Jhalla doesn't have that much trust in me yet. So, if you could just pay me for these two bags, I'll come back with another two bags just like that."

Allabva paused. The woman paused, too. "Really? That's not how it usually goes," she said.

Allabva shrugged. "I'm not usually helping out, am I?"

"I guess not," the woman said. "Well, here's the contract price." She plopped some coins on the counter.

Allabva glanced at the coins quickly as she picked them up. It was more than she had paid Master Jhalla.

"Thank you," she said. "I'll be back later."

"Alright," the woman said, "and tell Master Jhalla thank you. Is everything OK?" she repeated.

"I think so," Allabva said. "He just got slowed up this time, but you can expect the next delivery on time after today."

"Alright," the woman said, waving Allabva out.

Allabva wondered about the price but decided Master Jhalla must have given her a deal. Either that, or the contract price figured in the delivery she had just performed. It didn't matter to her, really. Without another thought, Allabva was jogging back to the southwest market square.

As she entered the square again, Allabva slowed to a brisk walk again. Master Jhalla looked up from his despairing reverie in disbelief when she plopped the mill's money down on the counter.

"You undercharged me," Allabva observed. "Here's your contract price from the mill. Two more sacks, please."

Master Jhalla blinked once slowly, then a few more times quickly. "Who are you?"

"Call me Allabva." *There's no point trying to hide it*, she reminded herself.

"Where do you come from? Why are you here? What do you want?" Master Jhalla was suddenly full of questions.

"I come from out west. I'm trying to help make the world a better place." *Or stop it from becoming a much, much worse place.* "And I want you to give me two more sacks of grain. I told the lady at the mill that you'd just run behind lately, and after today, she can expect her next delivery on time once again. But first we have to catch you up. Two more bags, please."

Dumbfounded, the grain distributor turned and grabbed two more sacks one at a time, a confused look on his face. He said nothing as he stood and placed them on the counter between himself and the Shrongelin's Companion.

Allabva grabbed one sack and placed it on her shoulder as before, and Master Jhalla lifted the other sack in the air for Allabva to wrap her arm around and swing it up to her shoulder. She turned and left for the second time, not waiting for the man to say anything else.

Another half hour had barely passed when Allabva returned and found Master Jhalla, red-eyed and sniffling, standing to place two more sacks of grain on the counter as soon as she appeared.

This time it was rice, which he asked with every bit of politeness anyone could have mustered, for Allabva to deliver to none other than the Tuna Tank tavern. After delivering some bags to a mill, at first she was surprised that he was sending deliveries directly to a restaurant. But a moment's thought made her realize it was much rarer that she saw dishes prepared with wheat that *wasn't* ground into flour, than was the case with whole rice, which was often steamed and served with many different dishes. She had delivered one bag of rice to the east mill, though.

Allabva passed the afternoon delivering grain to mills, restaurants, and two to the back gate of none other than the overduke's palace grounds.

"You'll need this chit," Master Jhalla told her, pulling out a scrap of parchment with an embossed pattern on it. "And just so you know, this delivery isn't late. I was going to close the booth a little earlier today and risk the chance of a moderate fine, but the Overduke Pymseet was going to get *his* grain on time, Avrekk being lame or no. Also, this one's already paid for, so they won't be giving you any coin."

"Got it," Allabva said, pocketing the piece of parchment.

"There's a bell you ring by pulling a rope next to the gate. You'll talk to them through the gate, pass them the chit, then they'll let you through. Can you do one more delivery for me today after this?"

"Of course," Allabva replied, feeling quite hungry now.

It was getting to be a good time to wind down and end the day she had spent so actively. It felt wonderful to be dashing about, though. After her scramble and run-in with Nillan's gang a week or so prior, she had been left with a body well-toned for physical activity. The Shrongelin's bond served to increase the amount and intensity of the activity she felt ready for. Adding to that the knowledge that she was making a difference for good in the life of this man and his family, and Allabva was pretty happy with how the day had turned out. If the Nightshade didn't like it, then maybe he could gallop into the city and make a big ruckus himself!

After a final check with Master Jhalla to see that she understood where she was going, Allabva marched off. As every time before, Allabva walked until she left the square, then ran on her light feet, just now beginning to register some minor fatigue.

"Oh," Allabva said aloud to herself, a realization hitting her. "I have submitted an audience request with the overduke. What will this delivery do to the likelihood that my request is approved?"

Thinking it over, it occurred to her that if she displayed her enhanced strength when she made her delivery right now, it might be noted as an attempt to enter the palace grounds as somebody more than just a young woman making deliveries. She didn't want to appear threatening in any way, though perhaps interesting or noteworthy would be acceptable.

But maybe the Shrongelin was right, that Allabva ought to be winning arm wrestling matches. When she took on large men and won easily, that certainly was noteworthy, right?

Allabva shook her head. Yes, of course that was noteworthy, but the Shrongelin in all his grumpy Nightshady-ness could have his idea of how to approach things, and Allabva would hold her own ideas. Besides, he *had* said she could spend some time any way she wanted. But part of her worried that he probably would have said certainly not this much time.

Allabva shook her head again. *Back to the question at hand: how to improve my chances of an audience with the overduke.*

As Allabva approached the palace, she saw that it was bordered by a stone wall, which was a relief. She was concerned that it might have a wrought iron fence, through which she could have been seen walking on the street outside it, easily carrying these two heavy bags. Allabva hated a lie, but she had decided that this situation called for her to act deceptively and omit sharing all the information she had.

Arriving at the back gate, which was wrought iron, and much wider than Allabva had expected, she approached one edge of the gate from an oblique angle so as not to reveal herself to the view of anybody who might be on the other side, set both sacks down on the ground next to the wall, and stood. Making a conscious decision to seem exhausted, Allabva assumed a heavy slump in her posture, then pulled the rope.

A bell sounded loudly on the other side of the wall.

Allabva heard footsteps approaching on the other side of the wall, then a woman appeared behind the gate.

"What's your business?" she asked, straight to the matter.

"I bring grain from Master Jhalla in the southwest market square," Allabva answered, making a show of wiping what little sweat she had on her forehead with her hand, then pointing at the load she had carried here with very little effort.

The woman leaned to the side to change her angle, peering to Allabva's side of the wall to see the two sacks.

"Oh, my!" the woman proclaimed, "how did you get that here by yourself?" She looked up and down the street, scanning for somebody to explain.

Allabva shrugged. "Carefully."

"Oh, I imagine!" the servant woman said. "Gio! Enore!! Come grab these grain sacks." She turned back to Allabva. "You have your pass?"

Allabva handed the chit through the bars of the gate and the woman studied it for a moment, then handed it back.

"Don't worry yourself any further," the woman behind the gate said, pulling out a keyring and unlocking the gate, then swinging it open wide enough for a person carrying a grain sack to pass through. "We'll have our men take it from here."

"Jain, why doesn't Avrekk bring the grain in himself?" a man's voice asked out of view of Allabva. Apparently, either Gio or Enore had shown up.

"Because he's not here, Gio," the woman replied. "It seems this young lass managed to get them here somehow. But you're going to take them from here."

Gio, a youthful man probably ten years Allabva's senior, came into view and saw her, then immediately turned to face the way he had come.

"Enore, you've got to see this."

Enore showed up and looked outside the gate, then commented as well.

"Well, what have we here? Do all Weslan Fields folk grow up so strong?"

Allabva shrugged but said nothing, deciding that anything she said couldn't serve better than silence right now.

"Ah, don't worry about him," Gio said to Allabva. "He just talks too much. Say, do all Weslan Fields folk grow up so strong?"

Allabva let out a laugh despite herself, but still commented nothing. She wished she could vanish from the spot where she stood and erase herself from the memory of the three people on the other side of the gate. Or that she could have changed her appearance so they wouldn't recognize her for who she was. Identification could ruin her chances of getting the audience with the overduke.

Gio and Enore picked up the grain, laughing to themselves about their good-naturedly feigned nosiness into Allabva's business, and disappeared into whatever space there was that Allabva couldn't see on the other side of the wall.

Chapter 24

Coughing Badger 2

As soon as it appeared socially acceptable to do so, Allabva receded into the evening and returned to the Market Square at a light run the whole way. Allabva arrived at Master Jhalla's booth as the sun was disappearing over the rooftops.

"Ah, you're good. You're back," Master Jhalla said. "Good, and thank you again so much. I cannot repay you for this kindness you have shown me today," he said as Allabva stood before him again.

"If you would be so kind as to help me out one more time? This is the last delivery for today."

Allabva handed the chit back and took the grain as she placed payment for the grain on the counter.

"I don't suppose I can convince you to keep the coin you just laid down?" Master Jhalla said.

Allabva grinned and shook her head. "That's not why I'm doing this."

"Alright. Well, this last one is just around the corner. You should be back fairly soon, and I thank you again for everything you've done for me today. Sincerely," he added.

"Not a problem," Allabva said. Then she was off with the grain again. It only took her a few minutes to get where she was going, but something tickled her mind. Master Jhalla emphasized his thanks with what sounded like some finality.

As Allabva made the delivery, she decided she would ask him about it when she got back to the square. But when she returned, he wasn't there. Allabva reached into her palm and looked at the coin she'd been paid for this delivery. The grain distributor had paid her, despite her refusal, for she had no way to hand the coins back to him.

His booth had a storage area where the grain had sat, and surely there was still grain inside that area, but it was locked. And while it was made of wood slats, and she could slip the coins in between, she worried that they could get lost, and then they wouldn't benefit him.

"I'll come back tomorrow," she told herself and then suddenly realized that she had definitely reached the end of the day as far as the Nightshade's license to do whatever she wanted applied. Now, though she would act as her own agent and decide where to go and what manner to use, she was compelled to seek some kind of attention with the intent to further the Nomord's cause.

So saying to herself, Allabva set her feet toward the Coughing Badger as a starting point.

She strode into the Coughing Badger confidently this time, having seen it the evening prior and knowing the layout of the establishment. The same young boy greeted her as before, and Allabva promptly ordered another banana drink and whatever the special of the day was.

"Coming right up, miss," the boy replied as Allabva took her seat to wait for her dinner.

"Ah, she comes back," Allabva heard a familiar voice say.

"She dares, after Jimlarnt whooped her right in an arm wrestle yesterday," Tank replied to Walrus's observation. Then they both laughed together. Allabva smiled, rising and walking to their table.

"How do you do, gentlemen?" Allabva asked. "Mind if I sit here?"

Walrus turned to Tank. "You hear that? We're gentlemen now."

At the same time, Tank said, "Of course, have a seat. But don't expect us to act like men right now."

The pair burst out in another peal of laughter, nearly covering up completely the sound of the music coming from a woman playing a pair of drums held snugly between her calves and a man manipulating strings on an instrument he played sitting down. But it was tall enough to rest on the floor and come up to his head. The pair sang in harmony while they played their respective instruments, a song that Allabva didn't recognize but suspected had been brought into the harbor on one of the many ships that moored in this city.

"How are you tonight, lass?" Walrus asked.

"Hungry," Allabva replied earnestly. "I've been running around all day and working up quite a hunger."

"Running around, you say?" Tank said. "Whatever for?"

"You know," Allabva stepped cautiously, "just taking care of business."

"Ah, business with a pair of sacks of grain on your shoulders," Walrus jumped right to the question that Allabva could see in Tank's eyes.

Allabva's eyebrows shot up, and her mouth opened involuntarily. Then she closed it again just as fast. Allabva's alarm was quickly quieted by the sly look in Walrus's eye.

"So," Allabva spoke slowly, "I guess you saw me."

"Ah, saw you, I did," said Walrus, laughing.

"I didn't," Tank said. "But if Walrus said it, I know it's true."

Allabva wasn't sure what to think, or feel. She had consciously decided not to try to stay hidden when she had begun carrying those sacks of grain and making the deliveries for Master Jhalla. That was true, but she hadn't expected it to come back around to her so soon. It seemed that Walrus and Tank picked up on her concern.

"Don't you worry, lass," Walrus said. "We're friends here."

"Yes, we're right envious about your level of energy, but we are no threat to you. Unless you start causing harm," Tank interjected.

"Aye, unless you start causing harm," Walrus agreed. "But even then, we already know to tread carefully with you," he reached up, gently massaging his right arm.

"Well, how are you doing today, gentlemen?" Allabva asked them, changing the subject.

"Oh, better now than an hour ago," Walrus quipped, raising his mug and clinking it against Tank's.

"That's a fact," Tank said.

"To be frank," Walrus explained, "I'm having a bit of trouble with a project I'm working on right now for a minor repair on the north wall of the city. It's an old section done a different kind of stone from what I'm used to working with. Can't seem to get the cuts quite right the first time, and it's slowing me down. I'm sure I'll manage it tomorrow, though."

"Well, best of luck," Allabva wished him congenially. "And you, Master Tank?"

"Never better," Tank smiled back.

"Huh, he's selling you the pleasant version," Walrus accused.

"He didn't really tell me anything," Allabva said.

"That's right, what we said. Nothing wrong, really. Just, the work was particularly heavy today. The nicer days are when I just chisel all day. Today I was moving stones around, reorganizing my shop. Took some heavy lifting, you might imagine."

"I suppose so," Allabva said.

The waiter came back with Allabva's banana drink, which she thanked him for before he scurried off.

"So, what can a lowly carpenter and stonemason do for the likes of an up-and-coming foreign lady such as yourself?"

"I'm not foreign, and I'm not a lady," Allabva protested.

"But you have an accent," Walrus opined.

Allabva relaxed. "And to me, you have an accent. But I thought I told you yesterday, I'm Eslarnan, just like you."

"Ah, but you do not fall under the High Dominion of the overduke," Tank surmised. "You come from west of those mountains?"

"Yes," Allabva admitted, "but I'm still not a lady," she insisted.

"Not a lady?" Walrus said. "With a grip like that, you can claim to be whatever you want, and I won't try to dissuade you."

"Ain't that the truth?" Tank agreed.

Walrus's eyes shifted, but he said nothing more at this moment, instead dipping a slender piece of bread into a bowl of some sauce they had on the table. Allabva thought it smelled of garlic.

Allabva took a deep sigh. "Yes," then, guessing that she knew what Walrus's eyes had shifted about, she let them in. "I got my strength from a Nomord," she told them plainly.

Walrus stopped chewing and stared at her while Tank slowly lowered his glass—or mug—to the table.

"Come again?" Walrus said.

"A Nomord," Allabva repeated.

"How does that work?" Walrus said. "Do you consort with the creatures? What did you—" He made a sour expression, then slid one finger across his throat.

Allabva almost jumped in her chair. "No, of course not! One of them came to me," she said, "and told me some things, that it was important to travel with him."

Walrus stopped chewing again. "Him?" he said through a mouthful of bread.

Allabva nodded. "There are male Nomord."

"Yes, and then you caught a jackalope and a fae-bird, and met with a dragon," Tank joked.

Walrus turned to him with a perplexed look painted across his face. "Was that supposed to be a joke? That was... Never mind." He turned back to Allabva. "Go on. I believe you."

Tank muttered something that sounded like, "So do I. It was just funny."

Allabva continued, "He said I had to travel with him to meet another Nomord." She chose her words carefully. "Said there's trouble coming."

Walrus stopped, hand halfway to his mouth with another bite of bread. "Trouble?" he repeated. "A Nomord said that?"

"Don't you worry," Tank said loudly. "We'll take him, whatever they—"

"Hush, Tank!" Walrus shushed his large friend. "Miss Allabva, don't say another word. Not here."

"Don't you think you're taking it a little quickly?" Tank asked Walrus.

"Don't you think you're ignoring the fact that she already proved she has a superhuman ability?" Walrus rebuffed. "She got that from somewhere, didn't she? Now she's telling us where, and I don't see any reason to doubt her." He turned his attention back to Allabva. "Say no more here about what happened. But if it's not sensitive information, perhaps you can tell us how we can help."

Allabva nodded. "I need…" She breathed in and out again. "Ultimately, what I need is something I don't think you can give me, but perhaps you can help me get there."

"Go on," Walrus prompted.

"I need to speak with the overduke," Allabva said frankly.

"The overduke himself? Is that all?" Tank asked.

"Well, you're right," Tank said. "We can't get you that. What's your plan to get there?" Walrus prodded politely.

"I already submitted a request for a summons when I entered the city," Allabva said.

"And they actually took it?" Walrus asked, surprised.

Allabva nodded. "I had to arm wrestle the sentry to convince him to take it seriously."

Walrus's face instantaneously jumped from intrepid concern to a grin so wide he threatened to swallow the tavern. "Of course, you did! Alright, so?"

"So, I still need to attract attention," Allabva finished. "I put in the request, but there's no real reason for them to grant it or for the overduke even to hear about it."

"That's right," Tank commented.

"I need to call attention so that I can explain the situation and my mission."

"How? Just how big is this mission?" Walrus asked slowly. "How much does its success or failure affect?" He eyed the room to ensure nobody was listening in.

The waiter boy returned with a plate full of long noodles heaped under a pile of meatballs and tomato sauce, topped with melted white cheese. Allabva took a deep breath, enjoying the aroma of the pasta as the three of them waited for the boy to leave.

When he was out of earshot, Allabva answered Walrus's question. "Everything," she said solemnly.

Walrus pursed his lips, while Tank began to appear as concerned as Walrus had been.

"Well, what kind of everything?" Walrus poked, apparently hoping to reveal that Allabva wasn't saying what he thought she was. "And who?"

"Everybody," Allabva said.

Walrus took a slow breath in, squinching his face in thought, then exhaled as slowly as he had inhaled. "And this is all real?" he asked.

Allabva gave one slight nod.

Walrus blinked, then shook his head furiously, snapping back to the conversation with a loud, "Oy! You got the special, and it is special indeed. You will love it." Allabva was caught off guard as Walrus turned back into his charming self. "I'll tell you what, if you want some real spin on it," he paused, "then come by my house, and you can see how my wife and I make the pasta together."

"Weren't you already eating?" Allabva asked.

He looked down at his bread and sauce. "Well, this is just a warm-up," he sputtered, then laughed. "Guilty as charged.

Now you see how I grew so large!" Walrus and Tank laughed uproariously together.

"Oh yes," he said. "How I got so large?" He grew serious again, though not as somber as a minute before. "I mean it, do come. Tell us all about your situation, and we'll do everything we can. Tank will be there too. It's easy to find. It's the yellow and orange house on Mulch Street. You have a map?"

Allabva pulled her map out, and Walrus pointed. "Go there anytime. Knock like this," he tapped the table in three groups of two taps, "and we'll know it's you. If it's the middle of the night, do it again. You have to wake us up the first time, and we'll come. Tank won't always be there, but he's nearby. We'll get him."

"Now, repeat back to me. It's the...?" He paused for Allabva to fill in.

"Orange and yellow house on Mulch Street," she pointed to the map, then lightly tapped the table six times in the same rhythm Walrus had used.

"Good," Walrus said. "If you don't mind, I believe I must away. I told the wife I would help her cook tonight."

Walrus stood and pushed his chair in. Tank looked up at his friend, apparently deciding whether he had to take off as well. Reluctantly, he leaned forward off of his chair, then stood.

"Lass," Walrus said, "I do hope you'll be coming by."

Allabva's mind raced. They appeared to be good men and interested in helping. Also, she knew that with the Shrongelin's bond, she was far stronger than they were. But she couldn't help worrying about her own safety if she went into the home of a stranger in a strange city.

After all, if she had this gift of enhancement from the Nomord that caught everybody off guard when they saw it, how was she to know that her adversary didn't have similar tricks of her own? Up on the mountaintop, the Nightshade Unicorn had said they had weakened Sacalai for a time when they successfully formed the bond. How long did that weakening last? Allabva wasn't sure. A single day? A week? Two weeks?

Walrus turned to walk toward the open door.

"Wait," Allabva said, placing her hand on his forearm. Slipping her free hand into her pocket, she played with the brooch. "Please tell me that everything you said is in earnest."

Allabva stared into Walrus's eyes, studying every expression. He nodded gently.

"Yes, lass," he said. "Every word."

"Then I will come," she answered.

"Wait two hours," Walrus answered. "That will give us a better chance to prepare, and hopefully we'll prevent you from being followed from here to there. Don't go there directly."

Allabva nodded. Then Walrus's congenial face was instantly pasted back on, and he said loudly and cheerfully, "That's what I miss! Maybe come back tomorrow, and we can laugh about Jimmy again from yesterday."

Allabva forced a smile on her face as well. It was only half genuine, but the genuine half was sincere. She was glad to have met these friends, but the weight of the situation impeded unfettered enjoyment of the moment.

"Have a good evening," she said to both men as they left. Her attention turned back to her pasta with meatballs. As she dug in, she took a moment to question her choice of ordering the banana drink before knowing what her meal was going to be. Independently, both the drink and the entrée were delicious, but they didn't exactly complement each other.

While Allabva ate, she studied her map, locating the Tuna Tank as well as Walrus's home. She finished her meal and washed it down with some water after her pul-pul was all gone. After leaving payment with the young boy, she wandered out into the night. Pulling out her map, she took one final glance before telling herself that she was confident on how to get to the Tuna Tank, and she put it away.

She heard a scuff and caught sight of a leg and foot disappearing around the corner. Was that...? No, never mind. She shook her head. Jim wouldn't dare bother her again after last night, would he? Deciding she didn't have time to worry about that, as she was pressed to get to the Tuna Tank so she could start hearing news and rumors before heading to Walrus's home, she broke into a run.

Only a few minutes later—what should have been a grueling course through the city except for her bond with the Shrongelin—she arrived at her destination.

Chapter 25

Tuna Tank

Allabva found the Tuna Tank easily, just as it had been described to her and pointed out on the map. As she approached, she saw people looking out the windows at her. There was a bar, or rather a long table, at which patrons sat facing outside. Having visited a few different places in the city already, she felt more confident with herself. The knowledge in her head—that she could more than go toe to toe with anyone in sight—was now finally reaching her heart. Allabva walked into the place and found a table to sit at. Looking around, she took a moment to see how people grouped themselves in this tavern. She saw a group of men sitting together, calmly sipping their drinks, while a couple of them ate meals. Another group of men spoke more animatedly, but with hushed tones.

Allabva could see that this Tuna Tank seemed to prefer serving the tuna steaks she had heard about, as well as some dish with stuffing placed inside a bread roll of some sort. A woman approached her, wearing local attire with an apron over the top.

"Miss, can I get you something?" she asked.

"How much for the tuna steak?" Allabva said.

"Five copper hafender."

"Hmm. Do you have a half serving of that?"

"Three copper."

"I'll do that," Allabva nodded, and the woman scribbled a small note.

"And to drink?"

"I've been hearing about the Southmarch festival coming up," Allabva said. "You have some sort of citrus drink in town, don't you?"

"Oh, you want the wassail?"

"Yes, please."

The woman left Allabva to continue observing the room in peace. As she did so, she saw a knot of women and a couple of men gathered around a larger table, speaking with excited tones. Allabva caught a couple of words, and her brow furrowed when she heard the word "overduke" in the conversation. This could be an opportunity to get some information about the man she was trying to get an audience with. Sighing, Allabva stood and walked over to the group of people.

Allabva distinctly heard the word "overduke" a couple of times. She made her way over there.

"Good evening," she said.

"Whatever you say, miss," one man said in a huff.

"I'm sorry," Allabva replied. "I hope it hasn't been too unpleasant, but I couldn't help but hear you mention the overduke. I'm new in town. Can you help me understand local society?"

The man looked at her with a raised eyebrow and a frown. "You want to learn about local society," he said flatly. "I hope you didn't come here of your own free will 'cause I sure wouldn't. I'm only still here because I can't afford to leave."

"It was of of my own free will," Allabva reasoned out loud, "but I kind of had to."

"My deepest sympathies," the man replied.

"Why?" Allabva asked. "What's wrong?"

"What's wrong? You hear that, Rallan?" he said to one of his companions. "She asked what's wrong. In Tallensworth of all places, miss." He shook his head, then stopped himself. "I was about to ask where you've been, but you just said you're new in town. Alright, let's back up."

He took a swallow of his drink and set it back down, spreading his hands to gesture as he spoke. "Our benevolent and wise leader, the overduke, has just increased the farm tax. Now every farmer in the High Dominion is going to have to pay more taxes on his land. He'll either have to raise his prices for the produce he sells or pay his hands less."

Allabva thought about how a farm worked. "Maybe they can find cheaper tools whenever they have to fix a plow or harness."

"Cheaper tools," he huffed. "She says cheaper tools. No, that's something else our kind ruler has ruined for us. The past five years, he has enshrined the Blacksmiths' Guild and put one of their members on his council. Everything that happens in this city, the blacksmiths have a say in. Now, I'm not saying blacksmiths are all bad," he held his hands up defensively, "but I'll tell you one thing, generally speaking, their prices aren't coming down anytime soon."

"I see what you're saying." Allabva seated herself at the table. "Do you mind?"

"Not at all," he replied.

"Koszh," Rallan said. "Don't forget to tell her about the harbor."

"The harbor? Why do I care about the harbor?"

"Fine, I'll tell her," Koszh said. "There are sections of the harbor that are for noble use only. You need a special pass to moor a boat there, and they don't sell them. I think the nobles have to pay a fee, and I'm sure it's a big one. Well, maybe I don't know that, but at any rate, not even wealthy merchants can use that section of the harbor. So you see these yachts and recreational sailing craft out there in the harbor, right in front of everybody."

"Why, I suppose they have to put their ships somewhere," Allabva guessed, trying to be understanding.

"Maybe," Koszh agreed, "but the spot they sectioned off is right in the middle. You have merchants on one side and, on the other, people shipping goods in and out. They have to go all the way around this segment of the docks, and it clogs up traffic all along the wharfs. If these nobles think they need a special section, they should put it on the east or west end, not in the middle."

"So this is who I have to talk to," Allabva thought. "The man putting in all these laws that these men are finding so troublesome. Is there any reason that you know of why the overduke is raising the farm tax and giving power to the black-smiths?"

"Oh, don't let Koszh fool you," Rallan said. "The black-smiths aren't truly powerful. Sure, they have a bigger voice, I suppose, and if I were a blacksmith, I'd be glad to keep my prices up." He looked down, swished his drink around, set it down, and grabbed his fork to stab a bite of tuna steak.

"Supposedly," Koszh jumped in, "it's for everybody's good. For defense or something."

"Defense against whom?" Allabva asked.

"Exactly!" Koszh nearly shouted. "Against whom? No-body's thought of attacking us directly in nigh on three hun-dred years."

"But supposedly the overduke is concerned that we could get attacked. One of these days, somebody could come against us, so I guess he wants to make sure we have plenty of blacksmiths to make weapons.

"But we don't need any such weapons," Koszh finished.

"I guess I see what you mean," Allabva said.

"You can see that? You guess?" Rallan echoed scornfully. "It's as plain as the nose on my face." He gestured at himself pointedly. Allabva wasn't sure she quite understood, though.

"What's as plain as the nose on your face?" she asked.

Rallan did an exaggerated double take. "That the overduke is meddling where he shouldn't."

"I see," Allabva replied.

The waitress came and left Allabva's half tuna steak in front of her.

"That was fast," Koszh said.

Rallan blinked. "What time is it? Oh, I've got to get going home if it's past the fifteenth bell."

"It just sounded before I walked in," Allabva said.

"My silver!" Rallan proclaimed. "I'm out." He stood, taking a final swig from his drink and digging some money out of his pocket to leave on the table.

The rest of the group also stood up to go, leaving Allabva about to be by herself. Truth be told, she would prefer to eat in peace, but she specifically came to the Tuna Tank for the gossip. So she felt compelled to gather as much while she was here. She also stood, taking her plate and her wassail with her, and made her way to the table that was speaking more animatedly but in hushed tones.

As she approached Allabva just barely caught a word more interesting to her mission than "overduke," rise from the table before the speaker glanced around and brought herself closer into the group. The word was "Nightshade."

"What's this you were saying about nightshade growing outside town?" she asked as she invited herself to sit at the table, trying to sound clueless about what they were really discussing.

The speaker replied, "Nightshade growing outside, you think it's an herb?" She leaned forward. "No, young miss. Have you ever heard of the Nightshade Unicorn?"

Just like that?, Allabva thought, blinking. "Alright, I'll bite," she said aloud. "Tell me about the Nightshade Unicorn. Does it eat poisonous plants?"

The woman rolled her eyes and shook her head. "You're obviously new around here," a man replied. "We don't talk about trivial things here. If this is where you want to find out what's really going on in this town, this is where you come. Now, some people say it doesn't exist, but I always knew it did. Didn't I, Shel?" He elbowed the man next to him.

"You're right, I am new in town," Allabva said.

"Excuse me," the woman interrupted. "The young miss asked me a question, and I intend to answer it." She turned back to Allabva. "The Nightshade Unicorn, you ever heard of him?"

If only you knew, Allabva thought, taking a sip of her wassail. She sat back.

"Why don't you tell me about him?" she asked.

The man eyed Allabva distrustfully but said nothing, while the woman opened up like a book.

"The Nightshade Unicorn, they say, looks a little bit like the Amorite, but he's huge and fierce. Some say he eats the Nomord."

Allabva suppressed a giggle. The Nightshade was gruff, sure, but she'd seen him graze on grass herself.

"So, what about him?" she asked.

"You really haven't heard?" the woman asked. Allabva said nothing, and the woman continued. "My great-uncle used to work in the Royal Library at the overduke's palace, and he says the old stories say the Nightshade Unicorn comes before calamity."

Allabva frowned. "What kind of calamity?"

"Every kind of calamity," the woman said. "You name it—plagues, pestilence, earthquakes, storms."

"I'll admit," Allabva said finally, "I've heard these old stories before. So why are we talking about them now?"

"Because they're not old stories anymore," the woman said.

"Oh?" Allabva asked, her interest now truly piqued. "What makes them not stories?"

"Because Foral over there saw him. Didn't you, Foral?" She gestured toward a man who was sitting quietly, leaning back and carefully studying the bottom of his goblet. He peeked over the rim of his glass, then lifted it higher before bringing it down to the table.

"Waitress, more wassail, please," he said.

"Calae," he turned to the woman, "I didn't come here to yak to the whole town and beyond," he added, gesturing at Allabva. "We have an outsider here, and we're just telling her everything. She was sitting over there with Rallan's crowd a while ago. Now that she knows all about politics, we're letting her into the personal gossip. She probably came here just to make fun of us for all these stories."

Allabva hurried to correct this misconception. "Oh no, I didn't come here to make fun of anybody." The man stared at Allabva for a moment, perhaps judging whether she was telling the truth or whether that even mattered.

"Fine," he said at length. "I saw something," Foral said, "and I swear it looked exactly like a big black Nomord." He waited a moment, watching Allabva to see if she was going to react. She didn't, though she certainly had some thoughts in her head.

Oh Nightshade, I thought I was supposed to get attention in the city, not you outside of it, she mused, but she could let it rest. For now.

"Exactly like a black Nomord?" Allabva asked. "But there aren't any, right? Doesn't everybody know that?"

"I thought so too," Foral said. "But I saw what I saw."

"Where did you see it?" Allabva asked.

"Out on the northern hills," he replied. "It was just walking.

"What time of day was it?" Allabva asked. "Perhaps it was a shadow. Or perhaps there was a shadow that made it look like a different color."

"It was mid-morning," Foral enunciated, "and it was in the clear. No trees, no shadows, except for the beast itself."

Allabva considered this information, then decided to probe.

"And what do you think it must mean? If that's the Nightshade Unicorn, then what kind of disaster do you think is coming to Tallensworth?" she said, gesturing at the woman who recited the old myth that the Nightshade was a precursor to a great calamity.

"You tell me, miss," Foral challenged back.

Allabva thought for a moment. "Well, if you ask the gentleman who just left the table over there, the calamity is likely to be a raise in taxes," she said with a grin.

Foral chuckled. "Isn't that the truth? That group is always going on about the overduke. Rallan knows he'd never leave town, though, even if he had the chance to take his family elsewhere. He likes it here as much as he does complain."

"Well, but that's not all," the woman said, bringing the conversation back around. "Foral saw the Nightshade Unicorn, but I have a friend who says she's heard stories about the Nightmare Beast coming from small towns outside the city. Today."

"Really?" Allabva raised her brows. "And did she say what the Nightmare Beast was doing?"

"No." The woman balled a fist and tapped it on the table. "Just said people saw it. Now, I don't know what's going on, but I tell you this: something is up. The Nightmare Beast and the red lightning. I tell you what, he's probably casting it."

"Perhaps," Allabva said vaguely. She knew the woman was wrong with that assumption.

"All I know," said another woman, "it had better not mess with Southmarch next week."

There was mention of the festival again. Allabva thought it was increasingly sounding more important to the locals than she had anticipated.

"I'm not from here," Allabva said, obviously. "Can you tell me what all this talk of Southmarch is?"

"What? You don't know Southmarch?" the second woman said.

"Nope," Allabva confirmed. "But I'd like to find out, if you'll tell me."

"It celebrates the battle hundreds of years ago," Foral explained, stepping in as the apparent local historian. "I guess it was almost 1,000 years ago. Not long. Well, I mean, it was decades, but it was after the expansion of the Holbonin Empire over Eslarna."

"Really?" Allabva said around a mouthful of food. The woman at the market was right; the tuna steak was good. "What was this battle about?"

"Oh, you know," Foral said. "The Holbonins crossed the gulf and slowly expanded, taking over this area and that, till they had an empire, which eventually included almost the whole continent. Of course, Weslan Fields has broken off, so Eslarna isn't a unique political entity on the continent like it once was. But the Holbonins set up their capital in Nolnarn. That's why we don't hold the whole country Holbonin anymore, but it resumed the name used for much of the eastern half of the continent before that time. Anyway," Foral continued, "Tallensworth became part of the empire. Of course, we got conquered like everyone else, but we got used to it. I say 'we,' you know, this is so many generations ago."

"You really don't know any of this?" Foral asked Allabva, who shook her head. "The Battle of Southmarch? Nothing?"

"I'm afraid not," Allabva said.

"Very well," Foral continued. "So the Holbonins had the continent—or mostly. And we had some neighbors to the south who didn't want to join the empire. Specifically, the Colnarn Protectorate states."

Allabva's brow furrowed. "But they're islands out at sea," she said. "What does that have to do with the Holbonin Empire?"

"Ah, let's just say the Colnarn states decided that the Holbonins were getting too ambitious and too successful. After they took Tallensworth, they thought the Holbonins might go for Tunglin down at the tip of Fonglan Point."

"Hmm," Allabva murmured. "I knew the Colnarn states joined to stop the empire, but I never knew these details. But you still haven't told me what Southmarch is."

"I'm almost there," Foral said, holding up a finger for Allabva to wait a minute and give him time to explain. "In those days, just like the Holbonin—or the Eslarnan—Empire included Weslan Fields, the Colnarn Protectorate included Tunglin, which you know now rules itself. So Tunglin invited the Colnarns to help fortify against a Holbonin invasion."

"I guess they succeeded, since Tunglin isn't part of Eslarna today?" Allabva asked

"Right," Foral confirmed, swishing his goblet to stir his drink before taking a sip. "But that's not so relevant yet. What happened was that they trounced our guys so heavily that it stopped the expansion of the empire altogether. Emperor Holinnin the Third decided to secure his borders better in the west. I suppose the Glosens were more seafaring in those days. He focused on building up infrastructure within the empire, rather than try again to take Tunglin from the Colnarns. That was really the turning point when the Holbonins stopped being Holbonin, in my opinion, and started being Eslarnan. But what's relevant here is that, twenty years later, the Colnarns—including Tunglin, mind you—got cocky."

"You see, if you look at a map of the continent, the Talons Range reaches down into Fonglin Point but stops before it reaches the Tunglin capital. They have some good stretches of plains down there."

"What do plains have to do with a battle here in Tallensworth?" Allabva interrupted.

"Almost there," Foral delayed her. "It has to do with their tactics. Those plains dictated how they defended themselves so successfully against the Holbonins, but it was the same reason they failed so miserably to take Tallensworth."

"You got me," Allabva said. "I'm officially confused."

"Alright, class," Foral said. "Does anybody else have the answer and would like to tell our new student?" He gestured to the others at the table.

The first woman who had spoken when Allabva sat down replied to Foral's question with a glint in her eye. "Horses," she said.

"Horses?" Allabva asked.

"And she wins top of the class," Foral said.

Allabva laughed uncomfortably.

"Horses? Does that sound so confusing?"

"I don't know," Allabva replied. "Horses are horses, I suppose. I know they can be useful in battle, but why would they make the Tunglins lose a battle?"

"Strengths and weaknesses," Foral said. "They had a mounted cavalry and a familiarity with the terrain. They rode up the coast to our fair city and quite successfully made the trip, mind you. But once they got here, horses were their downfall. They managed to break into the city—the walls are much higher and thicker now than they were before the Tunglin invasion—but once inside, they were unfamiliar with our streets."

He held up a finger. "Their horses were less maneuverable than our foot soldiers." He held up another finger, listing the reasons. "We specifically laid traps to stop their horses, and barriers through which only a man on foot could pass. Finally, they were not armed for urban combat as we were. We had men with polearms and crossbows set up in specific locations to make their horses as vulnerable as possible."

"Alright, I get why horses were good and bad for them," Allabva said. "But what does this have to do with anything... And the festival? What is Southmarch?"

"What is the festival?" the first woman asked incredulously. "Obviously, we're celebrating that we won the battle."

"Alright, I see that," Allabva said. "But the name—where does that come from?"

"That's obviously what the Tunglins had to do because we won," the woman said impatiently.

"Oh." The final piece clicked into place, and Allabva smiled. "I get it now. So, how do you celebrate? What do you do?"

The woman's jaw dropped. "The questions never end, do they?" she asked.

Allabva shrugged. "I'm afraid you'll have to ask someone else, Little Miss," the woman said.

Allabva looked to Foral. He shrugged, apparently also wondering at the woman's sudden impatience.

"That's fine," Allabva said. "I've made some acquaintances in town. I'll ask them later. But as for the Nightshade Unicorn..." She stopped herself from repeating the woman's label of *Nightmare Beast*. "It sounds like he's just walking around, at least for now. I don't know that there's anything to be done about that."

"I would be inclined to say the same thing," Foral said. "I admit that's the rational take on the beast's behavior. He was just walking, and there was nothing about the way that he stalked that looked like he was going to do anything."

He took another swig from his drink. "But the very look of him was..." He paused to search for the right word. "Fearsome. I have to correct myself from earlier. He didn't look exactly like a regular Nomord, but with a darker coat. He looked like he'd been through an ordeal. He was roughed up, scruffy, with scars running up and down him where the hair didn't always grow right. His actions out there were innocent, but he had this aura—and I don't use that word lightly or idly—but he had this aura about him of anger. I swear," Foral said, "I thought he was about to come and eat me, just from the look of him."

Allabva digested the man's words, idly chewing on a fragment of some spice she had found in her drink. She pursed her lips, then set her cup on the table, realizing her plate was emptied as well.

"You think I'm crazy?" Foral accused Allabva gently.

"No," Allabva breathed, taking it all in. "Please pardon me for not explaining, but I think you're spot on."

Now Foral's mouth dropped open. "What do you know, girl?" he asked curiously.

"As I said, you'll have to forgive me for not explaining," Allabva repeated. "And if you'll excuse me, it's time for me to be going. Thank you for letting me sit with you," she said.

"Where do you have to be?" the first woman asked. "You're not from around here; you don't have any commitments."

Allabva turned to the woman as she rose, leaving payment for her meal on the table in the local fashion. "I mentioned earlier that I have some acquaintances in town. I said I was going to meet them, but I actually do have somewhere else to be before that. Everyone, it was nice to meet you."

"Wait," the man said. "Who are you? You know something you're not telling. Will you come back and tell us another day?"

"Perhaps," Allabva said. "But even if I don't, you'll know it all soon enough, whether you want to or not. Now you have—" she froze, unsure of the appropriate farewell, "—a good week preparing for Southmarch. Thank you for the lesson."

Allabva departed the Tuna Tank with a few deep breaths as she found her way next.

Chapter 26

Three Wolves Mute

Allabva did her best to shrug off her distaste for the scene where she saw rude gestures and heard ruder words every other moment she was there. She leaned against the wall next to the door and rubbed her chin, wondering where to insert herself. She had eaten at the Tuna Tank to be polite, but she suspected there was no need to cultivate appearances here. Although, polite or not, she acknowledged the risk that she could be asked to leave if she weren't a customer, regardless.

A man at a nearby table looked up from his hand as he played a game of cards with his mates. "Hey, boys, we got a pretty face over here. Come on over, miss," he gestured genuinely.

Allabva looked at him, trying to weigh the moment in an instant. He appeared friendly, but she wondered about his fellows. One of them seemed to leer at her.

"I can leave at any moment," Allabva told herself, "and there's nothing they could do to stop me." She walked forward toward the young sailor who had invited her.

"Have a seat, miss," the sailor said. "We'll deal you in. You know how to play Novulm Towers?"

Allabva shook her head, seating herself.

"You're from out of town," the leery player said. "What brings you here?"

"Perhaps I should ask the same," Allabva asked the leery sailor. The leery sailor's skin shade made it clear that his family wasn't from here, generationally speaking. "But I'm just here getting to know the city," Allabva answered.

"That's why I came too," the leery sailor said. "Ten years ago." He and his companions laughed as if he'd said something funny.

"That's alright, that's alright," said the eager young sailor. "You can come get to know my place anytime," he grinned.

"Thank you, but I think I'm good," Allabva said.

"No, you're right. I'm just playing," he answered. "So look, this is how it works," he said, gathering the cards from around the table into one deck.

"But I had a good hand," the leery sailor complained.

"Deal with it," the third sailor spoke. "This game works better with four players, anyway."

"Hey, no worries. I'll *deal* with it," the eager young sailor punned as he handed cards out, face down, around the table. "Now look, miss. Each one of us gets a hand, right? And we hand out the cards like this. You try to protect your land. If you get a card with a tower on it, set it face up, because that's how you protect. But if you get a card with a trebuchet, keep it face down because you use that to attack. You don't tell us when you're going to attack ahead of time, so keep it secret until you play it."

There was a pair of dice on the table as well. "My name is Cariel, by the way. What's your name?"

"Allabva," Allabva replied.

"Nice to meet you, Allabva. This here is Redeok," he pointed at the leery sailor, "and that's Lewolnn." The sailor who had rebuked Redeok waved back.

As she got into the game and understood the flow, Lewolnn suggested they put some friendly stakes on it to make it interesting. Redeok seemed to have been waiting for this, and apparently they'd been betting some coin on their match before she showed up. Cariel seemed not to care much whether they did or not, but grinned and joked that he'd clean them all up in short order. Allabva decided to go with the flow, but agreed to bet only two copper pieces.

Allabva started seeing the personality of each player, bit by bit. It seemed to her that Cariel really was genuine, if rough around the edges, and even if he liked to hang in joints such as this, which she generally considered less cultured. Lewolnn didn't speak much, and everything Redeok said seemed to be a complaint or otherwise reflected traits that Allabva would rather not spend her time around. But she found herself enjoying the game itself, if not the setting.

That sense of enjoyment lasted up until she saw Jimlarnt, from her first visit to the Coughing Badger, walk in out of the corner of her eye. She drew her lips together and held her hand on the card she had been about to play. She glanced up at him to be sure that she hadn't mistaken his identity, then forced herself to ignore the man and nonchalantly play her card.

"No, you can't do that to me!" Cariel protested in feigned anger at the play.

Redeok rolled his eyes. "She didn't do that to you. She played a tower; that's a defensive move."

"Since it poses a disadvantage to anyone who would attack her, technically she did it to all three of us," Lewolnn observed.

"But I'm building a hand that would have been great against her defenses, right up until that card right there," Cariel moaned.

"I do what I can," Allabva shrugged, hoping her sudden discomfort at Jimlarnt's presence didn't show. She was sitting in a calmer corner of the room and had worked to find enough comfort in the relative quiet to appreciate the game, despite the present setting of the Three Wolves Mute. Jimlarnt's presence quickly began to erode any sense of peace she had cultivated.

Jimlarnt had a seat at a nearby table, where he joined what looked to be another game of Novulm Towers. Allabva tried again to ignore him, looking at the towers each player in front of her had played, then back at her hand. She had one Trebuchet—a good card—but it wasn't enough to launch an attack on anyone. She also had two Infantry Company cards, which she would have to hold onto so she could play them when she made a move. But first she would need more...

Jimlarnt leaned forward to whisper something to one of the others at his table. The recipient of his secret message nodded, and pointedly did not look in Allabva's direction.

"Ha!" Lewolnn gloated, laying down a Drought card in front of Allabva. "If you can't shake this in two turns, you have to put any infantry you have out in front of your towers, then they're mine."

Allabva shook her head, trying a third time to get her attention away from Jimlarnt while his compatriot stood and moved to one of the more particularly rowdy sections of the room.

"No point," Cariel replied to Lewolnn, while laying a Wall card in front of his towers. "I'm building an impregnable fortress. Maybe you'll beat her, but I'll beat you. Your turn, new girl."

Allabva blinked, looking over her hand.

Jimlarnt said something to somebody else at his table, then stood. "Barkeep," he called, holding a hand in the air.

Allabva tried to decipher which card would be the best to play during this turn. She needed at least two more Trebuchets before she could have any real effect against her opponents, but what would she do to protect her Infantry Companies right now? It came to her as she shuffled through her hand. Something nagged her as she selected her Keep card and lay it on the table.

"You have a whole Keep?" Lewolnn complained. "I just wasted a turn playing that Drought card. No use if you have food stores on hand."

"I..." Allabva began.

Jimlarnt was still standing, longer than he should have been if he were truly just calling the waiter. He stepped closer to Allabva. No, he walked up right behind her.

"You're cheating!" Jimlarnt shouted at Allabva, snatching the cards from her hand.

"No, I'm not!" Allabva denied, turning and standing.

"Oh, really? Then what's this?"

Jimlarnt slammed Allabva's cards on the table face-up, showing her Infantry Companies and a few other relatively low-value cards that she had held a moment before, but also among them were a couple of additions.

"You had a War Chest?" Redeok exclaimed, scandalized. "You said you didn't know this game, and you're hiding a War Chest in your hand?"

"I didn't—I'm not—" Allabva wasn't sure what to say. She looked to all three of her opponents, looking for trust in their eyes.

Cariel looked confused and Lewolnn wore a blank expression, but Redeok pulled his lip up in a sneer.

"I knew it," he said. "You girls are always cheating."

Allabva blinked in confusion. "What makes you say that?"

"The cards are there on the table, little girl," Redeok said angrily.

"Excuse me?" Allabva winced. Redeok had used the same pejorative that Nillan Protfund had while Allabva was his captive on the road to Palf Glen. That was barely over a week past, but it seemed so long ago now. He couldn't have known, right? She felt her carefully constructed composure crack and her eyelid twitched involuntarily.

"Ha!" Redeok pointed triumphantly. "You see it come out. Her tell exposes the lie."

"No!" What was happening here? How did this card game suddenly evaporate into confrontation?

"I told you she was cheating," Jimlarnt said, stepping in toward Allabva and grabbing her by the wrist.

Cariel looked at Jimlarnt suspiciously. "We were having a friendly game before you showed up. Maybe those cards were yours." He reached down, grabbing the War Chest card. "It's not as worn as the rest of the deck!"

"Are you calling me a liar?" Jimlarnt challenged.

Cariel flinched. "I don't know—"

"Obviously Allab—" Jimlarnt stopped himself in the middle of saying her name, "—the little girl's cards aren't as worn as the others because they're not part of the deck. *She* brought them here."

"What did you—you know her." Cariel hadn't missed the slip.

"My silver, what's a guy gotta do around here to get even?" Jimlarnt muttered quietly, then with a, "Shut up," directed at Cariel, released Allabva's wrist and threw a punch at him. The blow landed on the young sailor's nose and threw him to the floor.

"Stop!" Allabva said, turning toward Jimlarnt, incensed by his audacity.

Cariel jumped up and launched himself toward Jimlarnt, who danced around Allabva and placed himself next to Redeok. When Cariel collided with Jimlarnt, he also ran into Redeok.

Redeok supported himself on the edge of the table to avoid falling down, then shoved Cariel from the side. "Don't worry, little girl," he shouted at Allabva, "I remember whose fault this really is!"

Lewolnn laughed at the spectacle, then turned to the room at large. Pointing at Allabva, he said, "We have a cheater over here, are you all witness?"

The room replied in the affirmative, while a few more men stepped closer in anticipation.

While Jimlarnt, Redeok, and Cariel fought to Allabva's left, Lewolnn leaned across the table and attempted to shove her, but she drew back out of reach.

A newcomer to the nascent brawl grabbed Allabva from behind, lifting her into the air and proclaiming, "I've gotcha!"

Thankful for the Shrongelin's bond, she reached up to the arms holding her in a bear hug and easily pried them apart, releasing the unknown man's grip and dropping to her feet.

"How did you—" she heard the man say while Jimlarnt barreled into her, knocking her off-balance.

Allabva rotated as she fell and caught herself on her hands, Jimlarnt's weight on her back. She stood and threw him off. "Stop it!" she repeated uselessly.

"Some kind of devil. She's freakishly strong!" the bear-hug man announced to the room. "Come on, let's get her!"

Now it seemed the entire crowd launched themselves at Allabva. She held them off while looking for Cariel. She found him on the floor, being pummeled by Redeok and Lewolnn. She reached in and pulled Redeok off of Cariel. Redeok threw a punch at Allabva's face, which she caught with her hand. She held Redeok's fist so he couldn't throw it again while she pulled Cariel to his feet.

"Get out of here!" she told Cariel, the entire clientele of the tavern having joined the brawl, unknowingly playing into Jimlarnt's petty vendetta.

"Not without you!" he shouted back over the din.

"Don't worry, I'm leaving!" She pushed him toward the door.

In the next instant, Cariel's eyes flashed open wide, whites on proud display as his gaze looked past her in alarm.

Allabva twisted and grabbed behind her, catching Jimlarnt's arm as he attempted to swing a knife into her back.

Anger colored the man's face as he futilely tried to force the knife closer to Allabva's chest while she still held his forearm in her hand.

"Why won't you leave me alone?" Allabva cried, holding back tears of persecuted frustration.

She couldn't let Jimlarnt keep harassing her like this. Setting her jaw and gritting her teeth against the thought of her action, she squeezed the man's arm with her Construct-bond-enhanced strength. She heard the bones crack and Jimlarnt cried out in pain.

"Witch!" he shouted in fury.

"Go! Now!" she yelled at Cariel.

"But it's my deck of cards!"

"Now!"

Cariel turned to go, but two men grabbed him, while a third lunged at Allabva. She stopped her assailant in his tracks, shoving him back and sending him sailing halfway across the room. Jumping forward, she pulled the men off of Cariel, then shoved him stumbling out the door.

With a breath of relief, Allabva reached the door herself and stepped out into the night sea air.

"No you don't," Redeok's voice came from behind as he lay a hand on Allabva's shoulder.

She turned, grabbing his wrist and removing his hand while stepping back into the tavern. "You'll leave us alone now," she instructed. "Look at that man." She pointed at Jimlarnt, who was cradling his arm. "I did that. I didn't want to, but I had to. Now get back inside and leave us alone."

Redeok looked at Jimlarnt, then glowered at Allabva as she turned back around and exited the Three Wolves Mute. The rest of the people in the tavern seemed to be caught up in the moment of human knots temporarily decorating the room with occasional accents of red.

"Whud was dat?" Cariel asked through a plugged and swelling nose.

"What was what?" Allabva echoed, avoiding.

"Everyding you did in dere. Whud was dat?"

Allabva looked at Cariel, inhaled deeply, and exhaled sharply through her nose. "Nothing." She began walking away from the tavern. The direction didn't matter. Just...away.

Cariel followed. "Did you really cheat at the game?"

"No. Do you believe me?"

"I don' know yed." Cariel looked at her with a sidelong glance. "I thoud everding was fine undil dat man showed your hand wid de War Chest. I still could have believed dat he was lying. But den...you did all dat. You fought off multiple grown men at once."

"Maybe I did," Allabva conceded curtly.

"So, what are you?"

"Just like I told you at the beginning. I'm a girl trying to get to know this city."

"Well, you cerdanly got do know de Dree Wolves!" Cariel laughed.

Allabva couldn't help but laugh in return. "I guess I did."

"So now what?"

Allabva glanced at her new friend. "Now I go about my way and you go about yours."

"I s'pose so," Cariel considered. "But dell me where you're from. I want do make sure not do tangle with your kind!"

Allabva laughed, supposing there was no harm in telling him. "I'm from a place called the Cleft—it's out west, past the mountains and the plains, and into some other mountains. But nobody else has this strength." She looked at her hands, opening and closing them.

"Den how did you get it?"

"Honestly?" That brawl was sure to get word around. Combined with her jump to save the little boy this morning and the grain-running, there was no hiding it now. And it was probably for the better to let the rumors begin to flow, just to get the word out. The world needed to prepare itself, and it couldn't do that if nobody knew there was anything to prepare for. "A Nomord gave it to me."

Cariel looked at her sharply, then his expression softened. "I didden know dey gould do dat. And I diden actually expect an open answer." He dabbed his nose with the inside of his shirt cuff.

"They don't, normally," Allabva replied. "But they will again soon, for a lot of people."

"Why?"

Allabva let several moments pass in silence as they walked, looking out over the now-visible harbor.

"Why will de Nomord give people strength?" Cariel asked again.

"Because there's trouble coming. A battle to fight."

"Against whom?" Cariel puzzled. "There's nobody attacking us." He still held his nose, but he'd quickly overcome the temporary speech impediment caused by the punch he caught.

"Ah, but there is." Allabva's brow furrowed. "Slowly right now. There's an influence that's sowing dissent among people. Have you heard of the Disaffected?"

"Oh. They're going to attack?"

"Mmm. I'm not sure," Allabva mused. "But their leader will, and she's got the Nomord scared for the whole world."

Cariel stopped in his tracks.

Allabva stopped a few steps ahead of him, turning back around to face him.

Cariel contorted his face into consternation. "The Nightshade Unicorn is a female? After all those stories?" Then his expression shifted into acceptance. "It makes sense. The Nomord are all female, after all."

"Actually, no, he's a male. And he's one of the good guys."

Cariel released a laugh. "You expect me to believe—" He saw Allabva's serious expression. "Oh. I suppose so. Wait, how many Nomord have you met?"

"In my life, up close enough to touch? I don't know. Several?"

"You said 'close enough,' but I know they never let you touch them."

"Almost true. I touched one when I was a girl, and recently, two more, including the Nightshade."

"You're making this up."

"No, it's true," Allabva said simply. "And you'll know it soon enough."

"I guess I'll have to take your word for it right now, because if I don't you'll beat me up," Cariel joked.

"Wrong again," she countered. "If you don't attack me or others, I'll leave you alone."

"I know, I was just saying—"

"Hey. I need to get going. Can you keep a secret?" Allabva reached into her pocket and put her hand around the brooch.

"Yes," Cariel replied.

"I'll tell you where to meet me again if you'll keep it to yourself. Will you do that?"

"Yes," he answered.

"Good. If you want to help prepare for this battle, it's just getting started. You can see me around tenth strike at the Coughing Badger tomorrow. For now, I've got to run."

"Alright," Cariel said. "Be safe. Hmm. I guess you will, won't you?"

"You as well. You might want to avoid the Three Wolves Mute yourself for a time. Take care."

Checking her map of the city and mentally charting a route to her next destination, Allabva jogged off into the night.

Chapter 27

Home Away From Home

Allabva located Walrus's house on Mulch Street as he had described it. Reaching up, she rapped on the door smartly. She could hear the rumble of voices within and there was light in the window. The door opened soon, and Walrus stood before her.

"Come in, come in," he said, stepping back and welcoming her through a small entry hall and into their dining area.

Tank waited there, as well as a woman whom Allabva assumed to be Walrus's wife.

"Panli," Walrus said, "this is the girl we told you about, Allabva Companion."

"Pleased to meet you, Allabva." Panli reached out, offering her hand for Allabva to shake. "Just don't squash it, please," Panli joked as Allabva took her hand and shook gently.

Allabva smiled awkwardly.

"So," Panli said, "I understand you're here from the west, and you have some kind of important mission?" she asked.

"Yes," Allabva nodded.

"Why don't you tell us all about it?" Panli asked. "Walrus and Tank here have gotten me quite intrigued."

"Of course," Allabva said.

"Oh, and dinner's in the oven," Panli interjected before Allabva could begin.

Allabva smiled. "That's not necessary—"

"What?" Walrus scoffed. "Not necessary? I told you to come hungry. I told you we would show you the most delicious pasta. Do you have no room for pasta?"

Allabva laughed. "Well, I ate light before, so I could eat something."

"Yes, and you will," Walrus insisted firmly.

Panli laughed and slapped her husband lightly on the shoulder. "Keep it down," she said. "You don't want to wake the kids."

"Yes, you are correct." Walrus blinked, smiling back at his wife good-naturedly. "Alright. Allabva, our companion here, has strength from a Nomord, and she says there is something coming. Please tell us more now," he invited.

Allabva did so, beginning with how the Forerunner came to her on the canyon trail while she gathered rosemary with her brother, Mellier. She told them how he then came back and whisked her away in the wee hours. She explained what she knew about the Construct and the impending escape of Sacalai.

Then she told them how she traveled to meet the Shrongelin, who, Hronomon had explained, was entrusted with a special job. And then how Allabva had been shocked to learn that the Shrongelin and the Nightshade Unicorn were one and the same.

Allabva told them about how she traveled with the Nightshade to come to Tallensworth. She left out Lamtor and his brooch—there was no need to complicate this exposition with that.

"Then what are you here in the city to do?" Panli asked.

"I think we can help with whatever it is, within reason," Walrus said. "But please, Allabva, do tell us exactly what your plan is."

"Well," Allabva said, "I need to meet with the overduke."

"Naturally," Walrus said with a hint of sarcasm.

Tank joined in. "No worries; we'll just get you on his calendar—"

"What do you need to meet with the overduke about?" Panli asked.

"Well, kind of everything," Allabva answered. "We need to get things ready. We need to arm the people and ensure that we are prepared for Sacalai's assault. So I need to see the leader of the city—well, the whole High Dominion, and that's just to get the campaign started.

"We're on a tour to visit several nations and gather support and troops to face Sacalai at Amonfweer. Hronomon is doing the same to the west, and we are going to meet up with him again in Cylgiana. After we meet there, we will campaign east and then finally north to meet her in some kind of battle."

Panli asked incredulously, "You? You're barely a woman."

"I know," Allabva breathed. "Don't I know it? But I guess the Nomord doesn't care so much about that. Hronomon said that for some reason I was the right match to be the Shrongelin's companion, so that he can lock Sacalai back up."

"Do you even know how to do that?"

"No," Allabva shrugged. "I'll have to learn that later."

"So let us see how we can help you," Tank said.

Allabva spread her hands. "I'm open to ideas."

"You are here representing Nomord, are you not?" Tank asked.

"Yes," Allabva confirmed, wondering where this was going.

"Have you heard of Southmarch?"

"Yes," Allabva said, now intrigued. "What does that have to do with Nomord? I thought it was more anti-horse, if anything."

"That is true," Walrus said. "But the Tunglins, when they attacked on horseback, fancied themselves as similar to the Nomord, for they rode on four hooves and carried a sharp stick, like the Nomord horn."

"What's the connection?" Allabva asked.

"We, the people of Tallensworth, never viewed them as anything like the Nomord. They were invaders. While we disrespect the invading enemy, we scorn their aspirations to be like the noble creatures, and we honor the true creatures themselves."

"Yes, but if I show up with the Nightshade Unicorn of all Nomord, there will be chaos," Allabva countered.

"You're probably right," Walrus said, "if it is out of the blue."

"Well, perhaps she could win some of the contests," Panli suggested.

"What contests?" Allabva asked.

"The Avaunt, the Southmarch itself," Panli answered. "It means 'go away.' It's a run—a foot race. You know, it's all symbolic. You chase several men on horseback until you reach the Sunset Gate—the southwestern gate—and you chase them right out of the city. You grab a token to prove that you made it there, and you run back. The first one back gets a lot of attention and will get the opportunity to at least greet the overduke himself."

Allabva made the connection. "I see," she said. "So while I don't know if my request is going to result in anything, I can win this race to at least get close."

"It's not a bad idea," Walrus said. "Although it will probably bring suspicion as well when you beat all the men."

"I'll deal with that suspicion when it comes," Allabva said. She'd begun to understand there was no way to completely prevent it.

"Hey," Tank said to Walrus, "don't you know the chief magistrate of the northern quarter?"

Walrus's eyebrow went up. "I hadn't thought of him. How do you think?"

"Perhaps just an introduction," Tank said. "Or he could make it more likely for Allabva to get that audience she has already requested."

"I see," Walrus said.

"Oh, you have to introduce them, my sweet seabird," Panli said to Walrus. "At least take Allabva to meet Magistrate Spalgen, and then we'll go from there."

"Yes, yes," Walrus said. "But Magistrate Spalgen is a very practical man. I do not believe he will take any action based on stories alone."

"What if he met the Nightshade and saw him with his own eyes?" Allabva suggested.

Walrus's other eyebrow went up to join the first. "We can do that," Allabva told him. "I'll meet with him tomorrow at third bell strike, outside the Tallen Gate."

"Oh," Walrus thought. "The Tallen Gate. As it turns out, I have some business on that side of the city that I could take care of tomorrow morning. I will go with you."

"And you?" Allabva asked Tank.

"I cannot, Miss Companion," Tank said, dismayed. "I have a project ending soon. I understand that this whole thing with the Nightshade is of utter importance, but I have to keep up with my own life in the meantime, don't I?"

Allabva nodded, understanding. "That's fine. We can take you another day."

"Is there..." Allabva trailed off.

"Yes?" Panli asked.

"Is there a pot for winning the Avaunt?" Allabva probed.

"There is," Panli answered. "Twenty-five gold hafender."

Now Allabva's eyebrows went up. "That would be really helpful to have, even if I don't get to talk to the overduke."

"Of course," Walrus said.

"Walrus," Allabva said, "if you take me to meet the magistrate, I can share some of the winnings."

"Oh no," Walrus demurred. "That is not necessary."

"It may be that I will need other help in the future," Allabva said. "The more you help, the less of your own work you accomplish. Some of that gold can feed your family while you earn less from your craft."

"I suppose it could," Walrus agreed.

"And the same goes for you, Tank," she hastily added.

"As I said, I suppose it could," Walrus said. "But I do not see that it is necessary. Not at this time."

"Very well," Allabva said. "Where should we start? We should start meeting in public, I think."

"Already?" Tank asked. "Before you meet the overduke?"

"Yes," Allabva said. "I'm beginning to realize that the more I get people talking about me, the better chance I have of succeeding in my mission."

"As long as you don't tell them the wrong thing," Tank countered. "Maybe do mention the Nomord and the Guardian, but do not call him the Nightshade Unicorn."

"Right," Allabva agreed. "I have to practice. I have to exercise caution with that."

Panli suddenly leapt from her seat. "The pasta! I'll be right back."

Tank, Walrus, and Allabva laughed at Panli's manner of jumping up to go to the kitchen. Soon, she came back, and they ate together. Allabva left that night feeling quite full and with greater optimism than she had felt since coming to this city.

Chapter 28

Catching Up With the Nightshade 2

Allabva didn't wake up with that same optimism. Instead, she woke up feeling something of a sense of despair. It took great effort to climb out of bed. What was going on here? She wondered what was going on. She realized she didn't have her strength. Why?

She set about taking care of herself, getting dressed. She walked downstairs to ask for a basin of water, then brought it back. Did the stairs really take this much effort to ascend? She washed her face and her hands, feeling so weak. She understood that she was simply at normal human strength. She could bear that, as it was simply true normalcy, but it came with this feeling that nothing she could do would amount to any good in the fight with Sacalai.

Allabva checked the sun. There wasn't enough time to meet the Nightshade, even if she had to walk at normal pace the whole way. There was more than enough time, so she went back downstairs and requested the simple breakfast that had been offered when she checked in. As she finished her last bite, thinking she might vomit it back out due to this nagging sense of inevitable failure, she felt her hands grow strong again and the despair subsided.

The strength was my own, she thought. *But that emotion must be from Sacalai.* This bond had some amazing advantages with her strength and stamina, but Allabva had to admit she didn't enjoy sharing some of the spillover of Sacalai's attacks. At the door of a prison, she would have to ask the Nightshade about these moments when the bond seemed to flicker.

Shaking it off, Allabva set out into the city. She jogged to Walrus's house, resisting the urge to run faster than humanly possible. It called to her, but she didn't want to draw attention that way right now. As it was, she got a few looks in the street. She wasn't sure if it was because she was an outsider, or if they had heard rumors or seen her running with the grain the day before. When she met up with Walrus, they set out together, walking to the Tallen Gate. They stepped outside the city a few moments after third strike sounded.

"We'll walk a little way up the road here," Allabva told Walrus. "We're not trying to cause a ruckus in the city yet, so he stays out of view of the gate."

"A wise idea," Walrus nodded.

They walked until they got to the first bend in the road. The Nightshade stepped out from some brush and trees where he had been waiting.

"I see we have a newcomer," he said directly.

"Yes, Shrongelin," Allabva said. "This is Walrus. He and another friend, called Tank, helped me out."

"What help do you need?" the Nightshade commented.

"These are kind men, and capable." Allabva kept her voice level. "They want to help our cause."

The Nightshade looked at him, appraising only. "Very well. I suppose it is nice to meet you or something."

Walrus smirked. "Allabva warned me you didn't have the best temperament."

"It's true," the Nightshade spat simply. "I'm sorry, but my job wears on me."

"And thank you so much for it," Walrus said, tipping his head to the Nomord. He looked nervously to Allabva, with an expression that asked, *Is this fine? Is this normal?*

Allabva nodded reassuringly.

"Did you get anything else done yesterday?" the Nightshade said to Allabva, now that the introduction was done. Walrus could wait until he was relevant in the conversation. Allabva took a breath to augment her patience.

"I got to know the city some more."

"Yes, but what did you do to bring us closer to our goal?" the Nightshade interrupted.

"Hold on," Allabva said. "I'm getting there." She took another breath. "Look, we'll have more success if we exchange detailed information to update each other, don't you think?" she asked rhetorically. "I was trying to get to know the city better so that I can understand how to approach the problem. We've made a lot of progress since yesterday morning."

"Like what?" the Nightshade asked.

"You'd be happy to hear that, although I didn't do it to show off, I saved a child's life yesterday morning. Doing so required jumping from the ground up to a balcony in front of several people."

"Good," the Nightshade said encouragingly. "You must be noticed."

"How does this kind of spectacle help your cause?" Walrus asked.

"The more she's talked about, the more the overduke will want to meet her, yes?" the Nightshade said gruffly. "It's a simple idea."

"You are right," Walrus agreed politely. "I was just not aware of it."

"What else?" the Nightshade prompted Allabva, turning abruptly away from Walrus.

"Well," Allabva said, "I helped a gentleman deliver his grain."

The Nightshade had been leaning down to take a bite of grass, but he whipped his head up in alarm. "What kind of a waste of time is that?" he asked.

What has him on edge? Allabva wondered.

"Look," she countered. "You said to use my daylight hours any way I wanted to. This man needed help; his son has an injury, so he can't deliver his grain like normal. The father was stuck at his stall in the market to avoid facing fines. He needed to deliver his grain, and I was there and able to help, so I did."

"If you must," the Nightshade conceded begrudgingly, rolling his eyes and bending down to take another bite.

Allabva took yet another deep breath and mentally counted to five. "You'll be happy to know that I *ran* through the city with two large sacks of grain on my shoulders to make multiple deliveries."

Now the Nightshade brought his face up with a slightly more pleasant expression. "Alright. That's good, I suppose. I must impress upon you the urgency of our mission, and I can't accomplish as much out here. I need to get into the city, but I know it's not time yet. Do you understand my frustration?"

"Yes," Allabva said. "Speaking of you out here, what's this I hear about you running around outside the city in full view of people?"

"Ha!" The Nightshade laughed. "I was bored."

"You were bored?" Allabva repeated.

The Nightshade appeared to get serious now. "Not just that. If you must know, I am doing what I can out here, even though it is more urgent that I get inside."

"What can you do out here?" Walrus asked, curious.

Nightshade looked at Allabva expectantly. "You haven't told him much, then?"

"The Gha-Nomord have the power to influence the weather and minds," Allabva explained.

Walrus looked wary. "What are you doing with these powers?"

"Giving my Companion the best shot I can to be successful at her current task," the Nomord answered. "First, I'm standing by to prevent inclement weather while she's here. Second, I'm doing my best to keep the city receptive to her."

"You control the people?" The man appeared to be ready to run from the Shrongelin.

"No, he doesn't," Allabva answered.

"How do you know?"

"He can't do that. None of them can. It's about influence, not control. They can drop ideas or feelings, attempt to steer us. But we have our own freedom to make our choices."

"But that's just what he's told you. How do you know it's true?" Walrus was visibly unsettled by the idea of anyone wielding mental influence over another.

Allabva thought about the brooch in her pocket, but said nothing. While it might be possible to use it to convince Walrus that this was alright, it could have the opposite effect if he was concerned about mental or emotional influence in the first place.

"Do you remember what I told you at your house last night when Hronomon came to see me? With his power to see inside me and know my heart, it worked both ways, and I saw inside his. I know, without a doubt, that he is telling the truth about the Nightshade. What he knows about the Nightshade, I know I can believe. Aside from the fact that I can believe whatever Hronomon himself said in the first place."

"Alright," Walrus said, seeming to calm down just a little bit.

"As for the power they possess," Allabva said, "how is it so different from giving somebody a hug or making a rude gesture? You're suggesting thoughts and emotions to other people by those means, aren't you?"

"I suppose," Walrus conceded.

"Gha-Nomord simply have the ability to do that without needing the physical or verbal interaction."

"Very perceptive," the Nightshade said. "You stated that very well." This was another rare moment where the Nightshade appeared to be giving Allabva a compliment.

"Is that what you were doing then?" Allabva asked the Nightshade. "You were trying to keep people calm?"

"More like keeping people open to new thoughts," the Nightshade said.

"Good," Allabva said. "Because the man who saw you yesterday didn't seem very calm about it." She thought a moment. "I take that back. He was calm but unsettled. He was concerned about what it meant and what you might do."

"You spoke with this man directly?"

"Briefly, yes," Allabva confirmed.

"Well, there it is," the Nightshade said. "I am walking around in full view outside the city, beyond direct view of the city itself. Just as the more attention you garner, the more likely the overduke will want to speak with you, the same goes for me. The more rumors I begin by my mere presence, the more the overduke will be curious to settle any rumor he can. That includes you. Surely, he is already receiving reports of what you did yesterday. So let's keep it up."

Allabva thought for a moment. "Nightshade—"

"I would prefer Shrongelin or Guardian," the Nightshade interrupted.

Allabva grinned mischievously. "Alright, Nighty."

The Nightshade blew air out through his lips and shook his mane. Allabva ignored the reaction and continued. "Nighty, I was talking to Walrus here, his wife, and another man named Tank last night. There is a festival coming up, week after next," she said.

"Week after next?" the Nightshade asked. "That's too much time."

"Hear me out," Allabva said. "The Southmarch Festival involves a contest I should be able to win easily, and that will get me an introduction to the overduke, if nothing else. Also, Walrus knows the high magistrate over the northern quarter of the city. He can introduce me to him, and I can ask the magistrate if he can accelerate my request."

Now the Nightshade turned his head to the side and inspected Allabva through one eye. "Why didn't you lead with this? You spoke of helping a man with his grain. You did good work yesterday. You should have told me that first."

"What does it matter?" Allabva asked. "I'm going to do the work my way, the best I can make sense of it."

Walrus grinned. "There's something else you may not know, Nighty."

The Nightshade growled. "You may call me the Shrongelin, or you may speak it in your language as Guardian," he said firmly to the man, "though I allow more leeway to my Companion. I do not require these respects from you for my own sake, but that you may internalize this respect and share it with others. Thus, others may come to know of the importance of the Construct and how they can help us stop Sacalai."

Walrus tipped his head to the Nomord. "Very well, Guardian." He looked at Allabva and then continued, "What she hasn't told you, because perhaps she doesn't see the relevance, and she does not know that I know, is that there are indeed many rumors going through the city about her."

Allabva looked at Walrus, surprised.

"She will not tell you that she walked out of the worst brawl in one of the toughest taverns in the city last night—untouched. And every man there knew that she could have owned the place if she wanted to."

The Nightshade nodded. "Good," he said. "Let the overduke ignore that rumor," he said sarcastically.

"Nightshade," Allabva said.

"Yes, Companion?" he asked.

"Walrus and Tank are on board, as is a friend I made last night named Cariel. They will help us as we need it. But I feel strongly that we should aim to prepare for this festival. When I win the Avaunt, the overduke will have to invite me in."

The Nightshade pursed his lips, still nodding. "I was hoping to be on a boat out of here in a week's time," he said. "But I have to admit, though waiting for the festival does not necessarily put us behind schedule... Very well, it is planned. Now, how do we prepare, and what do we do in the meanwhile?"

Allabva looked at the Nightshade. "I think probably, we keep doing what you were doing yesterday and what I did the last two days in town. Our presence will get noticed more and more." A thought occurred to her. "Walrus, what about the Ladies' Council? Could working with them help speed this along?"

"Impossible to say," the stonemason answered. "You should have asked Panli that last night. She's not on the Ladies' Council, but she would know better than I do."

"I suppose regardless, there couldn't be any harm trying."

"Shall we begin visiting the outlying towns today?" Nightshade suggested.

Allabva hesitated. "I don't think so. There are a couple of people I should meet up with first."

"Nor do I," Walrus concurred, "unless you can do both that, and continue your work of the last two days concurrently."

Allabva thought about the continuity of personal interaction she had begun in the city. She had told Cariel the night before that he could find her at the Coughing Badger, and she intended to meet Master Jhalla again. Add onto that, talking to women wearing the brown shawl to tap that network.

"Let us meet here tomorrow, then," the Nightshade said, turning away.

"Wait," Allabva stopped him. "Walrus, can you give us a moment?"

The stonemason lifted an eyebrow, curious, but consented. "Of course. I will wait for you at the gate." He turned and walked off.

"Shrongelin," Allabva addressed the Nomord more formally, "I have had moments where my bond-enhanced strength is not there. My body was back to normal, I think, but I feel extremely...discouraged in those moments. What does it mean?"

The Nightshade nodded. "This can happen sometimes. When has it occurred?"

"Early in the morning, both times."

The Shrongelin looked at Allabva with a knowing gaze. "It is normal."

"Why didn't it happen until we reached Tallensworth?"

"You said you feel discouraged when it happens?"

He didn't answer my question, Allabva thought. "Yes."

"You share the bond. Unfortunately, that means that sometimes you feel the result of Sacalai's attacks. Expect it to happen again."

"But what do I do about it?"

"Don't get in any fights when it happens."

Allabva stared at the black Nomord for stating the obvious. "Will it happen at random times of day, or always in the morning?"

The Nightshade paused a moment.

"No," he answered, "it shouldn't occur randomly. For now, I would suggest it will probably only happen in the morning as it has already."

That was a relief, but Allabva still wondered what he was hiding.

"I will see you tomorrow," the Nomord said. Then he...grinned? "Be ready to have some fun."

Allabva rolled her eyes. She expected some wild reactions and awkward encounters over the next several days, not what she would consider fun.

Interlude III

CHAPTER 29

FORMALITIES AND LEGENDS

"Y ou've got it?" Ruldern asked Delgan with a smile.

Delgan nodded, trying to keep still. He held his arms up, grasping a pair of long-handled tongs, which allowed him to dangle a chain in the air. He had just finished helping Master Ntoffel forge and link it together, hammering each loop into shape as it hooked into the previous one. Now he resisted the pull of the chain's weight against his arms with difficulty, squinting defensively against its hot glow as it radiated the heat of the fire he had just pulled it from.

Ruldern gave a knowing grin at Delgan's effort.

"It's heavy, isn't it?"

"Yes!" Delgan squeaked.

"It's quite hot to stand so close to it, isn't it?"

"Uh-huh." The blacksmith apprentice could hardly find the strength to say anything right now.

"Hmm. I suppose that's not surprising," Ruldern said, seemingly in no hurry to let Delgan drop the chain. "After all, we had it in the fire for a good while, and we pumped the bellows enough to make it, frankly, hotter than it really needed to be."

Delgan grunted, his only reply to the master's musings.

"And...quench it!"

Delgan opened the tongs, allowing the chain to drop into a bucket of water on the floor of the smithy.

Clouds of steam instantly billowed up from the bucket, accompanied by a fierce hissing sound.

Delgan backed off, waving a hand in front of his face to clear the air, as Ruldern laughed good-naturedly.

"What did I tell you, eh? You'll get stronger, am I right?"

"I guess so," Delgan agreed, now able to smile back.

"And we'll get you used to the heat of the forge, too."

Delgan simply wiped his brow and flicked the gallons of sweat away.

"So, you're ready to hit the road tomorrow?" Ruldern asked.

Delgan nodded. "All packed."

"Good," the blacksmith said. "I'm glad to hear it. You have a horse to ride?"

"Yes," Delgan answered. "You told me to make sure I had a mount to go on horseback—"

"Because we can, and because we need to," the blacksmith interrupted. "I'm bringing tools with me that would make it somewhat difficult to walk all the way there."

"I understand," Delgan said. "And I have my mount, Blackberry."

"So you're all set. Good, good," Ruldern said. "I want to make sure you don't have any loose ends when we leave tomorrow morning."

"Loose ends?" Delgan wondered. Where was Ruldern going with this?

"Your mother knows she has one mouth less to fix breakfast and dinner for until you're back?"

"Of course," Delgan laughed.

"Good, so you talked to your parents. There's nobody else you might want to talk to?" Ruldern asked, probing with his eyes.

Not sure what to respond, Delgan reached the tongs into the water and grabbed the chain, pulling it out and placing it on the workbench beside him.

"Delgan," Ruldern said, posing as though he was waiting for an answer from his apprentice.

"Yes, Master Ruldern?" Delgan asked.

Ruldern cracked a smile. "I told you not to be so formal with me in private," he laughed, pointing a finger at Delgan's face. "Call me 'Master' in public when it's necessary for appearance, and decorum, and all that. But here in the workshop, we're all about business and getting things done."

Ruldern's expression changed as he tentatively opened a new topic with Delgan. "Speaking of being familiar with people, I know you have a thing for that Roalke girl, Allabva. I also know she's been gone the last two weeks, and nobody seems to know why."

Master Ruldern," Delgan started, caught off-guard, then correcting himself, continued, "Ruldern, I don't know what—"

"Go over there, Delgan, and talk to her mother this evening, just in case Allabva comes back while we're out of town. Let her mother know what's going on with you. I'll wrap up here. You go ahead and get out of here, and tomorrow we'll head up to Norl. Maybe we'll get to see some of that odd Nomord behavior while we're there."

Delgan's jaw worked, opening and closing his mouth, unsure what to say. "Wait, what did you just say?"

"Apparently the Nomord have been talking to people in Norl. I heard some rumors about it, anyway."

Allabva said a Nomord was looking at her during Green-stone Observance, Delgan thought. *What did it mean?*

"Go on," Ruldern said. "Get out of my shop before I call the dogs," he added with a grin. He didn't have any dogs.

"Uh, thank you, sir," Delgan said.

Delgan made his way to the Roalke orchard on unsure feet. True, he wanted to go there, but if he went, he wanted to get more answers this time. But would he? What would Mistress Roalke say today? Would she tell him anything else, or would she be just as tight-lipped as before?

But as Delgan walked, he realized the wisdom in his master's suggestion. Delgan couldn't do anything about what Allabva was up to. Perhaps he could convince her mother to tell him more, but he couldn't control that. All he could control was himself. And all he could do right now was talk with the orchard's keeper and leave a message with her in case Allabva came back.

He arrived at the orchard homestead presently and knocked on the door.

"Coming!" an animated young voice called from inside.

One moment later, Mellier opened the door and looked up at Delgan.

"Allabva is still not here," Mellier said and then started to close the door.

"Wait," Delgan said. "I know that—well, I didn't know she wasn't here, but I did assume."

"You are right," Mellier said. "She's not here." He started to close the door again. Delgan thought he saw something shifty in the young boy's eye.

"Hold on," Delgan said, holding the door open with his hand. "Can I talk to your mother?"

"I suppose so," Mellier said, holding something behind his back. "She's out in the apple trees right now, working."

"That makes sense," Delgan said. "And does she know you've paid a visit to the cookie jar?"

Mellier's jaw dropped. "How did you—no, she doesn't know."

"Well, why don't we go talk to her?" Delgan said. "You and me both."

"OK," Mellier said with a sullen air. "Come on."

Mellier opened the door wide, and Delgan stepped inside. The young boy walked to the kitchen and returned his pastry to the ceramic jar he'd removed it from.

After that, Delgan and Mellier walked out to the orchard behind the house.

They found Madam Roalke, as Mellier had said, working among the apple trees.

"Mother," Mellier called, "Delgan is here. I told him Allabva isn't here, but he still wants to talk to you instead."

The mother looked down from her work, trimming small branches off the trees, and smiled at her young son.

"Alright, Mellier."

Then she looked up at Delgan and gave a look of understanding.

"Madam," Delgan began, "I'm going with Master Ntoffel up to Norl for a smith's trade fair, and I just wanted to..."

He trailed off. What was he supposed to say?

"Of course," Madam Roalke said. "Why don't we go inside and talk?"

She slipped her shears into a pouch in the apron she wore.

"Thank you for your patience," she told Delgan, "It's probably time for you to know everything I do. Come on."

Madam Roalke led the way back inside, followed by Mellier. She reached for the ceramic jar and removed the cookie.

"Thank you for bringing Delgan to me," she said, handing him the cookie. "We need to talk now, if you'll run along and play."

"So you have no idea where she went?" Delgan asked.

"None," the hostess replied. She had told Delgan what happened in those wee hours when Allabva had to depart.

"Does Brelin know?"

"No," Faethlen answered, then said with a chuckle, "I think she is rather preoccupied pursuing Alvern now."

Delgan had to smile at that, also. He took a final sip of his mint tea, blinking and wondering what else he might comment or ask. Something occurred to him.

"Allabva left with a Nomord, and there have been rumors of odd Nomord activity in Norl. Maybe that's where she headed. Maybe I can find something out while I'm there."

"Maybe," Faethlen conceded.

"I suppose that if somebody kind were needed to save the world," Delgan said, "I'm not surprised that Allabva would be the one to do it."

"No, not at all," Faethlen Roalke agreed. "She's not perfect—nobody is—but she always did want the best for everybody. Now, I suppose she has a way of helping...well, everybody."

"Mhm," Delgan said.

"I'll admit," Delgan said, "Allabva's absence kind of threw me for a loop. On one hand, it makes it difficult for me to put my heart into my apprenticeship. But on the other hand, it makes me throw my back into it so I can stop thinking about all this uncertainty I've been feeling."

"You poor young man," Faethlen said sympathetically. "Does it help to know?"

"I think so," Delgan said, blinking, trying to decipher his own feelings. "At least I can stop worrying about whether it was something I said or did—or didn't say or do."

Faethlen laughed. "New courtships can be that way." Then, more sadly she said, "So can long marriages. My husband's been gone for some years. And, well, it's most likely that he drowned in the depths of the sea. I truly don't know what became of him. I can say," she said, staring into nothing and searching for her words, "that I feel confident that he wants—or wanted—to return. Our years together tell me that I can trust him. I trust him to love me and be true to me. What I can't trust is the wind and the waves...and pirates, and slavers, and great beasts of the deep."

She paused, taking a breath, and straightening out her face, which had become twisted in her worry.

"But for a time, I was preoccupied, as you are."

"What do you mean?" Delgan asked.

"I wondered for a time if he chose to stay away, if he had decided to no longer call this his home." Faethlen shook her head. "I never believed that thought, but it was there, nagging me."

Then she seemed to wake up.

"Delgan, you and Allabva still need to really get to know each other, but I can tell you this: you are not the reason she's gone. Do not worry yourself about that."

"Of course," Delgan said, nodding. Then, ruefully, he said, "But I can still worry about her finding somebody else."

"I don't think so," Faethlen said. "That Forerunner gave me the impression she'll be pretty busy. If I were you, I would keep my worries to the same thing that I worry about—that is, her safety."

"I can think of another thing," Delgan said.

His hostess looked up from her cup, expecting an explanation. Delgan provided it.

"The whole world should be worried about her success."

Eretuquein, the Forerunner, galloped into Parfall just as the shadows of the afternoon began to lengthen more quickly, then dropped his pace to a trot. Half of Parfall had resulted fairly well, he felt.

"Audience on the governor's lawn," he called as he trotted. "Audience on the governor's lawn, immediately!"

Parfall had been an experience similar to what he imagined his predecessors as Forerunners had been through.

"Audience on the governor's lawn," he kept calling, trotting among buildings of wood, mostly painted in oranges and browns.

In Parfall, he had made himself well seen before the public at large, as well as visiting a place of learning in an attempt to bring the reality of his cause into the minds of the people. He had seen people who were ready to welcome him and to support his cause, trusting in the inherent benevolence of any Nomord, but there were others who looked at him suspiciously and whispered in dark corners and alleys.

Eretuquein understood that this was a relatively muted and benign response, coming from those who would ultimately oppose the Nomord. He chalked this up to Sacalai's influence being temporarily weakened by her defeat on the Summit Above the Aspens. It would grow, and people would become outright violent against the Nomord with no provocation.

"Audience on the governor's lawn," he called again.

Parfall, on the other hand, was going to be something new and different. The guides had come to Mascaldinig by chance, and Eretuquein and the Shrongelin weren't going to pass up the opportunity to gain an advantage against Sacalai. Their knowledge informed the Nomord of governments in the world, which the Guardian and the Forerunner would have no way of knowing about before sallying forth to find the companion.

So now, rather than campaigning primarily to the masses in all cities he came to—with the occasional emphasis given to government leaders who might sway more people in their favor—Eretuquein was targeting the governor of Parfall. He didn't know whether it would make any difference for the public response in Parfall and the region roundabout, but this was still only one region of several within an empire.

"Audience on the governor's lawn," Eretuquein continued to cry.

He stopped in front of a baker's shop, where it appeared the baker was closing up for the day.

"Sir, madam," Eretuquein said to the bakers. "Can you point me toward the governor's palace?"

The baker couple looked up at Eretuquein as though he were rabid, and they thought he might rear up and trample them.

Eretuquein stood still and waited for an answer. Slowly, they each raised an arm to point.

"Thank you," Eretuquein said, then trotted in the direction they had signaled.

"Audience on the governor's lawn immediately," he called at the top of his voice.

Window shutters opened as he traveled through the streets. People could hear the difference between a human voice and the voice of one of the Nomord, so the sound of his voice would naturally immediately attract the attention of anyone who heard it.

"Audience on the governor's lawn."

He didn't stop repeating himself until he came to the palace. None of the Guides had been to this city, so Eretuquein had no description to match when he looked for the palace. But it was obviously a palace, with both size and styling setting it apart from the rest of the structures in the city.

Eretuquein took a small moment to wonder that the city had no wall. Many towns had no walls, such as the Companion's hometown in the Valley of the Five Moons and Parfall Glen. But Parfall was on the large side for a city to lack a wall.

Eretuquein supposed that it was not because its residents considered it to be unimportant and not worth protecting. Instead, he assumed that it was because of its location in the heart of Eslarna, where it likely had not faced any siege or invasion attempts for millennia—apart from when the Holbonins would have swarmed it easily. He wondered if the people of Parfall in those days wished they had built a wall.

Eretuquein came to a stop in front of the governor's palace. Then, considering all his shouting in the streets as he made his way here and wondering whether that might have caused concern, he lay in the grass on the lawn outside the wall surrounding the governor's palace.

Here he waited, resting his hooves and nibbling at the grass. He didn't have to wait long, as crowds of people showed up, having heard his calls.

As expected, people began to arrive, flooding in from the streets. As they approached, Eretuquein stood.

"Was that you talking?" a woman asked, followed by two girls who trailed in her shadow.

"It was I," Eretuquein answered.

"I told you the Nomo-Nomo can talk!" one of the girls said to the other.

"I always told you both that," the mother said. "But they don't normally run through the streets of the city shouting, nor do they tend to say the same thing over and over again."

She turned back to Eretuquein. "What does this mean? It means there is trouble in the world, no?"

"It should mean nothing," Eretuquein answered, "as the Nomord could always speak. But the fact that I am here right now, speaking to you at this moment, means there is trouble in the world."

"Why does it have a low voice like a man when all the Nomo-Nomo are girls?" the second girl asked.

"They're larger than people," her mother answered, "so their voices tend to be deeper than ours. But you're right. This one is male."

"Why is it a boy?" the second girl asked.

"Because I always have been," Eretuquein said.

"Why haven't I ever seen a Nomord stallion before?" a man asked.

"Because we've had to keep to ourselves," the Nomord answered.

"Why is that?" the man inquired.

"All will be made known soon," Eretuquein said. "For now, let the people gather. In the meantime, can you tell me how to request to speak with Governor Lonswil Esyll?"

"Well, normally you ring the bell, and you wait for the butler, and you make an appointment," the man said. "But I'm not sure how that works when one is four-legged..." he trailed off weakly.

"I'm sure somebody will be along," the woman said. "What with this crowd following us, they'll want to know the meaning of it."

"Good," Eretuquein said. "I wish to explain the meaning of it."

After several minutes, quite the crowd had gathered on the governor's lawn. A servant came to the gate.

"Can someone tell me what is going on out here?" the servant asked.

"I can do that," Eretuquein spoke.

The servant's eyes popped wide. He hadn't expected a Nomord to converse with him.

"I need audience with Governor Esyll of Parfall," Eretuquein said. "Immediately, or as early as can occur."

The servant looked deeply troubled to see a Nomord speaking to him in this manner, but he disappeared behind the wall. A few moments later, the great door at the front of the governor's palace opened, and the servant stepped out, announcing:

"Presenting His Honor, the Governor Esyll of Parfall."

Then, gesturing and bowing to one side, he stepped to one side and gestured, bowing toward the open doorway.

Governor Esyll stepped out and descended five of the ten steps leading up to the great door. He stood there tentatively, obviously wondering what sort of occasion this was. He spoke to Eretuquein.

"Fair Nomord," he said officially, "noblest of all creatures, what brings you to my humble steps today?"

"Thank you for deigning to speak with me," Eretuquein said. "I have urgent matters to discuss with you, and momentarily, I will request a private audience. But first, I will tell you what this is about generally, out here in front of everybody, that all may hear."

Now the governor seemed as troubled as his butler had been. Eretuquein imagined he'd interrupted the man's dinner. But at the moment, that didn't matter.

"Of course," the governor stuttered. "Please proceed, fair Nomord."

Eretuquein turned halfway back to the crowd and spoke, both to them and to the governor.

"My name is Eretuquein," he said loudly, "but you may call me Hronomon, the Forerunner. 'For who or what?' you ask. "I shall tell you. I come to make the way for the Guardian. For the Shrongelin."

An audible gasp passed through the crowd. Eretuquein had supposed—hoped—he would get this kind of response. He had their attention.

He told them of the soon-to-be-free Sacalai, which event promised to wreak havoc on the world. He told them of the Nomord's war with the evil being and of the construct created to imprison her.

He told them they would have to make the choice: to join forces with the Nomord to protect their homes and their families, or to take part in their destruction this side of three months hence.

He finished his speech.

"The Shrongelin will travel from west to east to meet Sacalai in the north. Answer his call and protect all that is good. As Sacalai's strength grows, you will feel her influence. You will feel her lies trying to pull you. Stand stalwart and follow the guardian's banner.

"I am Eretuquein. I am the Forerunner. Remember, and be prepared."

Now Eretuquein stopped and turned to look in the gate, where the governor sat on his front steps with his adolescent son, who had come to join him.

Now Eretuquein addressed the governor.

"Governor Esyll, I kindly request that private audience."

The governor looked over his shoulder and waved. A servant came forward to open the gate.

Governor Esyll stood, bowing his head.

"Great Nomord, please enter and accept my humblest hospitality."

The gate was opened, and the Nomord entered.

"He's lying!"

A shout rose from the crowd. Eretuquein had wondered when that would start, and he knew that more would surely come. Looking over his shoulder, he called back, "Be prepared, and do not heed the influence of Sacalai."

At least for the moment, it was only words, and the owner of the voice was using no blade against Eretuquein or against other humans.

Eretuquein followed the governor up and through the great door inside.

In the entry hall, the governor turned and sat on a couch that Eretuquein assumed was placed there for visitors who would normally await audience with the governor. The governor's son ascended halfway up one of twin staircases that flanked the entry hall, then sat to observe his father's parley with the Nomord.

"What do I call you?" Governor Esyll said to Eretuquein, "Forerunner, Hronomon, Or Eretuquein?"

Eretuquein lowered his head, acknowledging the point of confusion.

"Until Sacalai imprisoned once again, what is of most importance is stopping her. I would have you call me Hronomon, or Forerunner, in public. But as I recently had a good friend remind me that I matter individually, I would appreciate it if you can call me Eretuquein in private."

"You must forgive my confusion," Governor Esyll said. "All this show of formality outside, and now you come in here asking to be on a first-name basis?"

"Only if you desire it," Eretuquein said, nodding. "I live, and I fight to serve and to save. An innocent human girl has shown me how to do that—*and* to care about each person individually."

The governor breathed deeply. "Very well, though you'll have to forgive me if I miss the pronunciation."

Eretuquein tossed his head, nodding his assent.

"And what is the meaning of this private audience?" the governor asked. "I granted it because you are a Nomord, and I wished to have the novelty of this conversation. I hope that it also serves a purpose."

"Governor, I have need to speak with the emperor."

"I assume about what you told my subjects out front?" Governor Esyll asked.

"Yes," Eretuquein confirmed.

"Why don't you go and pull the same stunt you just did in my city?"

"I could do that," Eretuquein answered. "But my thinking is to do what I can to improve my chances of success."

"And?" the governor asked.

"And Parfall is a wholly subordinate province of the imperial crown," Eretuquein answered.

The governor raised an eyebrow.

"What do you Nomo-Nomo understand of human politics?"

"Only a little," Eretuquein answered. "But I know that you are governor rather than duke because the crown never placed an official noble title upon Parfall after conquering it all those centuries ago."

Esyll laughed, grinning.

"You Nomord *do* know politics! So you come here to Parfall specifically because we have a unique connection to the crown." He laughed again and clapped his hands together. "Oh, whoever thought you beasts were capable of such intrigue?"

Eretuquein didn't waste the breath to explain to the man about receiving information from the Guides.

"Please, Governor. If you or somebody you appoint could come with me to Nolnarn, then I can be presented in court as an official guest of the crown. My hope is that this will help add extra legitimacy to my cause in the eyes of the public. But even without your help, I will go to Nolnarn regardless—even if I have to do what I did in your city today."

"Well, we don't want that, do we?" Governor Esyll said. "I could just see it. Your hooves causing a ruckus on those alabaster streets of the imperial capital, shouting, 'Audience on the emperor's lawn, audience on the emperor's lawn!'"

The governor burst into laughter at his own joke.

Eretuquein wasn't sure what to think. "Will you help me or not?"

Governor Esyll took a moment to sober up. "Things have been boring enough here," the governor said. "There's not a lot... Wait a second. Do you have anything to do with that group called the Disaffected, gathering themselves in the eastern provinces?"

"They oppose us," Eretuquein said simply.

"Oh," the governor gasped with fascination in his voice. "I suppose you would say they're listening to Sacalai's influence?"

"Most of them, probably," Eretuquein answered.

"I have to say I find reports of their activity somewhat annoying. Troublesome, even," the governor said. "Where they gather or pass through, we hear more reports of thefts and assault. I will gladly act in opposition to them."

"Thank you."

"Alright," the Governor said, "I'll put it on my calendar and make arrangements for—shall we say—two weeks from now? And you'd be welcome to... Where would you like to stay? In the stalls at the stable or somewhere else?"

"I cannot wait two weeks," Eretuquein said darkly. "With or without you, I will depart in the morning, and be there in two and a half days."

The governor gaped. "How can you move so fast?" Then he blinked. "You really are magical creatures, aren't you? Still, I cannot leave so suddenly. I have affairs here in my own domain, which I cannot abandon so readily."

"Not even when the world hangs in the balance?"

"Hronomon, would it be so crucial for you to make this one visit so soon?" the governor asked.

Eretuquein nodded. "Perhaps not necessarily this one, but I must keep my schedule. I came here and performed my function as Forerunner in your city. It appears I was well received, and I must move on. There is no reason for me to tarry."

"What am I supposed to do then?" the governor asked. "Leave my lands to rot in my absence?"

"Not necessarily," Eretuquein answered. "Somebody should stay here and tend to matters. If you cannot go, perhaps another can present me in court."

"I can go, Father," the governor's son spoke up from where he still sat on the stairs. He stood.

"Father, I can go with Eretuquein."

"What? You're just a boy!"

"I'm the heir of Parfall, aren't I?"

"Look, son—Rhylian—it's one thing for us to let this Nomord in here and talk to us. They're well known for being noble creatures. But to send my son to travel with him so suddenly, with almost no preparation..."

The governor turned back to Eretuquein, scowling.

"Father, please," Rhylian said. "I'll be alright."

The governor still scowled at Eretuquein.

"I," he said slowly, "believe you have good intent. But I don't like you whisking me or my family members off on this journey at breakneck speed."

Eretuquein saw the man opening up to the possibility, so he pressed the advantage.

"Governor, your son will be safe with me. I told you how fast I can get to Nolnarn. And I can do that with him on my back. No natural creature can keep up with me."

"And unnatural?" the governor interrupted. "Are there unnatural creatures that can keep up with you?"

"If you mean magical, then yes. A jackalope can nearly match my pace."

"And I suppose the jackalopes don't talk because they're in some kind of haze, like the female Nomo?"

"No," Eretuquein answered. "They do not possess our intellect."

The governor took a deep breath, then let it out in a long sigh.

"You traveled with the companion from her home to meet the Shrongelin," he recited the lore he'd been told out front. "And in the morning, you march off with my son as well. Is this a hobby of yours—to call youngsters off on adventures?"

Eretuquein snorted. "No. But if it were, I wouldn't do it with the fate of the world in the balance."

The governor laughed weakly. "Well, you heard, Rhylian. Sounds like you'll be riding on Eretuquein's back and traveling fast. Pack light."

Rhylian's face lit up. "Of course, Father!" He jumped up and ran up the stairs.

Nolder grunted, twisting in his seat on the wagon as the city wall came into view. He signaled for the driver to stop so he could climb down.

"Aiwa," he called, signaling to the other wagon. "Let's walk the rest of the way."

Aiwa nodded and hopped down from the wagon she rode in. To Nolder's chagrin, Hugne also hopped down.

"What's on your mind?" Aiwa asked Nolder amicably.

Nolder liked Aiwa. She was from Noonan by birth and showed it with her blonde hair and slender nose. She dressed sensibly for the journey, with sturdy clothing that protected her from the weather.

"Mostly, I just wanted to stretch my legs on this last bit," Nolder explained.

The past eleven days had been a constant battle, where he was forced to pick between wearing his feet out walking or wearing out his backside and his back riding in the wagon. How did he miss this while he was at the Disaffected encampment? He shook his head at the thought.

"I can't wait to get into town," Hugne said, walking behind Nolder and Aiwa.

Nolder pursed his lips. "I'm a little worried about getting into town," he admitted.

"Into the city?" Hugne asked. "Whatever for? My father is the baron over the Fisherman's Quarter. We'll have no trouble getting into the city. That's one reason the Council of the Disillusioned sent me. Also, I was in good with the old Wise. She showed me some things that the council wishes they knew."

"I wouldn't be so sure about us getting inside, Hugne," Nolder told the younger Disillusioned.

"That's *Seer* Hugne," Hugne corrected, pointedly.

Nolder didn't say anything. He already told Hugne that he understood and respected the title they both held within the Disaffected organization, but he didn't believe it was necessary for them to be so formal with each other, since they held the same rank.

After a long pause, he replied.

"Very well, Seer Hugne," he said. "Think about it. Surely the overduke has heard reports of our gathering to the north. If I were the overduke, and I wanted to hold on to power, I would probably give orders not to let us into the city."

"Whatever you say, old man," Hugne dismissed.

Nolder looked at Aiwa, who gave a knowing glance in return. What was the point in Nolder and Hugne calling each other *Seer* all the time in order to maintain their status in the eyes of their company, if Hugne turned around and undercut that effort by using a derogatory term for his peer?

"I guess we'll see when we get to the gate," Nolder said at length.

When they arrived in front of the gate, one of the sentries approached. Seeing that Nolder was the oldest in the company, he spoke to him.

"I see you have a group here," the soldier said. "What is your business in the city?"

"I am the son of Baron Kawn Horrick," Hugne said, before Nolder had a chance to speak.

"Alright," the soldier said. "Do you have papers?"

"Of course, I have papers," Hugne said. He reached for a pocket.

"We are an emissary company from the encampment of the Disaffected," Nolder said, stepping in between Hugne and the soldier. "There are fifteen of us, and we come peaceably to request audience with the overduke."

"I see," the soldier said slowly, turning his attention back to Nolder, while Hugne dug in his pockets. "Sergeant Glonea over there"—he pointed to another sentry—"can help you fill out a request form. I'm afraid we can't let you enter the city, though. But you're welcome to camp at least one hundred paces away from the gate while you wait for adjudication on your request."

Nolder nodded, disappointed but understanding the reasoning.

"This is an outrage!" Hugne said. "I already told you, I'm Baron Kawn Horrick's son!"

He thrust his papers in front of the sentry.

"Now let us enter."

The sentry took the papers and inspected them wordlessly.

"One moment," he said after looking them over.

He walked over to the hut where Sergeant Glonea sat and showed the papers to the other sentry. After a moment, the sergeant nodded, and the first sentry returned.

"Very well. You may enter," he said, pointing at Hugne, and then turned to Nolder. "I apologize, sir. As I said before, the company cannot enter the city until—and if—your request for audience is granted. Also, I can't promise that your request will even be looked at very soon, what with Southmarch upon us. The overduke must be backed up on his normal work, making preparations for the festival."

Nolder sighed. Aiwa walked off and began giving orders to the rest of the company to turn the wagons about while they looked for a place to camp.

The librarian found himself once again staring at the rough visage of Leaf. This made at least ten days in a row. Was it twelve? More? As before, the visitor had knocked on the outer doors before the librarian had a chance to open them.

Sighing, Falndeg let the man in.

"Do you know what, Leaf?" Falndeg said to the man, "I'm going to let you view a few primary sources. You love the old stories so much, and you have been treating the materials with proper respect. Can I trust you to do the same with our originals?"

"Of course, and I thank you," Leaf nodded slowly.

"Very well."

Falndeg took the man upstairs, then left him at the table where he always studied his folklore. What was the shabby character looking for, anyway? Meaning? A clue missing from his father's will?

Bringing four ancient books back to Leaf, Falndeg recited the rules. "You can only study these books here at this table, you may *not* crack the spine, dog-ear, or write in any of these books, and there will be absolutely no eating or drinking anywhere near here."

"I understand," Leaf said.

All true seekers of knowledge, Falndeg recited mentally. He eyed the man, wondering if his pattern of proper handling of recent materials would transfer to giving the utmost care to these volumes. "Alright. Enjoy, and let me know if you have any questions."

He returned to his desk, dedicating himself to analyzing the writing from the New Fonglan scrolls.

An hour later, Leaf stood before the Head Librarian's desk.

Falndeg almost had a heart attack before he realized that what Leaf casually held in front of him was a common notepad, not one of the precious tomes that Falndeg had brought out to him this morning.

"I don't know if I really have time to get into the old—"

"Read this," Leaf directed, plopping the notepad in front of him. Directed, as if he had any authority in the royal library. Also, it seemed uncharacteristic of him.

Tentatively, Falndeg turned the book around, bringing it closer and placing it on top of the facsimile copies he was studying.

Leaf leaned in and pointed at a spot on the pad. "Right there."

Falndeg looked at the notepad, then back up at Leaf.

"What is this?" the librarian asked, folding his hands on his desktop.

"Can't you read it?" Leaf asked rhetorically.

No, Falndeg thought, *your handwriting is atrocious. Is that even in Eslarnan?* Had the man written with his feet, boots on and all, instead of nimble fingers?

Apparently, Leaf suddenly remembered this shortcoming of his. "Sorry, I know it's sloppy. But it's still important."

"Um. Why don't you tell me what you find so compelling about that precise story?"

Leaf leaned in and spoke quietly, wide-eyed. "I believe it ties the other stories together. It's the linchpin."

Neither man spoke for a moment while Falndeg wondered why he still let the roughly dressed visitor enter the library. He still didn't even know which story Leaf was talking about right now.

"If you'll excuse me, Leaf," he began, "I have a lot of work to—"

"Haven't you heard the stories? Rumors on the street?"

Falndeg gave his visitor a sidelong glance. "I don't think so. What rumors are you referring to?"

"Oh, oh!" Leaf held a hand over his mouth. "A great black beast with fierce eyes!"

"What, a bear? A black panther? Not around here, surely—"

"A black Nomord. The Nightshade Unicorn himself!" Leaf's mouth hung open, gasping for air and waiting for a reaction from his host.

Falndeg stared back at Leaf, then shook his head. "Master Leaf, I must ask you to let me alone. I have plenty to do as it is. Please..." He looked at Leaf expectantly.

Leaf nodded, giving Falndeg a feeling of relief. "Alright, sir." Leaf stood. "I will be on my way."

"You're always welcome back—"

"I can't tomorrow; it's Southmarch. After that, I don't think so." He shook his head. "Anyway, I have to run. You'll want to handle the primary sources yourself anyway, so I hope you don't mind that I left them sitting out."

Falndeg felt a second wave of relief that Leaf hadn't tried to move the old tomes himself. He began to lift him out of his chair to escort the visitor out. "Thank you, I will—"

"Primary," Leaf laughed, interrupting the librarian. "I suppose they're rather old compared to what you call contemporary, but some of your so-called primary sources just contain retellings of older volumes that I'd wager you don't have in your collection."

Falndeg raised an eyebrow. What did the man mean by that? "I'm glad you enjoyed what we have, then."

"Just remember," Leaf said as he turned to walk himself out, "they say he's the harbinger."

"Thank you, Master Leaf, have a nice...day."

Leaf had walked away so quickly that Falndeg doubted the man could hear him over his own footsteps.

Sighing, Falndeg left his desk to go upstairs and put away the materials the erratic visitor had perused. When he got there, he found one of the books lying open, not with the spine cracked, but with two other books holding the edges of its front and back covers apart.

Glancing down, he saw that it wasn't in Eslarnan, but in Old Tal, the language spoken in this region before the

Halbonins invaded. Falndeg couldn't read old Tal with any fluency, but he was familiar enough to translate phrases when he needed to.

Then he noticed something else. A line of text was underlined! That Leaf had defaced an invaluable, ancient volume. It was pencil, but who knew if it could be erased without smearing the old paper?

Falndeg scowled at the line of text, deciphering its meaning in his head.

The nightmare beast was never the problem, but the prelude.

Part V:

Southmarch and Sea Breezes

CHAPTER 30

A FAMILIAR FACE

Allabva entered the Coughing Badger laughing with Walrus, Panli, and Tank. They came earlier today than they had previously.

"But Allabva, did you see the way the little man looked at you yesterday?" Tank roared. "He could not believe that you could lift a bigger stone than I could! And then when he started to believe it, I could see the gears in his head turning, wondering how to use you to make money."

"It is sad, really," Walrus said. "People like that never understand how to truly connect with others, and they have trouble believing that many people do things for others just because they wish for the happiness of others."

Allabva nodded. "It reminds me of the Disaffected who chased me up the mountain. They refuse to let others be."

Allabva had spent the greater part of the past two weeks making rounds with the Shrongelin in the outlying communities surrounding the city. While she had visited several with Walrus and Tank, she and the Nightshade had also visited the communities that were within range of running there with the strength of the Shrongelin's gift. The reactions they got from people ranged from a few who instantly pledged support for their cause, to people who didn't know what to think, all the way to one man who instantly grabbed an ax and charged, screaming, at the fearsome Nomord. Fortunately, there were a few people who volunteered donations. Allabva didn't want to accept them, but she needed coin to maintain her bed and daily meals.

She had largely gone with the flow of the Shrongelin's plan, traveling with him and sometimes also with Walrus, Tank, or Panli to the outlying towns during the day between mid-morning and late afternoon. Although most of her time was spent visiting outlying towns, she continued visiting the Coughing Badger daily as a sort of base of operations.

"You know what I thought was a grand thing to see?" Panli said to Allabva. "I loved every time that ornery Guardian complained to you that you were holding up the itinerary."

"He hates it when I do things that he thinks are a waste of time," Allabva giggled. "Oh, but Panli, I'm sorry I made you miss the baker's last loaf the other day."

"Say nothing about that. It was fine," Panli said, holding her hand out as if to ward Allabva off. "Those people needed help digging that ditch." Then she burst into laughter. "The Guardian was so peeved! He said you were a waste of the power of the Construct!"

Allabva couldn't help herself from laughing, and Panli's use of a nickname for the Shrongelin got Walrus and Tank laughing, too.

"But it's supposed to help people, right? And that's what I was doing. It just perhaps wasn't the way the Guardian would have done it."

Allabva and her new friends had taken to using the trans-lated title "Guardian" in public places, deciding it was less likely to cause unexpected problems when somebody objected to disrespect for the Shrongelin, or insistence that there was no such thing as the Nightshade Unicorn.

Panli sobered up. "Allabva and Walrus, remember your meeting with the chief magistrate this afternoon."

"Of course," Walrus said. "We will be there, won't we, Allabva?"

As Allabva nodded, she noticed the music stop, and looked over to the small elevated stage set up at one end of the common room. A bard was setting down a lute while his apprentice held a flute nervously in his hands. A young woman who looked a few years older than Allabva and held a resemblance to the flutist next to her held a wooden horn that was curved at the lower end.

"Lamtor!" Allabva exclaimed, crossing the common room to talk to the musicians.

The flutist stood to meet Allabva while the bard stepped away.

"Allabva, I'd like you to meet Alial, my sister."

"Pleased to meet you," Alial said. "Lamtor seemed to think I should, so here we are." She smiled, reinforcing the image of her brother with their shared round faces, dark tan skin with freckles, and straight red hair.

"Nice to meet you," Allabva replied. "What do you..."

"We're on break right now," Lamtor said. "Can we come talk at your table?"

"Of course," Allabva answered, wondering what this meant.

Allabva returned to Walrus, Tank, and Panli with Alial and Lamtor in tow. Before she got there, she turned to a larger table and signaled the group over.

"Who do we have here?" Tank asked, gesturing to Alial and Lamtor.

"Lamtor and his sister, Alial," Allabva answered. "I met Lamtor on my way to Tallensworth, where he and Master Yalben performed in an inn common room. I know he is a friend to us."

"Ah! It is good to have more friends," Walrus smiled, taking a seat with the rest of the group. "And I hope Alial and Lamtor feel they can count us as friends, as well."

A banana pul-pul drink appeared in front of Allabva as Andamaln delivered known preferences around the table. She took a sip and noted something wrong. It was missing the cream. Allabva remembered today was Siege Day, the eve of Southmarch; many foods were carefully rationed today to recall the austerity of a city under protracted siege.

"How did you find us?" Allabva asked Lamtor. "Or are you here by chance?"

"Really? More like, how did we find *you*," Alial replied with a grin. "Lamtor told me about you almost winning an arm wrestle against five grown men at the same time. Knowing that, it was pretty simple to ask around for a girl doing impossible things and learn where to find her. Master Yalben pulled some strings—no pun intended—for us to play here today. No chance of luck about it."

Allabva's face flushed with embarrassment. "Am I that easy to find?"

"Probably, if you know the right people," Alial answered again before her brother could speak. "But we don't. It took us almost a week."

"You mean you looked for me for a week? What for?"

"We want to know how we can help. I'm glad we ran into that Cariel fellow last night. He told us where to find you."

"But you don't even know what our plan is," Allabva objected.

"We know your aim is good, and it will affect everyone. That's good enough for me to get started."

"But it is lucky that you found us today. Tomorrow is Southmarch, and I won't come here. I'm going to be traveling soon enough. You might be able to help a little while I'm here in town, but I think we have this planned out."

"Lamtor is tied down currently; I'm not." Alial was showing herself to be undeterred in working her way into the effort. "I can travel."

"You mean you're not apprenticed...?" Allabva let the question hang.

"No, I came here to perform for fun today. I normally do embroidery since my husband died."

"Oh, I'm sorry to hear it," Allabva empathized.

"I'm sorry to have to share it," Alial quipped, "but it's the truth. He fell ill with a fever. No babies yet, so I guess I'm just kind of still around."

"Just still around?" Lamtor sputtered. "She has more energy than anyone else I know. Her embroidery looks amazing, and everybody loves her."

"Thanks, Lammie, the girls are talking," Alial shut her brother up with a grin.

"Maybe the girls shouldn't talk so long," Panli interjected. "It's nearly time for Allabva and Walrus to meet with the chief magistrate of the northern quarter."

"Oh? So what's the plan?" Alial dug.

"I'm trying to meet with the overduke," Allabva answered. "I submitted a request when I arrived in town, and we're hoping the magistrate can bend some ears to precipitate the audience."

"It's not like you'll need the magistrate's help, though," Tank countered. "With the Avaunt coming up, you'll get that audience."

"You're running the Avaunt?" Lamtor asked with wide eyes. "Very few women do that, but... Wow, that will be something to see!"

"If she can have enough strength tomorrow, eating no meat today," Tank moaned.

"Don't worry," Walrus counseled his friend, "nobody else is eating meat today, either."

"Except for those who really want to win," Tank countered. "They say that if you're not cheating, you're not really trying."

"She won't cheat," Panli said firmly to Tank.

Allabva countered Panli. "Except for having magically augmented strength, stamina, coordination..."

"Well, you're not cheating with meat today," Panli said with finality.

"You know," Alial offered, "pasta would be a good way to prepare for the race."

"But, as I said, Allabva needs to get going."

Allabva complied, standing. "Will you be here later today? I understand that telling the story of the battle is a traditional part of Southmarch."

"We'll be here," Lamtor confirmed. "Master Yalben will tell the story at half past tenth strike."

"Alright, that settles it," Panli said before Allabva or Alial could say anything else. "Walrus, take this young woman to meet the chief magistrate already."

Walrus frowned, then downed his coconut pul-pul in one gulp.

"Let's go, Companion."

CHAPTER 31

A STRANGER

"Remember," Walrus told Allabva as he pulled a rope, which rang a bell out of sight. "The chief magistrate is a busy man. I was only able to get us this time with him because it is Siege Day. I do not know how much time he will give us, but I suspect it will not be much."

They stood outside a gate in a wall encircling the chief magistrate's home. Allabva could tell that it wasn't a large compound of any sort, as was the overduke's palace, but it was still a house of generous proportions.

Inside the wall, Allabva could see across to the front door of the house itself, which now opened, and a middle-aged man stepped out, wearing stylish but casual clothing.

"Walrus!" The man smiled. "Come in, come in, both of you," he said as he opened the gate.

Walrus and Allabva entered, and the man closed the gate.

"Young Miss Companion, was it? I am Chief Magistrate Spalgen. It is nice to meet you."

"Thank you," Allabva said. "You can call me Allabva."

"Come on inside the house," the magistrate said as Walrus and Allabva followed him in, and Walrus closed the door behind them.

The magistrate took a pitcher from the countertop, as well as a glass. "Cider?" he offered.

"Thank you, please," Walrus said, accepting for both of them.

"Now, I really do only have a couple of moments," the host said. "As you can see, we have a full house today." He gestured to the countertops, where there were several dishes piled high. "My wife's family is here on visit, and I can only excuse myself so long before they believe I am trying to avoid them."

"Of course, thanks," Walrus said.

"Chief Magistrate Spalgen, as you know, Allabva here has requested an audience with the overduke, and it is an urgent matter."

"Well, let's hear it from the girl herself," Spalgen interrupted. "Allabva, tell me why you're here today. We'll have the guilt, I'm sure, of how much to divulge and right now."

"I have spoken to multiple Nomord," she said.

"Multiple Nomord?" the magistrate echoed. "That's impressive if it's true. But what does this have to do with the meeting with the overduke?"

"I have a message from the Nomord," she said, "which I'd much rather deliver to the overduke himself."

"I see," Spalgen said skeptically. "And I suppose then the Nomord want the overduke to give you money or lands?"

"It's not like that," Allabva said. "They want to help people, and I would like to share the details with Overduke Pymseet."

"Of course you would," the magistrate said.

Allabva didn't feel like this was going as well as she had hoped.

"Remind me where I fall in this," the magistrate said. "You want to meet the overduke, and you don't want to tell me the details. So why are you even talking to me?"

Walrus answered, "We are hoping that you can put in a word so that her request for audience is granted soon."

Spalgen blanched. "You want the audience, and fast, is it? Who do you think I am?"

"You're the high magistrate of this part of the city," Walrus answered.

"Yes, but I'm just a magistrate," he said. "You might have better luck if you got some of the dukes on board first."

"We do not have that kind of time," Walrus said. "We do not know any of the dukes personally, so bringing them on board would add extra weeks. But we know you, and you know the overduke."

"I suppose you can say I know him. I am employed by the Crown, by the overduke's house, but I am not his friend. Miss Allabva," the magistrate turned his attention to her, "you seem like a nice girl, but you are essentially a stranger to me. With my tenuous connection to the overduke, I cannot advocate for somebody who is essentially a stranger. I'm sorry."

Allabva furrowed her brow. "Is there nothing you can—"

The magistrate interrupted, "I got my appointment as a magistrate because I was recognized for having integrity. I can relate to the overduke that I spoke with you briefly, but what would I say? The fact that I spoke with you in itself does not give you any credit, and you have declined to tell me the details behind your request. I'm afraid I have no recommendation that I can make."

Allabva felt flustered.

Walrus mused. "Is there any way you can give him a message? When do you see him next?" he asked.

The magistrate sighed. "I suppose I could deliver a verbal message—very brief, mind you. Again, I do not know you, Miss Companion, so I cannot make a recommendation. Why don't you tell me what message you would like me to deliver, and I will tell you if I can share that with the overduke."

Allabva thought hard about this. "When will you see him next?" she asked, repeating Walrus's question.

"Tomorrow morning," Magistrate Spalgen answered. "The overduke hosts our morning feast on Southmarch for the dukes, duchesses, and the chief magistrates. There will be a lot of people there, so I do not know if I will have the opportunity for a conversation. But at the minimum, I can pass on a simple word."

"Tomorrow morning," Allabva thought. "What can I tell the overduke tomorrow morning that might help get this audience?"

There was a burst of laughter from outside the house.

"I must ask you to be on your way," Magistrate Spalgen said, looking over his shoulder. "I have to get back to my visitors."

"Thank you for the cider," Walrus said, gesturing with his glass and then setting it on the countertop.

"Yes, thank you," Allabva echoed, setting her glass down as well.

The chief magistrate escorted Walrus and Allabva out the front door and to the gate.

"Any message?" the magistrate asked again. "I don't know you, so I can't make a recommendation. But you seem nice, so I want to help."

Allabva's mind was racing. What could she say that would connect herself, impress the overduke, or give him an extra reason or motive to see her sooner?

"Tell him," she said. "Tell him I'm the one who's going to win the Avaunt tomorrow."

The magistrate looked at her under two raised eyebrows. "You want me to tell him something you just made up on the spot? That will make him know that you are to be disregarded as absurd?" he asked.

"No," Allabva answered. "The Nomord that I spoke to gave me some gifts, and with them, I shall win the Avaunt."

Magistrate Spalgen looked at Allabva with a carefully examining eye. He obviously didn't believe that she was serious or capable of making good on her word.

"You know you're a nobody to the overduke?" the magistrate asked. "You are a common out-of-towner who, as far as I can tell, has no real claim to even seek the overduke's presence."

"I'm aware," Allabva said. "But I think he'll want to see me tomorrow afternoon."

"After tomorrow afternoon..." The magistrate inhaled through his nose, puffed out his cheeks, and then blew the air out of his mouth.

"I'll tell him," he said at last. "But you know, if you don't win, this will probably completely break your chances of ever getting that audience."

"Fair enough," Allabva said. "Then I'll just have to win."

Allabva made her way back to the Coughing Badger, where she was met by Lamtor and Alial. Panli had gone home where Walrus was now headed, and Tank as well to his house, but they both would return later in the evening.

"Any luck?" Alial asked Allabva.

Allabva shook her head. "The magistrate said I'm a stranger, so he can't make a recommendation."

"That's too bad," Lamtor said.

"I'll still get the chance to at least come close to the overduke tomorrow, right?" Allabva said. "After I finish the Avaunt, I mean."

"Tomorrow..." Alial mused. "What are you doing tonight and tomorrow for the festival?"

"I was planning to be here for the retelling of the battle," Allabva answered. "And tomorrow, my only set plan is to run in the Avaunt."

"Well, that settles that," Alial said. "After the retelling from Master Yoben, you'll come to our place for the Seeds Dinner, and then we'll go to the parade tomorrow morning."

"I don't know if I can do the parade," Allabva said. "I have to—oh, there's so much you two don't know."

She took the time filling in Lamtor and Alial about Hronomon, Sacalai, and the Nightshade Unicorn being the same creature as the Shrongelin. Lamtor and Alial showed surprise and anxiety as Allabva told her tale and asked questions to make sure they understood the whole situation.

Allabva was glad that she had taken up the habit of returning to the same tavern every day. The faces she saw nearby were regulars, and she didn't expect any trouble from them. Still, she made sure to talk softly to prevent being overheard.

"So you see," Allabva finished, "I have to check in with the Nightshade—I mean, with the Guardian," she corrected herself, "tomorrow morning. I don't know if that conflicts with the parade or not."

"It kind of does," Alial admitted, dismayed.

"No, it can work," Lamtor said. "You're forgetting her strength, Allabva. You can watch the parade with us. You'll just have to break off to go meet with the Guardian for a while, and then you can come back."

Alial looked at Lamtor with a sideways glance. "She'll miss a lot if she has to meet him outside the city."

"No," Lamtor said with a smile. "Anybody else would miss a lot, but Allabva here can run as fast as a horse, can't you?"

Allabva kept her mouth closed, looking around out of the corners of her eyes. Then she gave a slight nod. "Faster, I think," she said.

Alial gawked. "You can't be serious!"

Allabva blushed. "I am, but it's not like it's my own strength. It comes from the bond."

"Well, I want one of these bonds!" Alial said with gusto. "Where can I get one?"

Allabva laughed. "Maybe you can. But all the Nomord are holding the shield in place. When they are free so that you can bond one, that will mean the shield has broken. It won't exactly be a happy day."

The three of them paused a moment at the foreboding thought.

"Well," Alial said, breaking the silence, "then I still want one, but I'll happily wait as long as I have to."

Lamtor rolled his eyes. "Never try telling my sister no," he confided to Allabva. "It never ends well."

The door of the tavern opened, and a young sailor walked in. Allabva saw him and waved him over.

"Alial and Lamtor," Allabva said, introducing the sailor. "This is Cariel. He's another friend I've met here in Tallensworth."

"He looks a little scruffy," Alial judged. "Where did you run into him?"

Allabva hesitated a moment, then admitted, "Three Wolves Mute."

Alial nearly jumped from her seat. "Three Wolves Mute? That doesn't seem like your kind of place, Allabva."

Allabva shook her head, smiling. "It most certainly was not."

"Then why were you there?"

"To get to know the place."

"Why would you get to know it if it's not your kind of place?"

"I mean to try to get to know the city," Allabva clarified.

"Hmm," Alial said. "I guess if you must. What did you do at the Three Wolves Mute?" Lamtor asked.

"I learned how to play Towers," Allabva said.

"And she got in a brawl," Cariel added, taking a seat.

"Brawling?" Alial asked, incredulous. "More and more, I wonder if you're a bad influence on my little brother."

"No, it wasn't like that," Allabva laughed.

"It wasn't like that," Alial repeated, mimicking Allabva in a silly voice. "Look, girl, you were in a brawl, and in a seedy part of town!"

"She started it, too," Cariel added.

"No, I did not!" Allabva protested, laughing.

"Did she really?" Alial asked Cariel.

He laughed. "No. But it was started over her."

"Now you're getting men to fight over you?" Alial goaded.

"No, really," Allabva said. "There was one creep. He started the fight. I think he was hoping the crowd would trounce me because I handled him."

"Because you handled him?" Alial gawked again. "This tale is getting wilder and wilder. Please tell me how you *handled* this man."

"No, that's enough," Allabva said. "The creep was following me, and I made him stop following me. That's all there was to it—until, that is, he followed me to the Three Wolves Mute. I'm pretty sure he stopped following me since then, though."

Alial sighed. "Whatever you say, girly."

The four of them joked and laughed until the early evening, when Lamtor and Alial returned to the stage with the master bard. Alial and Lamtor played a soft accompaniment while the bard told the tale of Tallensworth's defense against the Tongans.

The crowd in the tavern ate bowls of watered-down soup containing vegetables and puffed grain. Some of them ate crusts of bread. No meat, cream, butter, or cheese was served this evening.

At the end of the evening, Allabva bid good night to her three friends, with plans for them to meet her at the Medicine's Roost in the morning. She walked home rather than ran. She had plenty of time, as she hadn't been out among the taverns late this evening, and the parade wasn't going to occur too early in the morning.

Allabva walked slowly, poking her head into this shop and that, wishing she could go shopping here with Brelin. There was so much variety, with all kinds of foods and clothing styles. Some of it came in through the port, as claimed by the man who had bought the shawl from her, and as Allabva had noticed some people who certainly traced their lineage through Iddypol, Tunglin, and other places.

She was grateful to the Shrongelin for helping with the weather as well. He didn't have total control of it, but he could do a lot for a short period, or small adjustments for longer. Speaking of the weather, Allabva realized that she was probably experiencing some calm before a metaphorical storm, as her efforts to see the overduke would come to a head the next day, for better or for worse.

Chapter 32

Parade

Allabva woke in the morning, feeling immediately grateful that the sensation of weakness wasn't there this morning. It hadn't come every morning, but she had grown to dread it for the nauseating emotions that attended it when it did come.

She got dressed and skipped down the stairs, where she eagerly ate the complimentary breakfast. This gave her another reason to be grateful, because the eggs were back. Yesterday they had only offered an extra roll of bread instead of eggs, on account of Siege Day.

While she ate, she was alerted to a small commotion happening at the front door, where Cariel was trying to enter. Allabva wolfed down her last couple of bites and went to meet Cariel outside. Soon after, Alial and Lamtor showed up, and the four of them walked to one of the city's main thoroughfares to watch the parade.

As Allabva heard trumpets blowing at the start of the column, which was still not in sight, she turned to her musician friends. "Do you have to work today?"

Lamtor shook his head. "My master is high ranking in the guild," he said. "Those who are higher up get major holidays off. Southmarch counts, but Siege Day doesn't, and guild funds provide payment for half of the holidays they electively take off."

"That sounds good for them—and for you as well, I suppose," Allabva observed. "But it doesn't sound very nice for those who pay dues and don't get these days off."

"It's all time-based," Lamtor explained. "The less senior Guild members don't get that benefit yet. But they will in the future, if they stay in the Guild."

"I suppose," Allabva said, dropping the matter. She wasn't out to fight every fight and supposed there was a fashion of fairness in this.

"And I'm not technically a musician by trade," Alial added.

"Right," Allabva remembered. "So how long have the two of you lived in Tallensworth?" she asked. "You don't look like you're native to the place."

"Might as well be," Lamtor said. "We grew up here, but old Ma and Papa come from Northern Westland Fields," Alial added.

Allabva nodded. She had heard descriptions from people in that part of the continent before, and these two siblings matched.

"Where are your parents now?" Allabva asked.

"They passed away," Alial said. "That's why it's just Lammie and me living together. No parents, no husband—all I've got is my kid brother."

Lamtor teased, "Yeah, me and your needle and thread."

Allabva watched the parade go by, headed by three trumpeters and a drummer, who played fanfares to announce the coming of the column. Behind them marched a few barons in uniform with a company of soldiers. Then followed a group of people carrying a banner depicting the silhouette of a black-smith at his forge.

Group after group of craftsmen and women marched by, along with some youths wearing quasi-military-style uniforms. Finally, at the very end of the parade, rode a lone man on horseback, wearing a military uniform and armor. He alternated between drawing his sword and holding it forward and above in a salute, and then sheathing it at his waist.

"Does the overduke not take part in the parade?" Allabva asked. Then she remembered that he must be at his morning feast right now.

"There are multiple parades throughout the city," Alial said. "This one is probably the standard—nothing too distinctive, just the basics."

"And you want me to go see another parade now?"

"Oh, of course!" Alial said. "This one is just a reference point. The next one that comes by has the best music."

"Why was there only one person on horseback?" Allabva asked.

"He's the baron-commander," Lamtor said. "He'll present the parade to the overduke later today."

"When's that?"

"At the victory feast after the Avaunt."

"Oh."

"Besides," Cariel said, "didn't you see the banners they were carrying? The soldiers, I mean."

Allabva thought. "Yes," she said. "I was confused by that. Did they have the banners upside down?"

The banners depicted the head and neck of an armored horse—upside down.

"No," Alial said. "That was the Tunglins' symbol when they marched on Tallensworth, so we put it upside down to mock them. Remember, most of our guys were on foot."

Allabva nodded, and third strike sounded.

"Oh, I have to go meet the Guardian," she said.

Alial took a quick glance at the sun. "Well, hurry up! You don't want to miss the second parade."

Allabva dashed off at top human speed. At first, she ran among the crowds, but when she found herself in empty streets, away from the parade, she opened up her stride and sprinted to the Tallen Gate.

She slowed again, walking out as two sentries were arguing about a shadow they saw at the top of the hill on the horizon.

It was the Nightshade.

"Why can't he let things happen more naturally?" Allabva wondered. Then she picked up her pace again, running at human speed to meet him. Fortunately, he disappeared from the city's view before she reached him, or Allabva would have been concerned about what the sentries would say when she re-entered.

"Report," the Shrongelin said.

Allabva was somewhat chafed by his manner. "Shrongelin, I'm not your servant. I'm your companion," she told him. "We both serve the construct."

The Nightshade said, "Anything I suggest that you do is purely out of service to that."

Patience, Allabva told herself. *Remember the battle he's fighting.*

"I talked to the chief magistrate," she said.

"And?" Nightshade prompted.

"He says he can't recommend a stranger."

"Ah." The Nightshade growled in frustration. "This is so useless. We have been here almost two weeks. This city has already taken more than its share of the time we have available. Why don't you just go jump over his wall, jump up his balcony like you did to save the child, and talk to him on your timing? I gave you the means to do exactly that."

"That's true," Allabva said. "But my physical ability to jump over his wall doesn't mean I'll convince him to help me—help us—when I get there."

The Nightshade growled again. "Figure something out."

"We *are* figuring something out," Allabva said. "I've made connections in the city. I'm running in the Avaunt this afternoon. That alone will bring me direct attention from the overduke himself."

"And somehow it doesn't grant you an audience," the Nightshade yelled back.

"Not necessarily," Allabva said. "But with the request and the race, how can he ignore me?"

"The same as he has ignored you thus far," the Nightshade drawled. "I guarantee he has received reports of your activity, and still he sends no summons. If he's not going to pay attention anyway, then jump over his wall, encounter the man who won't aid you, and let's get this over with. We have places to be."

"If we don't get some backing now, it will be the same in every city we go to."

"City?" The Nightshade scoffed. "We have *countries* to visit."

"We *are* getting noticed," Allabva argued back. "I went with you over the last week and a half to all the surrounding region. People saw you, and we spoke with people."

The Nightshade glowered. "We'd better hope my Forerunner is having greater fortune than I am. Otherwise, the world is doomed. Sacalai will escape and her armies will overrun us before you and I have the chance to imprison her again. Then she will rule this world unfettered, mightier than anyone who would oppose."

"I know the stakes, Nightshade," Allabva said softly. "I know that we have to achieve this. But we have to start somewhere."

"And we have to get somewhere, too," the Nightshade interjected.

"We *are* getting somewhere," Allabva said. "I'm sorry if it's not as fast as you would like, but we *are* seeing progress."

"Would that my companions were stronger, as they were in the days of King Edowan," the Nightshade said.

Allabva stared at the Nomord, confused.

"The Shrongelin's Companion during that cycle was King Edowan himself," the Nightshade explained. "It was easy for my brother to campaign for support."

"Did that make the battle easier to win?" Allabva asked.

The Nightshade was silent for a long moment. Finally, he answered, "There is no way to know for sure. Each battle is different. None of them is easy, and after each one, humanity has to rebuild their civilization almost from scratch."

Now Allabva was silent for a long time. Having the Shrongelin's companion be a king for instant political support sounded like a significant advantage. Yet, it sounded like the calamity was just as severe as every other time.

Why even fight? Allabva wondered. "Nightshade, I'm going to go win this race and try to speak with the overduke this afternoon. I will at least get noticed, if nothing else. It seems to me like it's all I can do."

The Nightshade nodded. "Yes, companion. Perhaps we will fail. Perhaps we will succeed. But you are right. All you can do is all you can do. I can ask nothing more."

The Nightshade Unicorn turned and slowly walked away.

Feeling disconcerted, Allabva walked back to the city gate.

"Did you catch the black shadow?" one of the sentries asked her. "What was it?"

"No," Allabva answered. "I'm not sure what that was all about."

Without feeling the emotional spring in her step, she jogged back to find her friends watching the parade.

"Allabva, you're finally here!" Alial half shouted when she found them, her face contorted in concern.

"Of course I'm here," Allabva replied. "What did you think had happened to me?"

She hadn't told anybody else about her weak spells in the morning, so she thought only Alial should have any cause for concern. Allabva checked the sun, even though she knew it was still relatively early.

"What? The Avaunt isn't until fifth strike."

"That's true," Alial said, "but you have to get a race band first."

"How do I do that?"

"They have sparring matches," Lamtor said, "and you have to win at least two out of three of your matches."

"I thought it was just a foot race," Allabva recalled aloud.

"It's all symbolic," Alial said. "It's a foot race because we drove out the Tunglin cavalry on foot. But first, the soldiers had to fight them to get them to run. So, before you can join the event, you have to show you can fight."

Alial blinked. "Why are we standing around here? Let's go!"

"We'll never get there in time," Lamtor worried.

"Allabva could get there in time," Cariel said. He had a concrete appreciation for her strength, having seen it in action.

"Where do I go?" Allabva asked Alial.

"It's the Market Square, three blocks east of the palace," she answered. "On the side closest to the palace, at the biggest entrance to the square, next to the fountain. Tell them you're entering for the Avaunt. Go!" she commanded.

Allabva set off running. She arrived next to the fountain just as fourth strike sounded. She found a man with a writing pad and spoke to him.

"I'm registering for the Avaunt," Allabva said.

The man looked down at her. "You? You'll get crushed in the challenge."

"I accept that possibility," Allabva said immediately. "I would like the opportunity."

"You're late anyway," the man said. "Didn't you hear the bell strike just now? Registration is closed."

"Please," Allabva said. "I really want to try."

The man looked at the list he was holding, then back at Allabva.

"Fine. I think I'll like watching you get crushed. What's your name?"

"Allabva Companion."

The man slowly looked back at her, raising an eyebrow. "That's an interesting surname. Were you born with it?"

"Does it matter?"

The man grunted. "No, I guess not. Congratulations, Miss Companion. You will be crushed at station number twenty-three over there for your first and only match. It'll start in a while. Now go wait."

Allabva walked along the side of the Market Square, weaving between vendor stalls. Lines were chalked on the cobblestones to mark boxes. There must be too many people wanting to enter the Avaunt to have single matches one at a time. As she walked, she noticed that each box had at least one person standing there, dressed in everyday clothes. Some boxes had one, two, or three people standing in various types of baggy clothing, and some of them had padding as well.

Allabva found box twenty-three and introduced herself to the man standing there in customary clothing.

"I'm here to fight to enter the Avaunt," she told him.

The man gave her a long, hard look. "You mean you're here for a pummeling to let somebody else into the Avaunt?"

"Either way, I'm here to try," Allabva said.

"Very well," he replied. "But I'm going to require you to wear padding. Nobody's getting concussed at station twenty-three, let me tell you that."

"That's not necessary," Allabva said. "I'll be fine."

"What did I just tell you?" the man insisted. "You're wearing padding, or you're not fighting at my station."

Sighing, Allabva grabbed the pile of gear the man pointed to on the ground. He had said nobody would be concussed, so she found a pad that went over her head, strapped it in place, and turned back to the box she was to fight in.

"You think that's enough?" the man said. "No, you're putting on the full getup."

Accepting that she wouldn't be able to change the man's mind without some demonstration, she dug through the pile and added more items until he was satisfied. She saw that people in the nearby fighting stations were doing similar things.

While Allabva had been gearing up to fight, others had gathered around the various stations, and the market had grown crowded. Wondering how many fighting stations there were, she looked to the far end of the market and saw they continued around the corner at the main entrance. A crier stood on top of something Allabva couldn't see and shouted, "Begin, begin, begin!"

Allabva assumed it was as loud as the man could shout, but she could barely hear him over the din of voices. The man running her fighting station turned and tapped two men on the shoulder, pushing them into the square drawn on the ground. Each man held a long staff, as if it were some kind of polearm.

"Alright," said the man running station number twenty-three. "Knock him down or shove him out, both feet out. Ready—go!"

On the command "go," the two men launched themselves at each other. Up and down the row of fighting stations, opponents clashed on the command of the station runners.

Allabva zoned out somewhat as the fighting continued, and one match followed another. Soon enough, it was her turn. Her movement was restricted by all the padding she had been forced to wear, but she accepted one of the staffs and prepared herself to clash.

Three times she heard the command "Ready—go!" against different opponents, and three times she won easily. She barely noticed the looks on her opponents' faces while she fought. Her heart wasn't in this; it was merely a necessary step to see the Avaunt, which itself was only a step in protecting her family. Three times, she knocked her opponent out of the box marked on the ground.

"Well, you, Little Miss, you've done it," the man running station 23 told her with a clap on the shoulder. "Now take off my padding and take this."

He handed her a strip of blue cloth with a stripe of yellow dyed near one end. "Put it on your left shoulder."

Allabva accepted the strip and stepped away from the box on the ground, where more people would still fight after her.

Allabva caught sight of Lamtor and Cariel watching her. Lamtor wore a loose grin that appeared pasted on, whereas Alial stood agape.

"Oh, you found me," Allabva said. She hadn't even known they were there.

"It wasn't hard," Cariel said. "We just asked where the skinny girl with curly hair went. You fought in those clothes?"

Allabva looked down. "They're the clothes I have," she said.

Now Alial, getting over the shock of seeing Allabva's strength in action, shook her head. "Come here. If that's the clothing you have, I suppose it'll do, but let's get you prepped to run in it."

Alial stepped forward and started manipulating the skirt of Allabva's dress, pulling the center of both the front and the back toward each other and tying it halfway up toward her waist so the two sides imitated the shape of trousers, each side hugging one leg. She also tied the blue strip as a band, high around Allabva's left arm.

Alial stepped back when she was done, and Allabva inspected herself. She felt like her dress was bunched up in an odd way.

"I don't know, Alial," she said. "I think I'll be alright just as I was."

"You can't be serious," Alial said.

"Of course I am," Allabva said, unbundling the skirt of the dress and letting it fall. "I already ran like this today, didn't I?"

"But you're trying to win, aren't you?" Alial said.

"Yes," said Allabva, "but I'll be fine. I ran down from Tallen Mountain wearing this dress."

Alial laughed, shaking her head. "Alright. You do you."

"Thank you. I will. But I really appreciate you trying to help me."

While they waited for the race, they walked around the square. Shopkeepers were hawking their wares, regardless of whether their booths had fighting stations in front of them or not. Allabva took some time to admire the decorations and appreciate the fact that nobody was using a horse today—except for the very few designated individuals, like the baron commanders in the parades.

This made her think of the grain vendor in the southwest market, and she wondered how his son's leg was healing. She hadn't told the Nightshade, but she had made a few more deliveries for the man. Despite his protests, Allabva had continued to refuse payment.

CHAPTER 33

AVAUNT

When the time came, Allabva and what seemed to be a few hundred other people wearing blue bands on their left arms were corralled at the east end of the square, away from the fountain.

A woman dressed in silk stepped out on a balcony over the east entrance to the square and held her arms up to call for silence. The noise of the crowd dropped to a murmur.

"Who is that?" Allabva asked the man next to her.

"The Duchess," the man whispered back.

"The overduchess?" Allabva asked for clarification.

"What? No. Duchess of Rralen, the lands east of the city."

Allabva looked up at the woman, who now spoke.

"Good afternoon, everyone, and a happy Southmarch to you all." A few cheers rose from the crowd.

"Welcome to the Avaunt. Please listen as I tell you the rules, or you could wind up confused and lost. It's pretty simple, really," she said, continuing. "Here you have our enemy—" she pointed down to several men on horseback wearing the old Tunglin symbol of a Nomord silhouette painted large on their backs "—whom you will chase out of the city, so to speak. Follow them—or the other runners in front of you if you cannot see the enemy cavalry—all the way to the Sunset

Gate. When you get there, you will be required to show your blue armband to grab another one. Its color is a secret to you until you get there, to make it harder to cheat. You must have the correct armband on the other shoulder when you return to prove you made it all the way to the gate.

"If any of you think yourselves clever and have already discovered the color of the return armband, be advised that your victory will be verified before it is recognized. Do not think that our so-called enemy riders are not watching and will not know who is tailing them the whole way.

"Also, be advised that the turnaround point is a loop, to avoid those in front running into those farther back. You will run on foot the entire way. After the turnaround loop, you will trace your steps back here. Run through this square, and leave the square via the gap by the fountain on the west side." She pointed toward the west. "Follow our horseback riders from here to the finish line in the quad in front of the royal court, where the winner will be presented to the overduke himself during our victory feast!"

A great roar erupted from the crowd, some people shouting hurrahs and others chanting, "Avaunt, avaunt!"

The Duchess held her arms up again, this time having to wait several moments for the crowd to calm down.

"Are we ready?" she called.

Another cheer rose from the runners and the hundreds of other people packed into the square to see the race begin. The Duchess had to wait again for the noise to subside, though not as long this time.

"Then, on my signal, you will chase the enemy from the city!"

She raised an arm high overhead and held it there for a long moment before chopping it down in an arc toward the eastern exit of the square.

"Southmarch force—Avaunt!"

The riders kicked their horses into a trot, leaving the square, while the crowd began shouting, "Avaunt, avaunt!" and making shooing motions with their hands.

Allabva and the sea of runners began moving, also making shooing motions with their arms toward the horseback riders. Allabva trotted at an easy pace, locked into a relative position by the runners around her. This took several blocks to loosen up and give her room to advance. She slowly maneuvered and edged between runners, ignoring their surprised looks to see a young woman running the Avaunt in a dress, and gradually inched closer to the front of the mass. Eventually, she made it to the front, running several paces behind the horses and alongside the other frontrunners.

These were all men now around Allabva. Allabva had seen the fastest of the few women who had made it through the fighting rounds several minutes before, a little behind the main group of male runners. One runner beside Allabva looked over, clearly trying to calculate how she was able to maintain the pace.

"Where are you from?" he asked.

Allabva didn't feel like getting into a full discussion. "Out west," was all she said.

"I can see that," the man said loudly, blinking at her. "What I really want to know is how you're doing this. I've been at the front of this race for the last three years. I train for it, and I'm dressed for it."

Allabva spared a glance at the man's lightweight, comfortable-looking boots and loose, short trousers. He wore no shirt.

"I can sweat and cool off. What are you going to do in your full dress?"

"I'm going to run," Allabva answered. "That's all there is to it."

"No, there has to be more!" the runner said.

"Well, that and a bit of magic," Allabva admitted truthfully with a wry smile.

The runner grinned and laughed, shaking his head. "There would have to be. Say, magic girl, my name's Rawaln. And yours?"

After everything that had happened in this city, after making several friends and a few enemies, after easily fighting her way into this race, now running with a salty wind in her face, Allabva felt more free than she had since leaving home.

"Allabva. Nice to meet you, Rawaln, and I'm sorry to say that I'll be waiting for you at the finish line!"

This got a laugh from Rawaln. "Not on your life!"

They ran on. Allabva pulled ahead of the Rawaln and the other runners, edging closer to the horses. As she did, the riders urged their mounts to a faster pace. Allabva matched it at first, but when the riders grew alarmed at her ability, she held back and let the distance between them and her grow to what they had set in the beginning.

She chased the horses through the cobblestone streets, turning left and right as she ruthlessly followed her quarry. She didn't slow down to let any other runners come near.

As she ran, Allabva saw crowds of people on either side of the street, chanting, "Avaunt!" as the shamed cavalry rode by, who turned to cheer the runners and stopped, utterly dumbstruck, as they saw the first runner was a girl. She saw their confusion as they pointed, told their friends, husbands, or wives to look, to see what they could make of this. She also saw some unfriendly glares, as some people considered that the source of her speed could be something dark, unsure if they could accept her ability as a good thing.

For her part, Allabva pasted a smile on her face and waved at all of them, then alternated that with shouts of "Avaunt!" as she pursued the supposed Tunglin riders.

As Allabva held a steady pace ahead of Rawaln and the others, she approached one corner where a large barrel had been left out, presumably to catch rainwater running off of a roof. It must have been empty now, for it hadn't rained since before Allabva had arrived in Tallensworth. The barrel wasn't in her way, as the road turned away from it and it was on the outer side of the turn, but it gave the people standing around it a clean view of the runners' faces after the horses made the turn.

One man caught Allabva's eye because he wasn't cheering like the rest of the crowd, but instead leaned against the barrel with his arms folded. As she noticed him, the man stared at her intensely and his face grew red. Allabva wondered for a moment what was crossing his mind, then she made the turn and raced off.

At length, Allabva and the horsemen neared the designated gate. The riders turned right a couple of blocks shy of the gate. After two more left turns, Allabva was following them along with the city wall to her right, and arrived at the gate. It was closed for the race, and when she got there, she found a table where a woman sat, looking pointedly at Allabva's armband.

When she saw the band was correct, she looked up at Allabva with a dark scowl.

"You're cheating," she accused. "How can you be here first?"

"I ran fast," Allabva said, shrugging.

She glanced at the riders ahead, hoping they would confirm that she had run the whole distance. They trotted on, ignoring the disagreement behind them.

"I ran it. That's why I'm behind the horses," Allabva told the woman.

She reached for one of the strips of cloth on the table—they were white with a green spot near the end.

"Oh no, you don't," the woman said. "You just ran out behind the horses right before this last turn, I know it. There's no way."

"I ran it," Allabva insisted again.

"Look, girl, I'm not going to stop you from grabbing one, but if you take one of these bands, go around the next corner, and jump on a horse to make it to the end, I'll tell them you cheated. You think you'll win a victory, but all you'll win is shame. I'll send word right now."

Allabva wasn't surprised by the woman's incredulousness, but she couldn't accept the refusal. She needed to win this race and get the overduke's attention, and this was the way she saw to do that. She really didn't want to go jumping over his palace wall like the Nightshade suggested.

"Girl, you're not even out of breath," the woman said. "You think I'll believe you ran here behind those horses?" She turned her head to see as the leaders in the group of runners rounded the corner into sight.

"I was running ahead of them," Allabva pointed.

"No, you're lying," the woman said firmly.

"Look," Allabva huffed, "if you ask the riders, they'll tell you I was behind the horses the whole time." She gestured toward the other runners arriving at the table. "And the other runners know I was ahead of them."

Rawaln arrived at the table first, nodded at Allabva, grabbed a band without a word, and waved at the woman as he continued running, tying the band around his right arm.

"Fine," the woman said, holding her hands up as more runners grabbed bands. She kept her eyes on the runners' left arms to ensure they had the blue qualifying bands before they grabbed turnaround bands. "It's no skin off my nose when you get caught cheating."

Allabva supposed that if it came to it, there were enough witnesses to back her up. She took a band and ran off with the crowd.

It took a couple of minutes to catch back up to Rawaln at the front. Allabva didn't want to draw too much suspicion by gaining ground rapidly.

"Oh, you're back," he said. "I thought you quit."

"No way," Allabva said. "If I stayed back there, how would I wait for you at the finish line?"

"Good point." Rawaln's voice showed he was starting to tire.

They ran on wordlessly as she kept pace alongside the man. She didn't dare pull far ahead after the incident at the turn-around table. She needed witnesses to see her win, so she kept pace and ran on, passing crowds cheering on either side of the road.

As Allabva ran through the streets back the way she came, she couldn't help but notice how the views looked different. She was coming at them from the opposite direction, and every left turn was now a right and vice versa. But also, she saw details in the houses and shops that she didn't notice before. As she ran, she saw a few taverns that she had not visited that seemed like somewhere she would like to go if she had the chance.

Allabva soon recognized a familiar view as she approached a particular corner. There was a large barrel in the corner, but this time there was no man leaning against it and glaring at her. She wondered for only a moment what he might be up to, and then put him out of mind.

With everything Allabva had done since arriving in this city, all her half-arguments with the grumpy Shrongelin, and all the uncertainty she faced as to whether her attempts to reach people with the power to move multitudes would garner success in the end, what she could do right now was simply to enjoy the feeling of the wind and some sense of companionship, as she did not run alone. She still planned to pull ahead at the end, but for now she kept pace alongside Rawaln, with other runners close at their heels.

Her thoughts were interrupted by sudden, rapid movement above. Looking up, Allabva saw the angry man from before standing on a rooftop, where he had just released something from his hand.

Allabva ducked and jumped out of the way, avoiding a rock that she had barely registered was coming for her head. Because of the angle of the projectile, offset to one side, while Allabva successfully dodged, Rawaln was still in the way.

In the fraction of a second since Allabva had become alarmed and began her reaction, Rawaln picked up on the sense of something wrong. But without the enhancement of a Nomord bond, he wasn't fast enough to dodge gracefully. As luck would have it, the rock delivered him only a glancing blow, striking the ground behind him. Then, as he stumbled, he fell and rammed his knee on the cobblestones.

Allabva took a moment to look at Rawaln to see that he was otherwise unhurt. Then she looked up at the assailant. She considered leaping up to the roof and confronting him, but he was already dropping down on the far side of the roof, out of sight.

Allabva turned her attention back to Rawaln.

"Was that somebody you know?" he asked her as he pushed himself to his feet.

"No," Allabva answered truthfully.

A cry from the crowd arose, calling out, "Constable! Constable!" Meanwhile, runners flooded past Rawaln and Allabva, continuing the race. A woman came to talk to the two of them.

"What was that about?" she asked.

"I'm not sure," Allabva answered.

"Well, you go on," the woman said, looking around. "We'll get the police after that man, and we'll catch that son of a dugong."

Allabva hesitated, still wondering if she should go after the man.

"Go!" the woman urged again. "We'll get him. You have a race to run."

Allabva turned to Rawaln and shrugged. Rawaln shrugged back, then started to run again. Immediately, he gasped and doubled over.

"What's wrong? I thought the rock—"

"I'm fine," Rawaln interrupted. "It's just my knee." He began to walk with a limp. "I'm going to finish, but I'm going to come in last place. I can't run any more."

"Oh, no, you won't," Allabva said. "We ran this far together. I'm going to see you finish with me."

"How am I supposed to—" Rawaln began.

He was interrupted as Allabva scooped him up. She was momentarily grateful that the other son of a dugong, Jimlarnt, had given her practice in carrying a man on her shoulders.

Allabva started running.

Now she didn't care if she drew eyes. She had already done that to a lesser degree while running only a little bit faster than most humans were able. And what had it gotten her? Shot at—that was what. Angry at the man who had loosed the stone at her, Allabva reminded herself she needed to direct her true anger to Sacalai, whose influence was evidently beginning to pick up again. Now, more determined than before to succeed in this city, she ran in great leaps and bounds, quickly overtaking the runners in front of her and arriving at the heels of the riders.

One of them looked back by chance, and his face instantly took on a pall of alarm. He turned forward again and kicked his horse into a gallop while he shouted at his fellow riders.

"She's a monster, following on our heels!" he called.

All the riders matched the first to react, and Allabva chased them at galloping speed back to the beginning of the race and through the market square.

When she entered the square where the Avaunt had begun, Allabva realized that she must be far ahead of the next runner. She slowed her pace, allowing the horsemen to pull ahead so they could ease their mounts—and their own nerves. As she assumed an easier pace and stopped bouncing so much, Rawaln spoke to her.

"What *was* that?" he demanded. "And what are you?"

"I'm a girl," she said, tongue-in-cheek, "from out west. And that was something called running."

"What about that guy with the rock?"

"Never saw him before in my life," Allabva answered.

"Then why did he throw it at you? Or was it at us?"

"Some people dislike me and a couple of friends I have."

"How would he know what friends you have?" Rawaln asked.

"Good question. Perhaps he just thinks I shouldn't be able to run so fast."

"Ha! Today, I would have appreciated if you couldn't run so fast."

Allabva continued to jog, keeping the horses just in view. As the street at last opened up into a wide and expansive courtyard ahead, Allabva stopped and set Rawaln down.

"I'm sorry if that was rough," she apologized. "Come on, let's finish this race."

Rawaln looked at Allabva with confusion and utter disbelief on his face.

"Alright," he said finally. "You first."

Allabva turned toward the courtyard and walked slowly across the finish line.

CHAPTER 34

VICTORY FEAST

The next hour and a half was dizzying. Lamtor, Alial, and Cariel ran to Allabva after she entered the courtyard. Or rather, they tried to, but couldn't even get close. The crowd pressed around Allabva and Rawaln, wanting to know the details of the run.

"I'll come find you," Allabva hollered to them.

"Later on," Alial hollered back, making a cutting motion across her neck with her hand. "You made it into the overduke's feast, but it's too costly for us to join you. We'll celebrate out on the street or in a tavern!"

Living in a blur as she allowed the events to happen around her, Allabva answered their questions the best she could. She normally preferred to stay out of the center of attention, to live her life quietly. But now? After having thought to be the center of attention, she actually was, and it felt odd to her.

A man came up to her and introduced himself as Baron Garien Scalleh. A *baron*. Talking to *her*. He then turned around and introduced his wife, the Baroness Clea Scalleh. Allabva recognized her as the woman from the southwest market, who had spoken to her after she saved the child from falling in the earthquake. Allabva didn't know if this was by chance or if the woman had sought to speak to her again. It didn't matter to her, but the woman's knowing gaze told Allabva that she held no ill will toward Allabva for downplaying her heroics when she had rescued the child in the southwest market.

What was odd was that this baroness, this woman who seemed to descend from the heights to speak with Allabva less than two weeks before, took her into a set of rooms built into a small building in the palace compound, and with the aid of a few palace servants, helped brush her hair and wash up. It would do no good to be presented to the overduke covered in dust after the run. Allabva even spent three quarters of an hour in her underclothes, waiting while the servants washed and heat-pressed her dress.

While the people spoke to her back out in the courtyard once more, Allabva thought back to home. All of this noise and attention was just so that she could help the Shrongelin stop Sacalai. It was partly selfish, in order to save Mother and Mellier, Brelin and Delgan. But at the same time, Allabva knew she did it unselfishly, to save these strangers she was meeting now, to save people she never would meet across the world.

Eventually, the time came for the official beginning of the feast. The overduke's presence was announced by a fanfare delivered by a fifty-piece band seated near the palace steps. The courtyard had been laid out so that everybody had a view of the front of the palace and access to the various vendors who had set up around the courtyard.

Allabva wondered what kind of fees they had paid for the privilege to sell their wares at the focal point of today's feast. Not everybody in the city was here in this courtyard. Many people celebrated in their homes. But those who attended the overduke's feast had the opportunity to purchase savory meals with beef, lamb, pork, and chicken piled high on beds of rice or different types of tubers.

The Baron and Baroness Scalleh invited Allabva to sit at their table as a magistrate walked out on a balcony and called the feast to order. Allabva tried to keep up with the niceties expected of her throughout the whole affair, but her thoughts turned from home to now and dwelled on what she might say to the overduke.

Finally, she realized that the overduke was standing on the balcony now instead of the magistrate, and he was speaking to the crowd.

"… I want to thank all of those who made preparations for this wonderful feast. I say we have the best chefs in the world right here in our city and the best produce and meat grown in this region. Can you imagine, then, what this would look like if we had fallen under Tunglin rule? Some say that the Imperial Crown does nothing for us, but I can tell you that without the strength of the whole bond in Eslarna, Tallensworth would have fallen that day. Even still, it is continuously impactful that we remain part of this great empire.

"Now, who enjoys a bit of sport?" the overduke said, rubbing his hands together.

Eager but polite applause followed.

"In case you missed it or haven't heard already, we had the most interesting outcome from the Avaunt this year. I am sad to report that the first-place runner is not one of our own. In fact, this athlete comes from clear across on the western side of the empire. But I will happily point out that this year's champion is indeed Eslarnan, just as much as the rest of us."

More polite applause.

"Please, if you will, welcome this year's champion, Allabva Companion."

"It's time, girl," Baroness Clea told Allabva. "Climb those stairs and stand before him. Speak when spoken to."

Allabva stood numbly, accepting the baroness's encouragement, and made her way over to a flight of stairs set into the wall at the side of the courtyard in her freshly pressed dress and carefully tended curls. She walked up the steps, nervous about whether she should appear to hurry, to display dignity with a slow gait, or something in between. Erring on the side of not making the overduke wait too long, she ascended the flight of stairs and stood at the top.

From where she now stood atop the wall, some five arm spans away from the balcony's edge, Allabva had a better view onto the overduke's balcony, though the floor upon which he stood was at the level of her knee. This would be her chance, if she could only broach the subject of preparing for the impending calamity in just the right way.

Overduke Afaln Pymseet stood at the front of the balcony, dressed in a silk vest and trousers, resting his hands and leaning on the stone balustrade rail before him. He smiled at the crowd through a neatly trimmed beard under a pair of spectacles housed in narrow frames.

Allabva could see behind him now, and realized the balcony and the room behind it were much larger than she had realized. A few dozen people sat at tables set further into the building, leading Allabva to wonder if this was the end of the brunch that Chief Magistrate Spalgen was supposed to attend. They certainly appeared well-dressed and important. She could believe that several of them were dukes and duchesses, though she didn't see the magistrate among them right now.

The overduke continued.

"Many of you remember last year's winner—the same man who won the previous two years, Rawaln Forllen!"

Several whoops emanated from the crowd, but subsided quickly.

"Perhaps it is no surprise that he should be bested by someone younger than himself, but I think you all must share my shock that the one to accomplish such a feat, this fair creature before us, should be... Should be..."

The overduke trailed off, staring into the distance, alerting Allabva's sense that something was distracting him. Identifying a moment of silence that could be an opportunity, and worried that it may not come again, Allabva dared to address him. She wasn't sure exactly what manner was demanded by protocol... What did she care? She was about to break protocol, anyway.

"Your Majesty, I had hoped—"

Time slowed as the overduke turned his gaze to Allabva, his brow furrowed into deep creases. At first she was taken aback, worried she had ruined her shot with a misstep. But he wasn't angry—he was confused.

"What can this mean?" the ruler said aloud.

What? Allabva thought, turning her head to look to the east as she began to hear the commotion that had caught the overduke's attention. She could just see the tops of heads; there were people shouting and moving in the distance, as if avoiding something.

No, she thought, *I can't let this go by!*

"My lord, I requested an audience, and—"

"Not now!" Pymseet commanded, holding up a hand to stop Allabva.

"RUN!" a voice screamed from the street outside the palace gate leading into the courtyard.

"Close the palace gates!" came another shout.

But it was too late, as people flooded through, running into each other as those in the street tried to flee into the compound while some of those inside tried to avoid being trapped. Individual screams quickly piled together to create pandemonium and general panic. In all the confusion, none of the crowd's shouts arrived clearly to Allabva's ears.

"Guards, protect the overduke!" a man in uniform yelled nearby.

The flood of people at the gates fell away from something moving toward the palace as if melting before a hot iron freshly plucked from the forge's heat, and the Nightshade Unicorn calmly walked onto the palace grounds.

Allabva was hurt. Why did he have to scrap all their careful work in one moment? No, she was furious.

"No!" she shouted at the beast she was bonded to. How could he ruin her chance to resolve this rationally with soft words? "Go away!"

"Avaunt!" a voice in the crowd yelled, its owner repeating the shooing gesture the whole town had used during the festivities two hours earlier. It may have been comical if Allabva weren't so incensed.

She leapt down from the top of the wall and ran toward the black Nomord from which everybody else fled like mice from a cat.

"You cannot come here! Go away, you out-of-touch, old relic!" Allabva's eyes burned as she approached the Shrongelin and sobbed, "Please, go. I was so close."

"I will speak with the overduke," the Nightshade said stoically.

"No! Not now!" Allabva ran to meet the great beast, and started shoving him, pushing him with her hands, with her shoulder, her back, sobbing the whole time, "Go away, go away from here! You can't ruin things like this!"

Enhanced strength or no, Allabva was no match for the Shrongelin. She didn't know how much he benefited from the bond, but he also gained increased physical strength like she did. Allabva didn't stand a chance of stopping the Shrongelin if he wanted to press on right now.

But he stopped, looking down at her. They locked eyes for a moment. Allabva wondered if he could read her in any supernatural way, as the Hronomon's gift had let Tuki see her soul. But right now, she assumed all the Shrongelin could see were the tears in her eyes.

He turned around as Allabva futilely kept trying to push him back. Then, picking up pace, he trotted out of the courtyard, Allabva hot on his heels, still screaming herself hoarse, "Go away!"

Allabva followed the Nightshade all the way to the north central city gate and out into the countryside. Once they were a distance away and they saw that no crowds followed, he turned on her.

"Why did you push me out?" he demanded.

"What do you mean, why? I was just starting to talk to the overduke!"

The Shrongelin was silent for a moment. "Was it a summons?"

Allabva blinked. "No, but he was right in front of me."

"It was nothing, Companion," the Nomord bit back. "It was festivities only. Give a little speech about how great your little human kingdom is, about how it fought off another little human kingdom. Talking about real issues was not on the agenda for today."

"I know, but I was in the act of *putting* it on the agenda for the day!"

Nightshade cleared his throat. "I see that you were near him. Maybe you would have been able to speak of serious things with him, though I doubt that. At any rate, it has taken too long to get to this point."

"That's it? 'It's taking too long', that's why you went in there? You think he'll talk to you?" Allabva asked. "Did you see and hear the people's reaction when the *Nightshade Unicorn himself* marched right into the city and onto palace grounds?"

"Some reaction is inevitable!" the Nomord shouted back. "Let them have their reaction, but then they will realize the world they live in is not what they thought it was. Then they will talk."

"And how long will that take? How long will it take to build up some modicum of hierarchy of civilization again, after you tear it down in the people's panic, before there's a designated person to talk to in the first place?"

Allabva stared at the Nomord, wide-eyed and trying to comprehend the line of thinking that had brought him into the city in the middle of the Southmarch festival. There must be something else, some other reason he would throw their plan away after all that.

The Shrongelin looked at Allabva with what she could only describe as worry or concern.

"What else is there?" she asked. "You didn't go there ignorant of the disastrous effect it would have."

"Our plans were made based on the current political structure of nations in order to rally together against Sacalai.

But if they never know there is a problem at all, there is nothing for them to rally against."

Allabva shook her head. "No, I know there's more to it. Please tell me."

The Nightshade lowered his head for a moment, then raised it, shaking his mane. His worried look now showed a hint of desperation. "Sacalai is growing stronger. I have tried to hold onto her prison for too long, and we *must* be prepared in time. I may have acted rashly, but my reasons are rock solid."

"Yes, it was rash." Allabva rubbed her forehead before speaking more. "Look, Nighty, just give me one more day. I will talk to people and pull strings as hard as I can. If that doesn't work, I'll jump over the palace wall and talk to good old Afaln. If that doesn't turn out, be my guest to walk back in. But please, give me one more day."

Allabva and the Shrongelin locked eyes. Finally, he spoke again.

"We will need a ship. We have the best bet at procuring one if we lean on the current social order without upsetting it first. Very well, you have one day. Meet me outside the Tallen Gate by sundown tomorrow."

The Nightshade turned and walked away, leaving Allabva wondering how she was supposed to pick up the pieces that he had left scattered this afternoon.

Falndeg passed the guards and entered the library alone, locking the door behind himself. This was no regular workday, so the library had been empty all day. It was late afternoon on

Southmarch, and Falndeg had come to search. He climbed the stairs and made his way to the special collections.

Which books had he shown that clown Leaf, only two and a half days before? The scruffy man hadn't seemed to be anything consequential, coming here and talking about old-as-time children's stories. Jackalopes and castles and stars and dungeons... What did he hope to find, puzzling out nonsense like that?

Falndeg located the library's volumes on folklore and rubbed his temples. Which books had he allowed Leaf to read? Which one had the man pulled his last mysterious-nonsense-snippet-of-the-day from?

Taking a guess, Falndeg selected one of the books and set it down on the nearest table. He opened it and flipped through its pages. This wasn't the right one.

He left the book on the table, returning to the shelf to grab another.

Wrong again.

His hand hovered over the shelf a third time. He had to find the correct book, had to find that passage the silly man had thought was so significant. Had to figure out what today had meant.

He grabbed a third priceless, ancient book and looked it over as he placed it on the table.

Leaf had been right. This wasn't a primary source, just a very old secondary source. Still, it was the best Falndeg could come by.

After a few moments, he found the passage he was looking for.

The nightmare beast was never the problem, but the prelude.

But that wasn't what Leaf had quoted; that was what Falndeg himself had spotted when he put the book away. He sat down and read on slowly, having to take out a pencil to make notes on a small pad he carried with him.

The librarian settled in. After the creature that looked like a dark Nomord strutted onto palace grounds today, Falndeg knew that he needed to be ready to advise his overduke on anything ancient or arcane at a moment's notice. However, first he needed to make sure his information was as accurate as possible.

He had a lot of reading to do tonight, and it seemed like he should have brushed better up on his Old Tal before now.

The nightmare beast was never the problem, but the prelude. As the harbinger…

CHAPTER 35

AFTERMATH... OR BEFORE

A llabva awoke the next morning to the sound of knocking on her door. That was unusual; nobody had bothered her in the morning before. She tried to blink away the sleepiness, grateful there wasn't too much light.

Then she groaned, realizing she'd been woken up quite early. After parting ways with the Shrongelin the previous afternoon, she had gone to the Coughing Badger and waited, hoping to meet up with people. They had all come eventually: Lamtor, Alial, Cariel, Walrus, Panli, and Tank. She had passed hours there into the night, discussing how to recover from the Nightshade's interruption and meet with the overduke after all.

Allabva had begged and finally relented with Walrus to get him to seek a chance to talk to the chief magistrate again. Panli had suggested Allabva make an attempt via Baroness Scalleh, as she stood approximately halfway between a regular commoner and the overduke, hierarchically speaking. Allabva decided it was worth a try, and intended to do so later this morning. Cariel had sided with the Guardian, suggesting Allabva jump over the palace wall and be done with it.

"Miss Companion?"

"One moment!"

She jumped out of bed and threw her dress over her head, pulling it down hastily. She had nothing else to wear, but at least it had been washed the day before. Glancing in her small desk mirror, she pulled her hair back and tied it with a simple ribbon, tucking spare locks behind her ears.

It was useless; she couldn't get presentable this fast. She didn't have to be seen, did she? "Who's there?"

"Miss Companion, it's Mistress Tofan."

When had the innkeeper stopped calling Allabva "Madam?" *Just as well,* Allabva thought. *I'm no 'Madam' to her. At least she didn't bother about me once she figured out I was no delegate.* Really, the innkeeper had handled the confusion the best way Allabva saw.

"Can I help you?" Allabva asked through the door.

"There's a messenger here for you. He insists on seeing you personally, or he cannot deliver his message."

Confused, Allabva took another look in the small mirror, then walked over to the door, walking staff in hand, just in case. Opening the door, she saw only Mistress Tofan standing there.

"Where is—"

"He's downstairs, in the common room. I won't have unnecessary noise up here among my guests' rooms."

Allabva pulled her boots on and followed the woman down to the common room, where a man stood wearing official-looking clothing.

"Miss Companion," the stranger said, "in light of your recent victory in the Avaunt yesterday, combined with the—" he coughed once "—rude interruption by an impossible hallucination we all seem to have shared, his majesty Overduke Afaln Pymseet wishes to continue the conversation he began with you at the Southmarch Victory Feast, but in a quiet setting this time."

Allabva's eyes widened. She got the audience! "How do I—"

"Come to the west entrance to the palace at third strike, no later. You may bring one escort for your protection—if you need it, though I imagine any bodyguard will be far weaker than you..." The messenger raised an eyebrow, evidently remembering how Allabva had been seen running with a grown man on her shoulders. "But any weapons must be surrendered at the gate. Do you understand your summons?"

Allabva's mind raced to take it all in. She repeated it back to the man. "Um—yes. West gate, third strike or sooner, one escort, no weapons inside."

The messenger nodded. "Perfect. Have a lovely day." Then, looking intimidated as he finished a conversation with a slight figure he knew could pummel him if she wished, he turned and left the inn, leaving Allabva standing there, wondering how to make sure she was ready.

What would she say to a willing ear today?

"Miss Companion, would you like your breakfast?" Mistress Tofan asked. "I can have the kitchen whip it up in a moment."

Allabva blinked, settling on a course of action in her mind. "No, thank you. I'll be back later; I'll take it then."

Allabva rushed to the Tallen Gate, giving occasional inaudible blasts on Delgan's flute. She had to talk to the Shrongelin. As she exited the city, she saw his indistinct shadow at the top of the hill and jogged at human pace to get there.

"Do you have news?" he asked when Allabva reached him, getting directly to the point.

"I have a summons," Allabva replied, breathless after her sprint through the city.

The Nightshade cocked his head. "When?"

"I have to report by third strike."

"Alright. You could have waited until sundown to tell me how it went; why are you telling me now?"

"I don't know what to do or what to say. The messenger said I can bring an escort, but I think after everyone's reaction yesterday, it will have to be a human escort."

"Not to mention your own reaction," Nightshade reminded Allabva.

She shrugged awkwardly. "I suppose I could ask Walrus or Tank, but they don't know any more about the situation than I do; the only one around is you. I mean, I was planning to ask Panli—I don't know where to find Alial at this hour—if she could help me prepare myself to be presentable in court, but—"

The Shrongelin cleared his throat.

Allabva stopped talking and looked at him, waiting.

"I know somebody here in town who could accompany you."

"Oh." Allabva paused a moment. "How?"

The Nightshade laughed, an unearthly, foreboding sound. "You have not supposed that I was taking naps when we were apart? I have been working on my own as well."

"Oh," Allabva repeated, realizing how little she knew about this enigmatic Nomord.

"He will come to you, a green-eyed man with graying hair and beard, wearing an old cloak. He knows much concerning the Construct and what is to befall this world if we should fail. Where should he meet you?"

Allabva thought for a moment, then replied. "If I need to meet up with him, that complicates things. He could meet me at Panli's house, but if she's not there, then I will be wasting my time. Have him come to the Medicine's Roost at half past second strike."

"He will be there."

"Alright! Then I will see if I can get Panli—"

"Allabva?" the Nightshade interrupted.

"Yes?"

"Did you have a weak spell yesterday morning?"

Allabva shook her head, suddenly worried where this might be going. "No."

"I suspected not. Be ready for one this morning, but your audience with the overduke is of utmost importance."

"I know."

"Do not miss it, no matter how you feel, with physical strength or emotion. You must attend and do your best."

"I will," Allabva said, feeling the morning chill now.

"I wish you the best, Companion."

"Thank you."

Allabva walked back to the city gate. With the prospect of another weak spell interfering with her long-awaited audience, she needed to conserve her energy. There wasn't time now to seek help from Panli; Allabva would have to do her own best.

She found a messenger as soon as she could after reentering the city. The common messengers in the street didn't wear the overduke's livery like the page who came to her inn this morning, but they could be found and hired. Paying the messenger, Allabva sent word to Walrus that he need not bother the magistrate this morning, then she walked all the way to the inn.

After looking herself over several times and leaving her knife in her room, Allabva descended the stairs again. She nearly fell down a flight as the wave of nausea, sadness, and guilt hit her. She caught herself with difficulty with her normal, human-weak arms, never more glad that a staircase had a handrail.

Allabva emerged into the common room and asked for her complimentary breakfast, requesting and paying for a side of bacon and fried, diced potatoes and vegetables. She ate her breakfast in silence, trying to fight off the sense of despair that plagued her during her weak spells. She failed in this, but held herself to the plan, determined to see this day through.

Allabva ate slowly; why bother hurrying? There was no point.

Around half past second strike, her escort arrived. Allabva knew she should have thought better than to trust the Nightshade Unicorn's judgment of a good candidate. The man fit the Nomord's description, but there was much that was left out. His torn trousers and worn-out boots. His unkempt hair. His beard that spoke of living in the street, or sleeping outside in general.

And yet...there was something in his eyes and his graying hair. A soft hardness, as though he wished he could be congenial with everyone, but life had dealt him a losing hand time and again.

The stranger approached and sat across from Allabva.

"You must be Miss Companion," he greeted her. "You can call me Leaf."

Allabva tilted her head as if she could catch more information falling into her ear that way, intrigued at his manner and name. Her despair and nausea were gently muted, imposed upon by a sense of surrealness.

"Yes. You can call me Allabva."

"I understand we're going to see the overduke. Shall we get going?"

"You don't have any weapons, do you? They'll take them away at the gate."

"It's just me here," Leaf said, spreading his hands wide, "though some people seem to think I can be rather intimidating." He smiled weakly.

Allabva took another look at the man's appearance. She was to meet the overduke with this man as her escort? Maybe she could do something about the way he looked; she had the gold from winning the Avaunt yesterday, after all.

"Let's go," she said. "Let me buy you a new cloak. There's a shop right down the street. Not the cheapest, but I happen to have the coin right now."

"But—"

"We need to hurry to make it in time, but this meeting is important. Vilna's Fashions will have something for you."

"I don't—"

"What?" Allabva asked. "I'm offering you a new cloak for free. I'd pay for a haircut, too, but there's no time for that."

Leaf shook his head. "Thank you, but I won't be needing a new cloak or anything else."

"We're meeting the *overduke*," Allabva stressed.

"I know. But I've heard some things this city is saying about you, and I'm sure he'll see you even if you show up with poor, old me."

Allabva clenched her jaw, seeing that the man wasn't going to budge on this.

"Fine. Let's go."

Chapter 36

Making a Case

Allabva and Leaf made their way to the palace and were granted entry via the west palace gate, a wide wrought iron construction bedecked with pieces of filigree in gold and silver. After Allabva's identity was confirmed and both were examined for weapons, the pair was led through several sets of doors, past guard after guard, through imposing halls hung with tall tapestries and expensive looking decorative pottery, then deposited in an antechamber no less elaborately decorated, to wait until called.

"Please wait here," said the servant who brought them. "The overduke will see you after his current meeting. He doesn't hold court until fifth strike most days, so you'll be undisturbed. You will meet with him in one of the side audience chambers inside."

Then he disappeared, leaving them alone, except for the two guards standing on either side of great, gilded double doors which Allabva assumed lead into the royal court.

Allabva turned to bedraggled Leaf awkwardly as it occurred to her that he was the first person she had met who already knew the Shrongelin. It was also the first time she had had to interact much with anyone during one of her weak spells.

"You've been meeting with the Guardian?" she asked him through a haze of misery, softly so the guards wouldn't overhear their conversation.

He dipped his head. "You could say that."

"He says you know about the Construct."

"That's right."

"Good," Allabva breathed, "I might need some help in there."

"I'm sure you'll do fine. I expect I'm just here for support."

"I'll probably need all the support you can offer," she prefaced. "I'm not feeling well right now, so I'm afraid my mind isn't as sharp this morning as it normally might be."

Leaf smiled. "Don't worry. Believe in yourself. If you're the Companion, I'm sure the Forerunner had good reason to choose you."

"I hope you don't mind me probing, but who are you?" Allabva puzzled aloud.

Leaf took a breath before answering. "I'm a humble servant of the Construct, like yourself. I'll do what I can to help out."

"You look like you're from western Eslarna also, like me," Allabva said. "Is that correct? What brought you to Tallensworth?"

"I think that will have to wait for another time, my young friend," Leaf said, looking up as a man entered the antechamber.

The man was dressed smartly, even ornately, but nowhere near as much as Allabva had seen the overduke and his guests on the balcony yesterday. The man carried a tall mug, and was that the smell of...oats and nutmeg?

The man stopped as soon as he laid eyes on Allabva's escort.

"Leaf? You have business with the overduke?"

"Not me," the unkempt man answered, then pointed at Allabva. "Her."

"You—you..." the man with the mug looked back and forth between Allabva and Leaf, as if trying to grasp something that was far out of reach.

Leaf turned to Allabva. "Miss Companion, this is Head Librarian Falndeg, of the royal library here on the palace grounds."

Allabva blinked, considering this information. "What—so you have been to the library?"

"Almost every day for the past two weeks," Falndeg answered distantly. "He's come to read esoteric children's stories and ask me odd questions about them." The librarian snapped out of his daze, focusing on Allabva. "And you're the Avaunt champion. The one who faced..."

Falndeg's eyes widened, rolled back in his head, and closed as he crumpled to the floor, out cold.

"Falndeg!" Leaf exclaimed as he and Allabva rushed forward to help.

The man had spilled his oat brew all over his trousers and shirt as he fell. Allabva righted the cup and set it on the floor off to the side while Leaf tried to revive him.

The guards saw the need for their assistance, and stepped forward from the gilded double doors, which began to open, pulled into the court inside.

Allabva heard voices coming out from within.

"I'm sorry, gentlemen, but if the overduke has told you he can't promise anything right now, that is that."

"He cannot ignore us forever. We grow by hundreds every day."

What? Allabva's ears were pricked.

"I assure you, he does not ignore you. But if he chooses not to grant your requests, that is his prerogative."

A third voice entered the conversation. "My father may be unimportant, but we are not."

One guard knelt next to Allabva and Leaf, pulling Allabva's attention back to this side of the great double doors; Falndeg still lay inert on the floor. "You have audience now," the kneeling guard said. We will help him from here."

The other guard seemed standoffish. "The librarian was obviously upset when he saw these two. Do you really think we should still let them in?"

"He was overwhelmed by remembering the Nightshade Unicorn yesterday, and this girl had the guts to face the beast. If she meant to hurt the overduke, she already could have done it yesterday."

The second guard nodded. "Fine. Go on ahead, you two. We'll take it from here."

Allabva's attention was pulled back to the conversation coming from inside the court as she heard the door open.

"We are not going away," the first voice said. "He may not grant us entry to the city, but our group will be right outside to remind him of his people's needs."

"But I will be right here," the third voice said. "Since my father is a baron, you can't keep me out of the city without the the endorsement of the Dukes' Council." This voice sounded younger, and very narcissistic.

Allabva looked up and froze. Three men stood there in a row. Two of them, the closest and farthest from the door they had just exited, were unfamiliar faces to her. The man in the center was Nolder Lawgrin, one of the party of five Disaffected who had abducted her on the road as she journeyed eastward a few weeks before. She stood slowly as she made eye contact with him, feeling a sudden, new tension in the air.

Nolder nodded to her, a suspicious expression crawling across his face. "Allabva," was all he spoke.

The man closest to the door wore palace livery, and must have been the second voice Allabva overheard. The younger man, farthest from the door, wore modest finery embroidered in a light brown color and a sneer on his face; Allabva suspected his face probably always looked like that.

The snobby young son of a baron looked to Nolder and back to Allabva. "So, this is the little girl who conspires with monsters."

"Yes," Nolder answered.

At the same time, the page in palace livery said, "I don't know about monsters, but Miss Companion is next for audience. Farewell, gentlemen. Have a nice day. Miss Companion and escort, if you will, please?"

Leaf stood next to Allabva, who took a step toward the double doors. Then she stumbled, having an image thrust in her mind of the overduke in the side audience chamber, with a knife in his chest. A hand still rested on the hilt of the knife, and the light brown embroidered sleeve on that hand...

Instead of stepping away from the doors, the baron's son turned and plowed through Nolder and the page as he shoved his way back into the court. He disappeared from view faster than should have been possible.

Nolder and the page were knocked to the floor as the young snob passed through. "Hugne, you fool!" Nolder shouted as he fell.

"No!" Allabva shouted, and mentally heaved herself through the nausea and dread she felt, willing herself to run forward. She had no weapon, she had no supernatural strength at the moment, but she *had* to stop that man. She broke into a sprint, heedless to the fact that it was too slow.

Allabva stepped over them, running.

"Your Majesty!" she screamed, "watch out for—"

"Girl, wait!" the guards called after her. It barely registered in her mind, but the guards were now also chasing the wishful assailant.

Allabva entered the royal court, a vast chamber of proportions she would not have believed if she only saw the building from the outside.

Hugne was two-thirds of the distance across the great chamber, sprinting to the far end, where a side chamber door was cracked open.

Allabva felt desperation, unsure if it was her own, or an effect of the weak spell. Her effort wasn't enough. Without the gift from the Shrongelin's bond, she couldn't hope to catch up to this man.

Then Allabva felt the surge of power, the strength of the bond flowing through her once more, the relief from the inexplicable sadness. Now unencumbered, she *sprinted*.

Without looking back, the too-fast Hugne reached the far side, opening the door and running inside the audience chamber.

Allabva reached the door a moment after and jumped inside, grabbing Hugne's arm as he held the dagger high, the alarmed overduke still sitting in his chair and looking up in panic.

"No, you pig dropping!" the young noble shouted in angry frustration, struggling to swing his knife at the overduke, at Allabva, anything.

An image of animal droppings flashed in Allabva's mind, confusing her. She held onto the man's wrist and pried the knife from his grasp as easily as if he were a toddler. Then she dropped the blade and backed away from the ruler, pulling the snob Hugne with her across the room.

Running footsteps approached across the royal court.

"Your Majesty, are you—"

The guards entered together, wide-eyed and breathless, then stopped when they saw Allabva had the situation under control and the overduke was turning the dagger over in his hands.

"You little girl, I will kill you," Hugne raved, and images of violence flashed through her mind.

What is he? she thought.

More pounding footsteps approached at a slower run, and Nolder and the page appeared.

"Your highness," Nolder said, "this girl is not what she seems! She—"

"Silence!" Overduke Afaln Pymseet roared. "Let me sort this out. For the moment, I see that she has restrained *your* companion," he pointed at Nolder, "who just tried to kill me. Yesterday, she chased off a frightful beast who entered the palace grounds on one of the biggest feasts of the year. Right now, I'm inclined to hear her out, which she duly requested two weeks ago!"

As he spoke, Allabva handed Hugne over to the two guards. The overduke continued.

"I already granted you audience, after only two days of you submitting the request, out of consideration for the size and novelty of the settlement you represent. Have I not been fair thus far, Master Lawgrin?"

Nolder's face was red, but he nodded. "Yes, your Majesty."

"I don't suppose you had any part in your fellow's plan?"

"No, your Majesty."

"If I may—" Allabva said, tentatively.

"Please," the overduke interrupted, "of all the people here, I must say you have me quite intrigued right now. Speak, if you will."

Nolder scowled and Allabva spoke.

"Master Lawgrin appeared just as surprised as the rest of us when Hugne bolted back into the court chamber. I don't think he had any violent plans today."

The ruler stared at Allabva, chewing his tongue before speaking. "Thank you, Miss Companion, for your candidness." He looked askance at Nolder. "I don't know what it is you and she have going on, but I'll find it out from her for now. You will be escorted outside of the palace grounds, but thanks to your apparent adversary's words, you will not be expelled from the city. Your company will still remain outside the walls. You will be permitted one guest accompanying you in the city. You will wait for my summons, or leave if you wish. Do you understand?"

Nolder's face was a mask of studied indifference. "Yes, your Majesty."

"Good, and don't expect a summons too soon, after what just happened. Page, please see that his pass is updated and escort him from the grounds. Guards, you may take Hugne to find a suitable cell."

The guards snapped to a salute and turned to go, guiding Hugne with his hands now bound behind his back.

"Can the guards wait a moment, your Majesty?" Allabva said quickly.

The guards paused to wait for the ruler's decision.

"Yes, what is it?"

"He..." Allabva reconsidered discussing her thoughts in front of Nolder. "Will I be able to speak with him later?"

"Of course, Miss Companion."

"Then never mind."

The guards turned to take Hugne away and the overduke stood. "Miss Companion, let us not be alone. I've learned that almost any conversation I have ought to have a few witnesses. Did you come with no escort today?"

"I did," Allabva answered, the surreal feeling returning. It had abated when she jumped into action to stop Hugne. Fortunately, it was not accompanied by another weak spell. "He must still be in the antechamber. There was a man who passed out, and we went to help him..."

"Sire!" Falndeg's voice called, nervousness dripping. He entered the court, walking quickly to cross the distance while the guards and page escorted the two Disaffected out a side door. He walked in an odd manner, trying to hide the stains from his spilled drink. "Sire, whatever she says, you have to hear this girl."

"Yes, I intend to do that."

"No, I mean you really must—"

"Falndeg, why don't you sit down with us and talk to her with me?"

"Uh, well, there's—"

"Oh, we were also just looking for her escort; have you seen him?" the ruler asked.

"Umm, I'm afraid I don't—"

Allabva heard the clopping of hooves on stone tile. *I didn't blow a distress call on the flute,* she thought.

"Sire, there's something else," the librarian spat out. "Don't be alarmed! Besides, we have Miss Companion here, right? She'll see that we're alright, surely."

"What are you going on about, you bookworm?"

The gilded doors were pushed open, and the Nightshade Unicorn walked in.

"Guards, to me!" the overduke screamed.

"Please, your Majesty," the Nightshade spoke, "let us discuss matters calmly."

The overduke looked to Allabva, seeming to expect some derring-do acts.

Allabva stood in place, staring at the Shrongelin.

"How can we be calm?" the regent asked, breathing rapidly and obviously struggling to keep from shouting more or running. "The creature is back, right here in my court!"

"He was never the problem," the librarian answered in a frightened voice. "The calamities—"

"I promise he won't hurt you," Allabva said. "Can you trust me?"

The overduke's eyes darted between Allabva, Falndeg, and the Shrongelin. Finally, he nodded slowly at her. "But the guards will be here in a moment. When they see..." He gestured to the great black Nomord and let the implication hang in the air.

"Not to worry," the Nightshade said. "Please, do not be alarmed. Companion, brace yourself."

What?

Then, before Allabva's eyes, the Shrongelin...melted. Stepping forward slowly, his blade-like horn and sinewy build shrank and contorted, replaced by the form of a man wearing shabby clothing and worn-out boots.

Leaf stood before them.

Allabva watched the librarian's mouth work, jaw opening and closing as he realized his recent acquaintance's true identity. Allabva felt no lesser shock herself. Meanwhile, she found herself gripping her midriff as she felt the nausea of another weak spell setting in. Her brow twisted and she squinted her eyes as it dawned on her that the Nightshade had known exactly when and *why* these weak spells occurred.

She looked at him and opened her mouth to say, *You*. Nothing came out. Leaf smiled and inclined his head at her, and she understood that this was not the moment. Right now she had to keep face in front of the overduke.

Leaf bowed to the ruler. "Your Majesty, we have much to discuss. I trust you will inform your guards there is nothing to be worried about?"

The overduke looked to Allabva. "My librarian came to me late last night, telling me the dark Nomord may not be the malicious creature we assumed yesterday. At any rate, combining that opinion with the many reports of your odd behavior... In the end, do you know what convinced me to ask you here? It was how you saved a child and helped a grain seller in the southwest market. Why? You had no ties to them. And just who are you, young woman?"

Allabva smiled meekly, sparing a glance to Leaf to see if he caught that. "I am just that, a young woman, but I am traveling for a very important reason with this Nomord known as the Guardian..."

CHAPTER 37

O'ER THE DEEPEST, BLUEST SEA

"Delgan, be a comrade and hand me that vial of oil and the rag next to it," Ruldern said, gathering his hand tools together. "I don't know why they hold this smiths' trade fair up here in Norl. The air is something else here on the Falren Bay. Keeps the whole city incredibly humid, and all these nice tools like to rust under those conditions."

Delgan complied, opening the vial for the master blacksmith and wetting the rag before handing it to him. He also continued his own work of untying the cover they had on their portable table, then walked off to the picket lines to come back with Blackberry.

"I'm sorry I didn't catch you," Ruldern said to Delgan when he came back, "but I'm going to cut you loose for the evening, if you'll just bring Homkin by first."

Cut me loose? "Of course," Delgan said aloud.

He walked Blackberry back to the picket lines, tied him back to his post, then untied Homkin and returned to Master Ntoffel's booth.

"Thank you," Ruldern said. "I've got him now, so I can carry everything back to the inn myself. You have a good evening. Don't get into bed too late."

"What do I do?" Delgan asked awkwardly, mentally unprepared for this kind of freedom.

"I don't know," Ruldern blinked back. "Do what you want to."

"What..."

Ruldern laughed out loud. "You really are a freshly minted adult, aren't you? Not sure what to do with your free time. Go...read a book if you want. Talk to another apprentice and complain about how I do things, or better yet, go find a journeyman and learn what he did to deal with his master's idiosyncrasies. If you're not too set on that Roalke girl, go find some female companionship for a couple of hours. I'm going to go talk to some old fogies like myself."

Delgan stood, holding Homkin's reins and wondering what he wanted to do.

"I suppose you could come with me if you really wanted to, but we'll probably talk about taxes, or how our wives keep moving our favorite mugs, or something else boring."

Delgan realized he still held the reins to his master's horse in his hand.

"Delgan," Ruldern said, stepping forward and taking the reins with a grin. "Go have fun."

Delgan sat at a table in the Bristling Boar, staring down a plate in front of him that he hoped he could finish. The meat pie hadn't sounded quite this large when the waiter had described it, and it was accompanied by a rhubarb tart just to make it more of a challenge. Next to his plate sat a mug of the local concoction, a Norl soft brew made from sassafras they liked to call bakine.

Across from Delgan sat two young men he had met at the trade fair. Each one had his meat pie and tart, along with a mugful of bakine.

"It sure is nice to be able to visit an actual city, don't you think, boys?" Joró said. "I think after dinner I'm going to have to swing by one of the more grown-up taverns in town, if you know what I mean."

"I don't know," Dass said. "I live here in Norl. I'm glad for the convenience of everything we have close by. And I appreciate the community we have here. I think people look out for one another. But what I do know is that those taverns? One thing I think this city could do without."

"What are you, some kind of child?" Joró asked rhetorically. "Those taverns are what it's all about. What about you, Delgan? You've been kind of quiet."

"I don't know," Delgan said. "I live in a smaller town, and I think we have the kind of community Dass is talking about. Maybe we don't have all the convenience. There is that—you can buy pretty much whatever you want here. Fabrics. Tools. I guess that's what the city has going for it."

"You're making it sound like you like living in a small town, Delgan," said Joró.

"Well, yes, I do," Delgan said.

"Let me tell you," Joró said. "I live in a small town myself. It's called Mosswood, and it's a little south of Parfall. You ever heard of it? Yeah, I didn't think so. And those small-town folk, man, they tell some crazy stories. Let me tell you. Lately, I've been hearing stories about one of them unicorns."

Delgan saw Dass's eye twitch.

"What kind of stories?" Delgan asked Joró.

"Oh, it's this crazy guy, I don't know. He came in to have his horse shod, but he was blathering on about how he's seen this unicorn following at a distance behind a wagon full of people."

"What do you mean?" Delgan asked.

"Just what I said. There's this cart, right? Couple of horses pulling the cart. The cart has people in it. And they're going down the road. And there's this unicorn following behind the cart. Far enough back that the people in the cart don't realize they're being followed."

"I wish you would use the proper name," Dass said softly.

Joró ignored him. "Anyway, that's just an example of the crazy stories you hear in a small town," Joró said. "Everybody knows unicorns don't do that kind of stuff. They're too dense."

Delgan saw Dass's eye twitch again.

"Joró," Delgan said. "Don't you think it would be more proper to call them Nomord?"

"Oh, shut up with that," Joró said dismissively. "They're just dumb beasts. I'll call them what I want."

Delgan took a breath to recharge his patience. "Well, I think they're fascinating animals. And, I don't know. Maybe it could happen—a Nomord following a wagon."

"Yes, but why would the unicorn do that?" Joró challenged.

"I don't know," Delgan said. "But I don't see why not, either. Who knows? Maybe there's something in the air this spring making a Nomord act funny."

"What do you mean? You heard something funny, too?" Joró asked.

Delgan hesitated. "I don't know. I'm just here to enjoy a meal. Right, Dass?"

Delgan lifted his glass in Dass's direction, and Dass nodded, seeming to recover from Joró ignoring his request to use the proper name for the Nomord.

Joró looked back and forth between Dass and Delgan, sensing that his attitude was in the minority at the table. "You know what?" Joró said. "I think I need to find a new crowd."

Taking his plate and his mug, he stood and left the table.

"I've heard about some odd behavior too, Delgan," Dass said once Joró was gone.

Delgan nodded his head. "Actually, I saw some myself, though it wasn't much. There was a Nomord standing on a hillside, watching our town festival. But I figure there's no harm in that. It was just watching, right?"

"Of course," Dass said.

Wait, Delgan thought. *What did he say a moment ago?* Out loud he said, probing, "What did you mean, 'too'?"

"I've heard of odd Nomord behavior near here."

"Has there been some?" Delgan proceeded cautiously, not divulging Mistress Roalke's tale of Hronomon coming to get Allabva in the night.

"You had already heard there was odd Nomord behavior in Norl?" Dass asked.

"Yes."

It appeared that Dass preferred caution as well, as he glanced from side to side before continuing. "Yes," he said, "there was a Nomord talking to people here a couple of weeks back."

Delgan leaned in. "I heard that too," he said. "I was hoping to hear more about it. What do you—"

Dass paused a long moment, searching Delgan's eyes.

"Do you believe it could happen?"

"I don't see why not," Delgan echoed himself from earlier.

Dass leaned back in his chair. "I see you're a little skeptical. You'll entertain the idea, but you're not sold yet."

Delgan could feel the opportunity slipping by. He leaned forward in his chair, opening up a bit about Faethlen's account. "Actually, only a little bit skeptical. I heard of another Nomord. I didn't see this, but I heard about it talking to this girl I know back home."

Now Dass leaned forward again, resting his arms on the table next to his plate. "Really? What did the Nomord say?"

Now Delgan searched Dass's eyes, not wanting to say more unless he could feel safe that Dass was going to be friendly to the news.

Delgan decided he would be.

"The Nomord said there'd be trouble."

"What kind of trouble?"

Delgan gulped. "Pretty big trouble," he said softly.

"What did he say had to be done about this trouble?" Dass asked, raising an eyebrow.

Delgan checked left and right again. Dass had said *he* when talking about a Nomord. Delgan now opened up and did the same.

"He asked my friend to travel with him."

Dass's eyes nearly popped from their sockets. "When was this?"

"About three weeks ago."

"Three weeks."

Dass looked at his hand, rapidly counting days on his fingers. "So the Nomord was here in Norl first, then went down to the Cleft."

"Where did they go?"

Now Delgan allowed a frustrated look to appear on his face. "I don't know where they went," he said. "I was starting to think I was super lucky that you knew something about them. I'm trying to find out where my friend went. And if the Nomord was here first, then she probably didn't come here."

"No," Dass agreed. "I imagine not."

"Right."

"Wait a second," Delgan said. "Was the Nomord stallion talking to you about traveling with him?"

"No," Dass said. "It was a friend of mine who works for the duke of Norl's game warden."

Delgan sat back, feeling a small sense of loss as this apparent near miss failed to produce any information on where Allabva had gone. Perhaps it wasn't a total loss, though. After all, now he knew that Dass was an ally, and he knew there was no need to ask Joró anything else about Nomord activity.

"Do you think I can meet your friend?" Delgan asked. "I'm guessing he and I would get along pretty well."

Wherever Allabva was and whatever she was doing, Delgan hoped she was safe and happy.

"A Lemnerox?" Alial asked. "What's that?"

"Somebody who has performed a dark ritual to steal magic from the world around them, but not from a Nomord," Allabva answered.

"Oh. Why not from a Nomord? It would seem there is more magic to be had there, what with the healing power and all."

"Because if a Lemnerox steals a Nomord's magic, that's a Binterox, which is more powerful."

"Oh," Alial said, "so this Hugne guy was a Lemnerox. What magic did he have?"

Allabva nodded her head. "He's fast, and he can send mental images. We think—the Guardian and I—we think he stole his abilities from a jackalope, or maybe several jackalopes. If he has any other abilities, we can't pin it down. He won't talk to us."

They walked along a city street behind a cart loaded with Allabva's few belongings, plus several outfits of clothing gifted to her by the overduchess and Alial's trunk.

Allabva could have carried the items, but she was having one of her Leaf-induced weak spells. She tried to think about the weather and how grateful she was for Alial's companionship, to keep her mind off of the weight of Sacalai pressure.

"I'm confused," Alial said. "If Hugne is so fast, how did you manage to stop him from killing the overduke?"

"Because I'm faster," Allabva smiled.

She was only faster when the Nightshade was in his true form, as the powers of the bond lay dormant whenever he took on the form of Leaf. But she didn't want to talk about that in public because she might make her vulnerability known to enemies.

Leaf walked alongside the porters who were pulling the small cart through the streets, glancing back occasionally, but in general, he continued talking to Tank and Walrus, who walked along beside him.

"So let me get this straight, Allabva" Alial said. "You march in there, save the overduke's life, and then he's totally cool staring down—you know—the Guardian?"

Allabva laughed. "That's an oversimplification, but it works."

After the incident, Allabva and the Nightshade—as Leaf—had returned to the palace to engage in discussions with the overduke for hours each day over a three-day period.

"He believes us. I think the Disaffected showing up on his doorstep helped edge him our way as well. And he's giving us—or rather, he's commissioning—a ship to travel with us, with a full complement of supplies and crew."

"Wow," Alial breathed. "Does it feel strange?"

"It absolutely does." Allabva breathed through her teeth. "I'm just a farm girl who knows how to take care of apple trees. What business do I have bearing a title?"

"All the business in the world, apparently," Alial affirmed. "Besides, your title is different from anything the overduke can give. Your title means actual power."

"I don't care about power," Allabva said. "Unless it's the power to protect and help people."

Alial turned her head to look squarely at Allabva. "Isn't that exactly the power you got? You know, as none other than—" she lowered her voice. "—the Companion to the Shrongelin himself."

The world was still going to have to get used to the idea that the Shrongelin was a Nomord, and one who had a demonic look to him, no less.

"I suppose," Allabva said.

"I'm confused about something else."

"What's that?"

"Did you know the Guardian could, you know, become Leaf?" Alial asked.

"I had no idea," Allabva answered.

"But isn't he the second Nomord you traveled with? Could the Forerunner do it, too?"

Allabva shook her head. "All Nomord can, but—"

"Why don't they? Why haven't people seen them do it?"

"Because the Ta-Nomord aren't fully in this world, so they don't have any reason to, nor do they of it."

"And Hronomon?" Alial asked. "Wouldn't that have been awfully convenient when you were trying to avoid people who don't like Nomord?"

"Nightshade says Hronomon probably doesn't remember how," Allabva said. "The Construct has some effect on his memory."

"Oh. Well, I heard you went to the Tuna Tank the other day," Alial changed the subject.

"What of it?" Allabva said, smiling because she knew that Alial was making no judgment.

"That place is full of gossip," Alial said, "and I know there are a lot of people who complain about the overduke's policies."

"That's true," Allabva agreed.

"Did you talk to the overduke about their complaints?"

Allabva took a moment to wave back at somebody who had recognized her as the champion of the Avaunt.

"Actually, the Guardian and I aren't here to get into local politics about things like that. There's no time. We're here to rally the world against the greatest threat ever known."

Allabva looked down as a wave of discouragement pressed on her. How could she hope to stop the greatest threat the world had ever known?

Steeling herself, she went on. "As long as a ruler will rally behind us and lend the support of his or her resources, that's all that matters—until the enemy is back in her prison."

"So," Alial prompted, letting the prompt hang in the air.

"But yes, I did." Allabva laughed. "I mentioned them to him. Just to help him be aware in case he wasn't."

"Was he already?"

"He was."

The group reached the docks, where Lamtor stood waiting for them. The porters set the front of the cart down and turned to grab the luggage. Walrus and Tank stepped in to help load the things onto the ship that would take Allabva across the Gulf to Iddypol and then beyond from there.

Allabva eyed the lettering on the side of the ship's keel and stern, trying to decide if *Featherstone* was a good name for a ship or not. Birds got places quickly, right? But stones had a tendency to find the quickest route to the bottom of a body of water.

"I'm glad I ran into you back at Greenstock," Lamtor said.

"So am I," Allabva replied, wishing that she could feel this gladness more completely, free of the weight of the construct as it pressed on her right now.

"You remember what I told you?" Lamtor said, opening and closing his hand and putting it in and out of his pocket while looking down at Allabva's hip.

"Yes," Allabva said, reaching into her own pocket and holding the brooch.

"I'm glad I can't go," Lamtor said with a pointed look.

"You liar," Allabva laughed, pulling her hand from her pocket. She leaned forward and embraced him in a hug. "But you're kind of going," she said. "You're sending your sister with me."

"Someone has to keep you out of trouble," Alial joked. "Who knows what will happen if I'm not there to stop you from charging at wild animals with nothing but your bare hands."

"Speaking of bare hands," Alial said, "how did that Disaffected guy get into the overduke's presence with a knife?"

Allabva paused. How could she condense the explanation enough to save time?

"He has a mild magical enhancement," she said. "It lets him cast images into other people's minds. I think when he was inspected at the palace gate, he must have cast an image of his belt without a knife on it."

Lamtor looked troubled. "The bad guys have magic too?" he asked.

Allabva nodded. "Keep on your toes, music boy."

"If you were here in the city doing all that work by yourself," Lamtor puzzled, "and the Guardian could turn into Leaf and come talk to people also, why didn't he? Wouldn't that have made things easier for you?"

"He did a little bit of it," Allabva answered, "in his own focused way. He talked to the royal librarian, after all, to prepare him for the idea of...well...himself." She laughed at the irony. "But he can't stay as Leaf all the time for a couple of reasons."

"What are those?" Alial asked.

"One, I'm not going to say right now," Allabva said. She was vulnerable, with regular human strength and speed, while the Shrongelin walked around as Leaf.

"Number two: when he is Leaf, the other Gha-Nomord—they have a heavier burden. He says if he stayed as Leaf all the time, Sacalai would break out faster."

"Ah, I see," Alial replied.

"Wait, I have a question," Lamtor said.

Allabva looked at him expectantly.

"We've talked about the Disaffected some. Why do they say they want to change the order of society, but they also always express hate for the Nomord? That seems like it doesn't necessarily match up, and it seems...I don't know, oddly specific."

Allabva nodded. "I thought so, too, and I was confused as to which one is their real goal. I think it's both. Remember, this is because of Sacalai's influence in the world. I think she wants them to think it's all about reordering society because she can convince more people to join her cause that way, but what she really cares about is killing the Nomord so they don't imprison her again."

Lamtor looked at Allabva through haunted eyes now. "That sounds very calculated. I wish I hadn't asked."

Allabva felt a shiver go down her spine. "Yes. I wish I hadn't answered."

Leaf remained over by Tank and Walrus, and although he looked at Allabva now as if he wondered if this conversation might cause trouble, he said nothing to stop it.

"All aboard!" a man called from the ship, interrupting the questions, for better or worse.

One moment, Allabva thought, approaching Walrus and Tank.

They smiled as she walked up.

"Thank you for your help since day one," Allabva said.

"We are only glad that Jimlarnt cannot bother you," Tank answered. "And we would like to voyage with you ourselves—"

"But our wives would be furious if we disappeared like that!" Walrus laughed. "Can you picture Panli that mad? It is not something even you would want to face."

Tank got serious. "We still have things to take care of here. There's a lot to do before joining the Guardian's fight in earnestness."

"It's true," Walrus agreed. "Lots of work to prepare, and somehow we must continue paying the bills until life as we know it falls apart."

Allabva felt a twang of concern at that remark, then an idea hit her. "Friends, I have something I don't need so much of—I'm set for now—but could probably use it."

She dug out her coin purse.

"I have the winnings from the Avaunt, but I will be provided for by the overduke's resources for now. Please, let this gold make the preparations easier for you."

The two large men's eyebrows rose in surprise.

"You cannot do this," Walrus said. "It is yours."

"But I can do this exactly because it, well, because it was mine until just now," Allabva insisted. "If you don't want all of it, share some with Lamtor, and could you give a little to Master Jhalla, the grain seller in the south market? He had some hard times recently, and he could probably still use the help."

Tank started blinking rapidly, eyes reddening. "You can't do this. I..." He smiled. "Thank you. This is why you are the Companion, isn't it?" He accepted the purse and turned to Walrus, beginning to divide the sum.

Allabva leaned forward, giving a hug to each of the two men, then turned away return to the siblings. With a bittersweet feeling, she gave Lamtor another hug.

"Thank you, I still have it," Allabva said, reaching into her pocket. "And I will give it back to you when I can."

She turned to Alial.

Alial gave her brother a hug and turned to Allabva with a wide smile.

"This is it, Allie, let's go."

Allabva appreciated Alial for her manner, which reminded her of Brelin back home, especially with the impromptu nickname. Allabva tried to reciprocate and get into a playful spirit.

"Alright, Allie, let's go," she echoed back to her friend with a laugh, and they walked up the gangplank, followed by Leaf, the Guardian of the world.

"Wait!" a voice called as the crew lifted the gangplank, causing Allabva to look back to shore.

The people in the crowd on the docks moved out of the way as a young man ran between them.

"Wait!" Cariel said again as he hustled toward the *Featherstone*, carrying a heavy-looking back over his shoulder. He arrived to where the sailors were untying the mooring lines from the dock, then heaved his back across the gap and onto the ship's deck.

"What is this?" Captain Harsok yelled back. "You can't just come aboard my ship!"

"No, it's fine!" Cariel said breathlessly, still standing on the dock. "Look, I got a pass..."

He fumbled in his pocket, growing wary of the ship's widening gap from the dock.

"We'll throw your bag back."

"No, I—" Cariel tried to remove some paper from his pocket, but it wasn't folded small enough to fit easily through the top of the pocket.

"Goodbye, son," Harsok said. "Men, cast off already!"

"Oh!" Cariel gave up on pulling the paper out and leapt, covering the distance just enough to land with his midsection across the gunnel, his legs dangling in the air. If the dock had sat lower to the water, he would not have made it.

"We will cast you overboard," the captain warned.

Cariel pulled himself onto the deck and managed to get the paper out.

"I know Allabva," he gasped, "so the commissioner of ships gave me a transfer to crew on the *Featherstone.*"

Harsok took the page, inspecting it carefully. Finally, he handed it back to Cariel.

"Welcome aboard, Sailor Cariel. Be sure that you learn our way of doing things quickly, yes? Carry on, men, and somebody take charge of this boy before he causes any more ruckus."

Allabva watched all this, happy to see another friend on board. She hoped he wasn't too rough around the edges to fit in here. If only Leaf were in his true form right now, she could enjoy this moment fully, free of the weight that plagued her.

The wistful thought vanished quickly as the *Featherstone* pulled away, leaving the docks behind, and the sadness and fatalism that hung in the back of her mind grew and consumed her at the sight she now saw. A form, standing alone on the docks, looked out at her, made eye contact with her.

Nolder watched Allabva sail into the gulf.

Allabva was met on board the *Featherstone* by an obsequious woman who introduced herself as Gali Kadarn.

"I am here by commission of the Royal Overduke Pymseet," Gali said. "I am the stewardess of this voyage and, where needed, will interface between you and Captain Harsok and his crew."

While Stewardess Kadarn spoke, Allabva watched Captain Harsok shouting orders to his sailors as they cast off from the docks and set sail.

Allabva was surprised at how much work was required to sail the ship. It took some time to transition from being moored at the docks to being under full sail at sea. While she watched this activity, Allabva became aware that Stewardess Kadarn was still talking.

"Keep in mind that your security detail—"

"What?" Allabva asked.

The stewardess sighed. "You have to keep in mind that your security detail is here to protect you."

Allabva looked over at Leaf, then back to Stewardess Kadarn. "I'm not sure I need that protection," she said, glancing at the six men she hadn't noticed before and which Stewardess Kadarn was referring to.

"Of course, you need the protection," the stewardess said in a patronizing manner. "You are on an official mission from the overduke of Tallensworth himself."

"That's not exactly how I see it," Allabva said.

The stewardess stopped dead. "What do you mean, not how you see it? This is the overduke's ship, is it not?"

"Yes," Allabva answered readily.

"These are the overduke's men all about you, are they not?"

"Yes."

"Then how can you say this is not the overduke's mission?"

"It's not *his* mission," Allabva said. "It's *his* mission." She pointed to Leaf.

The stewardess looked at Leaf, then back at Allabva. "Please, no jokes right now. I don't know who that man is, except that apparently, he knows some things about old stories."

"You mean you weren't told all the details about this mission—about this voyage?" Allabva asked incredulously.

"I was told enough," Gali huffed. "You're the Champion of the Avaunt, and we're to sail wherever you say is necessary."

Allabva cocked an eyebrow. "I see. You didn't talk to the overduke himself directly?"

"Of course not," Gali answered. "He is far too busy to talk to every ship steward personally. I got my commission from the overduke via the royal commissioner of ships. Who else?"

"I see."

Allabva looked back to the dock and saw Nolder standing there, staring at her.

"I see," Allabva said again. "Well, I think you're about to find out who that man is."

Leaf looked to Allabva and shrugged. Allabva got the message. She would have done things a different way, but she knew this was the Shrongelin's way—saying they needed to rip off the bandage and people would get over it.

As Allabva watched, Stewardess Kadarn looked over at Leaf and gasped.

Leaf began to grow. His skin bulged and darkened as he leaned forward. His arms and legs grew longer, and his hands and feet—boots and all—turned into hooves. Finally, his fierce, blade-like horn sprouted from his forehead, and Allabva felt the augmented strength of the bond return to her body.

Allabva felt an impulse to flex her muscles just to feel the strength restored, but this was interrupted by the sound of screaming from those on the ship. Allabva wished her escort had given her the chance to talk to the crew first and prepare them.

She spent the next two hours explaining to the captain, the stewardess, her unnecessary security detail, and several members of the crew that the Nightshade Unicorn looked evil, sometimes acted mischievously, but was only here to help the world stop a truly evil entity.

Of course, this came after a good half hour of her jumping into the sea to extract sailors who had thrown themselves overboard in panic.

Finally, when all aboard were at least outwardly calm—if not inwardly convinced—and after Captain Harsok had chided both Allabva and the Nightshade Unicorn himself for giving them such a fright, Allabva sat and thought. Meanwhile, Alial went belowdecks to lie down, suffering from seasickness.

Stewardess Kadarn approached Allabva slowly.

"Miss Allabva—" She stopped herself. "Miss Companion?" she said more softly. "I see why you thought you didn't need your security detail."

Allabva nodded.

"But, miss," Stewardess Kadarn countered, "please consider that you must sleep sometimes, I assume."

"You're correct," Allabva admitted.

"Also, please consider that there may be some people on board this ship who may not agree that protecting human society as it is, is a good thing, and who may harbor ill will toward your hoofed friend."

Allabva looked at Gali appreciatively. "I know that's true," she said.

Gali breathed a sigh of relief. "Thank you. Then the security detail will follow their training to protect you."

Allabva nodded, noticing that three members of the detail were on the deck of the ship at that moment, appearing to do their own thing for the most part, but glancing at her frequently.

Stewardess Kadarn departed, saying, "Let me know if you need anything, either from me or from the crew. I think I'm feeling a little unsettled in the stomach myself."

Allabva nodded, and the woman was gone.

No sooner had Stewardess Kadarn retreated than the Shrongelin approached, his hooves tapping their distinct sound on the wooden planks.

"Companion," he addressed her.

Allabva smiled. She had begun to feel seasick herself before Leaf had transformed back into his Nomord form, and she was grateful for the bond.

"Yes, Guardian," she replied.

"You have made good progress on your journey."

Allabva took a deep breath in. If it started sounding like a compliment, she felt sure he was about to point out where she needed to improve.

"You fought against the odds to join me at the Summit Above the Aspens. You agreed to the bond, and in so doing, became a true friend to all who seek peace. Most recently, you convinced a great leader among men to champion your cause. And as we sail away from Tallensworth, the overduke is preparing it for all-out war, even though it does not appear to be at his doorstep yet."

"Yes," Allabva said, trying to follow where the Shrongelin was going with this "and next, we will go to Iddypol to do the same thing, more or less."

"Thank you for all you do."

Allabva cocked her head. This was certainly unexpected. She breathed the sea air, taking in the Guardian's courtesy.

"You...were right," Allabva admitted at length. "I did need to be more bold in the end. After all, that is what caught everyone's attention so the overduke would listen to what we had to say. Truth be told, I didn't know how to put myself out there, but I am sorry I held back at first."

"No, Companion," Nightshade said. "You were just as right as I. The gift of strength from the bond could have called all the attention in the world, but it was your kindness that won the overduke's and this city's support."

Allabva smiled at her escort, feeling greater peace in his presence than she had since standing on the Summit Above the Aspens.

"Thank you, Nighty—" she ignored his irritated snort "—for listening to me in the palace courtyard. I still think you shouldn't have come in the first place, but ultimately you suspended your own judgment of what the situation needed, and respected the work that I was doing. I appreciate that."

The Nightshade nodded, obviously wanting to get back to business. "But we have a few days on our hands."

"Days for what?" Allabva wondered.

Without warning, the Shrongelin shrank into Leaf once more. Allabva resisted—with only marginal success—the emotional kick in the gut that came with it.

Leaf turned and walked over to a chest sitting on the ship's deck that Allabva had paid little attention to, thinking it must be full of ropes for the sailors to use. Leaf opened the top of the chest and pulled out two wooden practice swords.

Turning to Allabva, he tossed her a sword.

"Now we train. If you thought you were tired when you reached the mountaintop, let me help you realize—that fatigue was nothing."

"But...the other Gha-Nomord have to hold the prison without you right now," Allabva protested, confused at this seemingly impulsive and imprudent usage of his human form. "The prison will break faster."

"All part of the plan, unfortunately. We trade off letting our enemy out earlier in exchange for being more prepared ourselves. Now, come forward and learn how to hold that stick in your hands.

THE END

EPILOGUE: THE STORM ROILS

"Seer Falb, they are ready for you," Nillan told the Disillusioned who led the Emissary Company.

"Thank you, Nillan," Falb replied, adjusting his collar before grabbing his satchel and dismounting in front of the Lord Mayor's mansion in Palf Glen. He handed his reins to another Disaffected who was standing by, then turned to walk inside behind Nillan and the Lord Mayor's house servant. He stopped and turned back to his group.

"Remember, friends, we're only passing through. Whether or not we make headway in this town, we strike camp in the morning and head west."

"Of course, Seer," Halmon said.

Nillan couldn't help but smile to himself. He'd worked hard over the past week to position Halmon, Tunbloth, and himself in Falb's good graces. Then he'd schemed carefully to make sure the company of Disaffected led by Falb would accomplish its mission...according to Nillan's own vision, of course.

Falb left the small contingent outside and entered the mansion, where the house servant showed them to the Lord Mayor's study.

The Lord Mayor Issap Flanteh stood behind his desk, waiting for Falb and Nillan.

"Masters Relwater and Protfund, is it? Take a seat, gentlemen." He gestured to a pair of armchairs, then sat himself.

"Yes, Viscount, and thank you for seeing us," Falb said.

"Viscount only by technicality of this assignment; I hold the permanent title of just a baron," Flanteh corrected. "Now, I understand you wish to discuss how things are run here in Palf Glen. This isn't the kind of visit I get very often, especially from those who hold no rank. But I think you've got yourselves a movement going—there's fifty of you, and that's just the small group you brought—so I thought it no harm to give you the courtesy of a tour. I'd be happy to show you around town if you like, though perhaps most of it will have to wait until morning."

He glanced out the window at the dimming sky while he said the last bit. He stayed peering out a little longer than seemed necessary to observe the sky.

Nillan leaned forward, wondering what the baron was looking at, concerned he might see something he shouldn't.

"Thank you, baron," Falb said, holding a hand up, "a tour won't be necessary. We only wished to discuss—"

"The many injustices you and your ilk commit on a daily basis," Nillan interrupted.

"Excuse me?" Baron Flanteh and Seer Falb said in unison, turning to Nillan.

"Nillan, mind yourself," Falb admonished. "If a lack of decorum will help our cause, you are wrong, at least for here, today."

"Thank you, Relwater," Flanteh said. "It's good to see you police your own."

"Of course, we—" Falb began.

"I know how things are," Nillan interrupted again. "You mistreat your women, you abuse your servants."

Flanteh's face turned red. "I assure you we do not."

"Hmm," Nillan said. "Yeah, I don't care. I just decided, and you're done."

Baron Flanteh scoffed. "Done with what? You're nobody to—"

Nillan interrupted a third time, shouting at the top of his lungs, "Come in, boys!"

The front door of the house, visible from the Baron's study, opened, and several men rushed in.

"You can't come in like this!" the voice of the house servant sailed down the stairs in the entry.

Lord Mayor Flanteh looked up from Nillan and shouted in alarm and anger, "What is the meaning of this? Get out of here this instant!"

The invaders ran into the study and grabbed Flanteh, struggled with him and forced him into his chair, binding him with rope.

"I don't think so," Nillan rebuffed while his cronies worked. "We're taking over, see. I said you're done, and I meant you're done...with everything. Boys, did you bring a torch?"

"What? No!" a woman's voice screamed from the doorway.

"Right on time," Nillan said with relish.

"Nillan Protfund, what is the meaning of this?" Falb shouted. "This is not what we planned. You cannot—"

"Oh, but I am, *Seer*," Nillan mocked. "Would you like to know what else? You and your slow-to-act kind? You're done, too." He spat the condemnation at his superior with determination and derision. "The Disillusioned? No, now we become the Disavowed."

"Can't you see you're only hurting our cause?" Falb shouted and jumped at Nillan, but the other men pulled him off, and grappling with him, gave him and the baron's wife the same treatment they gave to Flanteh.

With three prisoners tied up and Tunbloth and Halmon standing there with burning torches, Nillan looked around.

"Oil. We need some oil to do this the right way."

"I'll check the kitchen," a man said, running out of the study. After a few moments and crashes, he returned and handed Nillan a bottle.

"Bring Issap around the desk," Nillan commanded.

Nobody moved.

"Issap Flanteh, you half-wits! I declare he's no baron now. Bring him around next to the other two."

A few men eagerly stepped in and lifted the baron in his chair, moving him around in front of the desk.

"Now's the fun part," Nillan smiled, insanity in his eyes.

He poured oil in the baron's and baroness's laps, then on top of Falb's head.

"You can't do this! I can't believe I worked with you!" Falb screamed, shaking his chair, trying to tip it off balance.

"Quiet, Seer," Nillan said, "can't you see beyond this moment and understand what I'll accomplish with you gone?"

"Fungus!" Falb shouted.

"You will never get away with this," the baron told Nillan. "We have police. The emperor will send his soldiers."

"Let him," Nillan defied the baron. "I'm getting away with this tonight, and the Disaffected—no, the Disavowed—will continue to grow."

He looked around. This needed...

A roar shook the house, shook the ground. Men out in the street, who had come at the beckoning of Halmon and Tunbloth, shouted in alarm as red lightning ripped across the sky. It shattered the evening, illuminating everything in scarlet like blood.

Aha, Nillan said, taking a torch. *I know what would be perfect.* He touched it to the two nobles' laps, lighting the oil he had spilled, then turned and tapped the flame to Falb's scalp.

As they burned, screaming in pain and fear, Nillan held a hand forward, touching them, burning his skin as they died.

"This is *my* power," Nillan spoke. "It once belonged to another, but I have conquered, and I have taken, and now it is mine. I will do as I please with my power. It is my right. This is my power. Let all who would challenge me wither!"

He pulled a knife out, pricked his palm in a cross and a circle, and touched his palm to each of the three foreheads.

"This is my power. Let it permeate my blood."

"Boss, what are you doing?" Halmon asked. "We need to get out of here before the house burns down."

Nillan smiled, slowly turning and following his men out of the mansion. Crossing the threshold into the night, he raised a burned hand to his face, index finger extended upward. As he watched with intention, a candle flame appeared, floating in the air above his fingertip.

Another peal of red rifted the sky, sending cracks among the stars, and Nillan's flame sparked and surged, growing larger. Nillan watched the gleam and licked his lips in anticipation.

"Who else needs his house burned down tonight, boys?"

Jashdin tilted her head, reveling in the feeling she got when the sky cracked with red lighting. It made her feel powerful. In fact, she wondered if...

She tested her hypothesis by Shifting out of existence and back in, pushing as far as she could. She looked back at her footprints to see the distance she had just covered. It was about seven paces, up from the five she had been so frustratingly bound to.

So, these emanations in the sky from the Alvewimon increase my power, Jashdin thought. That was good to know.

Things had been progressing over the past few weeks. The mind—the Alvewimon, she reminded herself—had been relatively quiet since the previous red lighting, about three weeks before. That didn't mean Jashdin would just sit around, though.

On the contrary, since the Alvewimon had shown Jashdin how to make a Lemnerox and a Binterox, she had not rested in her pursuit of power. She had started on herself with the fae-bird, followed almost immediately by making Ani'irad into a Binterox. Then, after sending the other woman west into Eslarna, Jashdin had followed it with augmenting her speed by stealing power from a jackalope.

That was a good memory for Jashdin. Fae-birds weren't too wary, proximity-wise. A person could get close to one, but it didn't matter. To most people they were impossible to catch, until Jashdin wove her net of woolly rhino and unicorn hair.

Jackalopes presented a similar but unique challenge. They were indeed impossible to capture to the natural human, requiring some magical aid to accomplish the feat. Jashdin had discussed it with Ani'irad, but they had no time to attempt it before Ani'irad went west. She recommended to Ani'irad that she could catch a jackalope by soothing it with her mental suggestion power gained from the Gha-Nomord horn. Similarly, Jashdin had caught her own jackalope by taking advantage of her power of Shifting right on top of one. No jackalope or rasselbock in the world could outrun that.

Then Jashdin had been partly disappointed. While the jackalopes were known to possess great speed, they also had strength disproportionate to their size, and Ephemery, or pictorial thought communication. To the chagrin of the young gray-eyed woman, she found that harvesting a jackalope only rendered one of the three magical powers to the Lemnerox. She had had to kill two more to finish the job, and even then her strength didn't seem augmented much beyond what she had already stolen from the mammoth.

Jashdin accomplished these hunts in moments while she was alone, apart from the mammoth. She'd needed to endow some advantage upon Ani'irad to send her west and build a following there, but there was no need to share that knowledge where Jashdin was herself. The strength of mammoths, she shared so she would have strong lieutenants. Mystical powers she preferred to keep to herself, at least for now.

During the day and evening, Jashdin maneuvered politically. In these few weeks without the extra aid from the Alvewimon, she had gained much.

Staying with Silomat, Jashdin managed to find an opportunity to cast doubt upon the chief in the Nafet'elu Glosen's minds, discrediting him to the degree that he was cast out completely, all based on a fabricated story. Silomat was installed in his place, and he formally elevated Jashdin to chieftess.

A wise decision, Jashdin thought, *because it let him keep his throat unpunctured.*

As she continued to pull strings, her followers in the Bas'naya Glosen, greedy for the power she promised, installed one of their own at the head of the tribe, making Jashdin all but the leader-in-fact of that tribe. Now commanding the Wetwood and the Ringwood, her influence began to grow among the Hal'p'non and the Nay'y'non Glosen on the plains as well.

Things were progressing, and while some might say it was fast, it wasn't fast enough for Jashdin. She wanted it all, and she wanted it now. The Alvewimon wanted it for her, and she wanted it for herself. Jashdin had a sense that the Alvewimon was restrained somehow, but that eventually the Alvewimon would be loosed. What this truly meant, she didn't know, but she knew that she was to have a place under the Dragonspeaker just as she had given Ani'irad a place under her.

With all that in mind, although Jashdin barely dared to think it, she craved to be the one on top in the end. Who was this Alvewimon, anyway?

To that end, Jashdin desperately needed to multiply her power.

She now stalked her next prey. Some would have thought it impossible to make this kill, but she had thoroughly discarded most people's idea of impossible. Fae-bird, a mammoth kill by herself, a jackalope—three times, no less. And *somebody* had killed that Nomord stallion she'd gotten the horn from.

So, undeterred, with augmented strength, increased speed, short-range Shifting, and Ephemery, the woman without a past slowly inched closer to an elusive Nomord mare for the second time.

Jashdin had already done all this a few days before, and all to no avail. She had stalked in close, projecting Ephemery of a clear landscape, trying to fool the beast, make her think

Jashdin wasn't there. Whether or not the Ephemery did the job was dubious, but she was able to Shift in and kill the beast.

But when Jashdin harvested the horn and performed the rite, nothing had happened. No power came. She had been furious enough that she almost decided to kill Silomat when he welcomed her back from her hunt. He'd had no right wishing her well in a moment like that; she could replace him. Only her desire not to start over training a new partner held her back.

Maybe that Nomord had been a fluke, or perhaps Jashdin had misspoken the words of the rite; she had to try again.

Now, as she pursued another one of the unicorns from a distance, she was blessed with the red rifts splitting the sky, a different view in the early morning with the sun fully in the sky. The light actually seemed to darken the sky rather than lighten it.

"What's that?" The Ta-Nomord spoke to nobody, while she looked up, alarmed, and bolted a few paces, but then seemed to realize there was nowhere to flee from the terrifying display of light. Instead, she stood still, quivering and darting glances about the landscape.

This gave Jashdin pause. All the Nomord she had seen appeared detached, mostly unaffected by what was going on around them. Was their detachment somehow the reason her harvesting rite hadn't worked? Somehow their minds and magic were apart from their bodies enough that their power couldn't be stolen?

Jashdin scowled at the thought, reaching up to rub her eyes.

Then how was a Binterox made? The thought had come to her, that evening in the woods when she killed the fae-bird, that a dead Nomord was the key. But if all the stallions were gone, and all the mares were somehow partially separate from this world, how had she succeeded with Ani'irad?

Jashdin looked at the terrified mare again as the red lights slowly dissipated and normal morning light returned. The spotless beast stood more at ease, eyeing the foliage around. Timidly recovering from her fright, she lowered her head and nibbled some grass. Her manner appeared more self-assured, and yet more carefree.

Jashdin blinked, staring at the Nomord for several minutes. Was that the key? Not the red lightning itself, but the effect it had on the beast. What if Jashdin could scare her, harass her into holding her mind solidly in this world, then killed her?

The hunt became more interesting, but also impossible. Jashdin could still Shift, of course, but she had limitations. She could only jump about 5 paces at a time, and usually could only do only three successive Shifts in about a minute. Even with her jackalope-powered running, there was no way she could terrorize the haughty, proud Nomord and also get in for the kill.

Then, to Jashdin's delight, sparks of red skittered across the sky once more. Maybe now...

She ran for it, zooming in toward the mare at a speed faster than any normal human could have run.

The mare, momentarily startled by the red lighting again, turned her eye back to the level to look at Jashdin. "Demon!" she shouted, and bolted, much faster than Jashdin could hope to run.

Jashdin, knowing this would happen, Shifted once, twice, three times, and just missed coming close enough to the Nomord to have any effect. Straining, she heaved and Shifted a fourth time, now finding herself alongside the unicorn.

The Nomord planted her hooves and shifted her weight to turn and take on a new direction of travel.

Jashdin had expected this, and was ready. Raising her arm, she wielded an obsidian blade she had acquired and honed for just for this purpose. She thrust it forward and slashed it across the Nomord's hindquarters.

"Help!" the Nomord screamed. "Help!" And with that, the mare was out of Jashdin's reach, galloping off.

Now what? Jashdin had injured the creature and still pursued her, but she had no more Shifts left for the moment and couldn't catch up while they both ran.

As the thousand red rivulets in the sky began to fade, Jashdin heard a wolf howl.

No matter, she thought, *I can fight off a few wolves.*

Jashdin kept running, losing ground. Looking at her obsidian blade, she saw that it was broken. Such was an obsidian blade sometimes: one strike, one usage. Mildly annoyed, she threw it away and pulled out another.

Then the Nomord changed direction again quite suddenly, heading a bit to the left.

What's this? Jashdin thought.

Then she saw a wolf directly in her path, ahead of where the Nomord had been a moment before. Fortune was with Jashdin. She adjusted her direction, going after the Nomord, as it appeared the wolf was also.

More wolves howled, raising an eerie din, no less so than if it had been in the dark of night.

The Nomord changed her direction again, going further left.

The wolves and I just might have her boxed in.

Suddenly a wolf jumped from in front a point of the Nomord, leaping toward her and catching her throat in its jaws.

The Nomord bucked, shaking the wolf off. Another wolf jumped on the creature's back, and she rolled, crushing it with her weight, then got to her feet again and bolted...toward Jashdin.

Jashdin saw there was too much distance between her and the Nomord; the creature would veer off again, staying out of reach. But maybe... Jashdin Shifted again, sooner than she should have been able to. One more Shift, and she was closing in.

The Nomord reared up, pawing the air, trying to kick Jashdin. Two wolves jumped on her haunches, biting her back. She rotated, easily knocking them off, and dashing...

Into Jashdin's blade as she Shifted a final time, placing herself in front of the white equine, and sliced the graceful neck, opening a wound in just the right spot that blood began to pour out.

"No!" the Nomord shouted, then repeated more weakly, "No..."

"Oh, yes, beastie," Jashdin said, walking behind the Nomord as the beast began to step unsurely, faltering.

The Nomord lifted her head, appearing confused. She spoke a single word. "Wolves?"

Jashdin stopped in her tracks and looked around, wondering. She spotted the wolves, but they merely watched her and the Nomord, curious, apparently having lost interest in the hunt. Jashdin turned back to the Nomord, who fell to the ground.

Jashdin breathed heavily, giddy at her second victory, this one having been drawn out by the convenient cooperation of the wolf pack. She approached the mare.

Tossing aside her second broken obsidian blade, Jashdin pulled out a proper steel knife and a mallet. She knelt, placing the tip of the blade at the base of the Nomord's single horn, and tapped the back with the mallet, driving the knife tip into the beast's forehead as it cried out in pain.

Finally, Jashdin separated the horn from the forehead of the dead beast, her own knuckles white, linked with red, from the work.

"This is *my* power," Jashdin said, holding the horn firmly in both hands. "It once belonged to another, but I have conquered, and I have taken, and now it is mine. I will do as I please with my power. It is my right. This is my power. Let all who would challenge me wither!"

She pricked her hand with her knife, then pressed the tip of the horn into each cut with great force.

"This is my power. Let it permeate my blood."

Standing, Jashdin, Oracle of the Alvewimon, turned away from the discarded corpse, carrying the horn as a keepsake to remember this victory.

A wolf whined nearby.

Jashdin looked at it, viewed its wounds, which the Nomord had inflicted while defending herself.

The unicorns can heal those they choose, she thought. *Could I...?*

Jashdin reached her hand out, but she knew within herself that she held no ability to improve this animal's health. Probing, she reached out with an invisible perception, touching the wolf with her intuition...and found it.

Jashdin took a sharp breath in when she heard the wolf yelp. Stepping back, she flexed her fingers. She brought her hand up to her face and inspected it. Her knuckles were clean, free of scrapes.

She laughed, then jumped high in the air, higher than she had expected to be able to. Coming down to earth, she turned on the wolves with a wild look in her eye.

The pack sensed danger and ran from the presence of the new Binterox.

She gave chase for the sport of it. She still wasn't as fast as the Nomord she had slain, but she didn't think anything else could outrun her now.

<u>**Before You Go**</u>

If you enjoyed this book, please help other readers find it by
leaving a comment on Amazon or on Goodreads.
The author will love you forever for it.

<u>**Coming Soon**</u>

Allabva's saga continues in *Nightshade Unicorn book 3*.
Find out where you can purchase it via
www.NightshadeUnicorn.com

Subscribe for updates at www.pedramon.com/

Pronunciation Guide

While many of the uncommon names appearing in this book will be easy for the reader to pronounce, I'm aware that I've included several difficult names. Therefore, I have provided this pronunciation guide.

Those names which are made up of common English words are omitted, while the names unique to the world of the Nightshade Unicorn, no matter how simple, have been included. If the reader encounters any names in the book which are missing from this Pronunciation Guide, I would appreciate being advised so they can be included in the future.

This guide is not cumulative, and has been pruned of a few names which appeared in book 1 but are not mentioned in this volume. A cumulative guide can be found at https://www.NightshadeUnicorn.com/pronunciation .

Please note that the tick mark (`) precedes the the accentuated syllable.

Ex.:

Apple: `App-uhl

CHARACTERS, CREATURES, AND CONCEPTS

Characters are listed in alphabetical order by first or only name given in the book.

Afaln Pymseet — Af-`aln (Uses 'al' from "pal.") `Pim-seat
Aiwa — `I-wuh
Alial — `Ah-lee-awl
Allabva Roalke — Uh-`lab-vuh `Rowlk
Allvron Pymseet — `Alv-ron `Pim-seat
Alvern Swiskopfel — `Al-vern Swiss-`cop-ful
Anastine Ntoffel — `An-a-steen N-`tah-ful
Andamaln — `And-a-maln (Uses 'al' from "pal.")
Ani'irad — Ah-`knee-'ee-rod (' represents a glottal stop.)
Aulbwin Tonalstga — `Ahl-bwin Ton-`alst-ga
Aumelle Calda — Ah-`mel Call-dah
Avrekk — `Av-rec
Banduchy — `Band-oo-key
Bakine — Buh-`keen
Bas'naya [Glosen] — `Bass-nye-yah
Binteroces — Bin-`tair-oh-sees
Binterox — `Bin-ter-ox
Brelin — `Brel-in
Brolfith Noteh — `Brol-fith `No-teh
Calae — Ca-`lay
Cariel — `Care-ee-uhl
Churloe Tunnigan — `Chur-low `Tun-again
Clea Scalleh — `Clay-uh `Scah-leh
Dass — `Dass (Rhymes with "class.")
Delgan Dlorovin — `Del-gun `Dlore-oh-vin
Eretuquein — `Air-too-cane

Enore — Eh-`nor-ay

Faethlen Roalke — `Fayth-len `Rowlk

Fae-bird — `Fay-bird

Falb Relwater — `Falb (Uses 'al' from "pal.") `Rel-water

Falndeg Tiweth — `Faln-deg (Uses 'al' from "pal." ) `Tih-with

Fiewren — `Fee-ren

Foral — `For-uhl

Gali Kadarn — `Gal-ee Ka-`darn

Gio — `Jee-oh

Garien Scalleh — `Gair-ee-uhn `Scah-leh

Gha-Nomord — `Gah-Num-ord

Glonea — `Glow-nay

Halmon — `Hal-men

Harsok — `Har-sock

Holb — `Holb

Holbonin — Hole-`bah-nin

Holwan — `Hall-won

Hronomon — `Hroh-nuh-mohn

Hugne — `Hyoon (Pronounced as "hewn.")

Issap Flanteh — Ih-`sap`Flann-the

Jain — `Jane

Jaldren — `Jawl-dren

Jashdin — `Jash-din

Jhalla — `Jaw-luh

Jilona — Jih-`lone-uh

Jimlarnt — `Jim-larnt

Jonatlu — `Joe-nat-lu

Joró — Jo-`row

Juilna — Ju-`ill-nuh

Koszh — `Kawzh (With the 'zh' sound from "treasure.")

Lamtor — `Lam-tor

Lemneroces — Lem-nair-oh-sees

Lemnerox — 'Lem-ner-ox

Lesala — Lee-'saw-luh

Lonswil Esyll — 'Lons-wul 'Eh-suhl

Lewolnn — 'Lew-oln

Liceln — Lih-'selln

Livim — 'Liv-im

Lussie — 'Luh-see

Lerran — 'Lair-uhn

Marlson — 'Marl-sun

Mellier — 'Mel-ee-er

Mhosorem — 'Mow-zoe-rem

Nafet-elu [Glosen] — Na-'fet-'eh-loo (' represents a glottal stop.)

Nillan Protfund — 'Nill-un 'Prot-fund

Nogtad Zoldril — 'Nog-tad 'Zole-drill

Nolder Lawgrin — 'Nol-der 'Law-grin

Nomord — Num-'ord

Panli — 'Pan-lee

Pontil — 'Pon-tul

Qurast — 'Cure-ast

Rallan — 'Ral-an

Redeok — 'Red-ee-ock

Rhaslemonor — 'Rahz-lem-on-or

Ruldern Ntoffel — 'Roll-durn N-'tah-ful

Rylian Esyll — 'Ril-ee-un 'Eh-suhl

Rralen — 'Rah-len

Rubiro — Roo-'beer-oh

Sacalai — Suh-'caw-lie

Saneii — 'San-ay

Scaltern Wold — 'Scal-turn 'Woeld

Shel — 'Shell

Shrongelin — ʽShrong-geh-lin

Silomat Veliti'Mon — ʽSi-low-mat Veh-ʽlee-tee-mon

Spalgen — ʽSpal-jen

Ta-Nomord — ʽTa-Num-ord

Tahonu [Glosen] — Ta-ʽho-noo

Thaler — ʽTah-ler

Tofan — ʽTow-fan

Trinva Yalben — ʽTrin-vuh ʽYal-ben (Uses 'al' from "pal.")

Tunbloth — ʽTun-bloth

Tunralger Faetlan — Tun-ʽral-gher ʽFayt-len (Uses 'g' from "gun.")

Tylonus — Tie-ʽlow-nis

Umblan — ʽUm-blan

Vlon — ʽVlon

Yalnan — ʽYal-nan (Uses 'al' from "pal.")

Yalrou Tonalstga — ʽYahl-roo Ton-ʽalst-ga

Yon'ir'fan — ʽYon-ear-fawn

Places

Due to the story in this book taking place mostly within the bounds of Eslarna, some place names appear only on the map, not in the story. However, you can expect these and more locations to appear in future books.

Alervayn — ʽAl-er-vane ("Al" rhymes with "pal.")

Amonfweer — ʽAy-min-fweer

Apthane — ʽApp-thane (Uses 'th' from "with.")

Arn — ʽArn

Arnlia — ʽArn-lee-uh

Bolsnard — ʽBowlz-nard

Colnarn — ʻCoal-narn

Colnuinard — Coal-ʻnoo-ih-nard

Cylgiana — ʻSill-gee-ahna (Uses 'g' from "age.")

Darlte — ʻDarl-teh

Dullsworthen — ʻDulls-worth-en

Eslarna — Es-ʻlar-na

Fonglan — ʻFong-len

Glosen — ʻGlow-zen

Holbonin — Hole-ʻbon-in

Grinswolder — ʻGrins-wol-der

Holbonin — Hole-ʻbon-in

Iddypol — ʻIh-dee-pole

Indoque [Alley] — ʻIn-doc

Littonwelt — ʻLitton-welt

Malmar — ʻMal-mar

Malnonny — Mal-ʻnon-ee

Mascaldinig — Mass-ʻcal-din-ig

Nolnarn — ʻNol-narn

Novulm — ʻNo-vulm

Nylorna — Nye-ʻlor-nuh

Palf [Glen] — ʻPalf

Parfall — ʻPar-fall

Roula — ʻRoo-la

Tallen — ʻTal-in

Tallens — ʻTal-ins

Tallensworth — ʻTal-ins-worth

Islewilds — ʻAisle-wilds

Rimewaste — ʻRime-waste

Turilnia — Too-ʻril-nia

Weslan [Fields] — ʻWess-lan Fields

Ylonga — Ee-ʻlon-ga

T.S. Pedramon grew up and went to school as a musician,
taught music, then joined the US Marine Corps and served as
a Marine Musician on the clarinet. After two tours he grad-
uated from Officer Candidate School and served as a Cyber-
space Warfare Officer. He settled into full-time story writing
upon leaving Active Duty service. He is fluent in English,
Spanish, and Dad jokes. He resides on the US East Coast
with his family, a parakeet named William Cutie, and a black
one-eyed cat named Skippy.

Pedramon has enjoyed reading *Animorphs*, *Dragonriders of
Pern*, *Wheel of Time*, *Fablehaven*, *Lord of the Rings*, *Born
to Run*, clarinet sheet music, *Bird Talk Magazine*, the *Holy
Bible*, the *Book of Mormon*, and much more.

*

You can connect with him at:
www.pedramon.com